Release
from Cibola

Release from Cíbola

Conquistadores, Eisenhower and Me

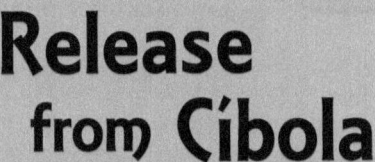

Andres C. Salazar

SUNSTONE
PRESS

SANTA FE

"River from Cibola" (Chapter 3) was previously published in *Azahares 2013* by the University of Arkansas-Fort Smith.

Sunstone books may be purchased for educational, business, or sales promotional use. For information please write: Special Markets Department, Sunstone Press, P.O. Box 2321, Santa Fe, New Mexico 87504-2321.

Book design › Vicki Ahl
Cover design › James Patrick
Body typeface › Minion Pro
Printed on acid-free paper

Library of Congress Cataloging-in-Publication Data

Salazar, Andres C., 1942-
    Release from Cíbola : conquistadores, Eisenhower and me / by Andres C. Salazar.
        pages cm
    ISBN 978-0-86534-951-3 (softcover : alk. paper)
    1. New Mexico--History--20th century--Fiction. I. Title.
    PS3619.A433R45 2013
    813'.6--dc23
                              2013010081

WWW.SUNSTONEPRESS.COM
SUNSTONE PRESS / POST OFFICE BOX 2321 / SANTA FE, NM 87504-2321 /USA
(505) 988-4418 / ORDERS ONLY (800) 243-5644 / FAX (505) 988-1025

Dedication

This volume is dedicated to those wonderful mentors in the Española School System in Española, New Mexico during the 1950s that took the time to inspire as well as teach. They saw in me what I didn't know was possible until I tried it. It took many years for me to realize what gift they had given me, an undying love of learning, empathy and tenacity. Especial thanks go to Sally Gonzales, Gary Kellogg, Robert MacNeely Norita Plummer and Charles Pompeo.

Preface

The narrative is done as a series of coming of age stories in the southwest in the mid twentieth century or during the epochal term of President Eisenhower. The backdrop is the mountainous region of northern New Mexico, the location of Spanish settlements started in 1598 that was part of the American annexation in 1848. The entries relate to the boyhood memories of Reyes Córdova who is caught up in the historical and cultural contradictions of growing up in a place that is part of the United States but still clings to traditions hundreds of years old in language, mysticism, poetic manners, Pueblo Indian relationships and delectable food. His journey to becoming "Americanized" occurs in a decade that witnesses the growth of the atomic age, the anti-Communist fanaticism, and the rights movements of Blacks and women. The young man attempts to assimilate into an American society grappling with the forces of these movements and that still rejects strangers who do not conform to stereotypical attributes of white skin, an Anglo-Saxon surname and unaccented English pronunciation. He yearns to escape from a milieu that appears to entrap its young by imposing old traditions at the expense of being successful in the new American society.

> *Memory is thus that aspect of human freedom which is most determinative in the construction of historical reality. It gives meaning to historical events without reducing them to natural necessity and recurrence; and it thereby gives the agent of action a dimension of freedom in the present moment which proves history to be a realm of freedom as well as destiny.*
> —Rheinhold Niebuhr in *Faith & History*, 1949

1

San Pablo Day
June 29, 1948

*We will be watching you and your
ancestors will be watching you, more
carefully than me.*

—Señor Valencia

Actually it was not San Pablo Day but the day before as I remember. Tito and I had our tires approaching the dip in the paved road just before the slight turn that takes you to Kramer's, the huge general store that sits right on the main plaza of the Pueblo of San Pablo. The dip is really an arroyo that carries water to the river in heavy rains. The road was simply paved over the arroyo so it always had sand on its surface left over from the last big rain. Most of the sand would be swept away by the road traffic but what remained was a reminder of the desert land and the memory of lost dreams. It didn't rain much in the Pueblo so there was plenty of sand and sun to whiten the day and darken our skin. There were a few trees, especially near the *acequia* or irrigation ditch, where you could see the brownish water carrying the silt from the mountains, its wetness cooling the air, the floating strands of alfalfa and mint creating a sweet smell, and the cottonwoods lending you shade as a breeze rippled the oversized leaves. Tito and I would sit on the *acequia* bank, each of us peeling a willowy reed and then pretending to fish with the greenish bark skin. We'd giggle and fish, giggle and fish, stretching out the time of another fantasy, another world of discovery and delight, blown in from the thin desert air.

The sun seared the village with no mercy despite its holy place in history as the ancient Tewa grounds remained intact and the ways of ancestors remained true. The ragweed plants would blossom after a rain and then wilt, their heads turned down, away from the offending sun. Only the scattered Siberian Elms stood tall where their roots had pierced the earth, digging deep into the bowels of the village where some moisture still remained. Otherwise, the parched winds would come and deposit plenty of gritty dirt and dust in your eyes and hair. You could collect stuff in your mouth when you talked outside during storms but the wise men said it was all right to eat dirt once in a while. After all, the dirt was holy in San Pablo, the mother pueblo of the Pueblo Indian tribes of the north and site of the first Spanish settlers; and there were minerals you needed in your body that the dirt would give you. Babies ate dirt. It was a natural thing.

It was early summer now and Tito, my best friend, and I were in command of two used tires, abandoned by a neighbor and rescued by us to be our sporty wheels of transportation around town. We would propel them with a slap of either hand once they were upright. Of course, if you didn't want to get your fingers blackened from the rubber surface, you could use a stick but you had to be good at it. You couldn't make the tire go by simply hitting it with the stick. You had to let the stick rest on the tire and then push the stick in the direction you wanted the tire to go. You had to run alongside the tire as you pushed and guided it with the stick. Tito and I had become experts in moving our tires, keeping them upright even at slow speeds, spinning them and crashing them headlong against each other but catching them before they fell over.

Today we were on our way to Kramer's with an errand to run, feeling the freedom of a summer day, testing our limits of tire control, off to buy cigarettes for my mother who really didn't smoke a lot, just with friends. She had given me a half dollar coin for a pack of *Kools*, the mentholated brand she liked best. Tito and I were driving our tires alongside the road making sounds with our vibrating tongues that imitated a car's engine until we'd stop at the top of the *arroyo* bank and let our tires go down the slope by themselves. We ran as fast as we could to keep up with them while trying to steer them with our sticks, all the time feeling the wind in our faces as we tried to keep up without running into them. With the momentum the downward slope generated, our tires could go part way up the opposite slope but never quite make it to the top. We would catch them before they started rolling downhill again and use both our hands to make them go the rest of the way until we reached the main plaza that housed the largest buildings in the Pueblo.

The tallest structure on the plaza was the Catholic Church of San Pablo, built from red fired bricks in 1889 after the last church burned down. Several others built before it on the same site had also been destroyed by fire, the first one built in 1599 which was burned to the ground in the Pueblo Rebellion of 1680. The current one had a tall bell tower and it looked out of place in the village comprised of mostly adobe dwellings in rows facing a plaza, their parapets uneven, all built without nails, concrete or sawn wood. The church looked sturdy and permanent, even fireproof, while other buildings made from the mud and straw adobe bricks with few windows and doors appeared tired and worn as if melting in the fiery sun. Directly across the road from the church was the Chapel built from huge blocks of sandstone; its steeple tall and imposing, challenging the church in permanence but not in size.

Kramer's was a large mercantile store built on a rise adjacent to the Chapel. Tito and I parked our wheels in front and went in the main entrance which had a screechy screen door that announced every customer. A gentle breeze created by huge ceiling fans would hit you as you entered, carrying with it a smelly inventory of all the items it had for sale—grain and feed for horses, cows and chickens and oil stained tools like axes, hoes and rakes. With no windows the store resembled a barn—dark, cavernous and mysterious.

The store had a counter near the front door that contained the cigarettes and candy, probably the most popular items. There were shelves behind the counter that had common food staples like canned meats, vegetables and fruit. Kramer's was the only general store in San Pablo and if you didn't find it there, you either did without it or you would have to go to San Isidro or Santa Fe.

There were quite a few people in the store, probably picking up a few items before the holiday tomorrow. Besides individual shoppers there were groups of men or women, two or three lost in conversation or occasionally laughing at someone's joke, their banter being part of the excitement in the air on the eve of the village's most festive day of the summer. Today many women in the village were probably preparing some of the food for the guests they would entertain tomorrow during the lunch and supper meals, the part of San Pablo Day resembling the American Thanksgiving Day.

The clerk behind the counter was Señor Valencia who knew my family. In fact we were related in a distant way. He was a small man with a slight limp, balding with friendly eyes and a thin moustache, and his engaging smile and almost imperceptible laugh made you feel at ease as if he were greeting an old friend from out of town.

"Reyes, *como estas, güerito?*" asked Señor Valencia as we got to the head of the line. He was always calling me *güerito* because my hair was so light colored. "Are you ready for San Pablo Day tomorrow?"

"I know I'm going to have a good time. Tito here will dance for the first time. He's taken his lessons," I answered. Tito nodded and laughed, half embarrassed.

"Well, I'm glad. We need more young dancers. They don't get tired so easily in the sun and they have spritely moves. We will be watching you and your ancestors will be watching you, more carefully than me" as he directed his comment to Tito.

"I know the drumbeats. My uncle taught me the steps," said Tito. "I have my outfit ready because my mother made me wear it yesterday to see if it was just right."

"Your family will be proud of you tomorrow. Your dance steps are important to the pueblo and the spirits," said Señor Valencia.

"Are you going to the dances, Señor Valencia," I asked.

"I have never missed them except when I was in the Army. It is out of respect for our Indian neighbors, the church that celebrates the birthday of our patron saint, San Pablo, and for the land that we love," said Señor Valencia, his face turning a bit serious.

"*Kool* cigarettes for my mother."

"Of course, *mi güerito*. Say hello to your mama. I will probably see her at the festival tomorrow," as he handed me the small pack.

She usually gave me money for one pack and the change I was allowed to use for myself. It didn't amount to much but it did cover the cost of hard candy for Tito and me. I was able to stuff the cigarettes into my front pants pocket and slip the hard candy into my mouth but keep the wax paper wrapper in my pocket in case I couldn't finish the candy. This left my hands free to drive my tire back to the house.

"*Adiós*, Señor Valencia."

"*Adiós, con cuidado*," as he waved and went to serve the next customer.

Tito and I ran out of the store and unparked our tires for the ride home. We did the same down-the-hill trick with them again, this time in the opposite direction so the slope wasn't as steep and we didn't have to work too hard to get them to level ground again. We were joined by a pack of stray dogs of different sizes. The pack started with five mutts but on the way home two of them peeled off and went their separate ways. They were attracted by our tires as we rolled them, running all the while. The dogs would circle us and bark from time to time, wagging their tails, perhaps thinking that Tito and I were playing with them. A couple of them usually stayed with us for part of the day. They were fed table scraps by different families and really didn't have a home but they survived as communal pets because they weren't pests and didn't seem to go after chickens that a few families kept in their backyards. They were not friendly with strangers though. People believed they were like guardian angels, protecting the community, and controlled by spirits so they left them alone.

We stopped briefly at Tito's house because we saw his mother working outside near the *horno* just like a lot of the Pueblo Indian women who were baking bread for the feast day tomorrow. She had taken out a batch of Indian bread out of the earthen oven and placed about six loaves into a large basket that was lined with a *trapo* or kitchen towel. She saw us approach her and knew what would please us. She took one of the smaller loaves and broke off part of it, splitting it again and gave Tito and me each a piece.

"*Dios los bendiga*," [May God bless you] she said as she handed us the bread that had a light brown crispy crust and a white interior that still had a little bit of steam coming out of it. My mouth started watering when I saw what she was doing for us. We parked our tires near the *horno*. Holding the piece of bread she had given us with our fingers blackened from the tire rolling, we looked at each other and laughed with glee at our good luck that we had caught his mother at the time she was taking the bread out. We bit off tiny pieces of the still warm bread and savored each one, hopping up and down, and made faces of ecstasy as we chewed and swallowed the glorious food. Friendship and a fresh piece of Pueblo Indian bread had to be something you found in paradise.

We sat with our backs to the warm *horno* looking westward at the setting sun amidst gathering clouds on the horizon so we knew the imminent sunset would have a spectacular reddish glow against them. A couple of dogs sat down next to us, their heads looking at the horizon and then turning to us with droopy eyes, obviously an invitation for us to pet them and approve the companionship. We waited a few minutes and admired the color-lit show. I got up finally and Tito decided to join me in delivering the nearly forgotten cigarettes to my mother.

Tito and I arrived at my house and we parked our tires on the north wall. We delivered the cigarettes to my mother who was preparing dinner and who warned me not to stray too far from the house. Tito and I sat against the wall near our tires and finished sucking our hard candy that we had saved in our pockets.

"I'm afraid of tomorrow," he said in *Tewa*.

"Why? Tomorrow is the happiest day of the Pueblo," I answered in *Tewa*.

He looked sad. His father was Hispanic but his mother was a Pueblo Indian so he knew the *Tewa* dialect very well. I knew a lot of words and could understand what someone said to me in that tongue. He was a little darker than me and he had high cheekbones like his mother.

"I don't know if I will remember the dance steps my uncle taught me. He said it was important for me to learn the Pueblo Indian ways."

"You will be fine," I said, trying to cheer him up. We were about the same age with his birthday being in October and mine in early December. We would be going to school in the fall because we would both be six by the end of the year. We had been great friends since my mother had moved to the Pueblo de San Pablo about two years ago to work as an adobe plasterer.

"Tell me about your training for the dance," I said. Tito went on about his outfit and the lessons he had taken with his uncle who was one of the tribal leaders. He had gone into the pueblo prayer room and been given a blessing and instructions for respecting the spirits of nature, the ways of the community and the memory of his ancestors. We continued in *Tewa* and laughed when he tried to teach me new words. He didn't know any English words and neither did I and we were both concerned about starting school where *Tewa* or Spanish speaking was not allowed. He said his older brother had been worried as well when he went to school but he told Tito that the teachers were patient with the kids that didn't know any English. My mother yelled my name for dinner and we both got up. Tito got his tire going and went home.

The house had the aroma of pinto beans and *chicos* and freshly made *tortillas*. My mother had made a little bit of red chili sauce to use as a condiment for the cooked bean and corn mixture. I washed my hands in a small basin that my mother had filled with warm water. After washing my blackened and grimy hands she asked me to dry them with a hand towel and then throw the water out in the front yard. The occasional water from the basin discarded this way kept the front yard moist and minimized the dust that one brought in the house. The floor in the house was always gritty, despite my mother's daily sweeping. The floor was made out of clay but had been plastered smooth and a piece of linoleum covered it up to the base of the wall where dirt always seemed to creep in from underneath.

The adobe walls inside had been plastered smooth and then had been coated several times with tinted calcimine. The ceiling had the traditional *vigas* or de-barked pine logs that had been shellacked and acted as the joists for the roof. The *vigas* were then held in place by a lattice of cedar poles that were strung together to form the actual roof of the house. The cedar lattice was laid in a chevron fashion to give some design to the ceiling. Either straw or more recently, tar paper, was laid on top of the cedar lattice to hold the four or five inches of clay that was spread atop to form the roof. The clay roof was virtually flat but was shaped so that water would flow down and out the *canales* (or spouts) that were built into the parapets of the house. If a roof leak developed it was because the clay had eroded or the rain water had become trapped on top of the earthen roof.

Adobe homes were cool in the summer and kept the warmth inside during the winter months. Heat was generated with cast iron stoves, one that doubled up as a cooking top in the kitchen and another that was usually placed in the sleeping area. Firewood consisted of *piñon* logs that emitted a pleasant scent when burned and whose smoke was tolerable as it wafted through the neighborhood. Cedar logs were also used but they splintered easily when tree trunks were split and made crackling sounds as they burned. White pine logs did not make good fire logs, burning too fast and creating a lot of creosote that clogged up the chimneys. Cottonwood logs were also avoided. They were pulpy and spewed out too much smoke and creosote as well. Kindling was brought into the house in a bucket and generally was nothing more than the chips created when logs were split into pieces that would fit into the fire chambers of the stoves.

My sister liked to listen to the news on the radio when she got up to go to work. The two room house we lived in had electric wiring for lighting and nothing more. There was an overhead light bulb hanging from the ceiling in the kitchen and one in the bedroom. We pulled a chain to turn the bulb on or off. When she bought a radio, we had to buy an adapter that could accommodate the bulb but also provide a receptacle for an extension cord that we strung along the ceiling and down a wall to plug the radio in. We had to have the light bulb on in order to listen to the radio. The news was given in English so I didn't understand much of the broadcast. Music in Spanish was available later in the day and sometimes my mother would turn the radio on during weekends when she wasn't working. That's when I learned that my mother knew a lot of Spanish songs and why she would take me to movie musicals in Spanish when we later moved to San Isidro. The radio connected us to an outside world that was hard to understand. English was an impediment, certainly, but what was talked about did not seem to be important in the Pueblo of San Pablo.

I went outside after dinner and noticed there was no moonlight at all but there was a mysterious glow so that nearby objects were still visible. The only lights piercing the darkness were from the houses that were close to ours. The lights were dim because many of the houses only had a hanging light bulb in each room and heavy curtains were used to cover the windows for privacy. It was quiet except for the far-off drone of cicadas from the *acequia* until I thought I heard drums off in the distance. I listened for the rhythm but the sound faded into the emptiness of the night.

It was the eve of the fiesta, San Pablo Day, and the last one I would celebrate before I went to school and learned English, the language of the new order. It would be a new world for me, one that my mother could not explain to me. I did not know whether I would fit in. Other kids that could speak English would be ahead of me in learning to read in the new language. My stomach tightened as this fear came over me.

As I looked up I felt a chill when I saw a distant shadow move quickly. My mother had warned me about spirits that become partly visible through a moving darkness. Seconds later, I sensed someone had touched me and I was scared. My feet began to tingle and my heart was now racing. I looked around but I could not see anyone. After regaining a semblance of calm I went inside, put on my nightclothes and jumped into bed.

The radio station news program woke me up in the morning as my sister was getting ready for work. My mother was up already and she had lit the kitchen stove and from my bed I could feel its heat on my face. Even though it was early summer, the nights were still cool and the heat from the kitchen stove was just right to make the house comfortable. The hot water from the whistling pot on top of the stove moistened the air and made our house seem warmer. My sister would have hot oatmeal for breakfast before she went to work. I got up and washed my face in the basin that my mother had prepared for me. She had laid out my Sunday clothes that were a little less worn and more color coordinated than my everyday stuff. After a light breakfast, she combed my hair after putting a little bit of pomade on it. The clock in the kitchen showed that it was 7:30 already.

My sister had just left and my mother looked in the mirror one last time. She locked the door with a passkey and then put it in her pocketbook. We walked northward toward the church after she took my hand. The morning chill was still in the air but the sun warmed our backs as we walked. I was excited. San Pablo Day had arrived.

Deep blue skies framed the background for the Black Mesa off in the distance, due north and west from the Pueblo. As part of the foothills for the Jemez range on the west, the Black Mesa was a sacred place for the Pueblo Indians and you could find many volcanic rocks painted there by their ancestors. The towering San Felipe Mountains were on the eastern side of the San Isidro Valley which contained many of the eight Northern Pueblos including San Pablo. The famous Rio del Norte flowed along the Black Mesa's eastern border while the Chama River flowed along its western flank before it joined the legendary river. Because of the waters that surrounded it, a bluish-white mist could be seen around its base in the morning giving it a mystical image.

We met neighbors along the way, my mother engaging them in trivial conversation as I trailed along behind them. We parted ways with the neighbors as we approached the churchyard, my mother excusing herself by saying that she was going to briefly visit a house behind the church. She took me by the hand again and said she was going to show me where I was born. I said that I had been there before but she insisted that it was important that I visit it again.

There were about three houses behind the church. A dirt road separated the church from the fenced yard that enclosed the adobe dwellings. The smallest of the three was toward the back of the yard. It was a one room house and it looked like it was about to fall down. There was someone living in it because you could see smoke coming out of the chimney.

"*Allí nacistes*," [You were born there.] my mother said. She had let my hand go and she stood there with her hands on her hips, staring at the sad looking house, not unlike many others in the village. "*Hace casi seis años*," [It's almost six years ago] she continued. I didn't interrupt her because she was so serious when she talked about my birth. She looked straight ahead at the house and I knew better than to speak when she was in such a trance. The house must have had more significance than just being my birthplace. She took my hand again as if to bring herself back to reality. She tightened her grip on my hand and then said something softly. Her eyes had narrowed but I didn't see any tears.

"*El nacimiento era duro. No sé cómo sobreviví. El Doctor Espinoza vino y te examinó. El firmó tu declaración de nacimiento. Él sabía de tu padre y su muerte. Él había firmado la declaración de muerte en Abril y tu nacistes en Diciembre.*" [The birth was difficult. I don't know how I survived it. Doctor Espinoza came and examined you. He signed your birth certificate. He knew about your father and his death. He had signed the death certificate in April and you were born in December.]

I had heard the story before. My father killed himself after murdering his estranged wife, chasing her down among the *chicos* [sagebrush] and shooting her in the back. My mother had had an affair with him. The murder/suicide had occurred in April and I was born posthumously in December. Before the affair, she had separated from her husband and her family had all but disowned her. A friend living in that house had given her shelter and assisted during the birth. I had never met the friend who had assisted my *Tia* Gregoria in the childbirth. All I knew was that she had moved away.

The story was important to my mother and it was many years before I could understand why. She later told me that he was not buried in the Catholic cemetery, the pastor at that time adhering to the church policy of not having murderers buried alongside pious churchgoers. There were few people at his funeral. She didn't know for sure she was pregnant at the time.

We were one of a few Hispanic families still living in the Pueblo, many leaving the Pueblo for other villages like Nambroca, my mother's birthplace which was situated across the Rio del Norte on the delta formed with the Chama. The Hispanic emigration occurred once the Pueblo was declared reservation land for Native Americans after New Mexico's annexation by the United States in 1848. There had been marriages between the cultures like my *Tia* Gregoria's but they were not common. Like other Hispanic families still living here my mother rented from the Pueblo the modest house we lived in. All homes in the Pueblo were community property of the reservation. My mother lived here because the rent was cheap and she had found work in plastering village houses.

We went to church a little late and many of pews were full. There were more people at this mass than the eight o'clock Sunday mass we usually attended. The air inside was stuffy and a smell of incense hung over the congregation like a cloud before a rainstorm, dark and foreboding. We found seats near the side altar. It was already warm inside with so many people present and there were signs that it was going to be a hot day. There had been no morning breeze so the open windows provided little ventilation. People were already fanning themselves. The priest gave a short sermon on the blessed life of San Pablo, raising his voice or using his hands to punctuate his remarks.

Just before the consecration, a young girl about my age, kneeling a couple of pews in front of us, jerked her head up and rose awkwardly with an arched back, her body stiffening with her head falling over the back of the pew into the laps of the people behind her. I could see her eyes looking upward until only the whites remained, her face becoming pale and her breathing irregular, the mouth half open and making a grunting sound, such conditions frightening the people around her. A lady sitting with her, probably her mother, tried to hold her back and soothe her while other people nearby prevented her from falling further back. Finally, a gentleman took her up into his arms and carried her out into the aisle and out of the church. Half of the congregation had become aware of the commotion and were straining to see what was going on. The rest of the attendees were focused on the holy part of the mass, most of them with their heads down. My mother always recited the rosary during mass and I don't think she skipped a prayer during the incident. She gave me a jab in the ribs that clearly meant that I should observe the mass and that the girl would be taken care of in due time.

After the mass, we went out and mingled with relatives from Nambroca. They greeted us warmly and gave my mother the traditional hug. They referred to me as *güerito* on account of my light brown hair and said that I had been out in the sun too long bleaching it like the earth in the village. They all laughed.

The members of the congregation who were going to participate in the dance ritual that day left quickly, presumably to get dressed and get organized in the prayer room. I saw Tito briefly after church as he accompanied his mother in the group that left early.

There was a lot more traffic in San Pablo than usual. People were parking their cars in the big square in front of the church and across the street near Kramer's. The pueblo celebration brought a lot of people from neighboring villages including farmers and ranchers whose lands bordered the Chama and Rio del Norte rivers.

Eventually we made our way to *Tía* Gregoria's house near the church. My aunt had been to mass also but she had not stayed around to greet family and friends but had hurried home to prepare the breakfast for us. She bore resemblance to my mother but she was taller and heavier, wearing her hair like the Indian women, bangs in the front and cropped at the neck. Of my mother's ten siblings, she was among the older ones, often acting as a surrogate mother to the younger children, my mother being one of them.

"*Mi hijito*, I am so glad to see you," said my *Tia*. My mother said she called me *hijito* because she had assisted in my delivery although it could be used when addressing other people's children. I gave her a hug when she greeted me with open arms. "*Eres bendecido y querido*," she said. (You are blesséd and loved.)

She had made *atole*, a creamy slate-colored mush made from ground blue corn that you ate with a little bit of brown sugar or honey and milk. She had boiled eggs with a creamy red chili sauce for us to have with *tortillas* made from the *Pansy* brand of white flour that came from southern Colorado. Actually, my mother preferred the *Royal Flush* brand but I couldn't tell the difference. Next to my mother she was the best *tortilla* maker. She made them on the cast iron top of the wood burning stove that most families had in San Pablo Pueblo. You had to get the right temperature of the stove top. The *tortilla* would scorch and burn quickly if the top was too hot. The center would not be cooked enough, making it doughy and the burnt section made it taste like carbon. If the stove top was not hot enough, the *tortilla* would dry out from the length of time you left it on the griddle and it came out looking and tasting like a communion wafer, brittle and bland.

But both *Tía* Gregoria and my mother were experts in getting the stove to the right temperature by fueling it appropriately and waiting for the heat range that would produce *tortillas* that were heaven sent. The perfect *tortilla* had light brown scorch marks on both sides, pliable enough to tear easily and crispy around the edges. There would be no burn marks and the taste would be bread-like as the warm chunk melted in your mouth

"*Tia*, your tortilla is better than anyone else's," I said.

"Well, what about mine?" My mother asked.

"Just like my mother's," I said. They both laughed at my silliness.

My aunt was a *curandera*, a healer of sorts in the village. She knew about herbs, roots, leaves and flowers in *remedios* that could be used for curative purposes and warding off evil spirits. Also, she had been the *partera* or the midwife who had assisted in my birth. When I visited her she liked to describe the cold weather and darkness of the night when I was born in December. She was a very popular person in the village and her house always seemed to have a client in need of her services.

My mother told me that her husband, Don Filigonio, also possessed knowledge of potions from the Pueblo Indian culture. His skin color was dark and his face had deep age lines, the eyelids filling up the sockets so that his eyes shown through narrow slits. His hair was thick and graying and was gathered in the back and his *chongo* or single braid was at least a foot long. The *chongo* had a reddish cloth woven through it. He spoke slowly and mixed Tewa words in with Spanish. Sometimes when he looked at you, despite the kindly smile, his eyes didn't blink and they seemed to reach inside of you to read your thoughts, pulling them out one by one, making sense of their context. My mother told me that he could see if you had a demon inside of you that could cause evil with your body. His father had also been a medicine man for the tribe and had taught him ancient rituals that had magical powers. Many of the Pueblo elders would consult with him about Pueblo customs and religious matters. In one story I heard, he had cured a relative of mine from a hex put on him by a jealous lover. Sometimes when I encountered Don Filigonio in the Pueblo, I saw that he held a small, round rock, bigger than a pebble and rather flat that fit nicely in the palm of his hand. My mother explained that the rock was used in rituals to cast or remove spells.

"Are you ready for school in the fall?" said Don Filigonio as he came into the kitchen addressing me before my mother.

"I don't know if I can learn English," I said. "They don't allow us to speak in Spanish or Tewa."

"You should do the best you can; that's important. Patience is a virtue in learning a new tongue. A wise teacher will see your knowledge grow and be a guide for learning new things in the Anglo's language. You will live in his world and not in the Pueblo. It is a new way with different views of the world and to survive you must learn what is important and accept it. But never forget our ancestors and our Pueblo teachings because they are part of your spirit," counseled Don Filigonio.

"I want to learn more *Tewa* so I can talk with my friend Tito. I don't know why I have to learn English," I said. Don Filigonio smiled as he finally greeted my mother and gave her the traditional Pueblo embrace.

"I understand," as he turned again to me. "You will never lose Tito as your friend as long as you respect and honor him and thank him for being your friend. Friendship is not just talk; it is like the corn we plant in the field. We must nurture it, water it and remove the weeds around it which try to stunt its growth. It is hard work. But in the end, friendship will be the nourishment that makes both of you strong." Don Filigonio took my hand and brought me closer to him. He lowered his voice to almost a whisper, and bent down so his face was close to mine.

"English is important for you because you must live with the Anglos who write the law of the land. They have knowledge too and you must learn from them just like you have learned from us. You are part of us and we are part of you," Don Filigonio said as he put his arm around me. I felt a sensation from his embrace when his eyes closed and his head nodded. It reminded me of the strange feeling I had had the night before. "Remember to honor, honor yourself as you honor your mother, your ancestors and the rest of us. The earth reminds us of the nature that cycles through our bodies as the spirits pass through our minds." He arose from the table and silently went into another room, leaving me with my mother and *Tia* Gregoria. My *Tia* explained that he was tending to a young lady who had had a seizure in church. Her parents suspected that an evil spirit had invaded her body and they were hoping Don Filigonio could drive the spirit away. Her name was Marla Garcia and someone I would meet again.

Tia Gregoria always had comic books for me to look through as she and my mother visited after breakfast. The books were in English but I could follow the plot with the sequenced picture panels. I had leafed through a bunch of them when my mother came and got me to go for the morning dance. I asked to go to the toilet first. Most of the houses in the pueblo had an outhouse since there was no running water. There were pumps with spigots scattered throughout the pueblo that people used to fill their water containers they usually kept in the kitchen. The outhouse usually had a lock that engaged from the inside or a lever that you turned that prevented the door from being opened from the outside. There were cracks between the wooden planks that formed the walls and the front door so you could tell if someone was approaching the outhouse.

My mother took me by the hand after leaving *Tia* Gregoria's house. There were a lot of people now standing around a residential square behind the Chapel that sat on the main plaza. The square was formed by two rows of houses that were about two hundred feet apart. The rows, each about a hundred yards long, ran east and west with no separation between the houses. The houses were all made of adobe and some were better kept than others. The exteriors were distinguishable by the number of windows, the shape of the door and how smooth the plaster was on the outside. Crude ladders were placed in front of a few of the houses. The long sidepieces of the ladder were pine trunks that had been shaved of their bark while the cross pieces were made from pine or spruce with smaller diameters and also shaved. The crosspieces were flattened at the edges and were bound to the sidepieces with twine or leather straps. The ladders had crosspieces that were nailed to the upright poles. The poles came together at the top and formed a long triangle as the cross pieces became shorter and shorter toward the top. Ladders were used to access the roof that consisted of clay and required periodic upkeep.

It was midmorning and the people standing on the north side of the plaza were now in full sun and were trying to shade their eyes. Many of them had shed their light jackets they had worn earlier in the morning when the air was a little cooler. My mother and I had taken a position on the south side where you didn't suffer the glare but the sun beat down on your back and neck. She had brought a bandana and had put it on to protect her neck from sunburn and she had lifted my shirt collar to cover at least part of my neck. Once the dance started you couldn't cross the plaza, this transgression considered an insult to the dancers, their ritual being both a celebration and a religious observance derived from their culture, thousands of years old.

The drumbeat started and the dancers filed out of the prayer room. A few headed to the small altar made from cottonwood branches and fronds that honored San Pablo, the patron saint of the Pueblo. They began a dance in front of the holy image, symbolizing the fusing of the Christian religion with the ancient faith of the Pueblo Indian culture. My mother explained it to me when I first saw the dance and she said that it was a tradition that was almost four hundred years old dating back to the arrival of the Spanish missionaries.

Others remained in the square and formed a double file with the dancers being five feet or so apart. They filled up most of the plaza and they formed straight lines oriented east-west. The senior dancers were on the east side and the smaller, younger dancers were on the west side. There was clearly an order of either age or height going east to west. One file was comprised of the women dancers who wore beautiful costumes, mostly white colored with artistic edges made from red or blue threads. Most of the dancers, both men and women, had bands of slotted bells, the small round kind that you see on horses. The men could shake the bells so that they sounded like rattles of a snake. The women wore white calf length boots made from soft white leather and all had hats that covered most of their hair. Their skirts were a bit fuller than those of the men. Their blouses covered their arms down to their wrists and the bodice was tight around their necks. Many of the women had small gourds with handles that they held in her hands. As the women shook the gourds, the seeds or pebbles inside the gourd would make sounds that were rhythmic to the drumbeats. The men had bands around their upper arms and foreheads. Tucked through the band were small pine or *piñon* fronds. The men also had white boots but only ankle length. The dancers were synchronized with the drumbeats which were regular but had accentuated pauses. The drummers also sang in *Tewa*, the words and sounds they uttered also synchronized to the drumbeats. Once the dance with the east-west lineup finished, the dancers arranged themselves in a west-east configuration and proceeded to repeat the dance. The drumbeats stopped and the dancers arranged themselves in a north-south orientation in a neighboring plaza. The onlookers followed the dancers to the new location. There was a brief rest period so that dancers could adjust their costumes and the senior dancers could instruct the younger dancers as to steps and rhythm of the next dance. This was also an opportunity for the parents to encourage the youthful dancers in their performance.

The drumbeats began again and the north-south dance began. This orientation was a lot more pleasant for the audience since only the side of the face was exposed to the sun. You could choose which side you preferred to sunburn. My mother adjusted her bandana so the side of the face was covered and she had a hood formed over her forehead as well. Small clouds of dust were kicked up by the feet of the dancers and beads of perspiration were forming on the foreheads of the senior dancers. The drumbeats were so loud I felt them in my chest. They seemed to replace the beats of my heart. The pounding of the ground by the hundred or so of the dancers also created a syncopated rhythm. The earth seemed to shake and you felt the energy come through your feet and up into your head. I felt my body rising above the plaza and I was soon looking down on the dancers, their movements like moving beads on a rosary, the linkage of generations, a vision of time on the desert ground. I couldn't make out where I had stood. I had disappeared. This frightened me and I found myself holding my mother's hand, back on the ground, part of the audience on the pulsing plaza.

Don Filigonio had told me that the dance was very old and had been modified only slightly since the Spanish came, the woolen garments and bells being small but noticeable additions. The constant movement required by the dance, although measured and slow, required both mental and physical focus. Those who had performed the dance many times made it seem effortless. The rays of the sun rained down on dancers and audience alike, binding us together during the transformative dance of nature. The shaking ground, the loud drumbeats, the bells laced to the dancers' feet put many in the audience into a trance, drawing them into a peaceful state, a glow that lasted for hours afterward.

I spotted Tito among the younger dancers. His costume was beautiful like many of the other young dancers. It seemed whiter, perhaps because it was new and a sign of a first-time dancer. He followed the movements of the older dancers very well. His face was expressionless and his eyes were busy making sure he was not an individual but part of the community of dancers keeping alive a heritage in earth and sky. He had tiny pine fronds on his arms and his face had similar markings like the men dancers. It was hard to picture my friend as being part of another world that would separate us. Even though there had been intermarriages and sharing of religion and food, the Pueblo and Spanish cultures remained distinct even after nearly four hundred years of searching for Cíbola. I still hoped we would remain friends and continue having the good times we enjoyed so much. I knew a bit of the *Tewa* language and I would continue learning more from him and other members of the Pueblo. My mother knew very few words in *Tewa* so she wouldn't be much help. It was not a written language so practice would be very important in mastering it.

After the north-south dance ended, the dancers re-oriented themselves into a south-north configuration and resumed dancing. Once the last dance segment finished, the dancers filed back into the prayer room. The crowd dispersed slowly since it was lunchtime and the families were making plans for the midday meal. Traditionally, the Pueblo residents invited visitors, even when they had not met before, to eat lunch in their home. All the houses in the main dance square and many others nearby opened their doors and invited the guests in. Once inside, the guests sat on long benches on either side of the largest table that the homeowner had. Sometimes two tables were shoved together and chairs were used to supplement seating accommodations. It was courteous to eat deliberately because other guests were waiting for you to finish. Don Filigonio once told me that San Pablo Day traditions, like inviting the public to lunch, were meant to remind us that we are a community, living in nature and sharing its bounty, united in the love of God and human kindness, thankful for health and the joy of life and family. A prayer would precede every sitting, usually led by a member of the host family. A Pueblo Indian family did this despite not having a lot of money or a fancy home. A house on the Pueblo square was often very old and had no running water or electricity. The furnishings were modest, the tables and chairs often crudely hand made.

My mother and I had been invited to the home of Marcos Maestas and his family. Their home was located on the north side of a residential plaza. We went in with other people they had invited for the first sitting. The table was already set with plenty of food including the traditional dishes of red chili stew with pork and potatoes, *posole* in a pork broth, beans in a slightly thickened sauce, *chicos* in a chicken broth, candied yams along with plenty of sliced Indian bread. A side table was laden with desserts of prune, apple and apricot *empanadas* or turnovers. The most popular dish of Pueblo de San Pablo was the red chili stew. Very few cooks outside of the Pueblo could match the flavor, consistency and texture of the smooth, almost creamy stew seasoned with San Pablo chili that had the soft potato morsels and bits of pork floating in it.

The chili was a bright red and had been grown for centuries in the fertile soil near the Rio del Norte. The seeds for the pods had been preserved and handed down for countless generations among the Pueblo Indian farmers. The ripe reddening pods were picked from the knee-high plants in late September or early October and tied together in a *ristra* with twine and dried on the *vigas* that jutted out from the adobe homes. Once dried, the pods were crushed and ground using crude implements into flakes and powder that were used to make the chili paste throughout the winter months and until the next harvest. It was said that the chili from San Pablo Pueblo was incomparable to that grown in other parts of the river basin.

I normally did not eat chili, especially the hot variety made from green chili pods picked during the summer months. But I had been introduced to the red chili stew at an early age and it had become my favorite dish, especially when prepared by natives of San Pablo Pueblo. I would eat the chili stew cooked by non-Pueblo people reluctantly and only because there was none available from San Pablo Pueblo.

Special guests were treated to a loaf or part of a loaf of Indian bread that had been baked in the *horno* the day before. Tito's mother had given us a small piece yesterday just as she taken it out of the oven. It was made from wheat flour from the Colorado mills in the San Luis Valley and used very little salt and baking powder. Fresh yeast was used as leavening and the dough was kneaded at least twice thus eliminating any yeasty taste. It was dense bread, not crumbly, with dark brown crust and it held together even when dipped into chili stew or any meat broth.

My mother prepared a plate for me and we both ate at the table with a bunch of strangers. The people from out of the village introduced themselves first. A few diners were Maestas family members that I had never met. The conversation was minimal since the objective was to finish eating so others could come in for the following shift. My mother and I split a prune *empanada* for dessert and took it with us after we got up from the table. The Maestas family gave my mother a loaf of Indian bread. My mother thanked them for the bread and inviting us to their house. The plaza was filled with people waiting for their turn to eat at one of the houses that lined the square. My mother knew a few of those waiting and chatted with them for a while. We walked around the village finishing our dessert as we walked. We went over to Kramer's and bought a bottle of soda and split it between us.

It was around two o'clock in the afternoon when the dancers came out again and basically repeated the dance sequence they performed in the morning. The temperature was a little higher in the afternoon and you could see that fatigue had set in for many of the dancers. The women seemed all right but the men, who exhibited more accentuated movements of their arms and legs, were perspiring profusely. When the dance was over and the dancers had retreated to the prayer room, the crowd dispersed quickly and many people were seen leaving the plaza in their cars for the trip home.

My mother and I walked slowly out of the plaza and out toward the church. She told me she wanted to recite one more rosary in honor of St. Anthony, her patron saint. I accompanied her and we took a pew toward the back of the church. It was much cooler inside and while my mother prayed her rosary, I sat back on the pew and closed my eyes, thinking about everything we had done today and what Don Filigonio had said to me. His words had signaled a passage for me. I was to enter the world of the Anglo, whatever that meant. All I knew was that I did not know how to speak English.

I thought about the house behind the church and the lady who helped my mother. I began to understand that I would always be different, *bendecido* or "blessed" as my *Tia* said. I would have no father to guide me, advise or comfort me when I hurt. I imagined all the things that could go wrong. There would always be a void that, despite her best efforts, my mother could not fill. I sensed that we didn't have a lot of money and she had no means to change that condition. My sister and my brothers, who were older than me by at least nine years, were also not going to be much help. They had their own lives to lead. There was no obligation to help a half-brother. I didn't even carry the same family name. But I had lived. Here I am in a Pueblo Indian village and I am not an Indian. None of this is my fault. Sitting in church I felt sacrilegious in believing that I had to help myself first and not others.

I could hear my mother whisper the prayers as she went through the rosary sections, her lips moving ever so slightly, as I tried to cope with my doubt and fear. It was as if the drum-laden music had stirred them up and now I didn't know what to do. She thanked the Lord for the blessings we had enjoyed and our continued safety. When she was finished, she took my arm and led me out of the church and we walked home, the drumbeats of the day pounding softly in my mind.

2
Screen Door
May 20, 1950

I did not think it possible to be quieter
unless we stopped breathing.

—Reyes

The banging came suddenly like a thunder clap in the middle of a storm. It frightened you before your mind could comprehend what was happening. I froze in my bed, crouched in a fetal position. My mother, sleeping nearby, sensed it also but she didn't move or say anything. In time I saw her head rise, like an animal, unsure of danger. My heart was racing and it was hard for me to catch my breath. It felt like I had a knot in my stomach. She gestured me to stay quiet and still.

It was our screen door rattling under someone's fist. The neighbor's dog had heard the banging on the door and started to bark. It was not a big dog but its barking was loud enough to wake up light sleepers in the neighborhood. There had been complaints about him by the neighbors. He was kept outside and he had no leash. There was a fence between our yard and the neighbor's and I imagined that the dog had its paws up on the fence and barking at the person pounding on our back door. The dog had sensed that the person was inconsiderate, the loud knocking clearly showing no respect for the peace and quiet that the neighborhood normally enjoyed.

My mother strained to tell me who it was in a whispery voice—"*Tu tío Federico anda boracho*' she said. It was my Uncle Federico who was drunk and probably wanted us to take him home. He was married to my mother's older sister, Maria Elena. She and my uncle were my godparents. My mother and I visited them often in Nambroca, a village across the river from the Pueblo of San Pablo. He had been known to physically abuse my aunt when drunk. This was not uncommon in the Valley, alcohol able to release the anger and frustration that infected men unable to cope with the storm of economic change pouncing on small farmers and ranchers in the San Isidro Valley. He had started out as a farmer and then when it was clear that he couldn't support his family from the income the farm could produce, he went to work at Los Alamos as a janitor, a position he considered demeaning. But the steady job did support the family but he had to swallow his pride and forget the independence he enjoyed as a farmer. His son, Abrán, was close to my age and we had been friends ever since I can remember. But I didn't see him much except during our visits to Nambroca.

We had no lights on but the wood burning stove we had in the bedroom was still warm, very likely emitting smoke up the chimney from the smoldering embers. I remembered that we had thrown a few coal lumps into it just a couple of hours ago. It must be after midnight, I thought, as I covered my face to control my breathing and not utter a sound in the gloomy darkness.

My mother got up slowly and closed the door to the kitchen to darken the house even more. I doubted that the noisemaker would be deterred by that simple act.

The banging continued as we heard the shout, "¡Abranme!" [Open up for me!] But the door held fast despite the fury being released by my uncle's fist as I wondered how the simple screen door could withstand the hammer-like forces. The extent of his stupor may have played a role in preventing him from being more dangerous but the terror was real as my body felt paralyzed. We were defenseless if he did get in the house. Reason could not protect us by talking to him and we were probably compounding his anger right now by not answering the door. The barking continued, more muted now, but the dog was not letting up on warning us that something was amiss.

My uncle had done this several times before. He gets drunk, finds no one to take him home to Nambroca, then remembers that his sister-in-law now lives in the town of San Isidro and might help him in his drugged state. We did have a car, a modest one generally in good running condition, parked outside and close to the house. My uncle had never tried to break into it, damage it or hot wire it. But I had heard tales about drunks from my friends, one of whom had been beaten badly by his drunken father. But the victim was usually the woman who tries to reason with a person whose mind has been taken over by drink. My mother understood this from talking with her sister, Maria Elena, and knew the danger of our situation.

The banging continued but the screen door held in its wooden frame despite the furious knocks. It had a couple of hook latches on it and the kitchen door was also locked but it had a window in it so a good blow to smash the glass would then permit someone to open the dead bolt easily. We had been fortunate in that my uncle had not figured that out. Maybe he had and feared the consequences of doing so. We lived less than a block from the police station. My mother could send me out the front door to fetch a policeman on night duty. The neighbor's dog had calmed down and only barked occasionally now. It could be that a neighbor had gotten up to see what the ruckus was all about.

My mother and I continued to whisper quietly, planning what to do if he did break down the screen door and smash the window in the door. By this time I had found my pants and shoes in the dark, put them on quickly and opened the door to the front room where I could make my getaway upon my mother's orders. I would rush out the front door and run down to the police station and explain the situation to the desk sergeant. He would send a police officer or he would come himself and arrest my uncle for disturbing the peace. By spending a night in jail, my uncle might stop bothering us in the future. I started rehearsing in my mind what I would say at the police station.

"*Qué no me oyen? ¡Abranme! ¡Qué chingada!,*" [Don't you hear me? Open up for me! What the blazes!] The voice continued. As his voice grew in volume, the barking would begin again. Perhaps the dog was sensing trouble with the swearing and threatening voice.

The voice became angrier and the banging grew louder and then nothing. Everything went quiet including the canine chorus from our neighbor's yard.

It was not clear what had happened. Either a neighbor heard the banging and said something or my uncle fell down in a drunken stupor. My mother and I grew even quieter. I did not think it possible to be quieter unless we stopped breathing. We were caught in a moment of terror, not knowing what could happen next. I felt my heart beating fast, my throat feeling dry. We listened for any sound in the house. There was no sound from the neighbor's yard either.

We lived in a three room house with a half bath. We didn't even have a shower or tub. We lived in town and this was considered upscale living. The house was rented, a concrete block affair, rectangular in shape with partitioned walls. The kitchen had a sink with running water, cold only since we had no water heater. The only means of heat was the small wood burning furnace in the bedroom and the kitchen stove, also wood burning. I admired her ability to start the fire in the morning and get it hot enough to warm the kitchen and the bedroom eventually when she opened the door between the two rooms. In high desert country, it was cold in the morning the year round. In the middle of winter I could see my breath in the morning when she first got up. I didn't appreciate this act she performed until much later, actually when I became a parent and felt the blind love for a child. We stayed quiet for a long while. I had found my shirt and put it on and sat on the floor with my back to the small bed I usually slept in. I lay my head back and closed my eyes, hoping this uncertainty would end. My head started to hurt.

Was my uncle picking on us because we were helpless against him? Was it our low status in life that brought this on, a single mother with a boy not quite a man? It was a time of hopelessness, I thought. I was seven, not a little boy anymore but too young and small to take on an adult male twice my size.

My mother had always been a slight woman, weighing a little over a hundred pounds according to her driver's license. She now worked as a housekeeper for the well-heeled folk in town earning a few dollars for cleaning the house, infrequently getting a tip for the effort. However, it had its perks. We would get some usable hand-me-downs, dresses for her, and perhaps household items for our modest home. Usually her employers didn't have boys my age so I was rarely the beneficiary of these gifts. We did get state aid to dependent children, namely me, the princely sum of thirty dollars a month. This did get us food on the table so her wages would then get us clothes and gas for the car. My sister owned the car and she drove it when she was in town. She worked for the national lab in another town and stayed there regularly for security reasons.

My mother said it had been half an hour since the last banging and she felt sure that my uncle had left to find someone else to bother. She murmured something else and I didn't quite hear what she said but I was not going to ask her to repeat it. The furnace was barely warm now but the room still retained some heat. I felt myself sweating when I was paralyzed with fear moments ago. I wondered whether these assaults on our screen door would someday result in something more serious than the two of us jumping out of bed.

But the banging had stopped, the dog felt no need to bark, and my mother was preparing to go back to bed. I climbed out of my clothes and went back to bed as well, pulling the covers over my head. It was hard going back to sleep, an air of fear still lingering that the banging would start anew. My head was still pounding. I could tell my mother was asleep already in the big bed on the other side of the room. Maybe she was used to living in fear. She knew when it was gone and there was time to rest and perhaps face it again tomorrow. It may be something you learn to live with, like a handicap. You don't notice it most of the time and you forget it's there, waiting to take you over like a crippling disease. I had not mastered that circadian rhythm or maybe you were born with it. I closed my eyes and hoped that I would outgrow the fear or at least know how to handle it better.

3
River from Cibola
June 5, 1951

It was possible to look back on yourself,
your friends and the world you live in.
—Reyes

Fidel and I were headed toward the river and we were deep in the *bosque* or river forest, the sun now only able to shower a ray or two to the forest floor through the tall, dense cottonwood canopy. The scattered Russian Olive trees were still in blossom emitting their intoxicating fragrance and we were careful not to get too close to them and their vicious thorns. They grew tall and wide with light green feathery leaves, their small yellow blossoms being pollinated by circulating bees so that they could later bear the fruit of the monkey peanuts in the fall. Our steps rustled the dry cottonwood leaves from last fall forming an inch high, yellow-brown blanket on the *bosque* floor. The rustling announced our entrance to the forest kingdom created by the river god and the giant trees that served as sentries. The cottonwoods were the masters of the river forest, growing to be eighty to a hundred feet high with huge branches that gave them a span that nearly equaled their height. Their bark was thick with deep crevices that allowed kids like us to grip the bark sections with our hands and lift ourselves with our rubber soled shoes whose tips fit nicely into the crevices, thus climbing up the tree to sit like birds on the upper limbs and view the world far and wide. In the summer, just weeks after school was out, we would pick the cotton pods or *tetones* before they opened up and use the individual *tetone* as the projectile for a slingshot. Each *tetone* would ripen eventually from a cluster of ten to twenty of them, rupturing and releasing the cotton ball that floated in the air, it being so light and fluffy, so when the tree released so many of its balls all at once, a moving whitish cloud surrounded the tree. The balls would float away and end up far from the tree as any slight breeze would carry them off like angels until they alit. Occasionally you would find them in your hair and you'd be lucky if a comb could get all the cottony angels out.

It hadn't rained the last couple of weeks and the air in the bosque had a cool prickly dryness to it. It was midmorning and we could hear the river rippling through the rotting stumps and other obstructions brought about by the high waters of the snow melt just a month or so ago. The other sound was the slight breeze vibrating the full-bodied leaves of the monster trees surrounding us. We could see sparkly reflections of the river current through the willowy reeds growing on the banks of the *acequia* or irrigation ditch that paralleled the river in town, sometimes only a few feet away and sometimes as much as a mile away.

"Should we go to the *acequia* or on a river branch?" Fidel inquired.

"Let's start with the *acequia* and then go to the river at the end," I said, not really caring one way or the other.

The *acequia* was built to draw water out of the river stream and channel it away from the river and along the fields that the farmers flooded once or twice a week for their crops of corn, chili and squash, the staples of the Valley that had been grown for thousands of years by the Pueblo Indians. Newer farms, planted by the descendants of the Spanish settlers of the sixteenth century, also had fruit orchards full of apple, pear and peach trees. Some trees had flowered already and there would be green fruit in Valley orchards soon.

The river was the lifeline in the high desert San Felipe Valley, first allowing settlements of Pueblo Indians and then the Spanish colonists who tried to scratch out a living here several hundred years ago. Generations later, families remain in the same farms and ranches, maybe because it was too far to go back in time or space and start anew somewhere else. The river helped us survive the dry winter, the dusty spring and fall and the scorching summer. And so it did for those early Spanish denizens, although not without complaints to Don Juan Oñate, the early settlement leader, about the long turbulent seasons that the Valley had in store for them. The river was the fount of life here and it knew your dependency on it. It was still a force throughout the year, torrential in the spring from the snow melt, full bodied through the summer, rising a bit during the seasonal rains in late summer and early fall and finally quieting down during the winter as it froze along its banks.

Fidel and I already sensed that the river owned us and pulled us almost daily to its shores during the summer, its ripples acting like an enchanting song.

It had always been this way, for the children of the Pueblos as well as for those of the Spanish settlers. As we went into its chilly waters, we felt its power, always here and drawing us in as it had for countless generations like a siren luring her prey. Was there a mutual need and dependency between river and youth, one feeding the other? Our parents worried when we said we were heading toward the river for a swim. Their warnings were pointless but had to be uttered, a ritual performed for as long as anyone could remember. They knew it was a passage that could not be avoided, like an unplanned baptism that had nothing to do with religion and everything to do with the allure and discovery of nature. As boys of San Isidro we knew that the river refreshed our bodies, purifying them from the dust we accumulated in doing things we didn't want to do, like pulling weeds, chopping wood, going to catechism and doing errands. The water around us took us back in time, to a consciousness we couldn't remember, inside a watery womb of a former life, before we had to think and make decisions, before we had to be careful of making mistakes, before we could offend someone, before the ceremony and obligation of being a person.

Fidel was the better swimmer and it was hard for me to keep up. Eventually, I would stand up in the waist high stream and rest and simply let the water flow past me, urging me to move forward. I would see the tiny ripples in the stream or little eddies around me. The duty of the river was downstream and I was getting in the way. There was no time to waste as the sun moved higher in the sky, making everything seem whiter and hotter. The tan colored water continued to push me, its tint coming from the brownish clay that formed the channel banks. The main river stream had clear water from the dominant Rio del Norte tributary that came from a northern mountain chain that stretched into Colorado. The confluence of the two streams, the Chama and the Rio del Norte, was where the Spanish settlers came in 1598, finishing the journey from Zacatecas. Like most settlements into unknown territory, initially called *Antilia* and later known as *Cíbola*, it had a foolish intention, the search for a richer life, not necessarily one dependent on gold or silver as the legend claimed.

"What's the matter?" Fidel had noticed I wasn't following him.

"I'm okay. I stopped to rest," I said.

"Let's go to the river for a while. We can see how fast the current is today," Fidel said, probably as a taunt.

He was a risk taker and didn't understand why I would sometimes stop to observe the trees, some flowers or an interesting rock. Everything was there for him, for his enjoyment when he wanted it. He was my best friend and we took care of each other when we were together. He spoke better English than I did and he didn't know much Spanish. His parents, although both Hispanic and native Spanish speakers, spoke only English at home. Fidel told me that they wanted the children to avoid having a Spanish accent when they spoke English. Fidel and I could understand each other despite the parental differences towards language.

We felt time was nothing to worry about, that our youth would last forever like the river and forest, drinking in the sun, becoming cool with an evening breeze, staying natural in a rhythm without end. Today we could enjoy the *acequia* for a while and then move on to the river itself. Our swim trunks were already soaking wet and our bodies had the skin bumps from the chilly water. We would shiver a bit until the sun rays hit us hard and gave us warmth, evaporating the little droplets, even those falling slowly like tears from our hair and nose. The sun was an old friend, as it joined the river and the desert to create a scene of enchantment for Fidel and me, the yellowish orb showering us with energy that purged, at least for a while, the fear of becoming adults.

In the east the sky was a deep blue framing the jagged San Felipe Mountains and to the west a blackened Jemez range was home to countless *mesas* formed from ancient lava flows. It was many a year before I realized that the setting at the river was unique and magical.

My skin was dry by the time we found a good place to take in a river channel that had a current that wasn't too fast. The river created large tongue-like sand bars as the water receded from the swollen spring flows. There were at least three river channels winding their way through the sand bars like capillaries. The one we chose was about four feet deep at the most and about ten yards wide and it emptied into a small lagoon about a hundred yards from the bridge. The main river channel still had a strong current and was too dangerous for us to handle. Standing in the deep current you could feel the suspended sand going around your ankles, the gritty edges biting into your skin. We couldn't take it in until late summer when the river went down and the current surge was something we could manage.

"We were here before! Do you remember that the lagoon was not as big last week?" Fidel asked.

"Yes, but we were seen from the bridge. People pointed at us, remember?"

I was always afraid of people realizing we were in the river. I didn't see anyone on the bridge that connected the commercial end of town with the downtown district on the west side. We had left our clothes in the reeds on the river bank. They were hidden but somebody looking for them in earnest could find them. We certainly didn't have any serious money, but losing our clothes would be humiliating as we would have to walk home barefooted in our soggy trunks. Fidel didn't seem to care. He would go swimming naked sometimes, oblivious to the world. The river waters freed his whimsical spirit, driving him into a euphoric state, splashing wildly and diving into the water repeatedly. He wanted me to be the observer or the lookout in case of danger. I sometimes thought he was in a trance when we did the river swim. Was it a primordial reunion with the river for him more than me? I wondered.

We floated down the river channel, slowing our movement with strokes in the opposite direction of the slow current. I left the water and lay on a sandy shore area for a while, letting the sun dry me out again. The water-soaked sand was cool underneath me while the sun warmed my face and chest. My feet touched the water's edge and this seemed like a perfect spot for me, the river energy radiating into my body. I was in communion with my distant past. It was like taking a deep breath of peaceful air, quieting my limbs, uplifting and dreamlike. I had closed my eyes and imagined nature taking over me, my body becoming part of the sandy river bank, the edge of the river's pulsing artery. My breathing slowed and I felt myself going backwards, my feet higher than my head as I floated into a darkness. I felt lost in a space whose span was limitless. I had discovered spots like this before. Such a spot gave you a sense of wellbeing and that you belonged there. You had found your place. It was like leaving your body with nothing holding you back. You were now a spirit free to go wherever your mind took you. It was possible to look back on yourself, your friends and the world you live in. You could re-live events, have different endings, re-live them again and have still different endings. It was a non-physical world. You could meet people and interact with them, people you never met before. Places you liked could be revisited again and again. It was an endless dream.

"Hey!" I shouted as I jumped up from my cozy place. Fidel had dumped chilly river water on me with an old rusty bucket he had found nearby.

"What are you doing sleeping here while the water's great?" he asked.

"I know, I know. I just wanted to feel the sun a bit. It feels nice after a swim," I stammered. Fidel had brought me back to San Isidro, the reality of swimming in a river channel near the bridge. I was still the boy from the west side of town with a mother who was a part-time plasterer. I became human again, feeling pain and shock especially when somebody dumps cold water on you.

"It's time to go," he said. "My mother will be looking for me. It's getting close to lunchtime."

I got into the water to clean myself off. The bucket was rusty and the water poured on me had a nauseous smell. I felt the cleansing water around me again and I dipped myself completely, doing one baptismal dive after another before heading home. Despite the shock Fidel had delivered I still felt refreshed and energized. The river had done its magic again, washing away the unsettled state that comes from not knowing the future. You are reminded that we live one youthful day at a time, an uncommon instance when the senses are sharp and joy and sorrow are intense. And there is so much to observe and learn each day, especially with friends, and there is a parent to protect you.

I walked fast to catch up with Fidel. We found our clothes and removed our trunks and wrung them dry. Our skin still had goose bumps from the swim. We dressed and put our socks and shoes on after cleaning the river sand and grass off our feet.

As we walked home I could hear the river ripples become dimmer until I couldn't hear them anymore. It felt like we were leaving a friend behind, an anxiety rising inside of me as we walked further and further away from the water. We went through the canopy formed by the cottonwoods, our shoes making a crunching sound on the leafy floor punctuating a step at a time our exit from the river kingdom. Upon reaching the band of Russian Olive trees, I could see bees that were going from blossom to blossom, pollinating them as they were attracted to the trees by the yellow flowers and their wondrous scent. They had been here forever while Fidel and I were nothing more than visitors to them. Our life was yet to come and we had no idea of what it would be like. Our future was not going to be connected to the *bosque* and the river. We had only a few more visits left before we would say goodbye forever to the river from Cíbola, the river of the Conquistadores. We left the *bosque* and entered the town proper again, ready for the rest of the day. A river swim had prepared us for anything. But first, we would have lunch.

4
Picking Chimajá (wild parsley)
March 16, 1952

*We were alone but survival was the
real goal as it had been for the Indian
pueblos before the Europeans came.*

                                              —Reyes

The March wind was picking up and I could feel dust in my mouth already, my lips already chafing from the cold, dry air. My mother was still climbing up the hill looking closely at the ground and all I could see were small rough grass sprouts, *Chamisa* or rabbit brush shoots and occasionally a sprig of Apache Plume. She was looking for the *Chimajá* herb that sprouted when the last snow was gone from the ground, usually in mid to late March. But I hated the caustic wind that seemed to signal the seasonal change, how it swirled and changed direction suddenly, kicking up the dust and dislodging tumbleweeds from their anchors and unleashing them to roll like spirits in random directions. Some people had a crazy temperament in the season, maybe a reaction to the changing weather or a dark uncertainty it created in your mind. The older *Chamisa* bushes usually had pollen left over from the fall still stuck to their prickly branches and the March winds would loosen it and float it up into the air currents and mix it with the dust. The pollen and dust powder would cause misery to the allergy sufferers. It was a dry, bitter wind, making it seem colder than it was on desiccated skin, your nose becoming bloody from the lack of moisture on its tender lining. The edges of my eyelids would redden; my hair would get gritty and I would get fissures in the skin between my fingers that wouldn't heal despite the best of ointments my mother would procure from my *Tia* Gregoria, a *curandera*. The gusts would make whistling noises past your ears, pushing you back, flapping your pant legs, and making sure you couldn't ignore the invisible power. We both wore light jackets to fight the shivers, especially when sudden wind surges spit more debris and caused a penetrating, grayish cold. I imagined that the annoying breeze came down from the Jemez peaks to punish penitents, the range still covered with snow this Lenten time of year.

I looked around and there was no one near. It was a Sunday afternoon, rather cloudy but it didn't look like rain, the ominous clouds moving quickly in the turbulence. The desolation made you want to go home and the weather seemed to question your sanity. But it was a ritual of early spring that my mother believed in and had to be continued.

She had a will that kept her going and that I was sure I did not inherit. It disappointed her that I couldn't keep up and I didn't understand the importance of her search. We always seemed to be looking for some herb, nut or vegetable— *verdolagas* (purslane) along the river bank, *yerba buena* (spearmint) along the *acequia* bank, *piñon* nuts in the mountains and now *Chimajá*, all of them cherished by the lingering Spanish culture of the Valley.

The Jemez volcanic peaks and their lava flows formed the western slope of the Valley and she claimed that this was the place for *Chimajá*. Looking northward we could see the peaks run for fifty miles or more on our left as they disappeared among the darkened *mesas* that often formed their foothills. To the south they curved around westward forming the widest span of the Valley floor. This let the river bed be flatter and slowed the current to a virtual crawl.

In the fall we would travel into the mountains and search for *piñon* nuts, going from *piñon* to *piñon* to pick the nuts that their pine cones had released and were now atop the needle mulch of the tree. The nuts were small and you had to pick quite a few to fill the one pound coffee tin that each of us used for gathering them. We would spend hours underneath the trees and eventually come home with five or ten pounds worth of nuts. I enjoyed being in the forest, sitting beneath the tree that spread its fruit on an apron knit of soft needles. It was quiet except for an occasional breeze as it softly whistled past the pine boughs that did gentle curtsys. I wasn't a fast picker and my mother said I put too much needle debris in with the nuts but I didn't complain and I did contribute a significant amount to the harvest. Picking *Chimajá* was a lot different. I wasn't sitting down and it wasn't easy finding the pesky plants.

"*Por aquí, por aquí,*" she would say with some irritation as if that would make me move faster. She showed me a sample of the herb she'd found. As I understood it, the root was the target of the search but you had to identify the leaves first before trying to dig out the root. She carried a small bag with the specimens she'd found already. I'd found none but she hadn't given up on me for she knew my training would take time and patience. She was intent on teaching me the ways of the ancients like being obedient, never talking back, never interrupting the adults, always walking behind them and focused on what others had to say. I didn't understand why the ways were important but she said I would come to value them over time.

I went in a different direction but still could see her out the corner of my eye. She was a small woman, an inch or two above five feet and weighing a little over a hundred pounds, her energy defying comprehension. Her hair, thick and shoulder length, made her look taller despite a slight hunchback. She had learned to fend for herself being among the last of her father's family. Married at the young age of eighteen, she had raised three children while separated from her husband who'd been a sheepherder for the big ranches that had herds in Utah, Colorado and New Mexico. He would be gone for nearly nine months, coming home for the hard winter months—November through January. In mid-February he would take off again and not come back until late October. When the three children were all in school, she left him and tried it on her own, asking the older children to help out. She was not alone and there were plenty of single mothers in the Valley who had left abusive, never-do-well husbands or had never married. Part of the problem was the lack of good work for the men, especially if they not finished school. The Valley was full of farms and ranches but they were too small to require workers outside the family. The nearest city was Santa Fe and there was government work there but schooling was mandatory. In their despair, the uneducated men turned to alcohol and often developed an ill temper.

One of my uncles had become quite abusive when drunk and had taken to physically fighting with the older children. One night, after having a fight with his wife and eldest son, he shot himself. We had gone to his funeral last week. He had had a stutter that he couldn't control and it was hard for him to find work after giving up on farming. The money from his crops wasn't enough to tend to the needs of his family, according to my mother.

We went to a lot of funerals, partly because my mother's numerous relatives kept dying; but it was also a social event requiring attendance even by people who hadn't seen the departed for years. The event had stages, starting with a wake, followed by a rosary, a mass and finally the actual burial. There were refreshments and snacks after each stage at the home of the deceased. There were different reasons for death, including simply—old age. That reason I could understand. You were born, you lived for a while, married, had children, lived some more and then you became old and then died. I could understand accidents also, like being thrown from a horse or run over by a car. What I didn't understand was the suicide. You were born and you learned the ways of your elders. You followed the life that was expected of you. That's what I was doing here with my mother. Why kill yourself?

At last I found a few plants behind the *Chamisa* bushes. I felt a power lead me to them; maybe it was concentration or the spirit of my ancestors giving me a head start. Brushing away the surface gravel I was able to dig around the stem of one of the plants and gently pull out the root without breaking it off. I brought the root up to my nose just like my mother did to verify that it was the object of our quest. It had a fresh earthy smell, its oils getting on my fingers and permeating the air that I breathed. I wondered how our ancestors knew about the plant and its healing powers. There were so many plants that grew in the semi-arid rocky soil in the foothills, most of them sad looking, more grayish colored than green. Valley fauna, including people, had a worn, despondent look as well, their faces rugged from the icy winters, dry chilly winds, the searing sun and the dusty storms in the spring. My mother's face was wrinkled prematurely and had been for a long time despite her age of forty five, her hair already graying, making her look older than she really was. Her hands, calloused from work in the *milpas* and chili gardens during the summer and her plastering jobs in the spring, summer and fall, did soften a bit during the winter when she worked indoors usually cleaning houses and ironing clothes for others.

"*¿Qué hayastes?*" My mother asked. She looked at the roots I had and nodded approval. It was a relief to have been successful in a small way but now was the time to get serious and find more roots, adding to the initial good will and engendered hope that I was not a lost cause.

I would get down on my knees once I spotted something that resembled the plant. More often than not, it was something else but eventually I did find a few good plants, their roots dug out intact. Persistence may have been the power I felt earlier and not a mystical power from the past. I had crossed into its domain. I was happy that I could please her with my own cache. We continued to search for more and within an hour we had plenty of roots. I never knew where all the roots went once we got them home. We certainly weren't big users and I suspected she traded *Chimajá* for other herbs. Sharing food, bartering and taking care of each other were customs in the community that my mother followed religiously.

Chimajá was just another currency for survival. You had to work to get enough of it and have it amount to anything. Sure, you didn't have to till the soil, bury the seed, water it, weed the mound to let the plant grow but it was a burden to overcome. It was part of living in the harsh climate, continuing the settlement begun years ago on the promise that there was a good life in the land of Cíbola. The generations had been loyal to the cause, finding ways to increase the yield of crops and livestock for community and never for personal gain. We were alone but survival was the real goal as it had been for the Indian pueblos before the Europeans came. But the tribes had long made peace with nature, accepting the sun and the wind as they came, avoiding the disappointment that comes with unpredictability. The rest of us still sought magical Cíbola, the land of the Conquistadores, the land that was promised then and remained elusive to this day. This was a quest that consumed generation after generation

I patted the little bag of the *Chimajá* stash as we walked back to the car. It was but a little step in my entrance into the community, learning its ways, for it had endured, intact in its belief in God and family, its love of language and customs, attached to the land despite its decline in value. I felt I was far from being ready to survive by myself but I was happy to be with my mother during this period of learning and uncertain passage. It was the same comfort and security felt under a blanket during a winter night, the rubbing of feet together to feel welcome heat, covering your face with the bed sheet, and converging on a fetal position that will bring on desperately needed sleep. You knew the cold night would end and daybreak would bring warmth from the bright, high desert sunshine and you would feel alive and ready for the wonders of the day in Cíbola.

5

Good Friday
April 11, 1952

They were not looking for sympathy so it
didn't matter to them or to the faithful
—Reyes

Clouds had taken the sun away making the Lenten day seem cold, dark and foreboding. We were on our way to Sonseca for a religious observance and it was mid-afternoon of a long, listless day, people looking aimless, waiting for something to happen, the town dead after a long winter and no sign of spring. My mother was driving silently and I was in the back seat of the car with a couple of comic books she wouldn't let me read. She said today was a day for prayer, penance and reflection, not entertainment. Already this morning she had asked me not to play basketball because it would be rude and insulting, knowing that we observe the death of Jesus today. Worse, we had had no breakfast or lunch since it was also a day of fast. I could have all the water I wanted though. For me this was the first observance of the strict Catholic rules of Lent. I had made my First Communion last spring and had accepted the faith with all its restrictions. There were easy and hard ones, not eating all day was one of the latter. Fortunately, the all-day fast happened only on Good Friday and Ash Wednesday. But every Friday during Lent my mother and I had only one meal which couldn't have any meat in it nor could it have meat flavor. Fish was allowed but usually my mother served up pinto beans and *tortillas*.

School had been dismissed on Wednesday afternoon so the students could observe religious ceremonies on Maundy Thursday and Good Friday. Most of San Isidro's residents were Hispanic and Catholic and many stores, especially those owned by Hispanics, were closed on Good Friday. There was little auto traffic in town and we had encountered almost none in our trip so far. I wondered whether driving a car on Good Friday was to be avoided as well.

So I sat there in the back seat with hunger pangs, trying not to think about food, staring out the side window at the sea of *Chamisa* that covered the *llanos* or plains between San Isidro and the villages north along the Rio del Norte. My mother had said that the *llanos* had been grasslands at one time and then sheep had been brought to the area in the last century by the thousands and by the time she was born in 1908, the grass was totally gone and only a form of sagebrush, the *Chamisa*, could grow on the land. The grass was gone forever and perhaps as punishment for desecrating the land we inherited more dust storms as a result, especially during the turning of the seasons in March and October. Although this was early April, a nasty wind was still around, bringing in a chill during the morning and kicking up dust in the afternoon, a grim reminder that we lived in the high desert. As we drove by the *llanos* you could see clouds of dust rippling through the *Chamisa* and building small sandy piles around the plants. Occasionally you would see tumbleweeds rolling across the road followed by trails of dust as if chasing the yellowish weedy orbs. We were going through empty reservation land owned by the Pueblo of San Pablo where I was born. The *llanos* were relatively flat, slowly rising toward the sandstone foothills of the San Felipe Mountains that formed the eastern rim of the San Isidro Valley. Ancient water and wind erosion had formed strange figures from the crimson and yellow sandstone, arches and domes, towers and animal shapes. The reddish sunsets heightened the colors so that they appeared on fire.

The Pueblo Indians considered the land sacred and had left it intact, never permitting any development of it for housing or commercial use. At night, spirits allegedly roamed the *llanos*, manifesting themselves in shadows that moved, animals that appear then disappear, a glow that surrounds a *Chamisa* and whispers sounds no one can understand. My mother says the spirits could scare the most fearless of men. There were stories of men in a drunken stupor who ventured accidently into the sacred *llanos* at night, who upon discovery the next day, never fully recovered their wits from whatever fright they endured.

My mother had told me that we were going to observe Good Friday by joining in a *Penitente* procession in village of Sonseca just north of the Pueblo of San Pablo. The *Penitentes* was the name given to those men who on Good Friday re-enacted the crucifixion of Christ by experiencing self-inflicted flagellation and the carrying of the cross. The Catholic Church in New Mexico did not condone the practice and so no ordained priest presided over the ceremony. But villagers, especially those in Sonseca, continued the tradition that went back to the Middle Ages and was brought here by the first Spanish settlers to Northern New Mexico in the sixteenth century. My mother thought it was a form of extreme redemption in which the *penitentes* sought forgiveness from mortal sin while the community participants professed their faith, conducted self-reflection, and internalized the pain of Christ's last hours on earth.

We arrived at a small church, a *capilla*, in Sonseca and there were several cars parked just south of the cemetery that formed the church's front courtyard. Like most churches in the region, it faced east and was built of thick adobe walls, sloped so the top of the wall was thinner than the bottom, and with small wings forming the transept. Many of the villages north of San Isidro had *capillas* and occasionally a mass would be held there by an itinerant priest, usually on the birthday of a patron saint or for a funeral of a village member. Sonseca's *capilla* was showing its age and looking tired from burning sun, torrential downpours in the summer monsoon season, and endless dust storms that had eroded the wall surface. It was even smaller than most *capillas* and its small tower had no bell. Its pitched roof had rust spots on its corrugated galvanized steel panels, a few of them twisted and partly warped or lifted by high winds.

We got out of the car with my mother taking her small leather purse and a black mantilla which she used to cover her head inside any church she entered. She took me by the hand (although I was in third grade and nine years old), a practice she used to remind me not to stray too far from her, not just physically. There was a gust of wind as we approached the *capilla*, blowing dust onto my face, and instinctively I shielded my face with my free hand. I could still see that the graveyard in front of the *capilla* was full and another one had been established on the north side of the *capilla* with a few graves already populating it. The mounds marking the gravesites had not eroded or collapsed like those in the front courtyard. The heavy wooden door to the *capilla* was difficult to open but between the two of us we managed to open it slightly and, using all our strength, pull it open against the wind. We went in and there were twenty or so people inside the darkened church. The *capilla* had a wide middle aisle and a very narrow one on each side wall. There were only ten pews on either side of the middle aisle and only a couple in each arm of the transept. There was a loud murmur from people saying the rosary and we slid into one of the pews towards the back. The *capilla* had an earthen floor and the crude wooden pews had legs that had been sunk into the dirt. My mother promptly kneeled on a crude wooden foot rest, took out her rosary from her purse, and joined in the prayer chorus. I kneeled as well and silently observed the rosary session. The *capilla* interior had a stale and pungent odor that you find when you enter a closed up room with cobwebs and lots of dust. There was one small window on the north wall and one on the south wall, both rather high so you couldn't see outside but sunlight could enter the *capilla*. The small altar at the front had been covered with a black cloth, a tradition observed on Good Friday. There were religious icons and figures, *santos* and *bultos*, above the altar and that hung on the walls but all had been covered as well. The drone of the loud praying went on and on, occasionally being broken by the *capilla* door being opened and the wind making a noise like someone whistling. After the rosary was over, the *capilla* became quiet. Many people sat back on the pews, the old wood creaking as it took on the load. My knees were all right but my stomach was still rumbling.

After a while, I heard the *capilla* door open and people outside, chanting. It was a slow, mournful chant whose words I didn't understand. I assumed that it was in Latin. The chanters were several barefooted women and men who came into the *capilla* on their knees, slowly moving in the direction of the altar, their torsos moving from side to side as they advanced one knee at a time. Each held a rosary in clasped hands. Behind them were three men, walking at a slow pace, dressed in black robes with hoods that hid their faces. They were also barefoot, their feet much more dusty than the others, as if they had been walking for a longer time. A large wooden cross was carried into the *capilla* by two other men, one holding the cross piece with both hands and the other holding the bottom of the cross with one arm around it on his side. Once the group was inside the *capilla*, the door was closed. The wind had become stronger and its whistling fury could be heard inside above the chant.

At this point the people in the pews stood up and the chant continued with other people joining in. When the chant ended, the kneelers got up. The women, all wearing dresses pinned up in the front to expose the knees, got up slowly and wiped the blood off their legs with pieces of cloth that had been handed to them.

All of the people were facing the altar and a prayer leader started the Lord's Prayer in Spanish. All joined in. Afterwards, three Hail Marys were said and an Act of Contrition. The prayer leader started the same chant again and all the participants in the center aisle turned and faced the back of the *capilla*. The heavy wooden cross was stood up and turned around. The three hooded men knelt down while the women with bloody knees unbuttoned a robe flap that covered each man's back. The chant continued as the women spread oil on the exposed back. Each hooded man was given a gripped leather lash with three tails, each about two feet long and each had three knots toward the end. The participants in the center aisle moved away from the three kneeling men. The chant ended. Each kneeling man, the *penitente*, in turn exercised the lash on his back three times. Every time the lash hit a man's back, there was a collective moan from the observers. Some looked away. A few had tears in their eyes and others cried openly. The chant started again, this time it sounded increasingly mournful, almost like a constant wail. The group in the center aisle starting leaving the *capilla* once the door was opened.

The wind blew small dust clouds into the *capilla* as everyone followed the procession that started with the two men carrying the cross. Several men and women led the chanting; women were crying, their sobs producing a general lament within the crowd. The three hooded *penitentes* with exposed backs still held their lashes at their side. Others in the group were prayer leaders. The rest of the congregation followed.

It was still overcast but the snow-capped San Felipe Mountains were still visible to the east despite the dust and sand swirling in the air. They stood like mighty sentinels of *Cíbola* watching over us like casual observers at a funeral. But no one was dead, the procession really a reminder of our own impending death or the death of our ancestors who had experienced the same blanched earth and dry winds. My mother often said that the weather in the San Isidro Valley could drive you to despair. She claimed that Jesus was there to give us hope for a better life, a hope that was nearly four hundred years old.

Sonseca was on the left bank of the Rio del Norte, just off the road to Taos. People here could irrigate and coax the earth to grow maize and squash like the Pueblo Indians had done for thousands of years, tilling the soil, weeding the crops and irrigating with crude implements.

My mother had taught me to weed our garden last summer. The sharp edge of the hoe was maneuvered around the corn or chili plant to scratch the soil and cut off the weed and dig out part if not all its root. The rows of plants seemed to go on forever. It was tedious, tiring work especially if performed in times of full sun. My mother and I would tend to the garden early in the morning with the goal of finishing our work before noon. After our work was done we would have a light lunch on the bank of the *acequia*. Often she would tell me stories of her youth and the chores she performed on her father's farm. The reward for our efforts came in the fall when we had an abundance of crops and my mother could sell or trade them for other things we needed.

The head wind became strong and snapped me out of my daydream. We all leaned forward against it but people still lost their footing and almost fell. Several people in the procession were elderly, slight in stature, each with a back slightly curved, their darkened faces bearing deep wrinkles, walking in almost imperceptible steps, their hips and knees nearly fixed, only their ankles flexing in the shuffle. The women wore bandanas tightly wrapped around their heads, making them seem smaller and frail and highlighting their wrinkly faces with bluish veins prominent on their temples. Many had brownish spots on their upper cheeks as well. The elderly men were clean shaven with their faces waxen and eyes droopy with bulges just under the lids, their hair all white and thinning. Their threadbare pants appeared too large, the cloth draping like folds over their emaciated thighs and legs, A few of the elderly braced themselves with canes, the veins on their hands becoming larger as they tightened the grip. Their thin, splotchy lips were moving slightly, mouthing the words of the chant. They kept their eyes focused on the ground, opened to nothing more than slits to keep the dust from blinding them further today or in life. They were here, like all the others, for penance, seeking forgiveness for sins perceived or real. Their tenacity in this horrible weather indicated they were running out of time. I was perhaps witnessing the future of my mother, my brothers, my sister and myself, saddened by our lives and nothing to guarantee our passage to heaven. We would be here on a Good Friday, grasping for comfort, wanting to believe that we could escape the dread that aging inevitably brings.

My mother held my hand with a firm grip as if clasping something solid and dependable and with the other she carried her purse and rosary. I looked at her and saw that she was praying, her lips repeating words that pledged her undying faith in God. I felt sorrow at what my future appeared to be.

After only a few steps outside of the *capilla* and just beyond its courtyard the procession stopped and observed the first station of the cross. Prayers were said, the self-flagellation ritual was observed by the three hooded men; and chanting was restarted. This continued for each station with each hooded man, in rotation, dragging the cross by himself. Part of the crosspiece rested on the *penitente's* shoulder. The pain must have increased with every station because their steps became slower and more deliberate as the procession went on. The tip of the cross made an ugly rasping sound as it was dragged on stretches of rocky soil. I cringed when I saw their bare feet go over the sharp edges of rocks and pebbles. The image caused a strange sensation in my feet and I gripped my mother's hand a little tighter. But carrying the cross on sandy stretches was not any easier, the weight of the wood causing the tip to sink deeply into the sand with the resulting drag becoming another impediment for the *penitente* as he pushed the upper part forward. The wind was unmerciful as well, whipping itself this way and that, pushing you to the left and then the right, increasing the misery of the chilly, overcast day. It was worse for the *penitente* carrying the cross when it became a head wind, making his burden even more difficult to bear. It whistled past your ear and sometimes lifted your hair. Women tightened their *mantillas* or bandanas to protect their exposed skin. Some men had taken a handkerchief and used it to cover their nose and mouth. The torture suffered by the *penitentes* and the terrible weather that seemed to accompany the scene saddened me. I moved closer to my mother, putting my arm around her waist, wanting to seek solace from the hellish scene.

By the fourth stop, even though there were several people between us and the *penitentes*, I could see that their backs were now reddened by the lashes they had borne. By the eighth station, the backs of the *penitentes* were bleeding, each new lash taking a greater toll. Women continued to nurse their wounds with a cloth. Between the last two stations, the barefooted men and women who had entered the *capilla* on their knees again fell to their knees and advanced in that position. At the last station, the prayers were repeated twice and the hooded men fell prostrate after their last flagellation ritual, their exhaustion and pain self-evident. The congregation surrounded the robed men in a large circle, still chanting although the voices sounded hoarse and raspy. The women nursed the wounds for the last time and buttoned the robe flap on each *penitente*. The chant ended and the entire procession fell to its knees except for the *penitentes* who remained prostrate. Even the elderly were able to get down with help from others while the prayer leaders said the Lord's Prayer. There was silence for a moment and then a prayer leader shouted the phrase—*Eli, Eli, Lama Sabachthuni*—the words echoing in the gloomy afternoon, the whistling wind continuing to beat down on the faithful with showers of dust and gritty sand. Sobs from women broke the eerie silence of the chanters who had raised their heads from a pious pose and started getting to their feet. Finally, two men helped each *penitente* up, pulling each arm as he staggered in a daze, and slowly carried him to a car. This was done for all three hooded men, each being placed in a separate car.

Miraculously, each *penitente* did not drag his feet while being held up by the men with his arms around the neck of each man. By now all the participants had stood up, a few requiring help from neighbors. There was a collective sigh of relief, perhaps because the hooded men were all right. We were never able to see clearly the face of any one of the *penitentes*. They were not looking for sympathy so it didn't matter to them or to the faithful. The procession then disbanded, many participants still showing tears.

Several worshippers went back to the *capilla* and meditated for a few minutes. Most were elderly, experiencing a transition back to reality perhaps, the ritual having taken a toll on their ancient bodies. My mother and I stayed a while in the *capilla* also. I pulled out a handkerchief and wiped off dust and sand from my eyes and face. She spoke to a couple of ladies she knew outside the *capilla* as we were leaving, her hand still holding on to me. The wind continued to be annoying, flapping women's dresses against their legs and billowing out men's shirts, making them look like hunchbacks. As she talked with her friends I looked eastward toward the mountains, their majestic peaks undeterred by the nasty weather and the grim ceremony we had just witnessed.

6
Jail Time
June 5, 1953

Sooner or later every male in the Valley could expect to visit the police station and answer for his errant behavior, the occasion considered inevitable.

—*Reyes*

She held the tray steady as we neared the screen door of the jail entrance. It was about eight o'clock in the summer morning, the usual time for breakfast delivery. The entrance to the police station had a main door that was always open in the summer because the station had no air conditioning. It was a huge metal thing that had dents on it, the mementos of people kicking it or of protests at entering the house that supposedly cures ill behavior. It opened into the receiving room with a window up beyond eye level, not to be opened perhaps, the sash painted shut anyway. It did let light in but the air remained stale and smelly despite the outside air that the open door provided. You could see dust particles suspended in the air as sunbeams bisected the area where the desk sergeant often sat. There was an ashtray on the desk with cigarette butts smashed into it, most of them sitting upright like dogs waiting to be patted. The jailer lifted his heavy-lidded eyes once we were in the room. He rose from behind the desk, a cigarette in his mouth, smoke curling up into his face as he quickly put away the magazine he had been reading. His eyes squinted; he drew one last puff and then he extinguished the butt like all the others, twisting it, pressing it into the tobacco graveyard. He wore an officer's charcoal-colored uniform, now wrinkled and stained from drips of milk-diluted coffee that he had taken during the evening duty. His thin face looked tired and his stubble bore a grayish tinge. He had sunken cheeks and a prominent Adam's apple which moved up and down when he spoke. He formed a slight smile as he oriented himself to greet us.

"*Pase Usted*, Señora Córdova," the jailer said. "The guests have been waiting for you."

My mother smiled at the warm greeting despite its false sincerity. The jailer knew my mother spoke very little English so he addressed her in Spanish with a few English words thrown in. The mix of Spanish and English was still common in the San Isidro Valley where quite a few members of the older generation still clung to the mother tongue as well as the old custom of using the unfamiliar form of addressing people. I was not allowed to use the familiar form except with my friends. This custom was a reminder to the younger generation that respect for elders was still important even for those that I thought deserved no respect. My trouble was that in learning American English I could draw no idiomatic comparison to this custom besides using the word "sir" or ma'am." It was another one of those cultural differences that made learning the language that much harder. Speaking English without an accent was another failing that Anglophones made fun of and in turn made me self-conscious. The fear of ridicule induced me to practice speaking certain multisyllabic words in places where no one could hear me. I would say them over and over again until all Spanish intonation was wrung out of the rope of polyphonic sounds.

"*¿Son dos, verdad?*" My mother said as she lifted the cloth covering the meals she had prepared for the two inmates. The jailer had left word at our house the previous evening that only two meals were necessary the next morning.

"*Claro que sí. Son los mismos de ayer.*" He answered. "I think they will be here a couple more days. No bail has been set for them."

The jailer took the tray after unlocking and opening the door to the cell area. It was a heavy, grayish metal door with a small window at eye level and a louvered vent symmetrically placed in the door's lower half. He left the door open and we could see the two jailed men sitting on a bunk bed with their heads down, staring at the floor. They slowly lifted their heads as the jailer walked in.

"*Miren aquí que les trajo la Señora Córdova.*" He said. "I think it smells pretty good. You guys are lucky today." The jailer elongated the words "good" and "today" as they are sometimes heard in the Valley, especially when enunciated in a mocking tone.

"*Eres un pinche cabrón*, Ramirez. You know that, don't you?" One of the inmates said.

"Don't be *necio*, Martinez, or you'll never get out!"

"*Pelamela*, Ramirez. Just don't go around town without your gun. There may be somebody waiting for you."

"You don't scare me, Martinez. I will come after you. So eat, that way you won't lose any of that pretty weight."

They murmured something I didn't quite hear as the jailer slid the tray through a slot in the cell door. My mother sat down on a bench near the main entrance door as the jailer gathered the dirty dishes from the previous meal delivery. I stayed where I was, leaning against the massive desk, taking in the scene of the barred cell area. It was starkly furnished with two bunk beds with thin, soiled mattresses with no sheets or blankets. The pillows were small and made from the same striped muslin used for the mattress covers. There was a toilet in the corner of the cell with the u-shaped seat, the kind of facility that doesn't use a tank for flushing. The walls of the cell were made from concrete block painted over with green-colored enamel that still had some sheen.

The first man was thin, looking frail as if life had sucked out the energy his body once had, his pale face weathered with deep age lines, a few prominent liver spots on his temples, bags under his dry bloodshot eyes looking like he had gone days without sleep. His hair was disheveled, longish and graying, with dust balls still clinging to the side of his head, probably the result of sleeping on the filthy bed in the cell. As he stood upright I saw that he wasn't much taller than me. Perhaps his stature had shrunk from the weight of misfortunes in his life? He looked more pathetic than other inmates I had seen before. Often they were sad men, recovering from a night of drunken behavior, now ready to go sober for a while until whatever bothers them overcomes their will to be normal. In addition to their breath, sometimes you could sense the alcohol seeping through their pores, emitting a rank, constipated odor as it evaporated and formed a distinctly putrid aura around the body. Or they were men trying to control an anger that led them to act impulsively and do damage to person or property. Often you could see the anger slowly consuming them as they fumed about being there, a sign of their failure to cope with the demons of life. This man seemed beaten, just waiting until the final blow, maybe coming today or tomorrow. Someone just had to provide the reason for ending the will to live.

The other man was much taller and bigger than the first and a little younger. He's the one that gave the jailor a hard time. His name was Martinez. You could hear his breathing a room away, the massive amount of air being moved giving his presence away. He had a few days' worth of stubble on his round face that fronted bloated jowls, a multi-folded chin, and dark eyes like bulging orbs set under bushy eyebrows. His hair was curly and light brown, needing a haircut so his head looked larger than necessary even for his massive body. His wide mouth showed big teeth with a gap between the two front ones, the nose bulbous and ruddy, and the tip a bit more reddish than his pimply cheeks. His belly bulged so that his pants were held up with a belt that was fastened just above his crotch. I wondered whether my mother's meal was going to be enough for him. Her meals were often filling since she normally prepared a healthy portion of an entree with a couple of *tortillas*. He looked annoyed that I was staring at him so I turned away and took in the rest of the jail waiting area.

The police station was depressing, probably intended to be that way, with nothing on the walls in the office area except a large bulletin board with "wanted" posters on it. The wall paint was peeling in places, perhaps the result of neglect and the dry, hot air of the summer months. Today the morning air was warm but it was sure to get a lot hotter in the station later in the day, the heat acting as another form of torment for its occupants.

You could hear the men starting to eat their meals. There was conversation with the jailer that I couldn't make out but it must have been a friendly one because everyone spoke softly. I could see that the jailer had gotten water for the inmates in two plastic tumblers and had placed them on a bench just outside the cell.

"Okay, Ramirez. Tell Señora Córdova that the food is good."

"Martinez, you would eat anything!"

"*¡Qué cabrón! ¡Jodido!* I mean it, Ramirez. You never believe anything."

The cuss words and the starkness of the police station frightened me and I felt a shiver. I imagined myself being brought here and charged with a crime. There was an unsavory history of many of my relatives, uncles and cousins especially, who had frequented this place. I could have those same genes that drove them here. It might be drunkenness or a jealous rage over a lover, an insult that went too far and angered someone, a friend or foe, all too eager to reclaim one's pride. I had seen fights already at school over petty stuff. Pride was an element that you couldn't ignore. Some people had too much of it and some too little, such extremes creating dangerous situations, at least in the schoolyard. I wondered whether adults behaved the same way as my peers at school. It was thought that jail time was a passage to be expected, every male in the Valley a likely occupant of this place. Who was I to think that I could break such a long standing tradition, ignominious as it might be? Was it even possible in the Valley culture that such a goal of avoiding jail could be realized, especially if you came from the west side of town, local scene of most errant behavior. I wondered what I would do to merit passing through the front door, perhaps handcuffed, on my way to being fingerprinted and photographed front and side with a number that would be affixed to a file folder along with my name. How long would I stay here, sleeping in one of those cells with concrete block walls? Would I repent and amend my life by spending the time alone, with nothing to do but relive events that led up to the poor choice I made, causing harm, violating rights of others, or disturbing the lawful order of things? Would there be punishment, in kind, that would coerce rectitude and reset my compass so I would not lose my way again? Is there reason and sanity that can be applied to me, like a compress around my head, like my mother's attempt to lower a fever with vinegar and potato slices? What would I do? How would I react to these treatments to make me moral and conform to the Valley's expectation of me? Maybe I would fight and make things worse, to the point where people give up on me and I am lost, a homeless person, wandering aimlessly, a dog without a master, until the elements get the best of me. But today I am humble, a mere boy staying close to his mother, staring at the starkness of what jail means.

She accepted this part-time job of feeding the inmates when requested which was not every day. The food was money to her, a couple of dollars per meal so it did amount to something significant for us. It was just hard for me to get used to visiting the place although she had been serving meals to inmates now for over a year. The town had asked restaurants to deliver the meals in the past but the restaurant owners had determined that the town would not pay them a fair price for the service. Hence, the town asked my mother if she could provide the service, especially since our rented home was across the street from the police station. The service was not needed every day but just on those days when inmates were jailed overnight.

The aroma of her food was inviting and it partially explained why the jailer was glad to see us although he was not allowed to partake of the nourishment it provided. She covered the food tray with a *trapo*, a light dish towel and the aroma permeated it. The warmth of the food underneath and the flavored air pierced the stale environs of the jail despite its acrid smoke-soaked walls. It was enough to stimulate conversation among the inmates once the tray was taken to the cell area, a welcome break from their boredom. The food was usually still very warm and, of course, it was freshly made. My mother did not believe in feeding the inmates leftovers. They were reserved for us. She believed they deserved the best she could offer, maybe because the town was paying for it or maybe she felt sorry for the men who found themselves there.

She would vary the menu according to the vegetables available during the year—beans or *posole* with meat flavoring during the fall and winter, green chili stew with pork or ground beef during the summer, squash soup made with chicken broth in the spring and summer, fresh corn on the cob or fried sweet corn with squash during the late summer. My mother's *tortillas* were always freshly made, soft pale disks with random scorch marks from the wood-fired *estufa* griddle. The recipe for them was automatic for her, never having to measure anything. She could feel how much flour, lard, salt and baking powder to use. She blended the mixture with her hands, slowly turning her favorite bowl with her left hand as she kneaded the dough until it had the right texture. The water had to be the right tepid-to-warm temperature and the *masa* was left to rise for a few minutes under a *trapo* in a warm place before rolling out the round forms. When prepared correctly, the rolled out dough did not stick to the wooden surfaces of the rolling pin or the table. She could lift the partially rolled dough and turn it so as to get it flatter and flatter as she pressed and rolled the pin. When it was the right thickness and about eight to ten inches in diameter she would toss it from one palm to the other, stretching it evermore slightly and place it on the hot cast iron surface of the stove. To this day I prefer her thinly rolled *tortillas* rather than thicker, more pliable ones. The even temperature of the stove top would scorch the *tortilla* and form a thin crust on the dough as it cooked. After a few minutes, she would turn the *tortilla* and cook the other side. There was no question in my mind that being given a fresh *tortilla* could conquer any amount of despair, lifting the spirit of even a hardened philistine.

I wondered whether the inmates thought the food was liberating like I did. I felt a comfort and calmness when I ate the food my mother cooked. There was a kindness and love for me in the spoonful's of her chili stew or in her *sopa* with vegetables and diced potatoes floating in a warm, meat-flavored broth. Her *tortillas*, hot off the griddle, a little crispy but pliable enough to tear easily, could be eaten alone as an appetizer. *Tortilla* pieces could be dipped in a stew or broth for added flavor. I would sometimes lather them with chips of sweet butter that melted and would then ooze over their surface as I tilted them to keep the butter from dripping onto the floor. What did the food liberate us from? Yearning to be satisfied? Pangs of hunger caused by walking in the desert air, or a respite from troubles that plague us all, differently for each one of us? I couldn't stop thinking how each jail inmate might be freed from despair, at least for the moment, by taking of my mother's food. For a moment there could be escape from this dreary place as the food was consumed.

I loved her food and looked forward to coming home for lunch during the school year. She would have canned peaches in syrup for dessert, those that she had canned herself during the previous fall. Sometimes she would open a jar of pears, in their syrup, again preserved last season in their glorious white color. Pears had to be canned at a certain temperature with a hint of salt in their syrup so they wouldn't turn pink and ruin their whitish inner glow. She let me open one of the jars from time to time to hear the pop as I opened the lid and took in the preserved aroma from the fall. The fruit would be firm, not squishy like the canned stuff from the store, not overcooked so that it's almost tasteless. I wondered whether everyone ate as well as I did. People would raise an eyebrow because we didn't eat American food like macaroni and cheese but I didn't question their judgment. I just knew I liked my mother's cooking.

The jailer returned from the cell area and went over to the desk. After placing the tray with the dirty dishes from the previous meal on the edge of the desk, he sat down.

"*Esperese un poquito*, Señora Córdova, *aquí tengo su cheque*. I believe they brought your check in last night and it's around here somewhere."

"*Muchas gracias, le agradesco*," my mother responded. I could see a look of satisfaction in her face as she said it.

I sat there on the bench with my mother, waiting for the jailer to search his desk for my mother's paycheck. If we were lucky we would clear twenty dollars for the week, enough to get by and still have money left over for modest savings. I didn't realize until much later how important the money was to my mother who wanted to earn her own money and be proud that she was taking care of her youngest son. The New Mexico Public Welfare Department allowed her to earn a few dollars a week to supplement our assistance check. Perhaps we weren't living in style but she was grateful for the job. She took the check, folded it and stashed it inside the pocket of her apron. After my mother asked to be excused, I took the tray of dirty dishes covered with the *trapo* and followed her out the station house as she held open the screen door for me.

7
Sheep of Cibola
August 1953

A sudden chill came over me as I thought
I might be lost just as I dreamed before.
—Reyes

Tranquelino was my mother's husband but he was not my father. My mother had separated from him after bearing him three children. He liked to be called Tranq and that's what I called him. He treated me like his own son, certainly with the respect and courtesy that he showed my half-brothers and half-sister that were his own. He had been a sheepherder in Colorado and Utah for most of his working life but occasionally he would get a job pasturing sheep near our town.

Sheep had been introduced to Northern New Mexico by the Spanish settlers in the seventeenth century but they really became an industry with the advent of the railroad in the nineteenth century. Sheep outnumbered people in New Mexico until the early decades of the twentieth century when the grasslands began to disappear from overgrazing. Despite the plentitude of buffalo when the Spanish arrived, the grasslands had survived because the natural enemies of the buffalo had kept their numbers in check. There had been no natural control over the numbers of sheep. The plains of New Mexico are now more arid than before the settlements of the Spanish and later the sheep men that came after the American annexation. Dust storms are stronger now and instead of grass, the flat land is filled with *Chamisa* and *Cholla* cactus.

Sheepherding had become a vanishing trade with the only remaining grasslands up in the mountains. The season for grazing was shorter by a month or two and the mountains had more predators. Moreover, skilled sheepherders were scarce; Tranq was one of those men who had not abandoned his love of nature in general and the mountains in particular.

My mother left me with Tranq one summer day while he was taking care of a flock of sheep about thirty miles from town. She told me she would pick me up in three days after she finished her work in another town. I had not stayed overnight with Tranq while he was herding sheep. I had come to visit him for an hour or two with my half-sister or one of my half-brothers at various pastures through the years.

On the way to drop me off, my mother had taken an unpaved road about halfway there. The car ride was bumpy since the road was nothing more than an old logging trail that had been abandoned long ago. The county did little to flatten the washboard surface created by the mix of gravel and dirt driven over by hunters and others who had need to go to the higher elevations of the San Felipe Mountains. It hadn't rained recently so we didn't have to worry about getting stuck in any muddy stretches as the grade increased when we hit the foothills. Finally the road became one lane wide and there were some spots where it became rather rocky but my mother seemed to know how to manage them with the car. We had gone through stands of tall pines once we had passed the long stretch of *piñons* that covered the lower foothills.

Eventually the road opened up to meadows that allowed us to see the peaks of the mountains clearly. My mother spotted the smoke from a campfire and she drove in that direction to see if Tranq was near there. She parked the car about a hundred yards from the campfire since the going had become quite rough. We got down and walked the rest of the way.

Tranq must have sensed our arrival and he approached the campfire, waving a welcome as we got closer. After the traditional embrace with my mother and me, he said he was glad to see us with a broad smile pasted on his weathered face. My mother spoke to Tranq a few steps away with her back to me, presumably about leaving me with him for a few days while she went to work at another town. I heard her say that she would be back in three days. She would arrive in the late afternoon around four o'clock so that we could get back to town before dark. While the two adults continued talking, I went back to the car to get a small bag that she had packed for me. It was partially open and sifting through it I saw a shirt, a pair of jeans, a small towel, a change of underwear and socks, toiletries that included a toothbrush, toothpaste and a bar of soap. I was already wearing an old sweater that had a silly deer design on it and I wore it over a flannel shirt. She made sure I took my jacket out of the car before she left. She had often said that the nights are cool in the mountains and it was wise to have plenty of warm clothing.

Back at the car, my mother handed Tranq a couple of small packages that contained dried chili pods, both green and red, kidney beans and a five pound bag of whole wheat flour. As she drove off, Tranq put his arm around me and we both waved goodbye.

I had been left with relatives before while she went off to work for a day or two out of town. She had become well known for her plastering jobs on adobe houses. After several coats of mud on the raw adobe walls to seal the walls from the outside elements, a finish coat was applied that was more resistant to rain and wind erosion. My mother had become a local expert in applying the finish coat for houses being built or on those whose adobe walls were being repaired.

This time Tranq was stationed on a high plateau at the foot of the San Felipe Mountains, a range whose snow-capped peaks had lured Spanish explorers and the early Indian settlers before them in search of water, arable land and game. The plateau was several square miles in area and during the summer it was nourished in water from the snow melt of the western slope of the mountains. A few small creeks crossed the plateau in its slight downward slope toward the Valley and the wild grass that grew in the open spaces provided plenty of feed for the sheep. The upward slope of the plateau from west to east eventually hit the rocky foothills where huge boulders jutted up from the ground as the terrain became more uneven and difficult to navigate. The sky was an incredible blue and formed a perfect backdrop for the mountains and the pine forests that rose up to the point where rocky ledges and canyons took over. It took a while for me to get used to the open space with no sign of human presence. All that you could hear faintly was the rushing water from a nearby stream and the wind as it whistled through darkened stands of pine trees at the edges of the plateau. Occasionally you would see an eagle or a hawk overhead on a hunting mission for small game as it played nature's version of hide and seek. The altitude and air that carried an unspoiled scent of this mountainous world made me dizzy as I made my way to Tranq's campsite. I stepped carefully on the pristine ground of gravel and broken rock with sprigs of grass elbowing their way through the random crevices. I was awed by the places where Tranq chose to camp, always with mountains in the background, a stream nearby, a place rugged and soothing at the same time, taking you back to a serenity of the past, when nature took its course and survival had simple rules.

The immensity of the camp scene settled slowly in my mind while I felt an eagerness to savor the unspoiled surroundings. The contrast with the town was startling, the streets and people, the noise of traffic, concrete expanses, and unkempt buildings had been replaced with the coolness of grass and woods, mountain shadows, melting snow and the sounds of gentle creatures large and small.

"*Pon tu maleta ahí*," said Tranq, pointing to a spot near his tent where I could stash my bag and jacket. He had made camp near a stream and had assembled a fire pit with large rounded stones. The fire had dwindled but smoke still rose and curled in a light intermittent breeze. The tent contained his bedroll and a few items, the bare essentials for maintaining a temporary household in the mountains—tools like an ax, a shovel, rope, a lantern, a duffle bag full of toiletries and a mirror and a book or two. For his kitchen he had a water can holding maybe five gallons, a large tin barrel with airtight lid that contained flour, lard, dried beans, dried peas, chili powder, salt and jerky, each in its own container or bag. He had a large iron pot, a smaller pot and a frying pan that fit inside it along with a few utensils. A majordomo would visit him once a month to check on things and replenish his supplies. I was amazed that he could survive for months at such a minimal level of food and shelter.

"*¿Tienes hambre?*" he asked. [Are you hungry?] I had had a snack in the car and I had become nauseous on the bumpy road. I told him I wasn't hungry although I had always enjoyed the simple meals he prepared. At many campsites he told me that he would find plenty of wild mint and berries to harvest and in the early fall he would find *piñon* nuts as well. Although there was often rabbit and wild turkey available he didn't have a gun or traps for capturing them. His meat came from an occasional slaughter of a sheep that had suffered a bone fracture or was weakened badly from lamb birth. He would dry the lightly salted meat filets under gauze and, once dried to a paper thin and brittle form, save them in a tightly lidded container.

Tranq always seemed strange to me but it may have been the difference between people in town and those who lived in the open spaces. People in town talked a lot while Tranq spoke little. He stared into the distance when he wasn't talking. I would see his eyes narrow and then flutter. His body would be still, even standing up, like being in a trance, interpreting signs from the rugged world that was his home. He survived in this mountainous paradise. He knew secrets of survival you don't learn in school.

Tranq showed me the place on the plateau where the sheep were grazing that day. We climbed a bit higher into the foothills so we could see the expanse of the meadows that made up most of the plateau. The rocky and steep slope of the foothills formed the eastern edge of it while stands of pine trees several hundred yards further down the slope formed the western edge. To the north, may be a mile or two away, following the plateau you could see the dense pine forest that eventually rose up higher into the mountain range. His campsite was at the southern edge of the plateau where one of larger streams came out of the mountains and flowed down into the Valley. Further south brush consisting of reedy plants had taken over because of the wet ground from the small tributaries that fed the stream.

The sky was now darkening and soon a light rain started to fall. We retreated to the camp and sheltered ourselves in the tent until the rain stopped. As the sky cleared we saw the rise of a crescent moon yielding a dim, eerie light. The sheep became very quiet, a few resting on their folded legs. Tranq had relit the fire as we had a light supper of jerky and a hard biscuit. He had cold coffee and he made hot mint tea for me with a little bit of sugar. He talked about his travels in Utah and Colorado and his knowledge of the mountains in those states. He knew about grasses and trees and animals that were his life. His eyes narrowed as he spoke. He continued talking but in a muted voice and I was able to catch a word once in a while. After an hour or so, despite the warmth from the fire, I became drowsy and wrapped myself with one of Tranq's blankets on a spare bedroll he had laid outside the tent on a canvas atop the damp ground. Tranq was now nothing more than a silhouette against the night time sky. I must have gone to sleep because I awoke when I heard the sheep stirring with strange cries. It was very dark despite the crescent moon in cloudless skies. At first I sat up and noticed that the fire was almost out with few embers still glowing. I got up and looked over the flock and they seemed to be calming down with fewer and fewer bleats. But a hundred yards away I could barely make out a group of animals running away and something with antlers chasing them. Soon they disappeared into the woods at the far end of the sloping grassy plain we were camped on. I walked over to the flock which had become quiet again and I couldn't see any more movement among the sheep or in the woods off in the distance. There wasn't much moonlight to make out anything that far away.

I found a few more *piñon* logs to throw into the fire pit and soon I had a good fire going. There was a slight breeze and an accompanying chill. I put my jacket on and got back into the bedroll and waited for Tranq to come back. I assumed he had gone out to relieve himself. I must have laid my head down again and gone to sleep because I awoke at daybreak. Tranq was up and about and he had a fire going. I asked him about the commotion last night and he said that there had been a pack of wolves that had threatened the sheep but they had been turned away by him. I told him I had seen what appeared to be animals with something chasing them. He said I must have been dreaming.

"*La noche mete miedo,*" he said. It was another of his utterances that superficially made no sense to me. Literally it meant—*night scares you.*

I went over to the stream nearby and brushed my teeth and washed my face in the icy water. I found a small towel in the bag to dry my face and hands. My jeans, undershirt and flannel shirt had kept me warm last night in the lumpy bedroll that Tranq had laid out for me with a heavy blanket. I had taken my shoes off but my heavy woolen socks had been just fine under the blanket. After the morning stretching exercises, a routine that Tranq had followed ever since I had known him, we had coffee and more of the hard biscuits that Tranq had baked over a griddle placed on an open fire a few days ago. The morning air was crisp and carried a mountain scent of pine and grass. The sheep were gathered a hundred yards away across the creek. There were four hundred and twenty at the last count a week ago according to Tranq.

"*Hay que hacer otra cuenta. Ya vamos a ver si hemos perdido algunas.*" He said calmly. [We should count them. We'll see if we've lost some.]

Loss of sheep was the measure of a sheepherder's work. The smaller the number, the better, of course. Sheep were lost when they strayed from the herd and got lost and eventually became prey for mountain wolves or other predators. Tranq did not use dogs to help him keep the herd together. He said dogs were unreliable and needed food and attention to function well. They added to the expense of the sheepherding and their expense was deducted from his pay.

Without dogs, the number of sheep that could be tended by one man was limited to a number between 200 and 400. An inexperienced herder could mind the lower number without too much trouble while an experienced one could handle almost twice as many. The challenge was keeping the flock together compactly, not necessarily in one big group but in a controlled way. There were natural barriers that could be used to harness or limit movement and the good shepherd knew the methods. Sheep did not like steep hills and kept away from big rocks or difficult soil.

Tranq would use his voice to accentuate his presence to the flock. I would hear him use a certain tone to calm the animals when they were startled. He would emit a cackling sound to move them along in a certain direction. There was a hidden form of communication between Tranq and the flock. His voice and whistling were signals the sheep interpreted. There was comfort and protection from him as he kept them together. Their utterances and calls became muted when he walked among them, spreading a quiet leadership and calming spirit. His walk among them was deliberate and slow as they made way for him.

"*El conjunto tiene inteligencia*," he once said. "*Una no puede entender y decidir.*" [The whole has a mind.] [One (flock member) cannot understand and decide.] He continued as he tried to explain how sheep reacted to things. "*Cuando hablo, les hablo a todas, no solo a una.*" [When I speak, I address them all, not just one.] He was convinced that the flock reacted as a whole, without a designated leader, much like birds flying together.

As I spent time with Tranq I wondered how the experience and knowledge of sheepherding was passed on to a new generation. Was it all word of mouth and apprenticeship? I wasn't sure I could become the self-assured and reliant person that Tranq seemed to be.

He was at peace with the range of solitude and natural beauty the mountains provided him and the sheep. The sky was a vast sea of blue with a puffy cloud or two at this altitude and the air was intoxicating despite its thinness. The sun showered its warmth on the slope as it gave up its morning dew with a gentle breeze that stirred the smoke from our breakfast fire. The taller blades of grass bowed in rhythm to the breeze as well.

My mother had told me about Tranq's way with nature. He had conditioned himself to live in the wild with a discipline that few people develop well enough so that they retain their sanity. She said that he could meditate and appear to be oblivious to the outside world. He needed less nourishment than what most normal people require and he could go days without food. His night vision was astounding. She said that these attributes, although animal-like and strange, were commonly found in sheepherders. She said there were folktales, told by superstitious fools, that sheepherders had been known to change into animals that could protect the sheep.

At midmorning Tranq had moved the flock against a sharp rise in the foothills and he began the count by funneling the ovine congregation through a group of boulders that had a narrow passage through them. It was a process of "threading the needle." Sheep would be urged along the path through the boulders and Tranq could count them as they passed through. It was amazing that Tranq could control the flock and continue the count at the same time. The counting was sometimes slow but the method allowed for the counting to be deliberate and accurate.

This activity took most of the morning and Tranq was satisfied after the count. He had gained back a couple of sheep that had been either miscounted or had been lost and came back. The count was 422. Tranq led the herd to another part of the plateau where they could feast and find shade under bushes near the brook. There were a few clouds but not enough to temper the sun's relentless rays on the mountainside. It was time to slow the flock's movements and ours as well.

Tranq had no watch and neither did I but we could tell it was past mid-day, probably one o'clock in the afternoon and it was time for lunch. The sheep had migrated to a more level portion of the area and were happily grazing. The breeze had picked up a bit so it was still cool even with the open sky and unsheltered sun.

Lunch consisted of a chili stew made from dried green chili pods and mutton jerky that Tranq had pounded on flat rock to make it softer and into bite size pieces. He boiled the meat and chili in a pot over the open fire for a while. After he declared it done, he poured the stew morsels and broth in bowls and set them aside to cool. He went back into the tent and fetched a hard biscuit and broke it into two and gave me a piece. He handed me one of the bowls and a spoon and we ate together like work mates.

Tranq was thin and wiry. He ate slowly, always attuned to where the flock was and keeping an eye on the fire. His face was weathered despite wearing a hat all day while in the sun. He was strong, both real and imagined, given how he lived. He could pick up a one hundred and fifty pound sheep out of a hole into which it had fallen and lift it onto safe ground. I was there to observe and wonder about this work that had bridged generations, timeless and spiritual as it's bound with nature's way. It was my challenge to understand and learn a few of its mysteries. Tranq embodied the mastery of nature and living things that were essential to the passage of human time. I wondered whether he could teach me if I asked him.

"*Me ayudas con los frijoles.*" He said. "*Los atiendes mientras que voy al fondo.*" [Help me with the beans.] [Mind them while I go afar.]

Tranq told me he wanted to explore grazing areas at lower elevations. He said the flock would be fine where it was for the afternoon but he would move them back closer to the camp when he returned. I was asked to cook pinto beans in the large pot, making sure they didn't spill over in the open fire. They had to be cooked slowly for about two hours over medium heat with water being added from time to time. This required watching the fire and adding firewood when necessary to keep the heat relatively constant. The last water to be added would have a tablespoon of flour to thicken the bean broth. I found a few kernels of dried sweet corn (*chicos*) still clinging to a corn cob in his makeshift cupboard in the tent. I added those kernels to the pot after the beans had cooked for an hour. While watching the beans and the fire, I picked up a book from his tent and began reading it. It was a novel written in Spanish about a family living in the mountains, eking out a living, farming and ranching, always on the watch for hostile Indians. The family would travel to town for church services on Sunday and mix with the rest of the congregation until lunchtime when they would picnic on the way home again. While reading the book I found loose pages that were handwritten. I wondered if Tranq had written them. One page had the following verses:

> Sueño
> Me espantó el sueño
> Y espero que me lleves
> Lejos, con pies de hueso
> No tengo miedo de soltarme
> De mundo oscuro y neblina lenta.
> Cuanto tiempo falta
> De ser lo débil con vida larga.
>
>
> Sueño, que me espanta
> Libre como el aire
> Me lleva con las penas
> Lejos de mi madre
> Través países que no cobran
> Años de mi vida
> Que no cuestan
> La mente de juventud.

[Dream

I awakened
And I imagine you will take me
Far, with feet of bone
I have no fear of leaving
A darkened world and lazy fog
When there is no time
To be weak in the length of life.

Dream, that startles me
Free like the air
Takes me with the ills
Far from my mother
Through lands that do not ask
Years of my life
That do not take
The youthful mind.]

The other pages had poems as well and were rather abstract. Tranq had not told me about any poetry but he did know a lot of songs many of which I had never heard before. I folded the pages again and put them back in the book.

I was halfway through the book when I thought the beans were ready to take out of the fire and set aside until it was time for supper. After covering the beans and setting them between rocks that had been warmed by the fire, I threw thicker logs on the fire to keep it going. My reading and the warmth of the fire had made me drowsy and I lay down on the bedding from last night. I closed my eyes and imagined myself living in the mountains just like the family I had read about. My mother would be home taking care of me and my brothers and sister while our father would be hunting or grazing animals on the grassy areas in the Valley. I was sent one day to fetch my father so he could arrive back home in time for dinner. I followed the path that led to the usual pasture lands but I couldn't find him and I couldn't hear the usual sounds of our cows and sheep. I followed the nearby stream further down the Valley for quite a distance and found no trace of him. On my way back, amidst the sounds of birds and a whistling breeze through stately pines, I thought I heard a human yell, the kind you hear when someone wants your attention. I stopped and looked around for the source. I spotted movement among low lying Mugo pines ahead and hoped that it would be one or more of our animals. I ran in that direction and searched the area but I found no tracks, animal or human.

"*Oye, oye*," [Hello, hello.] I heard from Tranq as he awakened me from my afternoon nap.

"*¿Comó salieron los frijoles?* [How did the beans turn out?] He asked as I tried to regain my wits and utter an answer.

"*Muy sabrosos*, Tranq." [Delicious.] I finally said as I got up from the bedroll and walked over to fire pit. The logs I had thrown in earlier in the afternoon were nearly gone but the embers were hot enough to enflame a few twigs that Tranq had added. He was bringing in more firewood to last us through supper and into the night. It was twilight now and the flock had compressed itself much like the previous evening and had settled down. Several sheep were actually resting with folded legs and looking toward us.

Tranq warmed two plates of beans for us by placing them near the fire and covering them with metal lids to prevent flying ash or embers from getting into our supper. We ate what I had cooked and I was finished long before Tranq. He didn't say anything and I didn't ask about his trip to the lower elevations. He had made me the same sweet mint tea from the night before. I drank it slowly while he finished eating. He left to wash the dishes in the nearby stream.

Night fell and there was a half-moon with no clouds to dampen its brightness. The night breeze was gentle and helped direct the campfire smoke away from us. You could hear owls in the woods. Eventually Tranq came and sat near the fire after taking a look at the flock to see that it was calm.

After a while I heard Tranq utter something. I thought he was talking to me so I stretched a bit in his direction to hear what he might be telling me. His face glowed from the light of the campfire. But it was Tranq singing, his voice a bit raspy but melodious. It was not a song I recognized.

Me dice la luna,
Calma tu miedo,
Estoy en el cielo,
Cuando me oyes,
Estrella de alma.
¿Donde me guías?

Las nubes me llaman
A tu corazón.

[The moon tells me
Stay ever your fear
I'm in the sky,
Whenever you hear me,
Star of my soul.
Where'st you guide me?
The clouds summon me
To your heart]

Me dice la luna,
Ella te encuentra,
Amor de tu alma,
Vives contento,
Unido con hijos,
Cariño estraño,
Quitándote vida,
Viejito te mira.

[The moon tells me,
She will find you,
Love of your being,
Live in delight,
One with children,
Strange fondness,
Aging your life,
It sees you as old.]

Me dice la luna,
El sol es tu padre
Conde de tierra,
Te cuida con manto
Que sepas de muerte
Llora si quieres

La senda será dura
Pero llegas por fín.

[The moon tells me,
The sun is your parent
Master of earth,
He shelters with mantle
Of death you'll know
Cry if you will
The road will be hard
But the journey will end.]

Tranq sang the last verse twice. He sat there, looking at the steady flames from the fire. His face still seemed aglow from the firelight and I could see his lips still moving slightly, perhaps repeating the tune again, only this time it was inaudible. I picked up the book again and tried to read in the dim light. After a few pages I became sleepy and bid Tranq good night and went to my bedroll.

The next morning Tranq had already started a fire and had boiled water for mint tea. He had left a cup for me and half a hard biscuit. I could see him walking among the flock, uttering sounds that must have meant something to the sheep. I must have slept through his exercise routine. After sipping my tea and munching on the biscuit I joined him near the flock and asked him what we were going to do today. He said that he was going to lead the flock down the plateau about half a mile where we could find a stand of *piñon* trees. With an ax he handed me, I was to gather firewood by cutting and splitting branches from dead *piñon*s. He also handed me a coffee tin, the one pound size, and told me to search for *piñon* nuts that may be left over from last fall. He would come for me at lunchtime and bring me something to eat. Afterwards, we would gather the firewood and bring it back to the campsite.

I followed Tranq's instructions and spent half the morning looking for dead *piñon*s, stripping them of their branches and trimming them of twigs. I cut down the tree trunks and split logs that were about eighteen inches long. The wood emitted a sweet resin-ey odor after being split. The yellow-colored logs were heavy indicating the denseness of the resin, *Piñon*s only grew at elevations between 6000 feet and 8000 feet above sea level and this stand was probably the last one. There was nothing but white pine beyond this point up the mountain range. You could see the tree line maybe 2000 feet below the range peaks that rose to 13,000 feet. I stopped to rest from time to time and looked at the snow crested peaks. At our level we had no snow on the ground but the streams nearby were sourced out of the ground saturated with snow melt coming from the range peaks. After I had several woodpiles that were three or four feet high, I took a drink from a nearby stream and started to look for *piñons* that still had pine cones on their branches. When they shed their nuts in the fall, some cones remain on the branches with their jaws open wide to allow the nut to disperse at the slightest breeze. *Piñons* do not shed their nuts all at once. They have a rhythm or cycle that requires several seasons of good moisture and a stage of first shedding needles for a mantle to protect their roots against the winter freezes. They show a spurt of growth of new branches and needles, finally growing the cones that spawn the nuts. My mother told me that *piñons* used to have cycles four years long but now it appears that the weather patterns have caused the cycles to be about seven years in length. I went from *piñon* to *piñon* that had cones still attached and found nuts at each one. They weren't bountiful since squirrels and chipmunks have a taste for them and often harvest them in the fall as well. I was picking what they had left behind. After a couple of hours I had picked half a coffee can of nuts and my legs were cramping up. I would stand up and stretch but the cool ground would slow the circulation as I crouched underneath each tree. Trees had needle mantles that were thick and the freshly fallen needles would prick your fingers as you tried to extract the tiny nuts from the mantle surface. I started moving back toward the area where Tranq had left me and I heard a yell, much like the one I had dreamed about. I thought it might be Tranq trying to find me so I yelled back, calling Tranq's name and saying as loud as I could. "*¡Estoy aquí! ¡Estoy aquí!*" [I'm here! I'm here!]

After several shouts I listened for a response but there was nothing. A sudden chill came over me as I thought I might be lost just as I dreamed before. I had had so much confidence in Tranq and the thought of being left alone in the mountains had never crossed my mind. How would someone find me? I had reached the woodpiles I had created earlier in the day and sat down to rest, now out of breath. I put the coffee can down near the stump where I was sitting and put my head down. I wasn't out of breath from being tired but from the fear that had engulfed me. I knew I could make it back to camp from here. Even if Tranq didn't show up, I could wait for him there. I felt a little better and now was breathing easier.

"*¡Hijo! Tienes hambre?*" [Son, are you hungry?] I heard the comforting sound. It was Tranq and he was carrying a small jar of beans. He handed it to me along with half a biscuit that he retrieved from a sack he was carrying. He saw that I had been scared and he put his arm around me. I buried my face in his shoulder as he continued to hold me with his arm around my back. There was warmth I felt from his embrace. He knew that being alone took strength and I had not been up to it. The tears had welled up in my eyes and I wiped them away as I slid from his embrace to have my lunch.

"*Descúlpame, hijo—me detuve mucho,*" he said, apologizing for something that was not his fault. He went on to praise me for the firewood piles and the half-full coffee can. His words were few but they went a long way to calm me down from the fright I had gone through. After waiting for me to finish eating the beans, he handed me mutton jerky that had been marinated in red chili before the drying process. The piquant taste was welcome after the bland lunch of beans. He started loading firewood onto a flat canvas with handles. He had brought another piece of canvas for me so after loading that one up also, we each strapped a load to our back and started back to camp. The flock had been moving slowly back to camp as well. We passed them and reached camp about 1000 yards ahead of them. Tranq unloaded his firewood load and went back to make sure the sheep came all the way back. He said it would take him an hour to round up any stragglers but I could see where he was from camp.

I sat down for a while to rest and then lay down on my bedroll and closed my eyes. I didn't want to go to sleep like I did yesterday so I lifted my head and rested it on my hand using my elbow to keep it off the ground. The fire had gone out so I went to the edge of the grassy plain where I could gather small branches for kindling. I brought several loads of kindling and then stacked up the two loads of firewood that we had carried. It would be enough for tonight's fire and the one Tranq would relight tomorrow morning. Eventually I re-joined Tranq higher on the plateau to search for any sheep that may have strayed from the larger group. We walked down and back up again along the edges of the grassy plain and assured ourselves that the flock was pretty much intact.

We replenished the water supplies by bringing several buckets back to camp and pouring the water into a holding tank that Tranq had positioned near his tent. He had shown me the copper and silver coins he had placed at the bottom of the tank to mitigate any bacteria growth. He boiled most of the water he used so I surmised that it was just another precautionary measure. He could not afford to get sick out here. There was no one to help him if he couldn't make it to town. His *mayordomo* only saw him once a month so it was prudent to be careful.

By now it was late afternoon and Tranq started a fire and boiled water for mint tea. We each took a cup after a few minutes of brewing it. He took his cup and went to the flock and made the rounds, uttering the unusual sounds that seemed to make sense to them and only them.

By the time he got back, it was twilight and I had fed the fire with more logs. We rested a while before warming some beans and mixing them with a broth made from dried green chili pods and mutton jerky. He set the pot of beans beside the campfire stones. Tranq said he was out of biscuits but he was going to make *tortillas* on a griddle he had placed atop a few stones at the edge of the campfire. First, he went to the stream and washed his hands and then filled the pot we used to boil water. In a mixing bowl he mixed a couple of cups of whole wheat flour with a tablespoon of baking powder, a couple of tablespoons of lard and a pinch of salt. He had taken water that had boiled and become lukewarm and added it slowly to the dry mixture using a small knife. After getting the dough to hold together, he started kneading it by pulling it apart and folding it again onto itself. He did this over and over again carefully with a smile on his face, content with things, whistling a tune I didn't recognize.

Me amas cuando sueño,
Me amas en el día,
Estoy listo siempre
Con cariño
Solo para tí…

[You love me when I dream,
You love me in the day,
I'm ready always,
With tenderness
For you alone…]

Finally, he put the kneaded dough in the mixing bowl and covered it, setting it beside the campfire stones in a warm place. I joined him again at the stream where we washed our hands, some dinner plates and spoons, drying them with a cotton dish towel. He was still whistling while he fetched a small wooden *tortilla* press from his tent. It was a banged-up contraption but its flat surfaces were well seasoned and their sheen was a golden brown. By now the dough was plump and smooth and he partitioned it into ten little balls. He took each ball and used the press to form a thin disk of the dough that he easily pried off the flat surface and slapped on the hot griddle. He did three *tortillas* at a time on the griddle, turning over each one after a minute or two on the hot surface. Each *tortilla* showed some scorch marks on its surface when it was turned over. He handed me the first one and it tasted delicious. It was hard to chew it slowly since I was so hungry and it was welcome nourishment. I had eaten two *tortillas* before he was finished grilling the others. Finally, he poured the beans with chili broth into two plates and handed me one. Eating the meal he cooked near an open fire, under the darkening sky, with the mountain scent of pine forests, grass and wild flowers was nothing like I had done before. Tranq and I ate in silence, enjoying the simple meal he and I had created out here. He let out a sigh when he had finished. As usual, I had been done with my meal long before him. He stood up and picked up the dishes and went to the stream to rinse them out. He came back and poured hot water over them and then dried them with the dish towel. He looked at me and smiled and left to see after the flock. I picked up my book and resumed reading where I had left off the day before.

Tranq came back after an hour or so, carrying a sheep that was kicking its leg from underneath Tranq's arms. "*Está herida.*" He said. " *Se calló en un pozo.*" He explained that a sheep that breaks its leg, after falling into a deep hole, probably wouldn't heal the break by itself. It would become prey to wolves or other predators. He would tie it up for tonight and have it sleep next to us. We would probably have to slaughter it tomorrow.

Tranq had put the injured sheep inside the tent after moving his bedroll outside on the other side of the tent so his bedroll and mine were separated by the tent. He explained that the scent of the sheep would be masked by the tent walls and our bedrolls. Predators always seemed to know about injured sheep and he hoped that between the two of us we could protect this one at least until morning.

During the night I sensed that Tranq had gotten up more than once. I imagined that he was worried about the flock and wanted to make sure that would-be predators knew he was around. I hadn't heard any strange noises. The drone of crickets and the occasional hoots of owls had been steady through the night.

At dawn I saw Tranq working inside a pit about twenty feet from the stream. He was cleaning it out. There had been some debris in it and ashes at its bottom. It had been lined with flat stones up to about two thirds of its depth and at its bottom it had very large stones with crevices between them. The pit was about three feet in diameter and Tranq had a metal disk about thirty inches in diameter that he fitted on top of poles that were jammed into the top layer of stones lining the pit. It appeared that he had used the pit several times before and I imagined that it had been used for cooking mutton.

He greeted me and got out of the pit and we both walked back to the camp area where he had prepared breakfast. He explained that he was going to slaughter the injured sheep. He saw that the leg was badly broken and it had to be put out of its misery. He had a place near the pit that he used for the slaughter. He needed my help in getting the pit fired up with plenty of firewood as soon as possible. We would burn a fire for two hours this morning to get the stones very hot. Once the fire was out he would place most of the sheep's carcass that had been cut up in the pit and placed over poles and it would cook for six hours. The pit would be covered with the metal disk to keep the heat inside the pit and he would place pine fronds atop the metal disk to insulate it from the outside air.

Once I was finished with firing up the pit he wanted me to filet the large masses of mutton meat that he would cut away from the carcass. These thin filets, after being dipped in a briny broth, would be hung on a tight string that he had installed between two pine trees and covered with a roll of gauze that he wrapped around the filets. The string was ten feet high so animals could not reach the filets. We would use a small tripod stool that was about five feet high to reach the string. There was no time to waste since all this work had to be done in a single day. He reminded me that my mother was due to pick me up today in the late afternoon.

While Tranq strung up the sheep, hind legs up, and slit its throat to let the blood drain from the torso into a small drum, I started the fire in the pit and brought up more firewood from the *piñon* stand where I had left the woodpiles the day before. Fortunately, it had started out as a beautiful day with no wind at all. With a cloudless sky the sun had already burnt off any dew on the meadow.

The sheep were quietly feeding near the eastern edge of the plateau not far from our campsite. After half an hour or so I had a raging fire going in the pit with flames leaping all the way to the top. I felt the heat on my face as I added fuel to the fire. I continued adding fuel for another half hour and then Tranq told me to stop and let the fire go out naturally.

By this time he had skinned the sheep and opened the torso from the hind legs to the neck so that the internal organs and intestines had fallen out into a large pan. He asked me to start digging a hole about three feet deep for burying the sheep's blood and entrails. I was to fill the hole with sheep manure on top of the entrails and then put rock and stones. I was to fill the last foot or so with clay from the side of the stream and pack it tightly with grass tufts at the top. This burial process would make it difficult for animals to dig up the entrails.

After finishing the burial of the entrails, Tranq asked me to wash my hands and start filleting the meat. He pointed out where the sharp knife was that I was to use for this stage of making jerky.

He had a wooden plank; maybe twenty inches by twelve inches, that he had me wash in the stream for placing the clumps of mutton that I was supposed to fillet. It was slow going at first since I was afraid of cutting myself but I got to be pretty good and holding the squishy clump steady with one hand and slicing away with the other hand that wielded the knife.

Meanwhile Tranq had separated the two hind quarters and the two forequarters of the carcass and now was cutting them up into smaller sections by using an ax on them atop a tree stump. After this stage he now had about twelve pieces of the carcass that had had most of its meat removed. The fire had gone out in the pit and it was time to poke at the dying embers down at its bottom. Tranq used a long pole to do this. Since the pit was so hot he covered his arm with a wet rag and put on a glove. He lay on the ground next to the pit and created a roasting rack for the carcass section by placing short poles across stones that jutted out half way up the stone lining. This number of poles he secured inside the pit was enough to hold the twelve carcass pieces in place. After carefully spreading them over the rack so that there was space for the air to circulate around each of them, he took the metal disk and placed it over the top layer of stones. This way, the meat was halfway up the lined pit, between the bottom stones and the top lid of the pit. He then covered the lid with boughs that he cut from pine trees nearby. He filled the pit to the top with the pine branches. When he was finished, he looked up into the sky to mark for himself where the sun was. He figured it was midmorning, 9:30 or closer to ten o'clock.

At this point I had finished filleting about half of the mutton Tranq had brought over to me. He took the fillets and dipped them in a salty broth he mixed earlier. He filled the large frying pan he had with the salted fillets and took them over to the *percha* (clothesline) he had rigged up. By standing on the crude tripod stool he was able to gently lay the fillets onto the string. They were long enough to actually fold them over the string. He did about ten feet of fillets strung out this way. He came back and with another knife help me finish filleting the rest of the mutton. With this batch he added red chili powder to the briny mixture and dipped the rest of the fillets. When he had strung all the meat on the string, he asked me to hold the roll of gauze while he unwound it and placed it around the mutton hanging on the string. There was just enough gauze to cover the twenty or so feet of hanging meat. He went back to the tent and brought back a large needle and a ball of twine. He took enough twine that stretched the length of the gauze and cut it with his knife with about two feet extra. After threading the needle with the twine, he asked me to keep the twine straight as he commenced sewing the bottoms of the folded gauze together by going through the edges every six inches or so with the needle the entire length of the string that had meat on it.

When we were done with the meat hanging, Tranq asked me to gather the knives and pans and wash them in the stream. He was going to move the flock to a part of the plateau that had more feed. He would be back in an hour and we would then have lunch. It had been a busy morning and I was ready to take a break. I got the book I was reading and folded my bedroll to form a soft chair and sat down on it. The sky had been cloudless this morning but you could see a cloudy front coming in from the west. I wondered whether we were in for any rain this afternoon. It would be difficult for my mother to get here if the mountain road became muddy late in the day.

Tranq was back and said the flock was doing fine further north on the plateau. I had restarted the campfire and had placed the griddle atop stones that formed the fire pit. In a small pot I had water boiling in case he wanted to make stew. He had set aside a couple of unsalted mutton fillets in a covered pan from this morning. He took them out of the pan and laid them on the hot griddle. They had a little bit of fat on them so they didn't stick to the hot surface. A little bit of blue smoke came off the griddle as they cooked. He turned them over after a few minutes and when they were done, he put one of them on a leftover *tortilla* that had been grilled on the same surface and handed it to me. I bit into the sandwich and I was surprised that the fillet wasn't stringy but was very tasty and juicy. He brewed mint tea with the hot water I had prepared and gave me a cup. I had devoured my sandwich by the time he sat down to eat his.

"*Estuvo bién*," grinning as he looked at me and then nodded. [It was okay.]

I laughed out loud, almost dropping my cup of tea but managing to spill a few drops anyway. He grinned again and I heard him chuckle. I was happy that he was happy. I had managed to not disappoint him and he was grateful for the little help I provided. He could have done all the work himself but I still think that he was happy that I was there that day. We had supported each other as I did what he asked without requiring a lot of instruction. I had learned to do things that I didn't think I would ever do. Getting it all done was the reward in itself.

He started talking about the string of jerky and that it would take about three weeks to dry provided there weren't too many rainy days. The string was in the *resolana* or a sunlit place running east and west so it got maximum sun during the day. If the air remained dry, the jerky would cure faster. The salt prevented putrefaction and the gauze kept the flying bugs away from the surface of the meat and from laying their eggs on it. In three weeks he was going to move the campsite further north on the plateau about a mile away where there was another stream with abundant water for the sheep and himself. He asked me if my mother was thinking of bringing me back for another visit.

"*No lo sé*," I responded. Because I really didn't know what my mother's work schedule was going to be the rest of the summer. I didn't know that I was coming to visit until a few days ago. I asked whether I had been a burden on him. I didn't know why I had asked him that question.

"*No hay pena*," he said. "*Puedes venir a visitarme cuando tu Mamá te déjà. No debes preocuparte de eso.*" [No problem, he said. You can come and visit me when your mother lets you. You shouldn't worry about that.]

He got up and I thought I had detected a teary eye. But the lingering smoke from the campfire could have caused it. He said he was going to look after the flock and he would be back in a couple of hours to see about the barbeque pit or el *pozo de barbacoa*. I was to restock the firewood pile for tonight's and tomorrow's fires along with kindling while he was gone.

Today was my last day with Tranq so I took my time in completing the tasks he assigned me. I stopped periodically to gaze at the horizon high above me where the mountain peaks seemed to float against the sky, their snow caps still showing even at midsummer. The snow would be gone by late August or early September. The peaks would receive their first snowfall in early November and the clouds would hide the peaks during most of the winter months. It was still warm and the cloudy front had not reached the sun's position in the sky. The front was a lot closer but my mother had a good chance of getting here before any rain.

By the time Tranq got back to the campsite, it had become a little cloudy with the sun now coming in and out of clouds. We were in mid-afternoon and about five hours since Tranq had covered up the barbeque pit. He got the paper sacks that my mother had used to bring him chili and flour. He got out a wax paper roll that he had in his modest cupboard. He placed both the sacks and wax paper roll beside the wooden plank he used as a cutting board. He took the large frying pan and asked me to accompany him to the pit. I helped him get rid of the pine branches that he had used as insulation on top of the disk that covered the pit. He lifted the disk lid and a wonderful meaty aroma lifted from the pit. He skewered two of bony carcass sections and put them into the pan. For the first time I realized that he had also put the sheep's head on the rack as well. He put the disk lid back on top of the pit. We walked back to the campsite with the cooked sections in the pan. They appeared smaller than when he had put them into the pit. Of course a lot of the fat had melted off and the meat had shrunk to a degree. We sat down and he took a fork and lifted pieces of meat off the section. He did it so easily without having to use a knife or much of an effort. He put a small portion of the meat on a plate and handed it to me along with another fork. I tasted the meat and it was stringy but tender. It had a little bit of a smoky flavor to it but it was moist and delicious. In no time we had stripped one of the bony carcass sections of any meat and had started on the other. Tranq had brought out the last of the leftover *tortillas* and he tore it in half and handed me a piece. I used a bite of the *tortilla* to complement each small meat piece we were able to strip from the second carcass section. There had not been a lot of meat we had taken from the two sections but they had constituted a nice snack.

Tranq said he would be back in half hour or so and I was to clean up my bed roll and tie it up with twine, fill up the small water cistern beside the tent and pack my own things. He expected my mother to show up within the hour and I should be watching for her car.

I performed the chores and then I walked down the side of stream beyond where Tranq had slaughtered the sheep and looked for any wild mint growing on the banks. The stream was not very wide and quite shallow in a lot of places so it was easy to go from one side to the other. I found quite a few wild flowers growing on the banks especially where the sun was able to penetrate the shade of the pine trees for more than a few hours a day. But I found no mint growing anywhere.

I walked back to the campsite and saw Tranq out in the distance. He was standing very still, looking northward, perhaps toward where the flock was grazing. Then he disappeared. I hurried my pace thinking that maybe I had gone into a hollow and had simply lost him in the horizon. I reached the campsite and didn't see him anywhere. A chill came over me similar to the one I experienced the day before when I thought I was lost. I found the campsite the way I had left it and decided it was best to sit down and rest. Perhaps my eyes were playing tricks on me. I closed my eyes and let the world be whatever it was going to be. I tried to relax and felt myself going backwards, floating as if in a dream. When I awoke, everything was the same and I got up and dusted myself off and stretched to make sure I was breathing normally. In the distance I heard the whir of a car engine and the car did look familiar. The car stopped and later I heard the door slam. I hurried down the slope to get a better look and I did see my mother walking in my direction. She waved at me and I waved back and soon we were in each other's arms. By the time we reached the campsite we could see Tranq walking toward us. He waved at my mother and she nodded back with her right arm around my back.

Tranq explained that he had slaughtered an injured sheep and he had some *barbacoa* meat that he wanted to give her. He went to the barbeque pit and extracted the rest of the carcass pieces including the sheep's head. He wrapped six of the pieces in wax paper including the head. Seeing that the wrapped meat would not fit in the paper sacks, my mother asked me to run down to the car and get a cardboard box she had in the trunk and to empty its contents in the trunk and bring back the box.

The wrapped carcass sections and head fit in the box. Tranq would keep the remaining pieces and have them for tonight's dinner and tomorrow's lunch. My mother thanked him for taking care of me and he responded with a smile aimed at both of us. My mother and I carried the box back to the car and placed it on top of newspapers in the back seat. She was afraid that the pieces were still warm enough to drip some greasy juices through the wax paper and through the cardboard box.

We gave Tranq one last wave and got in the car. As we drove off, the sky darkened and it appeared that the rain would arrive soon. If we drove fast enough we may be able to reach the paved portion of the road before it came down.

My mother asked me how I liked staying with Tranq. She asked what I did during the three days. It was not going to be easy answering her questions. I would use words and they wouldn't make sense to her and to me. Tranq's world didn't use words to communicate. The sheep understood his will. He took from the mountains only what he needed to survive. There was a silent harmony; what he took was replaced; what he did was only what was necessary. He knew the rules of paradise and they were few—know thyself and that around you.

8
Apple Harvest
October 24, 1953

There was a culture of mistreatment of women in the Valley, especially during her time.

—*Reyes*

It was late October and my mother and I had crossed into the apple orchard through the barbed wire fence. In turn, we held the prickly wires away from each other carefully as we had done many times before. But the four inch scar on my arm was the constant reminder when we hadn't been so careful. It had happened about six years ago.

I was not quite five years old and we were crossing into the irrigated fields in San Pablo Pueblo, my birthplace and home for the first five years of my life. It had been twilight during harvest time and maybe I was so small that my mother thought that the wires didn't have to be so far apart. I screamed and the blood rushed out as a barb tore into my flesh mid-way up my left arm. The pain was intense and it scared me as the blood continued to pour out of the wound. I was shocked that my arm had so much blood. I stared at it because I could not believe it was happening to me. My mother squeezed my upper arm to slow the bleeding and asked me to continue squeezing with my right hand the upper arm area that she was holding. I followed her instructions even though the throbbing pain was forcing me to scream. Then she quickly tore a piece of her cotton underskirt to create some bandage material. She ripped the piece again and again to make several bandages each about a yard long. She used one as a tourniquet on my upper arm and others to wrap the wound tightly until we could get some help. We raced home while I felt the throbbing pain in the arm. She had loosened the tourniquet a little so my arm wouldn't go to sleep but there was nothing she could do for the pain. My head was beginning to hurt as well but I ran with her and kept up as she held my hand from the good arm. I knew I was crying but I didn't hear any sobs. When we got home, I was dizzy and I sat on chair while she treated my wound. She poured alcohol on it, this action making it sting some more, and she bandaged it again, this time more carefully with linen gauze and sterile bandages made from old sheets. She didn't have a lot of money and the nearest doctor was over four miles away. The wound was deep and should have had stitches to close it. It eventually healed but left an ugly four inch raised scar at the elbow bend. Today, the mark is still a reminder of how little support we had back then even to treat a nasty gash in the arm.

She hadn't had any plastering jobs lately and we were waiting for the welfare check we got at the end of the month. This rendezvous into the orchard was intended to get us apples still left in the trees now that the harvest was done. The remaining apples were often misshapen or bird-pecked and eventually would fall and form excellent mulch for the trees. Of course, there were apples that had fallen to the ground during the harvest and were never picked up. They sometimes gathered those and buried them under leaves to store them on the cool ground for later jelly or cider making. Because the cool, dry air in the Valley during the late fall season slowed the decomposition of vegetable matter, it was possible to have apples preserved in this way until early winter. In fact, Winesap apples preserved on the cool ground under the trees beneath a leaf cover would ripen and turn juicier. They would have a core that was darker and sweeter than the rest of the fruit. They became my favorite apple no matter where they were grown, even those that came from outside the Valley. Of course, I would always believe that Valley apples were the best. The minerals in the water used to irrigate the trees may have had something to do with their distinctive flavor. Those minerals came down from the San Felipe Mountains, composed mostly of granite and quartzite and other minerals. I believed, without any evidence, that the minerals had healing powers and that those powers made them taste delicious and unlike any other fruit grown elsewhere. The Valley residents believed in magic and this belief of mine was in keeping with the Valley culture.

The large farming area in my mother's village of Nambroca included the apple orchard that belonged to my *Tio Miguel*, my mother's oldest brother. He had willed a portion of the orchard to his eldest children who were my mother's age. There had been twelve siblings in my mother's family and she was second youngest. My uncle treated my mother like a child, looking down on her, an attitude bordering on contempt. My mother explained that this treatment was normal since the oldest boy of the family always grew up to be the surrogate father to the rest of the family. He certainly had a haughty air about him. He rarely looked at me, possibly because I was small and not worthy of his time. He knew I was a posthumous child and born out of wedlock. People still believed illegitimacy was to be punished on the child. And one form of that punishment came in ignoring the presence of the person.

Tio Miguel had had five children by his first wife who had died at childbirth with the youngest. He married again and had eight more children, the youngest being a couple of years older than me. My uncle had built a big house with a front porch that spanned the length of the house. It was screened and a pleasant place to be in the summer afternoons since it faced north. The house was 20 yards north of the *acequia* or irrigation ditch and about a hundred yards away from the orchard and rather hidden behind tall elms planted on the west side to shade the house in the afternoon.

We looked around for any apples still on the trees and they were few and quite high up on the trees. The apple pickers had probably found them too difficult to reach with the tri-pod ladders they used. Although I could climb to within a few of them, I wasn't sure it was worth the time and effort given the darkening sky. My mother had brought a small sack, probably able to hold no more than a dozen apples. I thought we should choose them carefully if we were not going to take too many of them since it would take time for me to climb up onto the tree. These would be eating apples and were not intended for making jelly.

"*No dejaron mucho,*" my mother whispered.[They didn't leave many.]

"*Muy pocas,*" I answered in a normal voice. [Very few] I didn't understand why she was whispering.

She acted as if we were stealing them when in fact my cousin had invited us to take some when we had seen her earlier in the day. Of course, my mother assumed that this part of the orchard belonged to her and not to any of her siblings.

As I looked upward to find any that would be easier to pick, I stumbled over a pile that had been covered with leaves. It was indeed a cache of apples. I went down on my knees and brushed the leaves away to uncover the extent of the hidden treasure. It took me a minute to register the luck of finding them. This would save a lot of time and energy of climbing up and down several trees to harvest a few apples. My mother prayed the rosary frequently and I stopped to wonder whether this find might be a case of answered prayers. I wanted to make sure I wasn't dreaming. My mouth was already watering with visions of savoring their natural glory.

"*¡Mire, aquí hay bastante!*" I blurted out. [Look, there are plenty here!] I may have said it loudly in my dazed ecstasy because she sshhed me instantly.

I looked over the jewels in front of me, an array of gorgeous orbs of natural bounty. They were beautiful apples, perfectly formed and their stems were a solid green, indicating a delightful freshness bursting with honey-flavored juice. My uncle had planted nothing but the Delicious variety. They weren't Winesaps but Delicious was a great tasting apple in the Valley. They were not like those you find in the town's grocery store, coming from the west coast, beautifully formed but tasteless and turning mealy quickly. I looked for the biggest ones, reddish with the greenish freckles that gave away their ripeness and juiciness. They would be crisp and once you bit into them the juice would fill your mouth and it was hard keeping all the juice from oozing out. Sweet fluid would inevitably dribble out of the corner of your mouth no matter what you did with your tongue. But you had to try preventing its loss and you got better at capturing the juice as you got older. First, you learned to suck at the bite hole to prevent the juice from escaping with the vacuum being created. Each bite would yield another crispy section, a crack being sounded as the portion was bitten off and the sweetness would captivate you and your hand would become sticky with the honey-water inevitably falling out of the apple meat and onto your fingers holding the heavenly fruit.

My mother had put a few into her sack and we were about to choose the last one or two that we knew could be squeezed into it. The sack already had at least a dozen large apples and a few medium sized ones that could be used for a pie. I was delirious just thinking about what my mother could do with them in *empanadas de manzana* or apple turnovers with a cinnamon flavored filling. They would come out of the oven of our wood fired stove with a light brown tinge on the top and around the edges. She would have sprinkled granulated sugar on the turnover top and a few of the sugar granules would crystallize during baking and add to the sweetness. If you split the hot turnover, there would be a tiny puff of steam that would come out from the ragged edges. You knew then it was ready to eat that wonderful treat. It was hard not to gulp the pieces down and there was discipline necessary to eat the turnover with smaller bites and chew the morsels slowly to make the delight last longer.

"*¿Qué hacen aquí?*" a voice growled in the growing darkness, snapping me out of my dream. [What are you doing here?]

A figure had appeared at the entrance to the orchard and now had caught us in our frenzy to choose the best apples in the cache we had found. My mother stood up and handed me the sack and she went over to the figure that she had identified as *Tío* Miguel.

"*Pues sí, habíamos venido por invitación de Elvira, mi sobrina,*" my mother answered. [Well, yes, we came by invitation from Elvira, my niece.] "*¿Es su arbolera, qué no?*" [This is her apple orchard, is it not?]

"*Estos no son sus manzanos.*" My uncle said with a sharpness to his tone. [These are not her apple trees.] "*Están al fondo, pero ya está muy oscuro para encontrar manzanas. Estos son mis arboles y esas son mis manzanas.*" [They're in the back but it's very late to try to find apples. These are my apple trees and those are my apples.]

"*Hemos recogido solo unas pocas.*" [We have gathered but a few.] My mother pleaded in a meekness I rarely witnessed. My mother was trying to salvage something out of the situation.

"*Pues, hay que ponerlas donde las hallaron y se deben despedirse.*" [Well, you should put them back where you found them and you should take your leave.] My uncle said using a condescending tone and obviously incensed to find us there. He was not about to show any compassion for us. A few people in the Valley were very possessive of their land and the benefits thereof, a curse of the Conquistador region of Cíbola. The original Spanish settlers had believed in common lands called *ejidos* to be farmed or ranched by groups of families. Amazingly, this concept had been intrinsic to Pueblo Indian culture as well. But over time, perhaps because of the scarcity of arable land, its ownership became tightly held among Hispanic people causing friction even among family members.

Mi hijo tiene solo las que trae en el saquito." She tried again, hoping for a bit of compassion. [My son only has those in the small sack.]

Ya les dije que deben de hacer, retírense por favor." The unyielding reply came. [I've already said what you should do, please take your leave.] There was no moving the large figure. He was at least twice the size of my mother. I didn't understand his firmness nor the urgency for us to go. Twilight was fading fast with only the western horizon barely visible because of a reddish glow. In the distance you could see someone's window light from a kerosene lamp. A few of the houses in the village still didn't have electricity.

I felt I was shaking my head as the two adults carried on the conversation. Even today, I do not know whether I actually shook my head or not so that my uncle could see. He was denying my mother a few apples that had not been harvested and sold. It was not even clear that he would ever use them this late in the season. I knew my dreams of enjoying the apples were not to be realized. Apple turnovers were not to be, not in the near future anyway. I felt a slow anger rising inside of me and envisioned myself throwing the apples at my uncle. Apparently I controlled my feelings since I found myself still holding the small sack full of apples. After both adults had finished talking, I saw both of them just standing there, each a few feet from the other. I didn't move or say anything. We all just stood there but I was focused on my uncle whose outline I could clearly make out against the darkening, deep blue sky. I felt there was a struggle, silent and invisible, occurring between the two. The figures still did not move. My mother was facing away from me and looking at something in front of the larger figure, her staring made her body shake a little. This went on for a while and I became afraid of what might happen next. I saw my uncle first sway a little and then step back. His large head nodded again and again like someone going through convulsions. My anger turned to shock as I watched the head move back and forth uncontrollably. His arms were motionless as if paralyzed. Finally, he turned westward toward the fading light as if he were recovering from something. All I could see now was his silhouette moving mechanically. Finally, my mother said, "*Vamos,*" and that sound broke my trance and I felt a chill. I wondered what I had just witnessed in the twilight. The thought crossed my mind that maybe I was seeing things. What I saw really didn't happen.

At that point I reluctantly emptied the sack onto the other apples in the cache and covered them again with the leaves as they were before. I continued to control my fear and anger and kept looking at my uncle in the eerie light, not for approval but for communicating that this treatment was not something one forgot easily. I was astounded that someone would be so cruel in demeanor over a few abandoned apples. He was my mother's brother. Was there no feeling for family, especially over something of such little value? Was it that he thought we were essentially stealing apples since we didn't check with him first? Had a protocol been violated and now he thought tough punishment for that was in order?

My mother and I walked away liked scolded children. She said "*Buenas noches*" softly and mechanically. My uncle did not respond, still standing there, facing westward toward the faint light. I turned around and he was gone, perhaps walking further into the orchard. Off in the distance, toward the river, I saw what appeared to be a large dog-like animal running. There had been no dog with my uncle so I wondered whether I was seeing things again. It made me afraid. I kept looking at the scene, walking backwards slowly behind my mother, in shock from what had happened. It was getting darker and harder to make out forms. Out here in the irrigated farms, it really became dark before moonrise. I felt a shiver come over me suddenly and I put my arm around my mother's waist instinctively as if to get warm.

There was no feeling left after the humiliation we had both endured. It was yet another attack at my mother's self-worth, another reminder of her low status as a younger member of the family with no rights, no inheritance, and no pity. It didn't help that she was separated from her husband. A single mother deserved little respect in this place. I always wondered whether the humiliation was unbearable because it was her brother who brought this down on her or whether that it was done in front of me, someone she hoped would respect her for the things she did for me.

"*Es un hombre malo*," [He is an evil man] she said as we walked back to her cousin's house where we were staying overnight.

She always said this when we met up with a meanness in a man. I learned that she had had unpleasant encounters with men in her life. There was a culture of mistreatment of women in the Valley, especially during her youth. It was a culture that would improve but not totally die out. We continued walking before either of us said anything more.

"*Como tu padre.*" [Like your father]

She said this softly like she didn't know whether she should say it or not. This was not the first time I heard her say it. I sometimes thought she looked at me to see if I was going to be like him, like the man that harmed her in a way that was too painful to remember. My arm slipped away from her.

As we walked back, I wondered how my uncle knew we were at the orchard. I could not believe that he was that vigilant, especially at twilight, when families were normally finishing their suppers. I believe he had had a premonition, primal in nature, and he had walked all the way to the orchard on that strange sensation. The whole incident was to be, maybe, a lesson for my mother and me. There was a hidden message that I had to interpret. I figured the answer would come in time.

9
Mesa de Cíbola
Summer, 1954

Nevertheless, the area engendered
dreams of grandeur to someone who
wanted to believe in a magical place.
—*Reyes*

It happened about once a month for it wasn't worthwhile if you went more often. There wasn't enough new stuff to look over. The town dump was about half a mile from the western edge of the town of San Isidro up into a bluff or mesa in the lower foothills of the Jemez Mountain range. The mesa had been formed from a lava flow and was now covered with layers of dirt, the result of wind erosion from neighboring hills made out of sandstone. The dumping grounds went on for about a mile. It gave you the illusion it was longer because of the rise in terrain, climbing up about a hundred feet from the lowest elevation to its farthest western end.

The Jemez range formed the western slope of the Valley with the Rio del Norte flowing through the town. The mountain range was volcanic in origin and its lava flows and basalt rock created a dark backdrop for the pine forests in the lower part of the range. From afar the site glittered, seductive like a fabled city of gold sitting up on a ridge, beckoning an unknowing mortal to visit only to fall victim to an endless search for fame and fortune. Of course, the glitter came not from gold or silver but from sunlight reflected from the piles of de-labeled tin cans and broken glass bottles whose millions of shards formed prisms that scattered light in all directions. Nevertheless, the area engendered dreams of grandeur to someone who wanted to believe in a magical place. Growing up I called the place *Mesa de Cíbola*, abandoned city of the long lost treasure. The whole area had a fence all around it and its entrance had a cattle guard to prevent any stray horses, cows, goats or other smaller animals from going in. People never brought garbage so it really didn't have much to attract animals anyway. There were no rules for what could be left there but there was little to no vegetable or animal matter to be found. I guessed that people had better uses for garbage—feeding the dogs, pigs or just using it for compost.

The place had always attracted me, especially during the spring or autumn. It seemed that people cleaned out their trash during those seasons. I would wander from pile to pile looking over the items people had abandoned. As I stepped on the heap, unsteady platform that it was, layers of vessels and shells, the discarded skeletons of glass and tin, the markings erased by sun and wind, some broken and others cracked or bent, hanging on to be whole but lonely in a graveyard of empty servings, I sought the alchemist's dream in the unlikely place. It was a balance of mind and spirit lest I fall into the dung and dregs of the past.

Mixed in with the usual bottles and cans there were other household items, usually broken or obsolete, and over-used or faulty car parts, discarded furniture, scrap from building materials and appliance parts. People didn't discard paper, possibly because paper was good kindling to start the fire in wood burning furnaces and stoves or for a simple use in the outhouse.

It was a treasure hunt for me and there was excitement in wondering whether you would come upon a valuable that someone inadvertently discarded. It could be an under-appreciated item, its value hidden from the owner and waiting for someone to uncover its true identity and reveal its glory. I looked at the site not as a wasteland but as a vast field of wonders to be found, like the gold or silver that miners from the last century sought in western fields or the lure that brought the Conquistadores to the high desert country of Cíbola, enduring the torture of searing sun, hostile natives and scarcity of game and edible fruit. Although I thought Mesa de Cíbola a magical place, other visitors were more pragmatic and harbored no illusions. They knew that trash was the waste of human living and it wasn't worth spending a lot of time looking for something. My mother worried about my interest in the site but she never prevented me from going there. We had always lived in rented quarters in the west side of town and had very little furniture or other forms of wealth. Maybe she hoped that I would find something valuable in my visits to Mesa de Cíbola.

Furniture, usually broken or well-worn, was an attraction for many visitors. People would come in their trucks to look over discarded chairs, divans and tables. In those days, the furniture items were made from solid wood and sometimes the wood could be used to construct some other items or simply to repair a piece of furniture. I never found the discarded furniture interesting and left those items alone.

Sifting was a personal matter because only you knew what might interest you. Sometimes a friend would go with me and we would spend an hour or so reviewing the additions to the old inventory. Of course, there were layers to the site, the result of trashy deposits over many years, at least twenty I guessed. I was sure future archeologists would date the periods of the grounds by the strata, analyzing carefully each year's discarded materials. Over time the wind would blow sand and dust over the heaps and coat them with a gritty glaze once an isolated rain came and made a paste which was then baked by the high desert sun. Additions to the site would be made on top of the coated layer and the process would repeat itself.

While visiting Mesa de Cíbola I would watch people unload their trash and look over other people's divested belongings and sometimes pick up one or more items and take them away. It was a free exchange of sorts, randomly occurring but which could stir some excitement among participants.

From time to time I would see Don Marquez at Mesa de Cíbola, sitting on a large flat rock that jutted out from the hillside at the far southern end of the hallowed grounds. He looked straight ahead, oblivious to me or the occasional bird that flew over the grounds. He was like a sentinel, keeping watch or waiting for something to happen.

The rock was a horizontal outcropping of sandstone whose softer layers had eroded. It was unusual in that there were no others like it around. On the road to Santa Fe you could see the state's most famous image of eroded sandstone—Camel Rock—that had the outline of a camel's head and its single hump. This rock at Mesa de Cíbola was certainly much smaller but it still had a strange position in its environs. When you sat on it and closed your eyes, you could feel a sensation like the early morning winter sun swallowing you when leaning against an adobe wall with a southern exposure. There were spots like that in the Valley that people sought, claiming that they had healing powers. But I never saw anyone else sitting on the rock except Don Marquez and me.

I had learned his name from my mother who seemed to know who he was after I described him to her. He was much older than my mother, his beard grayish as was his hair whose tufts spread out like straw from underneath the cap he always wore. His face was wrinkled and dark with a small mole above his left eye. He wore old work clothes like baggy denim pants, a heavy cotton shirt and ankle-high boots that had seen better days but were probably very comfortable. They looked like they had been re-soled. He lived in a house at the western edge of town, alone since his wife's death years ago, his children gone from town. A faint smile and a nodding of the head told me he was always glad to see me but he rarely spoke.

I often wondered why he visited Mesa de Cíbola because he never ventured into the mounds while I was there. I searched for something of value, the practical reason for my being here. At least that was what I thought until I met Don Marquez. His eyes became more alert when I came near him and I could see a welcome in his eyes. I would sit on the rock as well and view the expanse of Mesa de Cíbola from this great vantage point. I would close my eyes and imagine the Mesa de Cíbola treasure that had brought me here and others before me. Don Marquez would also close his eyes and there were slight movements of his head from time to time as if he felt the power of the rock or the ghosts that lingered in Mesa de Cíbola. I came to realize that he meditated at this spot. There had to be an internal conversation going on inside. I was not part of it. I belonged to the external world.

We could see if anyone approached the grounds long before they actually arrived. As we sat, facing north, the sun would warm our backs and the rays seemed to penetrate with a healing power that stayed with you after you left. The warm sensation was wonderful in late fall or early spring, even when a chilly breeze would blow in from the eastern slope of the Jemez range. In the summer, the sun was not in our eyes and the same breeze, when it blew, cooled our faces just enough so we could stay a little longer.

"*Yo los ví,*" [I saw them] were the first words Don Marquez uttered when I first met him at Mesa de Cíbola.

"*¿Quienes?*" [Who?] I replied. I thought he might be talking about some Mesa de Cíbola visitors he had seen recently. He was quiet and nodded. He continued moving his head slightly, up and down, in a nodding manner. I looked over in the direction he was gazing to see if I was missing something. All I could see beyond the trash heaps were the usual *Cholla* cactus here and there and some *Chamisa* plants, the denizens of the foothills. I actually got up and walked over to where he was looking. Of course, the *Cholla* cactus was just as ugly and the *Chamisa* simply had the sage oily smell, especially near its younger shoots.

He never replied to my question at that first meeting but I always remembered his first words. It was often that I was the only one to speak during our meetings. Sometimes I spoke in Spanish and sometimes in English. I sensed he was also bilingual but the few times he spoke to me, his words were in the

Spanish spoken in the Valley, full of archaic words that modern Spanish speakers would shake their heads at, wondering whether we had just stepped out of a time capsule from an ancient past.

I would talk about school and my friends and what we did during weekends. I would talk about my mother and where she was working. I would ask him if he knew my half-brothers who were much older than me. But he never responded to my questions. He would nod occasionally as he listened to my monologues. After finishing what I had to say, I would look over to him and his gaze would let me know that he heard and understood. At times he would put his right hand over my head and nod.

Llegaron cansados. [Arriving exhausted.]
Sus animales con sé, [Horses dry-mouthed,]
Se pusieron a pie, [Dismounting, they stood,]
Fueron al río, [Ahead to the river,]
Descanso por fín. [A rest at last.]
Hablaron de Quivira [They spoke of Quivira]
Montes que llaman [Forests that call]
Al hombre y cielo. [To man and to sky.]

"*Vineron y me hablaron,...*" [They came and spoke to me...] he said once after sitting quietly next to him for a long time. He continued with what seemed like words to a song. I remember it was getting to be late in the afternoon and I was about to head home. What he said reminded me of a parable but I understood very little of it.

"*¿Quienes?*" Again he said nothing after this question. I waited a while longer but it was getting close to supper time so I left.

" *El oro esta cerca pero mas hondo,*" [The gold is near but deeper] he continued on another occasion. The reference to gold caught my attention. There had been no gold mines in the northern part of the state, much to the chagrin of the first European visitors to the area about four hundred years ago. I didn't understand what he might have been referring to.

"*¿Dónde hay oro? ¿Hay oro aquí?* [Where is there gold? Is it here?] I asked these questions with no expectation of answers I could understand. I thought of asking my mother about Don Marquez' sanity when I got home. Surely the people in town would know whether senility was affecting him and I was wasting my time trying to understand what he was saying. I quizzed her and she said she had not heard anything untoward concerning my Mesa de Cíbola friend.

" *Hay que vivir quieto,*" [One should live calmly] he said on yet another occasion. This didn't help at all and by then I stopped asking questions. He tapped his foot when he finished. This was the usual sign that he would not speak again. Despite the enigma of his words, I remembered them clearly, maybe because I thought they could be clues to a puzzle.

Don Marquez was not always at Mesa de Cíbola when I visited. I never actually saw him come or go. When leaving the grounds I would look back and sometimes he would be gone and a fear would come over me. But I always enjoyed his company despite my inability to carry on a conversation with him. There was a certain kinship that our meetings engendered and I felt refreshed after our visits. Once I had brought a fresh apple for him and one for me. They were early season apples, Jonathans, available from the Valley in August. They were crisp and juicy with a bit of tartness. Don Marquez and I ate the apples. I had been hoping that the snack, partaken together, would loosen up the conversation so that it would be more bilateral rather than the typical monologue of mine. But I had no such luck. He smiled when I handed him the apple. He proceeded to take out his pocket knife and slice it up into sections and pick the seeds out with the tip of his knife. His way of consuming the apple left no core and he ate the whole thing. I could nibble the core down until all that was left was the inedible cover around the seeds and the stem. But there was a core and I had to bury it or leave it for the birds.

After finishing the apple, he wiped his knife off with his handkerchief, put it away in his pocket and then put his hands on his knees. He had a satisfied look as he turned to me and smiled. I went on with my prattle and didn't get any response.

My friend Lloyd was in town one summer day and visited me to play basketball. He knew where I lived because he sometimes came home with me for lunch during the school term. His parents were going shopping and dropped him off. His dad and mom were driving a new sporty car and I could see they were overdressed for going shopping. Lloyd himself had dressy pants on and a white shirt. But his shoes were scruffy so it must have been okay to wear them for playing ball on my clay-floored basketball court.

"I don't think my parents will be back for a couple of hours," he said.

"Good, we can play awhile and then maybe go to the store across the street for a soda."

Lloyd was clumsy in basketball much like other boys who came from the east side of town which had the nicer homes. All the houses there were newer and were of frame construction with stucco exteriors. Of course, all of them had running hot and cold water and indoor toilets and bathrooms. The river bisected the town. On the older west side of town where I lived, the houses were usually made of adobe with mud or cement plaster veneers. Quite a few still had no running water except for a faucet somewhere in the house, usually the kitchen. Some had outhouses for toilets. I lived in a house that had a kitchen sink with a faucet and a bathroom that had a toilet but no bathtub. We had no hot water and the kitchen sink drain ran into a street drainage ditch. The house lots were larger in the west side of town so there was plenty of room for erecting a hoop and laying out a half court. I had cleared out the weeds and leveled the area myself a couple of years ago.

We soon tired of playing ball because of the summer heat and decided to visit Mesa de Cíbola after cooling ourselves with a soda. He had never been there and was curious why I found it so interesting. It was a fifteen minute walk to the outskirts of town from my house and then another few minutes to the entrance. We talked about school and what we had been doing during the summer. I had only seen him once or twice since May when the school term had ended. His father worked in Santa Fe for the state government and his mother was a schoolteacher. Although his parents could afford to send Lloyd to a private school, he had stayed in the public schools.

"Wow, this is fantastic!" Lloyd exclaimed. "Look how it shimmers," he said excitedly as we approached Mesa de Cíbola. He hurried his pace once the excitement took hold of him. I told him that Don Marquez may be there, sitting on a rock, looking distantly into the northern parts of the Valley, with Black Mesa appearing prominently where the confluence of the Rio del Norte and the Chama rivers come together. I told Lloyd I had never seen Don Marquez either come or go. He was always on the rock whenever I arrived at or left Mesa de Cíbola.

There was nobody there. I had not seen Don Marquez for a few weeks now and wondered whether something had happened to him. The dry air was calm so we didn't have to worry about the dust that usually blows in from the west. From a distance, the thousand reflections of the sun from tin and glass were in stark contrast to the blanched earth of the Jemez foothills. It was the usual mirage in the desert landscape that had fascinated Lloyd.

We visited pile after pile just I like I had always done. Lloyd was probably overdressed for the visit to Mesa de Cíbola but I didn't say anything. He was careful in not getting himself dirty anyway. He examined each pile a lot more carefully than I did, partly because I had been over them so many times. I was more interested in the new additions.

He picked up some broken toys and a taped up baseball bat. It had a bad smudge on the end, as if someone had used it to pound a black colored item.

"I could use this bat for hitting rocks into the field behind my house," Lloyd said.

He used the bat to sift through other piles and he became excited that there may be other items that would be useful to him.

"It's amazing what people throw away," he continued. "I could spend the whole day here looking for stuff."

We had been at Mesa de Cíbola for over an hour and I thought it wise to start heading home. I suggested that we turn around and start going back to the gate. I looked over to the rock where Don Marquez usually sat but there was no one there. I felt a sudden chill come over me despite the dry summer heat surrounding us.

"Nah, let me look over here a bit longer," he said. By this time he had a few items accumulated in a bag that he was hauling around.

I heard the car pulling up and I thought it might be just another visitor. Then I saw the glum faces—the driver and the passenger—Lloyd's parents obviously displeased. It was clear to me what must have happened. My mother told them to look for Lloyd and me at the town dump. They must have been aghast that my mother would even sanction such an outing. They must have asked her where exactly the place was, gritting their teeth and admitting they had never been there. Cheerfully, in her naiveté, my mother probably described the way to get here. She might have mentioned Don Marquez, the strange old man. In tense disbelief and perhaps growing concern for their son, they must have followed her directions faithfully through town and on to the west side where there were few housing units and the dusty road that led to Mesa de Cíbola.

Lloyd finally noticed them and he walked over to them after dropping the bag and his prized find, the baseball bat. After some words he got in the car and waved goodbye to me. His father backed the car rapidly out of the grounds, not bothering to find a place to turn around. The car tires spun a bit as they tried to grip into the dusty road surface. A great cloud of dust was created as the car backed out of Mesa de Cíbola. His mother had her face turned to the back seat, saying something to Lloyd. Even though I couldn't make out what she was saying, I could imagine it. The words didn't matter and it was the disgust in her voice that probably hurt Lloyd the most. The cloud of dust lingered in the still summer air, dissipating slowly like a mist over an imaginary river in the setting sun.

As I walked back to town, I realized that they didn't offer me a ride home. I guess it was to be expected. They wanted me to know they didn't appreciate me taking their son to the dump, probably a place they associated with filth and vermin. Their son certainly didn't belong there. I often forgot that there was a separation between families. The Hispanic families who had more money lived in the east side of town, in Rockview. They spoke English at home and Spanish only when they had to. They ate American food like macaroni and cheese, steak and potatoes and hot dogs.

But money wasn't the only separator between families. There were other barriers, like skin color, physical handicap and in my case, being illegitimate. I remember walking into one family's home. I had been playing with a boy my age and he had invited me to meet his parents. Their home was even more humble than mine. It was simply a large room. There were four double beds in the room. They were all same, each with an iron frame and a single mattress placed on wire mesh strung on the frame. The beds were made with sheets and a handmade quilt with a single U.S. Army surplus blanket folded neatly on top of each one. There was a single chest of drawers in the room along with six straight backed chairs and a wooden table. There was a kerosene lamp on top of the chest of drawers. There was no evidence of electrical service to the home. The boy's mother was tending to a wooden stove off in the corner of the room next to what appeared to be a small cupboard. The stove was obviously the only source of heat. She nodded when she saw me walk in with her son. The house floor was made of pine planks that were unpainted and had been worn down in the high traffic areas. The only decoration in the room was a rather large, framed religious print of the Last Supper. My friend's father was seated on the edge of one of the beds. He was haggard looking, his face long with sunken cheeks and hair that was thick, graying and combed straight back. He greeted me by my name, Reyes, as if he knew who I was.

¿Dónde vives, Reyes? he asked. [Where do you live?] I told him where I lived, describing the neighborhood and a few landmarks.

¿Sabes de tu papá? [Do you know of your father?] I shook my head and at first wondered why he would ask me that question if he knew who I was.

"*¿Cómo no sabes? ¿Que eres bastardo?*" [How do you not know? Are you a bastard?] It was clear that he was trying to embarrass me. He obviously knew of my father's suicide after killing his wife. He also knew that I was posthumously born eight months after his death.

"*Mi papá murió en Abril y yo nací en Diciembre. Él era Teófilo Rodríguez, dueño de una cantina y separado de su esposa.*" [My father died in April and I was born in December. He was Teófilo Rodriguez, a tavern owner who was separated from his wife.]

The gentleman sat up with a surprised look on his face. I supposed that he was trying to make me cry or at least cower with his insinuations. I might of shocked him with my matter-of-fact answer.

"*Pues, entonces sabes que eres bastardo,*" he continued in a haughty tone. [Well, I guess you know that you are a bastard.]

"*Con permiso; me despido. Creo que se hace tarde y mi esperan en la casa.*" [Excuse me; I'm leaving. I believe it's getting late and they're expecting me at home."] There was no point in carrying on the conversation. The gentleman reveled in trying to make me feel inferior. It was only one of many experiences I would have in meeting people who were bitter with their lot in life. It had not turned out to be what they had expected. They let others know when they thought they had an advantage, petty as it may be.

I continued going to Mesa de Cíbola but not as frequently, possibly because there were fewer and fewer good things to be found. I never saw Don Marquez again to ask him about the gold. I asked my mother if she had heard anything about him but she hadn't. I continued sitting on the rock the times I did go, hoping that I would get inspiration about what Don Marquez said to me with those cryptic words. Sitting on the rock made me feel good, the perfect place for leaving doubts behind, opening up pathways to something new and a chance for filling a void that I couldn't describe. Black Mesa was far off to the north set against a cosmic sky because I could see for miles and miles with amazing clarity from that rock. The scene might have brought Don Marquez here, its natural beauty posing as the treasure that few people bothered to take in. He had sat like a guardian angel, watching over the Mesa de Cíbola. The rock was a place to rest and release shackles that we often place upon ourselves. It was a place to be alone and feel a surge of dreams that take you on a fateful journey. I would go home, happy to be alive. Maybe this was the magic of Cíbola, what kept some of the early settlers here, instead of going back to Zacatecas.

But I continued to think about Don Marquez' words. I looked for clues in the history books I found in the library about the settlement of the high desert country, the various battles with the native tribes, the occupation by Mexico, then claims by Texas and finally the annexation by the United States. I was growing older and maybe my standards for discarded items became elevated or maybe I believed less in magical places. Mesa de Cíbola still looked like a treasure site from afar, the optical illusion that lured me there in the first place. It was the nature of things. You want to believe.

10
That Accidental Home Run
August 13, 1955

*It was one of those times when you
think you have done a good thing and
someone finds fault in it.*

—Reyes

Little League started in San Isidro in the summer of 1952 when I was nine years old, the minimum age for qualifying. I was fairly good in athletics but not terrific. There were a lot of kids who went out for tryouts, most of them nine or ten years of age. About half of the boys didn't make the cut and I was happy that I was assigned to the Rockview Market team with green trimmed uniforms. I was given a uniform with the number 13 but I was not superstitious so the number was fine with me. I took it home and showed it to my mother who didn't seem to think it was a big deal. I played one game in the uniform and then my coach informed me that more 11 and 12 year olds had tried out for the team and he wanted to assign my uniform to someone else. Hence, I was sent to the minors after only one game.

Out of the boys who didn't make the uniformed teams, a minor league was formed with six teams of 12 boys each. The teams were designated colors—red, yellow, blue, white, green and black. Most of us were either nine or ten years old. Joseph Sanchez was my coach of the "blue" team and he called for practice every day for two hours starting at eight o'clock before the weather became too hot. The games in the minor league were only five innings long and were played at 4PM while the major teams played after our games at 6PM under the lights and in the coolness of the evening. We played two games a week for eight weeks—the length of the season. Joseph was a great coach, fair-minded, patient and interested in having us learn the rules and improving our skills. He expected us to be at practice every day and told us that if we missed practice two straight days, we were off the team.

The baseball field had been flattened out from a couple of rolling hills in the west side of town. A huge front loader and tractor had worked together for a couple of weeks to create the area for the baseball field. The town had built a fence that encircled the field and there was a crude scoreboard placed atop the centerfield part of the fence. Wooden bleachers had been built behind home plate and on the first and third base sides. Although the large stones had been removed from the field, it was still gravelly and sandy. There was no soil for sod on the hills in this part of town and certainly no clay. Steamrollers had been used to flatten the area and to compact the surface and the process did tamp down the gravel and sand mixture quite a bit but we still had to contend with bad hops caused by small stones and soft spots in the sand. The stones would rise to the top after a rain or after the winter freezing and thawing of the surface. When playing the infield we practiced grounders a lot so we could get used to the unpredictable bounces. Kids got hurt with bad hops that hit them in the face. The ears seem to attract the ball, perhaps because we would try to protect our face as we tried to scoop up the ball. I played infield, normally shortstop or third base, and I played deep so the ball would lose some momentum by the time I would go for it. My arm was pretty good so I was able to get the runner out despite my deep infield position.

The second season I made the Harris Ford Motor team in the majors and I stayed with that team for three seasons. I became a starting pitcher and pitched at least one game a week. The rest of the time I played shortstop or third base and never in the outfield, which looking back, may have been a mistake. At that time, speed, throwing accuracy, good lateral movement and skill in scooping up the grounder were rarer traits so if you didn't have them, you played outfield. As an outfielder you developed good sense of depth and speed in reaching the line drives and you improved your placement for the pop flies and grounders that got through the middle.

My pitching improved every year and in my final Little League year, I had four pitches, some better than others. My best pitch was a screwball that didn't have a lot of speed but it fooled a lot of batters. The curveball broke only a couple of inches toward the outside for a right hand hitter. My fastball was okay but it didn't break any records so my off speed pitch wasn't very effective. I had a winning record every season so I thought I was pretty good. Throwing so many different pitches did make my arm ache, especially since I didn't wear any warm up jacket to keep my arm at an even temperature. I threw a lot of strikes and never learned to control the placement of the near strikes. I didn't walk a lot of batters but I got hit a lot. Fortunately, we had a good infield team so we often got the batter but there were plenty of hits beyond the infield.

My batting performance was fair. I got a lot of singles and doubles but I had trouble hitting the long ball. During the season I would hit one or two home runs, none of which really helped my team. I weighed just under a hundred pounds and my upper body strength really didn't develop until high school. Players in other teams often registered ten home runs or more in the season. Yes, some were stocky and weighed a lot more than me, but some were about my size.

The spectator sections were filled with parents, friends and retired people. The loudest crew consisted of boys slightly older than the players. They had missed playing in the league or never qualified to play for one reason or another. They booed when errors were made, made fun of an unusual batting stance, and poked fun at those of us who went hitless far too long. We developed a discipline to ignore them and our coach made sure we didn't antagonize them by arguing with them or protesting their antics. Because of their noise, we learned to concentrate on the game and slowly grow self-confidence. My mother never made it to a single game and none of my relatives seemed interested in following my play. So in my case, I had to distinguish for myself when I was doing okay and when I was not up to par. As teammates we supported each other, not just with idle banter but with advice that more times than not helped our morale and spirit.

In my last year we had post season play for the first time. An all-star team selected from San Isidro was allowed to play in a tournament of four teams in Los Alamos, the town that was home to the national laboratory and whose residents consisted mostly of white professional families. The boys from Los Alamos seemed to outplay the boys from the Valley at San Isidro in all sports they competed in—basketball, football, baseball and track. There were many theories about the lopsided scores, some of them ethnic or even racist in nature. But there were never any fights after a game, at least not during any time I can remember. The other two teams were from Santa Fe and Las Vegas, towns that had also formed Little Leagues and had had them operating for a couple of years. We were slated to play the Santa Fe All Stars in the single elimination tournament game opener of seven innings on August 13, 1955.

Santa Fe was the capital of the state and was several times more populous than San Isidro so we figured that we didn't have much of a chance to winning the game. They had a lot more players to choose from and had more experienced coaches. Long odds never seemed to bother us and nobody really expected us to do well anyway.

We showed up at the field in Los Alamos in our regular uniforms but we all had black baseball caps with an "SI" on the front and "All Star" stitching in the back. The loud gallery from San Isidro followed us to the game and they started calling us the "si si" gang. We couldn't get away from them.

The field at Los Alamos was beautiful. It had grass in the infield and outfield with wide base running paths. The pitcher's mound was well groomed as was the home plate area. Home plate was at the northern end of the field so the sun was not going to be a factor for the batter or the infield. The view from home plate was spectacular with the majestic Jemez range in the background and pine forested foothills that seemed so close we could almost make out the deer roaming them.

The Santa Fe newspaper had an article about the match up and it made it seem that we would be a walkover. Their star pitcher, Tiny Martinez, had hurled several no-hit games during the regular season and was slated to pitch against us. We had several good pitchers, all with better records than me, so our coach picked Red Garcia as our starting pitcher. He was a strong pitcher with a good fastball and a sinking curveball. He had problems with control so he gave up too many walks. I was assigned to play centerfield against my protestations. I told everybody I had not played outfield during my three seasons in Little League. No one would listen and I had a bad feeling about the situation. I had had a few friends hit me a few fly balls during practice and I was able to get to them but they had been more high pop-ups and not line drives.

We were in the third inning before anyone scored. Red had walked two batters and a then line drive was hit to right center field. I ran up to meet the ball and stopped short to catch it on the first hop and then whipped it to second base. Our team captain yelled at me something and I knew he had wanted me to try for a running catch. But I had played it safe. The unforgiving gallery booed my play as well. One runner had scored and now they had runners on first and second with two out. Another liner was hit and this time it bounced just past second base and rolled hard into centerfield. I ran forward to meet it and I hoped to catch it in the second or third hop but it sank close to the ground and I had to stop it with my body. I had lost time but I was able to get it to the second baseman off balance with very little speed. The runner from second base had scored and now we were down two runs. My team captain didn't say anything this time but his look wasn't encouraging. Red finally got the last out with a strikeout. I got to the dugout and heard the gallery's unhappiness with my play. Tiny retired our side, three up, three down. We had had only two base runners, one on a walk and one on an infield hit and now we were in the bottom of the fourth inning with Santa Fe batting again. They put two runners on but they didn't score.

I had hit a hard grounder in the second inning but had been thrown out. In the top of the fifth we were up and I was the first batter. Tiny was short and he had an unusual windup, the kind that throws your timing off. He had a blazing fastball and he played the corners. His pitches were low and the umpire had been kind to him in calling anything around the knees a strike. I was kind of mad at myself and was ready to take it out on the ball if I could get a hold of it. I took two pitches on the outside for balls. I stepped out of the box and looked back at the coach but there was no sign. He figured I was good for a single if I could get a hold of the ball. That's what I had done for most of the season. The natural thing would be to take the next pitch and get the third ball and maybe get a walk eventually. We would at least have a man on base. I really don't know what happened next because I remember swinging straight through and heard a sweet crack of the bat. I figured the hit would be at least good for a single or a double. I saw the ball sail into right center and both outfielders were too far from where it might land. As I rounded first base I took a look to my right and saw both fielders looking over the fence. At first I thought I had hit a ground rule double but the third base coach waved me in as I approached second base. The damn ball had never hit the ground in fair territory. I had hit a home run.

It was one of those times when you think you have done a good thing and someone finds fault in it. My teammates were yelling, jumping up and down and they all patted me in the back as we were wont to do back then. But I did hear from the gallery "Why didn't you hit home runs back home?"

My coach congratulated me and said, "Don't pay any attention to them. You know you hit a home run against Tiny Martinez."

Unfortunately, we didn't score again that inning or the next. Tiny had become more careful, especially with 2-0 pitches. His team protected the 2-1 margin well and it was our bat at the top of the seventh, the final inning. I was up again after one out and a base runner at first base. I walked over to home plate, expecting another rejoinder from my anti-fans in the gallery.

Sure enough, I heard "Hit another accident!"

But the Santa Fe coach and Tiny played it safe. They remembered me and gave me an intentional walk. We now had the winning run on base. But Tiny bore down and struck out the next batter and got the last out on a pop-up. Tiny was the hero and his teammates made sure he knew it. We were proud that we had given them a good game, especially since we had not been shut out, thanks to an accidental home run.

11
Going to the Movies
September 18, 1956

And you don't seem interested in
getting along with all of us.
                              —*LeRoy Maestas*

Entertainment in San Isidro in the mid 1950s was going to the movies. There was a feature on Sunday and Monday, another only on Tuesday and another that showed on Wednesday and Thursday and then a blockbuster on Friday and Saturday. There was only one indoor theater in town—El Rio—named so because it was close to the Rio del Norte. *Cinemascope* and *Vistavision* had just been introduced into movies. It was the age of musicals with movies like "*Oklahoma*," "*My Fair Lady*," "*Damn Yankees*."

I had just started my freshman year at the high school and I got to meet a lot of new students who were from neighboring villages. They had gone through eighth grade in schools located in the villages. But we all met as freshmen at the high school, all 252 of us. It was the largest freshmen class ever at Fernandez High School. Now when I went to the movies, I frequently recognized one of my new classmates.

The El Rio did big business on Sunday afternoons when young people in the Valley filled the theater. The matinee show always had previews of the coming attractions, a newsreel short, a cartoon and the main feature. The show was anywhere from two hours to three hours long starting at 1PM. In the early 1950s the movies were mostly family rated with musicals and comedies playing a dominant role, at least in a small town like San Isidro. "*The Thing*," the "*Creature from the Black Lagoon*" and their ilk were horror films that came a little later in the decade.

On my way to the theater on this evening I spotted something that did not belong under a store window. Finding a purse is really not a stroke of luck as all events that happen to us could be. It was one event in a string of many that shape a life and can bring to question what values we hold. We can choose to make it an important event or we can try to forget it, pushing it out of our consciousness as much as we can. I have never been able to suppress the image of finding that purse.

I looked through the purse and found only a couple of dollars and loose change. There were receipts, a folding strip full of pictures of people I did not recognize, keys and makeup items—lipstick, a face powder tin and small hairbrush. There was no driver's license or other form of identification. Instinctively, I took the money and put the purse back where I had found it.

As I continued on my way to the theater I kept asking myself whether there was justification for what I had just done. Was there an obligation to take the purse to the police station? Was it easier for the person who lost it to retrace her steps and find it under the store window where she had placed it while waiting for someone? Why did I take what little money there was in the purse? I wanted to find a reasonable argument that would convince me that my actions were acceptable. Since there was no identification in the purse, was taking the money the same as finding it on the street by itself? The other items in the purse could be far more valuable to the lady than the small amount of money. Was I fooling myself into believing that I really had not stolen the money because it was impersonal, the purse had no ownership markings and so technically belonged to no one? The purse had been left on the sidewalk, a public place, and had been there for awhile. These arguments continued even after I arrived at the movie theater. Who was I kidding?

"How are you, Reyes?" said Emilio Montoya, a cousin of mine who was the theater manager. He was a short man, portly, balding and wore black framed glasses that made his head look larger than normal.

"Not too bad. How's Wilbert? I haven't seen him in a long time." Wilbert was his adopted son, about my age. Emilio had married a divorced woman who had two children, Wilbert being one of them. Then Emilio and his wife had two more. Those were still too young to go to school.

"Wilbert is visiting his Dad in southern Colorado. He'll be back next week. So you started the high school this fall?"

"Yes. Mr. Wainwright transferred from the junior high school to the high school also."

"Yeah, I've seen him. He sure looks like a homo. Maybe he should wear a dress. He's one of these Anglos from Texas, isn't he? There's too many of them at the high school. That's all that fucking Superintendent hires. We gotta get the school board to kick him out."

The Valley had its share of homophobes and Emilio was one of them. It was hard carrying on a conversation once the topic was launched. He also thought there were too many Anglos in high paying positions in the Valley. In his view they had gained economic and educational control of the Valley at the expense of the Hispanic contingent. In politics, however, it was all Hispanic in the legislative representation of the Valley.

"Mr. Wainwright is a very smart person. He's a good teacher and really wants to help students complete their education." I said it without trying to sound defensive. But what I said was true. The school had very few teachers we could complain about.

"Is that guy, Granger, still the high school principal?" Emilio asked. I knew this would start another tirade. Emilio had never met a Texan he liked. This was an attitude in the Valley that stretched all the way back to claims that the Republic of Texas made to lands bordering the eastern banks of the Rio Grande. We were claimed as a colony of Texas, not Mexico in the 1830s when Texas declared its independence and sought statehood under Sam Houston. Of course, the rampant prejudice against Spanish speaking people in Texas really increased soon after that era. As a result there was still resentment against Texan-born Anglos who moved into New Mexico or Southern Colorado since we became part of the United States.

"Yes, he is still there. He's tough, yells at us to clear the halls when we're changing classes."

"I heard he doesn't have a single Hispanic secretary on his staff. Is that true?"

"Yes."

"Does he have a single Hispanic on the administrative staff? A counselor, the truant officer, a student advisor?"

"No."

"But all the janitors and bus drivers are Hispanic, right?"

"Yes."

"That fucking asshole. He's as prejudiced as they come. We gotta get rid of him. You see what the colored people are doing now in the South. School segregation is now illegal. The Supreme Court says so. They are standing up for their rights. We Hispanics should be doing the same thing. "

"Well, he's not overt about it. I mean he doesn't call us names. I don't think you can compare the discrimination against Hispanics in the Valley to what the colored people put up with in the South. We don't have overt segregation here." I didn't know why I said this. It sounded like I was supporting Mr. Granger and defending Texans. Hispanics were in the vast majority in the Valley unlike the colored people in the South. Most of the private land in the Valley was owned by Hispanic families. But I knew there was discrimination by Anglos. It had been blatant in Los Alamos from the very beginning in the 1940s when it became an employer of many residents of San Isidro.

"He knows we would string him up if he did. He's too smart. He gets away with his brand of racism, not hiring anyone from the Valley. He goes to Santa Fe to hire Anglos and brings them here. Meanwhile we pay the taxes to support his brand of people." I had heard all this before. Emilio really got riled up about any Texan that got an important position in town.

"How do you get along with him?"

"Well, I met him once when I went to deliver mail to his office. He was okay."

"Let me tell you something, Ray. Don't let anyone tell you that you are not good enough. You can learn as well as anyone else. We tend to get put into remedial classes because we speak Spanish. They assume we can't do math so we get put into the slowest classes. Don't let them do that to you. By the time you graduate you are so far behind because you've taken all the slow classes. Then you can't get a good job even if you finish high school. Often Hispanic kids can't even pass the written test to get into the armed forces."

"But a few students can't do the math, especially those that went to the village schools. They can't be put into the regular classes. It's unfair to them." I had heard this. Here I was repeating it without knowing whether it was true or not. But I had seen my own classmates unable to keep up with the math instruction. They never really passed math classes or they dropped out of school. Fernandez High School had never had a graduating class numbering more than a hundred. Nearly half of the students entering the school as freshmen never graduated. Most of the dropouts were from farming villages or from the pueblos in the Valley.

"Well, if we put them in the slow classes they are doomed for life. And we are doing that at an early age. Students can be late bloomers and they should be given the chance to catch up."

"Eventually we have to make a decision about where a student should be, don't we? I assume the administrators and teachers have our best interest at heart."

"That's where your mistake is, Ray. They do not have your best interest at heart. They do whatever is convenient for them especially if they are tenured. Their first priority is keeping their job and not getting blamed for failure of the student. This is sickening. I'm getting upset just talking about this."

His face had reddened and had gotten a little puffy. I got the feeling we were talking about his personal experience with the school system. But I didn't want to aggravate him any further.

I moved slightly over towards the candy counter, pretending that I wanted to make a purchase. Emilio saw someone coming in the theater entrance and went over to meet them. As I approached the counter, I noticed a lady who looked familiar. She turned and looked at me.

"Ray, how are you? It is good to see you." It was Miss Maria Zamora who had been my fourth grade teacher. She was with a friend of hers, also a grade school teacher, Miss Ann Haley. Both were still wearing nice clothes, presumably those that they had worn to school earlier today.

"I'm okay. I hadn't seen you in a while."

"Ray, this is Miss Haley. She teaches second grade at the school and this will be her third year there. Ann, this is Ray Cordova, one of my former students. He has done very well for himself and is now in high school. I remember him being the subtraction champion in my class. He won second place in addition but he came out on top in subtraction. I would have a student challenge another student at the blackboard to see who could solve the problem the fastest. It was the math equivalent of a spelling bee. Do you remember that, Ray?"

"It's nice to meet you, Miss Haley." I turned to face Miss Zamora who was still grinning. "First, President Eisenhower. I remember you asked us who the President was almost every day." She burst out laughing and Miss Haley smiled. "Sure I remember the subtraction contest; you gave me a small box of candy as the prize. But I'm not sure I could win that contest again, though."

"I'm sure you could. You were a very good student and I understand you've kept up your grades. Good luck with high school. I expect to hear good things about you."

Both ladies finished their purchases and left to go into the orchestra section of the theater. Miss Zamora was one of the few Hispanic teachers in the

San Isidro Elementary School. She had been a stern teacher and had insisted on strict discipline in the classroom. When you dealt with her one-on-one she became a different person, a caring and sympathetic person who would help you with any problem. She shared a rented house with Miss Haley and the rumor was that they were lovers.

The El Rio was like a second home to me. It was one of the largest structures in town, one of the few that had two stories. The neo-Moorish styled theater had been built in the 1930s at the beginning of the Hollywood era of national distribution of films. The nearby bridge across the Rio del Norte had been built by the WPA in 1934 and the downtown section of San Isidro's west side grew because there was easy access by automobile. The theater had thick curtain sections that opened and closed the movie presentations. It had a large stage with the huge movie screen sitting at least 30 feet behind the edge of the stage. The stage had the elevated ceiling so that several backdrop curtains could be raised or lowered in front of the screen. The side walls of the theater were curved so that the narrowest width of the orchestra section was near the stage and then it flared out to its fullest extent at the rear of the section. The side walls had cloth-like covering up to a quarter of the height of the ceiling and on either wall there were four ensconced lanterns in Moorish style half way up the walls. The second floor had the rest rooms and the entrances to the balcony area. There was a hallway entrance to the elevated projection room. Both lobby areas in the main and second floor were fully carpeted with plush carpet featuring large floral designs. The orchestra aisles also had the same carpet. It was comfortable inside, warm in the winter and cool in the summer with the aroma of freshly popped popcorn always wafting through the aisles. The snack bar had no means to sell soda or hot dogs as did the drive-in theater—the *El Chico*—located about four miles outside of town.

I had gone to a lot of Mexican movies at the El Rio with my mother before my eighth birthday, as frequently as twice a week. The late forties and early fifties had been the golden age of movies made in Mexico. They enjoyed wide distribution in the Spanish-speaking areas of the United States—Texas, New Mexico, Arizona and California. We watched musicals with *Jorge Negrete*, *Antonio Aguilar* and *Pedro Infante* and comedies with *Tin Tan* and *Cantiflas*, dramas with *Sara Garcia* and many others. My mother spoke little English so she really enjoyed those movies. After 1954 the El Rio got new management and started showing more American made movies. My mother's interest in the movies dropped to only going occasionally but she did enjoy the westerns with Gene Autry, Roy Rogers, Rocky Lane, Lash LaRue and the like. Sometimes during a western she would lean over and ask me what it was that was said, especially if the audience had just laughed heartily.

I was able to lose myself in the movies, entranced by the flickering images which took me to an alternate world. There was a lapse in reality, a tunnel I would go through and come out different, apart from my body that was anchored and could not move. I would be one character and then another. It was a way to transport oneself out of San Isidro and into an imaginary existence, the proverbial escapist paradise. We knew the world portrayed in the movie was not real. There was no place where people lived like that, talked like that, and had music accompaniment announcing important action or speech. Watching the movie was hypnotic.

Often I would eat a whole box of popcorn and not remember eating a single kernel. One time I forgot I had eaten a pocketful of piñon nuts while watching the show. An experienced consumer of nuts could crack one in the mouth with the top and bottom incisors and access the delicious meat inside by only using the tongue. It became mechanical. I had discarded the shells where I sat. After the movie I made loud cracking sounds as my shoes crushed the shells when I exited the row.

What the El Rio represented, especially to people like me who had no means to travel beyond a few miles from home, was the window to the rest of the world. Before television, which was destined to arrive in the Valley in mid 1956, movies provided an inexpensive, rapid and intensive medium for not only entertaining but also informing the public what was going on in the rest of the country, if not the world. I was the first, or perhaps the second, generation in whom movies engendered a desire to leave the Valley despite the gravitational pull of family and familiarity. The admission fee was fifteen cents; a box of popcorn was a dime while most candy bars sold for a nickel. At those prices, poverty was not a valid excuse for avoiding the movies in the 1950s.

The theater had smoking sections in the balcony and the far rear of the main seating area. There was an extensive snack bar with popcorn and candy being the popular items. I know this because I worked at the theater in the summer when the regular snack bar attendant couldn't show up. On Sunday afternoon the theater was the date destination for the pre-teen and early teen crowd. The date consisted of holding hands and at the advanced stage, kissing and maybe petting. It was hard to keep your date's identity secret at the movies. The screen occasionally projected bright light back into the audience and people could recognize you even if you tried to slump down in your seat.

The movie tonight was "The Egyptian" with Edmund Purdom. There was a light turnout for the movie, maybe twenty to thirty patrons. The image of the purse kept coming up in my head, interrupting the movie so much that it was hard for me to follow the plot, as thin as it was. After the movie I saw Emilio again and we exchanged pleasantries and I left. Leaving the El Rio was like entering, or perhaps re-entering another world. In the daytime it was actually disorienting. You had to get your bearings, despite recognizing the familiar surroundings. You saw more clearly when your eyes adjusted to the bright sunlight. At night, it was less disconcerting, perhaps because you went from one darkened area to another with real people and stuff interacting with you in three dimensions.

Regaining my wits after walking a few paces from the theater, I met up with LeRoy Maestas who had been in the theater as well. LeRoy had been two years ahead of me in school. I was a freshman and I imagined he was a junior. Although he was older, we were about the same height and weight. He was known for his sour disposition. His face was pockmarked and reddish from a bad case of pimples. I supposed that the malady did little to improve his outlook toward life. He had been involved in a number of fights at school. In the eighth grade he was involved in a knife fight with my friend Tito from the Pueblo of San Pablo. Tito had always been shy and kept to himself. LeRoy picked on him one day even though Tito was in the sixth grade. They were about the same height and weight. Tito was getting the better of LeRoy and that was the time when the knife came out. Fortunately, Tito was able to avoid getting slashed. A teacher finally came and stopped the fight. LeRoy was suspended for a week and he had to stay after school for an hour every day for the rest of year. Tito transferred to St. Catherine's Academy in Santa Fe, a school for Pueblo students, and I never saw him again.

I wasn't sure I was up to having a conversation with LeRoy.

"Hey Ray, *que pasa*?"

"LeRoy. I didn't see you at the movie."

"I sat in the back with all the smokers."

"What did you think of the movie?"

"It was okay, nothing special." LeRoy was fingering a cigarette in his hand. He wasn't in a hurry to light it. He was limping noticeably. I knew he had a club foot and it had always affected his walk, maybe even his attitude.

"Doing anything this summer?" He started walking westward, toward the main intersection in town, the same direction I was going. I never paid attention to where he lived since I tried to avoid him as much as possible. He was part of the "cool" group of boys who wore their hair combed straight back on the sides, heavily greased, with a curl from the top of the head brought back onto the forehead. The shirt collar was worn straight up. It was the new generation of the *pachuco*, a style that had mostly run its course about four years ago.

What annoyed me was he seemed to be interested in my affairs, my friends and what I was doing. We weren't related in any way. He had an older brother who had killed a student in a fight and he had been sent to reform school in Springer. His mother had died and LeRoy lived with his father who was a construction worker, a carpenter I think.

"Yeah, my father got me a job as a mason's helper. We're doing a job over in Riverside."

"Good. That'll get you money this summer."

"Hey, I saw you with Sharon last Sunday at the movies. Did you fuck her afterwards?"

"She's not that kind of girl. We're friends; that's all."

"She's a bitch, kinda stuck up and all."

"She's okay. She keeps to herself, likes books and music."

"I think she acts like she's better than the rest of us. You guys are a matched pair."

"How can I be better? You know my mother and I are on welfare. I never had a father. It doesn't get too much worse than that."

"Yeah, but you act like you're smarter than anyone else. You look down on us, *ese*." He elongated the *ese* part in a mocking tone.

"I don't know if I'm smarter. Most likely, I'm not. But I do want to graduate from high school so I try to get good grades."

"Why are you trying so hard for? You make the rest of us look bad."

"That sounds like envy. I'm not trying to make anyone look bad. I just know what I want. I want a good job and I am tired of being poor. Aren't you?"

"You make it sound like it's a crime or something evil. Having money may not make you happy, Ray. Being smarter than everyone else may make you lonely."

LeRoy stopped and lit his cigarette. He took a couple of puffs and then kept looking at me. I wanted to get home so I paused to see if he was still interested in walking along.

"All I know is that it is important to be nice to people, Ray. And you don't seem interested in getting along with all of us. It looks like you're laughing at us. Are you ashamed of being one of us? You should be proud to be from the Valley. Our families have been here since forever, you know. We've survived. In the middle of a desert valley we've survived. You've got an idea that we're no good. Maybe not good enough for you."

LeRoy resumed walking along but at a slower pace, perhaps trying to aggravate me. He was driving the conversation so I had to change the topic or come up with a reason for leaving him.

"Well, I'm not into popularity contests if that's what you mean. I have my interests and others have different ones so I don't go out of my way to meet with them."

"Hey, I think you're too smart for your own good. Nobody likes someone who's too smart. You scare people. You're an alien. You have to go with the flow in the Valley. Take it easy. Don't be a *zonzo, ese*. [silly person, buddy] Are you listening? Are you ashamed of your mother? Maybe all your relatives?" He stopped and took in a long smoke. He let it out slowly with his eyes looking upward at the starlit sky. I continued walking and then stopped. I turned and looked back at him. He was this dark shadow talking to me, leaning to one side, favoring his bad foot, the smoke circling around his head. I didn't answer and he wasn't finished.

"My cousin was in your English class last year and he said that you always got the highest grade in the class and the teacher wouldn't grade on the curve. My cousin got a "D" because of you. He said you were a *cabrón, ese*." [fucker, buddy]

"It seems to me that he's the one responsible for the grade, not me. Does he like to blame others for his mistakes?" I was starting to get a little testy with LeRoy, acting exactly like he described earlier. He gave himself another puff again and exhaled. He flicked ashes away from the cigarette with his little finger of the hand that was holding it, the end of the cigarette becoming a crimson red. It seemed to pulsate as he spoke.

"Nah, he's a regular guy. His parents farm and have a few cattle. His mother is a secretary at Los Alamos. But he doesn't have any fancy ideas about who he is."

"Look LeRoy, I gotta get home. Why don't you come over sometime and we can shoot baskets on the basketball court in the back yard." LeRoy was taken aback by my initiative to end the conversation. He may have been shocked that I was still courteous with him despite his taunting remarks.

"Sure, sure. Take it easy, Ray."

I breathed a sigh of relief as I crossed the street just to distance myself from the unpleasant encounter. As I walked and took in the cool night air I wondered what exactly made me uncomfortable when I talked to LeRoy. He represented something that bothered me. The image he described of me was a person not fitting into the expected mold of the Valley. His was only a subtle nudge back to where the stereotypical Valley resident was. There was a collective pull back to the norm, the inertia of hundreds of years, the search for Cíbola's treasure. Why wasn't I cooperating and becoming one of the regulars? What was wrong with being a Valley person? I wasn't going to starve and the Valley would take me in if I got sick. I made it seem like it was a crime to continue to ride the wave like everyone else. I convinced myself that I wasn't holding anyone else back. I wasn't intentionally into malice of my kind.

As I approached the store window where I had found the purse I could see that it was still there. I crossed the street again and went to the purse, opened it and replaced the money. I had not been able to convince myself that taking the money, the small amount that it was, was worth the trouble. A greater amount would have forced me to take it to the police station. This way, the purse was intact, almost as if I had not come across it.

I was coming to the realization that I couldn't change anything in the Valley. Taking the money was malice, doing harm to someone. All I could change was me. The choice was mine and I had already made it. I had to leave the Valley as soon as I finished high school. I would be old enough to work in the city like Albuquerque or join the Army if I had to. LeRoy was right in noticing that I was going in a different direction. I wasn't a believer in the things that were important to the Valley—being nice to people even when they didn't deserve it, looking out for relatives or friends regardless of the ethics involved, and propagating the family line even when I couldn't afford it. I was slowly being released, maybe cast out, and repelled like a foreign particle, toxic to the preservation of the cultural stream. In a not so subtle way I had rejected the promise of Cíbola and now it was rejecting me.

I thought about where I had come from. My mother had no land here and I wasn't interested in land. What little I had learned about American culture, it was that a person was judged on what he or she could do. You could get a head start with money or land. But eventually you had to prove you could do something useful. I had filled my head with what was possible, with what I wanted to try out for and experience. I knew I had limitations but I didn't know how far I could go unless I took the risk. All those books, movies, concerts and discussions with teachers who cared about my success had given me encouragement to enter a world with greater potential. What was I giving up? Certainly the Valley would go on without me. My ancestors had done so for hundreds of years, the Indians for thousands. But the American way of doing things was here, like it or not. It was time to learn about its potential. The only way to do that was to learn the language, associate with its education, its business and people. Was it possible to be accepted so that I could do this? There was prejudice against colored people, women, Jews and other minority groups including Hispanics, especially by the Texas types. I had to learn to nullify that prejudice. My teachers all said that education was key to becoming Americanized. Maybe being subtraction champion in the fourth grade could lead somewhere.

12
Los Pastores, A Christmas Play
December 1956

*Maybe he goes for older women. I have
not advanced to that point.*

—*Reyes*

Tuesday, December 4, 1956

Dear Chris,

Thanks for the sweatshirt you sent me. It is has that military look to it, being gray and thick. It's great to wear during the winter when I'm playing basketball at Fidel's place. The freshmen year at the Fernandez High School is going okay. It would be better if you were still here. I enjoyed visiting you at the Roswell Military Academy last month when I went down there with your Mom and Dad. They paid for all my expenses –meals, the hotel room and the ticket to the ball game the night we were there. I thought I would write you this letter to let you know what your friends (Manuel and Daniel) and I are up to. I mean besides the usual stuff like going to movies, hanging out after school at the café on Hunter Street, and playing basketball whenever we can get at least four guys together. The latest thing is that we are in a play, a Christmas Play called *Los Pastores*. I don't think we've ever put it on before at the high school. Usually for Christmas we have concerts with all Christmas carols and readings and stuff. You and I were in such concerts in sixth grade, remember? Miss Ely was our teacher and we went around town singing a dozen carols at each place two Fridays in a row right after class. At Bond and Willard's downtown store we were given snacks and candy and we did an encore. We didn't get home until six o'clock. You and I walked Betsy home because you had a crush on her that year. She got a little heavy the next year when we got to junior high and all of a sudden, boom! It was over. I still don't know whether it was her weight that turned you off or the fact we just didn't see her often enough that year.

Getting back to what we're doing with *Los Pastores,* let me finish that. The play is done in Spanish so the guys and I are polishing up our pronunciation with Miss Vigil who studied in Spain. You might have met her during freshmen orientation held last May when we were about to graduate from eighth grade. She is young, thin with curly hair and very pretty. She is the only bilingual teacher we have this year. The superintendent really wants us to learn English from native English speakers, all Anglos. We hear that he really wants us to get rid of our Valley accent that has that tinge of a Spanish sing-song with elongated final syllables. This is hard since so many people in the Valley have it and you hear it so much. I personally think it is contagious and as long as we are here, it is going to stick to us no matter what.

She has run through the play with us. Manuel thinks he is in love with her. He stares at her too much. I have talked to him about it but he says he can't help it. Daniel says she reminds him of his sister and he hates his sister so there is no problem there. I remain very professional around her, whatever that means. I'm there to clean up my Valley Spanish. Damn English contaminates it so much, you know. Every time we forget the word in Spanish, boom! We use the stupid English one. Anyway, she has a Master's in the Classics and a Master's in History from the university so she supposedly knows her stuff. She has been very nice to the gang despite our hormonal antics. We are the three shepherds with speaking parts in the play. I am kind of the head shepherd (Bártolo) since I see the guiding star first and I go and alert the others and clue them in about the Messiah and stuff. Manuel and Daniel are still kind of stiff in their parts but they are getting better. Mr. Levine, the high school librarian, is our drama coach for this play, not Mr. Cochran, who is still the drama instructor for the high school. Anyway, Mr. Levine doesn't know too much Spanish but he is smart and tries hard. He knows what the words mean and he does try to help us with the blocking on stage, intonation and arm movements. This is my first time in a serious play and remembering all the acting stuff is hard. The play is about forty five minutes long if we remember all our lines, much longer if a player needs a prompter and we have to re-take scenes again and again. Acting is kind of fun once you get the hang of it and nobody starts laughing. That was the problem when we first started. A student in the play would say their lines the wrong way and we would crack up. We could not stop laughing. Mr. Levine would get mad and start yelling at us. We rehearse in the main stage in the high school gym and our first performance is Friday for the entire school. As you might know, the seniors get the orchestra seats in front of the stage, the junior class just behind them and the low-life sophomores and freshmen get the bleachers, each on either side of the main floor. So there will be over seven hundred attendees at our first performance. I still don't know if our voices will carry to the entire student body. The acoustics in the gym are so bad. Manuel says it doesn't matter because few students pay attention anyway. His brother is a senior and he's been to all the plays for four years and he said few are worth watching or listening to. I want to do a good job because I would like to try out for other plays. The only reason the three of us are in this one is that we had been volunteered to work in the library during our study hall and Mr. Levine got to know all three of us and knew our Spanish was decent, probably better than all the other snooty Hispanics whose parents speak English at home. I am sure they mean well but they still have the dumb sing-song accent, regardless. Anyway, Miss Vigil has been a godsend to the three of us. I am hoping Manuel will get over his swooning very soon before he embarrasses us all. I have asked her to attend our dress rehearsal once or twice to help us in *sitio* as they say. She suggested different blocking to Mr. Levine which allows the speaker to be at stage front in order to be heard more clearly. Manuel, of course, lost it when she was there. He forgot his lines, got red in the face and generally made a fool of himself. I think Daniel and I are going to have to have a heart to heart with him and shake him loose from this infatuation with the lady. He says that Daniel and I are just jealous that she pays more attention to him than to us. He has got to be kidding. That boy has gone zonkers. He got a hold of a pornographic comic book; you know the small size you can carry around in your back pocket. He told Daniel and me that he and two teammates stayed in the boys' locker room after freshmen football practice and got excited after seeing it. They masturbated together and had a cock spitting contest as to who could send their wad the farthest. Manuel said he won with a distance of three feet eight inches. Daniel and I were supposed to be impressed with the feat.

Anyway we have improved a lot since the start of rehearsals about three weeks ago. We have dress rehearsal tomorrow so we will all be in full regalia. My mother has made a costume from a drawing that Mr. Levine gave me. Daniel's mom works so she went to Santa Fe and bought him a costume. He showed it to me and it is very nice, perhaps even too nice. Shepherds are supposed to be poor from what I understand. I guess we are going to have an upper middle class shepherd in Daniel. His headdress looks more like one that a sheik would wear than a poor schmuck shepherd. Mr. Levine hasn't seen it and I suppose he would be the one to ultimately approve the costume. Manuel made his own costume because his mother is an invalid as you might know. His sister doesn't know how to sew so he did what he could. He also showed the damn thing to me. He chose crazy colors for his cloak from an old curtain, I guess. I tried to stay serious when he showed it to me. It was all I could do to prevent myself from laughing. He found a headband that his sister had used for pinning up her hair. At least the damn thing was black so it was more or less acceptable. Manuel found a pair of baggy baseball pants that his older brother had and so they look okay for sheepherding activities. But Manuel's cloak (really, old green damask curtain) and his headdress which is a small, pinkish tablecloth may be too much for the audience; I don't know.

You might ask about my costume. Well, my mother seems to remember, in her ancient past, that she saw the damn play performed in town and she remembered the shepherd costumes. She is pretty good with the old foot-driven sewing contraption that she owns and made me a gray and brown color coordinated costume. The pale gray pants are outrageously baggy and my brownish cloak is very poverty-stricken, kind of shaggy with frayed ends and patches here and there. My ochre-colored headdress is cut so that there is clearly a front to it. The sides fall away to my shoulders and it has a long furled back that falls to my mid-back, very fashionable, I'd say. The headband that holds it in place has color, namely red but of a muted shade, and features knots that are evenly spaced. I told you it was stylish, but poor-ish looking. Anyway, we will do our fashion show tomorrow night and get our first feedback from critics, I'm sure. I think the only one to worry about is Manuel and what he may have to do to get a decent costume. Fortunately, I do not think Miss Vigil will be there to pass judgment on his outfit.

What I really want to tell you is about the play's nativity scene. The players don't have speaking parts and they are on stage the whole time, staring at the baby Jesus. Unfortunately, Mr. Levine has decided to make the baby visible so it is, you guessed it, a life sized doll. It took a long time for the nativity players to get used to focusing on the damn doll. Frankly, I think they took zombie pills in order to do it without laughing. So Bert Archuleta is Saint Joseph and Cindy Blankenship is the Virgin Mary. The three wise men are there as well and they are Joe Racine, John Applewhite and Eddie Garcia. As you may remember, Eddie is a short guy, kind of dark complexioned already but he will have dark makeup.

Joe and John will be the Anglo guys that they already are. Remember they are members of the Stompers from Rockview. They wear the big belt buckles and cowboy boots and heavy black leather jackets.

They don't know any Spanish but that's okay since they don't have to say anything. They have been pretty good during the rehearsals. I think they want to get in good with Mr. Levine. I guess he complained about them because they caused trouble in the library. Bert is doing great. He is still going with Anita Lopez and she has got his senior ring so it is very serious between them. Cindy is a dream. Daniel and I have our eyes on her but she won't give us the time of day. We were hoping that we'd be able to thaw her out by now since we see her five nights a week at rehearsals. She is not that great looking but her reddish hair just drives us wild. She carries herself very nicely. You might remember that she was with us in Miss Ely's class in sixth grade. We ignored her then because she had those big freckles and was skinny and gawky. Well, she has blossomed and you cannot ignore her figure any more. It takes a lot of self-control nowadays to not stare at her. And as we have talked, those hormones that stir in us don't seem to have a lot of discipline. Anyway, Cindy has become a big distraction in the play, at least for me. Daniel might confess the same thing. You might want to ask him when you are next in town.

This letter will bring you up to date. My studies are doing okay. The teachers I got are so-so and I will talk about them when I see you. Before I close I want to tell you one other thing about the play. Next week, starting on Monday, December 11, we will present the play in *Chimayó* at the Sanctuario, in *Las Trampas*, that little hamlet near Truchas where the padres were massacred by Indians back in 1680, and at Abiquiu, the artist colony on the road to Chama. Mr. Levine will be driving us up in the school van. You know who I am going to try to sit next to. Hmmm. I will give you one guess.

So long for now but I will write you after each play performance starting with the one in *Chimayó*.

Your friend—Ray Córdova

✠✠✠

Monday, December 10, 1956

Dear Chris,

I saw your Dad taking tickets at the movie on Saturday and he said you would be home on Saturday, December 22. I will be over at your house at nine or so that day and we can catch up on things, maybe take in the movie that night if you have no plans. I want to hear about your first few months at the military academy.

Well, we had the dress rehearsal last Wednesday and it was a riot. The laughter started again as we looked over all the costumes. It may be sacrilegious laughing so hard at a play that is supposed to be so solemn but we couldn't help ourselves. We finally got started after everybody calmed down and took their places. There was a giggle here and there afterwards but nothing that seriously interfered with the flow of the play. Nobody forgot their lines. One or two students were still a little wooden in playing their roles but we were pretty good considering where we started. Manual showed up with his stupid outfit and Mr. Levine got the Home Ec department to help him get something more reasonable. He wasn't embarrassed and now he fits in fairly well.

The performance in front of the student body was punctuated with laughter at first but the Principal, Mr. Granger, was stern as he went up to the microphone and told everybody that he would cancel the assembly if students didn't behave. Everyone was quiet after that, quiet enough so that our voices could be heard by most of the students. The bleachers, as you may know, have the worst acoustics. I want to believe that the students enjoyed the show. A couple of students did come up to me and said they were impressed with our delivery in Spanish. Miss Vigil came up to the cast and congratulated us and even joined our cast party that we had Friday night. All the cast members attended the party along with the stage crew that consisted mostly of freshmen and sophomores. We had sandwiches and punch that Mrs. Valdez from the Home Ec department prepared with her students. Mr. Levine was happy that the performance came off as well as it did. He took a chance with us and it was risky for him because he is not the drama instructor at the high school. I took tape recordings to the party and played the popular songs I had recorded off the radio. The high school has A-V equipment and it has a recorder similar to mine and the sound was not bad. We had the party in the band room and we cleared away the music stands and pushed the piano off to the wall in order to make space for the food and a small dance floor. The girls were willing to dance and I wasn't turned down by Cindy Blankenship. Of course, she only wanted to dance rock n roll stuff so I wasn't able to get close to her. I didn't have a lot of ballads on my tapes anyway because everybody wants to dance rock n roll. Manuel even asked Miss Vigil to dance but she declined. She told him that it was inappropriate for teachers to dance with students. I guess there are rules at the high school I don't know about. I think he was gutsy to even ask her. He seems to be a little more in control now when he is around her. Maybe he goes for older women. I have not advanced to that point. I am still dreaming about Cindy. She still is aloof, not just with me but everybody else also. Maybe her parents have warned her about us Latin boys. By the way, did I tell you I am taking Latin I with Mr. McNair? I can conjugate a few verbs and I know about declinations. The pronunciation is nothing like we hear in church. The c's are hard and sound like a "k." There are about twenty students in the class and he makes learning Latin fun. The boys who have been altar boys thought they would have a jump start in class but they have to un-learn stuff in order to keep up.

Tonight we had our first performance on the road, at the Sanctuario in *Chimayó*. The church was packed, although it is a relatively small one. The floor is still made out of hard clay and the benches are still those old wooden ones with straight backs. The priest there is out of Spain (Padre Arrellano) so he speaks the old Castilian dialect with the heavy hissing "s" or the "th" substituted for the regular "s" or soft "c" in Spanish words. He was very kind to us and accommodated us with setting up the nativity scene with his own props.

The audience consisted partly of pilgrims from out of town who had heard about the play. Two of them were on crutches, one was in a wheelchair and they had been at the church earlier to take a little of the "holy" dirt from the pit in the side altar. The rest of the audience looked like they were from the mountain villages around *Chimayó* and from Santa Cruz Lake. They had that "mountain" look about them and spoke nothing but Spanish.

We were more comfortable playing our roles in such a religious setting. We were more in character and Mr. Levine even told us that after the performance. Padre Arrellano gave each of the cast members a small Miraculous Medal as a token of appreciation from him and his congregation. It was a very touching moment and even the Anglo students were appreciative of the gesture. None of them are Catholic and several of them told me that their parents rarely go to Protestant services. Many had never been to the Sanctuario and had not seen the source of the holy dirt that pilgrims talk about after visiting the site. The students were very attentive and wanted to know more about the church and why it was a pilgrimage site. They had a chance to hear about the alleged miracle associated with the church as one of the English speaking pilgrims volunteered to relate the story. They even had a chance to see the source of the holy dirt. They were amazed at the number of crutches and canes that healed pilgrims had left behind. They stopped to read one or two of the numerous testimonials from pilgrims who claim that they were healed of their maladies by the holy dirt. They were silent as we left the church and piled into the van for the ride home.

At the intersection with Highway 76 Mr. Levine stopped at the Chuck Wagon Café and bought a cup of cocoa for each of the cast members and a couple of the stage crew members that had joined us in our first road show performance. I thought it had been an outstanding success in more ways than one.

Changing the subject a bit, I did get to sit next to Cindy and I did manage to put my arm around her. It was kind of crowded in the van and the gesture was taken to be not unusual. My hand didn't actually touch her shoulder (although I wanted to) so I am not sure it counts as a romantic advance. Daniel later told me that officially I had nothing to brag about. I didn't ask Manual about it because he slept most of the way home, perhaps dreaming about Miss Vigil.

Anyway, it is getting close to midnight and I have to close this letter. I will mail it in the morning and will continue keeping you up to date on my budding career in theater.

Your friend—Ray Córdova

✦•✦•✦

Wednesday, December 12, 1956

Dear Chris,

We just got back from *Las Trampas*, the village on the High Road to Taos, where we did our second road performance of *Los Pastores*. If you recall, it is a few miles past *Truchas* in a small Valley with lots of pastures going up into the San Felipe Mountains. There was plenty of snow on the ground but the roads were clear. Late in the afternoon it really gets cold up there. The village is at about 8500 feet. I had not been in the church. It is no bigger than the Sanctuario at *Chimayó*. It has a clay floor and its thick adobe walls slope up to the ceiling that's about 15 feet high with the giant *vigas* like most of the old churches in the Valley. It might be narrower than the *Chimayó* church because we seemed a little more crowded up in the altar area where we put the nativity scene players. The cardboard sheep kept falling down because we couldn't find a level area for their supports. Fortunately the manger was made out of wooden tripod so it didn't need a flat area to stand on. The church didn't have a lot of lighting. They had a couple of chandeliers with about four incandescent bulbs on them. The priest, Padre Mondragon, is very young but astute enough to have lit a lot of candles in the side altars. I think that helped a lot and it did give the play a mystical image also. We were again perfect in delivering our lines despite having to change our movements on the very narrow stage. St. Joseph had caught a cold since Monday so he had to blow his nose a couple of times during the performance. He had brought his holy handkerchief and had cleared his snot with minimum interruption to the flow of the play.

We played to another packed house, although I have already admitted that the church is quite small so our audience maybe hit twenty five patrons. I may have forgotten to tell you that we didn't charge admission although Mr. Levine did leave a jar for anyone who wanted to donate something to offset our expenses. I am beginning to think that there isn't much entertainment up there so we may have been the only action in town. I did see a couple of Anglo people in the audience. They were an older couple and they may be retired and they may have come over from Taos where there is a growing retirement community. The audience, like in *Chimayó,*, consisted mostly of villagers, farmers and ranchers who still eke out a living out of the mountainous land. I saw a few middle-agers who were well dressed. They probably have jobs at the national laboratory in Los Alamos. Missing were any people our age. There were kids who sat in the front who looked like they were first or second graders, not many though. The audience spoke Spanish natively. I heard the conversations before and after the performance. Several audience members came up and spoke to us in Valley Spanish. They were very grateful to Mr. Levine for producing the show and bringing it up to them. Padre Mondragon had asked his parishioners to prepare snacks for us. They had *biscochitos*; the anise-flavored shortbread cookies were thick with lots of sugar and cinnamon on top. They had a pot of hot chocolate, made with fresh milk and honey. It was a lot better than the restaurant stuff they make out of little bags that they throw into a cup of hot water and stir. What was also interesting was that Padre Mondragon introduced us at the beginning, stating our names and the roles we would play. He had the audience join him in prayer and then he gave a blessing to them and then turned around to us and blessed us as well. This was unexpected and this may explain our flawless performance, I don't know.

We rode back in the van and Mr. Levine had to stop halfway home because Cindy was feeling sick. She jumped out of the van and threw up on the side of the road. She got in after composing herself and sat next to me. She may have gotten some splatter on her shoes or clothing because there was an acrid smell in the van that almost got the rest of us sick as well. Mr. Levine said that maybe she had drunk the hot chocolate too fast and that had upset her stomach. Let me tell you that vomit goes a long way in killing ardor for a girl. I did sit next to her but I kept my arm to myself this time. She was kind of distant tonight, more than usual. There was probably something bothering her and she didn't talk much. Daniel noticed the same thing and told me there were rumors in the school about her but he had not heard any details.

The weekly paper, *The Valley News*, came out today and it had pictures of the play from our performance last Friday at the school. The nativity scene with St. Joseph and Mary was featured prominently. All our names were in the article and the places, dates and times for our road shows. Mr. Levine was interviewed by a reporter and he said that the students had done a great job with the show. He thanked Miss Vigil for helping with Spanish diction and cultural research. The article may get us a few more attendees at our last performance in Abiquiu slated for Friday night. It is not a big village but it is off US Highway 84 so it is probably easier for Valley residents to get there.

It is getting late and I will write you after Friday's performance. These road trips take a lot out of you. I do not know whether I was cut out for show business.

Your friend—Ray Córdova

✛•✛•✛

Friday, December 14, 1956

Dear Chris,

We have completed all the performances for *Los Pastores* that had been scheduled but Mr. Levine told us tonight that we have been invited for a command performance in Santa Fe. This is by invitation from the Drama Department at St. Michael's College. They have invited us to perform on their main stage on Tuesday, December 18. They will invite the college students that live in town because the out-of-town students will have left by then. Christmas recess starts tomorrow. They will publish an article in the *Santa Fe New Mexican* newspaper about the history of the play and the famous author, Antonio Machado, will do a Christmas themed reading of his works before our performance. Mr. Levine told us that their theater sits 500 people and that they expect about 200 or more attendees. No admission will be charged but they expect about $200 in donations and the college will turn over the amount to Mr. Levine to offset travel and other expenses. Mr. Levine said that he would treat us to a dinner at the La Fonda Hotel before the performance which is scheduled for seven o'clock in the evening. Most of us were excited to hear the news and we sang most of the way home. What was strange was that Cindy's parents showed up in Abiquiu and took her home after the performance.

The Abiquiu show was nothing short of sensational. The priest at the church, Padre José Sandoval, had a beautiful nativity scene that was life size with realistic renderings of donkeys and sheep and goats. They were made out of papier mâché and had been donated to the church by artists that live in town. He had a wooden manger as well, filled with straw and a life sized baby Jesus. So we used his nativity scene figures instead of our cardboard ones. He also had St. Joseph and Mary and wise men figures as well but they were made out of wooden planks that had been painted by artists in town. We performed inside the church which was a lot bigger than the ones in Chimayó and Las Trampas. There was plenty of stage area in the transept. The church is old and made out of adobe but it is has a wooden floor that had nice woven rugs near the altar.

Padre Sandoval is an expert in New Mexican history and he persuaded Mr. Levine to start the play outside the church and have us precede members of the congregation. That kind of start to the play has historical significance. Well, it was cold out there while we were waiting to go in. We only had our costumes on with no jackets. I guess it never got cold in Bethlehem because herding sheep in those outfits in the winter would have been tough. St. Joseph's cold got worse so Bert had to drop out and Mr. Levine got Angus O'Hara to step in. He did well and the show went on. We don't have understudies, you know, so we have to grab whoever is available. The church is heated with wood burning furnaces and it was nice and warm inside when we finally got in. The introductions were brief by Padre Sandoval but he did manage to give an overview of the tradition of *Los Pastores* in New Spain that was followed in New Mexico as well.

We performed to a standing room only crowd. Apparently the newspaper article in the *Valley News* did the trick in bringing more people to us. More chairs were brought in to accommodate the overflow crowd but they ran out of chairs and so late comers had to stand along the walls of the church. Most of the attendees were adults and a good number of them were Anglo. I am sure they included members of the artist colony in the Abiquiu area. Padre Sandoval even had spotlights from the high rafters of the church and they were positioned on the nativity scene but one was focused on center stage. I was the first actor to speak so I had the spotlight on me for the first few lines of the play. It was another flawless performance with no one forgetting their lines. We didn't rush through the play and we had plenty of room for our movements. The audience gave us a standing ovation and Mr. Levine asked us to take three curtain calls, the last one with all of us holding hands like they do in the big stage productions. Quite a few attendees came up to us to view our costumes and congratulate us on our sterling performance. Padre Sandoval also has an altar society of women who helped prepare snacks for the parishioners and our cast and stage crew. This time we were treated to a little cup of *posole* with a condiment of red chili. They had hot apple cider with cinnamon flavoring and miniature *biscochitos* that were thin and crunchy. Daniel snacked on them all the way home. Mr. Levine told us we succeeded at the gate as well. Padre Sandoval gave him nearly $85 that had been contributed by the audience. I took a look at the jar when we were partaking of our snacks and I saw at least two twenty dollar bills in there.

We saw Cindy's parents come into the church after the play had started. They were among the people standing and they were very noticeable. None of our parents had come to our performances so it was unusual to see them there. While we saw many attendees smile, or sometimes giggle during the play, her parents were unsmiling the whole time. They did not stay for the refreshments either. They spoke briefly with Mr. Levine and then they took Cindy with them. I thought maybe they were going to take off early on a holiday trip. So I didn't get to sit next to Cindy in the van but we were all overjoyed on the news about the Santa Fe encore performance. Like I said earlier, Mr. Levine turned the radio on to a top 40 station and we sang the hit songs all the way home.

Well, it's been another long night in show business and I have got to close. I will write you a letter on Tuesday night, hoping you will get it before you leave on Friday night next. If you don't, we can catch up when I see you on Saturday, December 22.

Your friend—Ray Córdova

✤ ✤ ✤

Tuesday, December 18, 1956

Dear Chris,

It is almost eleven o'clock now and we just got back from Santa Fe where we performed a finale for the gentle folk of the old capital city. For the seasoned stage veterans that we are, it was another night at the opera. But this time we were treated to a dinner at the La Fonda Hotel before we took the stage. They had prepared a long wooden table that sat all fifteen of us. Mr. Levine sat at the head and there were seven on either side of the long table. There was a red tablecloth in keeping with the season and it was nicely decorated with fresh flowers and pine fronds. There were pots of poinsettias on the buffet counters behind the table so the corner of the restaurant they had prepared for us was especially festive. We ordered ala carte so we looked over the menu very carefully since a couple of the students had never been to a formal restaurant. Their parents had always taken them to the Woolworth counter in Santa Fe or to a diner with the plastic tables that had jukebox meters on the wall side. Although there were New Mexican dishes on the menu, the students could order a steak filet or a pork chop dish. Apparently when they ordered the meat dishes they didn't understand the waiter when he asked how the meat was to be cooked. When we were served, a couple of the girls were aghast that there was "blood" on the dish. Mr. Levine had to call the waiter back and have the meat cooked to a "well done" stage. The girls had never had meat that had been cooked rare or medium rare. I supposed we looked like country bumpkins to the rest of the restaurant diners because the girls were quite vocal about being served "raw meat." Despite our provincial behavior, we enjoyed the dinner and even had a great *flan* for dessert.

We arrived at the college about half hour before the performance was to begin. The stage was huge with an actual front curtain that dropped down and it was deep allowing a lot of set construction if necessary. Our cardboard sheep looked puny in the giant stage. The college had a giant star that they pinned to a plain gray curtain backdrop. There were markings on the stage floor so we enlarged on a graduated basis the distances between characters and the nativity scene. The acoustics were a lot better than our gym so we felt comfortable using a more regular voice volume. The lighting was fantastic and Mr. Levine worked with the technicians so the scenes could be accentuated. The nativity scene had a mix of colored lights that really made St. Joseph and Mary look holy with a mystical aura around them. The wise men had a yellowish glow on their costumes with the lighting that Mr. Levine ordered. The bright spotlight was on center stage where I was to come on at the beginning of the play. Apparently Mr. Levine and the Drama department instructor at the college had collaborated since last Friday and some epic music was piped into the theater, the kind you hear in biblical movies like "The Robe" or the "Ten Commandments." It was to be used during our production between the speaking parts of the play and as a medley before the play started and afterwards. A podium had been placed at center stage front for the famous author—Antonio Machado. The curtain was pulled down behind his podium and he joined us as we finished placing all the props in their new position. He was a very cordial person and spoke to all of us in Spanish. He wished us luck and said he was going to stay for our performance. During the reading of a selection of his works, we were to go into the dressing rooms or remain backstage but be very quiet. Since I had never heard him read his work I chose to stay seated back stage close to the podium.

Before Mr. Machado was introduced, I peeked to see whether we were going to have a sizable audience or not. The theater was full near the stage but there were plenty of seats toward the back and in the balcony. To start, the college drama instructor went out to the podium and gave a brief introduction. He had had a nice program printed and he read our names and urged the audience to stay for our play after Mr. Machado's reading. Then he went over a brief biography of Mr. Machado who had been the winner of many international literary prizes for his novels and poetry. He was originally from Costa Rica but was spending a sabbatical year at the University of New Mexico but resided here in Santa Fe during that time. As Mr. Machado approached the podium he got tremendous applause from the audience and he took a bow to acknowledge the kind welcome. He spoke in English, good grammatically but heavily accented, and gave a background on each of the works from which he would read. He then did the same in Spanish. He started and the audience was very quiet. His works were in Spanish and he spoke in a fluid and powerful voice. His passages were mostly about historical events in Latin America and he used conversations between characters to move the story line along. He read from his poetry that appeared to have religious significance and whose passages were centered on the Christmas season. When he had finished, he thanked the audience for its kind attention. He got another thunderous applause from the audience. There were shouts of "Bravo" from the more enthusiastic fans. He bowed again while the applause continued. The drama instructor appeared again at the podium and asked for another round of applause for Mr. Machado and they responded with vigor. When the applause died down, he asked the audience to stay after the intermission and view our play. Many members of the audience got up from their seats and went to the large theater lobby where smoking was permitted. Mr. Levine had explained to us that during intermission, a cash bar in the lobby would serve soft drinks, beer and wine to the theater patrons. A jar would be place in the lobby for our benefit to collect contributions that would be used to offset expenses for our travel.

When the theater bell summoned the patrons back to the seating area, it became clear that we had lost patrons, especially those that were very well dressed. Strangely enough, we picked up other patrons that had not been at Mr. Machado's reading. In general the theater reached the same attendance level that Mr. Machado had drawn. The famous author took a seat in the front row with a few admirers that had stayed to chat with him after his reading. Before the curtain was raised, the college drama instructor went out and introduced Mr. Levine and asked him to relate the significance of the play and say a few words about the student players. When he finished, the music came on and the curtain was raised. We were to start the play when the music died down and the spotlight hit me.

Chris, I do not know what happened next. People tell me that it was another person who recited the lines. I was smooth and dramatic and I spoke perfectly accented Spanish. They tell me that I looked at the audience and connected with them. My arm movements were synchronous with the lines that announced the coming of Christ. Mr. Levine told me that my opening sequence set the stage for everybody else. I had recited the lines so many times they seemed to come out automatically. I do not remember doing anything special. Maybe I was in a trance. I remember other sequences a little better. The audience was kind to us and even clapped after each sequence during the play. I do remember that they clapped after my opening lines. That interruption did not throw me off nor did any other spontaneous applause throw the others off either. We were flawless in our delivery again. Not only did we not forget any lines, there were no costume problems, sneezes or coughs and no one blocked anyone else during scene changes. The play was over and the curtain came down. The applause continued and we took three curtain calls. We held hands again at the end. Finally Mr. Levine came out and brought the Nativity Scene players out to bow. Then surprisingly, he yanked me out from the group and brought me to the front for a bow. The audience applauded and we took one final bow together.

As we drove home feeling the buzz from a memorable night, Mr. Levine told us that the audience had donated $345 into the jar in the lobby. Someone had put in a hundred dollar bill and there had been many twenty dollar bills in the pot as well. Almost no one had put in coins, unlike our take at the other performances. If he did his math right, he said the plays had grossed about $500 but there were expenses he would have to total up but he was sure that we would net over $400. He would make sure that the administration would bank the sum and keep it for drama productions in the future. That made us all feel good and got us really ready for the Christmas holiday.

I wish my letter would end at this point with kind of a happy ending. What had started as a laughable play with an inexperienced drama coach like Mr. Levine ended up with a month's worth of effort that we will never forget. We learned a lot about ourselves, gained stage confidence, and got to see people react to us in recreating a traditional work of art. But I must tell you awful news.

Cindy did not participate in the Santa Fe production. We have since learned that she is pregnant with Curly's baby. Yes, it's the same Curly Armijo who graduated from high school last year. He was always driving around in this black expensive convertible. His father owns the gas station in the "Y" formed by the Los Alamos highway and US 84. The news is that her parents will not permit an abortion so she will finish the fall semester in January and then drop out of high school. She will be home schooled and then try to pass the GED in another year or two. At this point we do not know if Curly will marry her. It appears that her parents are not in favor of a marriage since she is only sixteen. There are state laws about sex with a minor but we have not heard whether her parents will pursue that course against Curly who is twenty.

Daniel and I were shocked when we heard the news on Saturday. He and I were, of course, silent admirers of her and even had designs of dating her in the future. It goes to show you how naïve we are. We didn't even know that she had been dating Curly.

Manuel is still in love with Miss Vigil but he has gained a little self-control. I expect he will get over it in time. He told Daniel and me that he is now jerking off five times a day because of her. She seems like a responsible person and she will help get him back to reality.

Daniel and I saw Sharon at the movies on Sunday afternoon. We talked to her about the development with Cindy. Sharon is a serious student where Cindy never was. Of course, Cindy could put on the charm and she was always nicely dressed and groomed. All that made her a popular girl in school. Maybe that's why she was picked for the Mary role in the play. Sharon is pleasant and understanding but she is also self-confident. She comes from the poor side of town but I think she will make something of herself. I like her. As for me, the Cindy incident has shaken me perhaps because it took me by surprise and because it is so serious. She will be a single mother if her parents do not relent on the marriage thing. I am sure that having a baby is a wondrous thing but the price the single mother pays and the handicap that it imparts is just too much for my teenage brain to understand. You have not been part of the Cindy scene so maybe you can give me counsel. I still have feelings for her but they are now more of the sympathy kind than anything resembling romance. I do not know whether I have anything to say to her because in a sense I am still a child compared to her. I have had a great freshmen year so far. I plan to study hard in the coming semester and continue being on the honor roll. Mr. McNair has already urged me to take Latin II next year to strengthen my vocabulary even more. Now with a little thespian experience he thinks that I can improve my English pronunciation as well. He believes he can help me get rid of my Valley sing-song accent and speak the King's English. Miss Bell is my homeroom teacher and she has become a believer in me as well. I don't know how long she is going to be here at the high school since she is getting on in years. But it is gratifying to have these teachers supporting me already.

I will see you on Saturday morning. I have been telling you about stuff here in San Isidro. I am ready to hear about things in Roswell and the military academy.

Your friend—Ray Córdova

13

The Americans for Democracy and National Unity (ADNU) Contest Spring 1957

I think their dismissal of the culture
here in the Valley is shortsighted and
borders on racism.
—Sharon Archuleta

The Recruitment—February 4, 1957

Ned Wainwright was our History teacher during our freshman year and he pulled me and several other students aside after class and told us about the annual ADNU oratorical and essay contest. I remember the other students were Sharon Archuleta, Marla Garcia, and Tom Armstrong. The deadline for submitting an application was about a month away. He said that Fernandez High School had never had a student enter the contest and he would like to have several entries. He thought we were all capable of assembling a good essay and preparing a speech that summarized the essay's content. The theme this year was "Manifest Destiny" and represented the belief that the United States was pre-ordained to be the greatest country in the world. It had been destined to occupy the land that it does now and that every one of the forty eight states contributed in an "invisible" way to the strength of the country. He thought that we should think of ideas on how New Mexico performed well in its duty of making America strong.

The ADNU was a patriotic society started in the east coast soon after the civil war with the aim of bringing Americans together again. The founders took a proactive role in healing the wounds of the war and also welcoming the new states in the far west into the American fold. Members of ADNU ranged from those who were ardent constitutionalists to those who were willing to adapt the spirit of the nation's founding principles to modern times. In San Isidro we had ADNU members who were older people from the Midwest or from the eastern seaboard who had retired in the Valley and a lot of ex-military people who worked at the national laboratory or in governmental jobs in Santa Fe. The ADNU always had a float in every parade held in San Isidro and they were seen as a pro-American, patriotic group, the kind that prospered during the Eisenhower years.

Mr. Wainwright volunteered to be our advisor and mentor for our individual entries. He wanted to know if we were interested in working with him and that he would permit us to use the class period to work on our entried. We would be excused from doing homework and taking exams during that period. He would talk to the other teachers who taught history classes to see if they would be interested in having their students submit contest entries. He had copies of prior winning entries at both the regional and state level. The essay was limited to 5000 words and the speech was supposed to be between 10 to 12 minutes long. There would be judges at the district, regional and state level. The winner at the state level would receive a four-year full tuition scholarship to the state university of his or her choice in New Mexico. The district championship would be held in San Isidro, the regional in Santa Fe and the state in Albuquerque, each one about a week apart next month, starting on Friday, March 7. Entries were due on March 1. He wanted to know if the four of us were interested. He would choose others if any of us wanted to opt out of the offer. He was surprised to learn that all of us said that we were interested although Tom and Marla wanted to talk to their parents first. Sharon and I committed ourselves right then and there.

To me this seemed like a great opportunity to improve my English both in written and oral form. Mr. Wainwright had been a fair and conscientious teacher during the school year. So far we had had a couple of opportunities to give speeches in class and the four of us had done pretty well. We had slow learners in class and he had been patient with them, not pushing them beyond their limits. They had not checked out like they had in other classes, frustrated that they couldn't keep up with the rest of the class. Many of the Anglo teachers had had trouble relating to the heavy Hispanic makeup of the classes. Many of them had never lived in the Southwest and had only a passing acquaintance with Spanish. Hispanics made up three quarters of the student population, the remainder was mostly Anglophone with only a handful of Pueblo Indian students. The high school administration was all Anglophone and only a fraction of the faculty was Hispanic. About half of the teachers were from New Mexico but not from the Valley. Most had been educated at

Highlands University, St. Michaels College or at the University of New Mexico. Mr. Wainwright was among those Anglo teachers who had no trouble relating to students regardless of ethnicity. He knew the history of the state very well and had worked at the New Mexico Historical Archives in Santa Fe before becoming a high school teacher.

Mr. Wainwright was a slim, wiry man with a pale face, thin nose and blue eyes. With a bird-like face, there was an effeminate air about him including a high pitched voice. He was suspected of homosexuality but I never saw any evidence of it. He was unmarried and he had been seen escorting Anglo women to faculty social gatherings. His intelligence overwhelmed you when he spoke yet it never came across as condescending. He was readily available for student conferences and generally had an agreeable disposition. He wore suits that were thrift-store shabby and too big for him. He drove a ten year old Plymouth sedan with a loud muffler that was easy to spot in traffic and I was among those students who kidded him about it. He said that it helped other drivers know that he was coming and that pedestrians were forewarned in plenty of time.

What I admired about Mr. Wainwright was his attention to detail in his history lessons. It was clear that he appreciated the impact of certain historical events in the course of American history. But his expertise in the history of the Southwest was unmatched by any teacher or scholar that I had ever met in my young life. Several of the students in our class had joined me in just being spellbound by the breadth of his knowledge. He took me to concerts in Santa Fe and introduced me to classical music and poetry, interests that I still have today. He introduced me to the nihilism of Sartre and Camus and urged me to read beyond the Hemingway and Faulkner stuff. An ardent Stravinsky fan, he could also recite long passages from *The Prophet* by Gibran or the "Prufrock" poem by Eliot. He knew written Spanish but spoke it clumsily and he urged me to improve my mastery of it in written and oral forms.

Sharon and I had become students that he liked to challenge in class, using us to pace the rest of the class. Sharon was bothered by this dynamic because she didn't want to separate herself from her friends in class and to seem like a "teacher's pet." She and I talked about this and she asked why this sort of thing didn't bother me. But she knew I was a welfare kid and already disenfranchised from Valley society. In a way this freed me up to take chances in breaking away from any societal tradition or cultural conformity. The teachers who judged me on the work I could do were my friends, regardless of ethnicity. Mr. Wainwright was such a person and I was grateful for being given the chance to prove myself through my own efforts, not because of who my parents were.

Sharon had been in several of my classes during the junior high school years. She was well read and did very well in her studies although lacking the drive to be the best student in class. She said she was a girl and America did not appreciate the brainpower of women. A lover of music, she had possibly the best collection of Spanish music in the Valley.

Of course there was something between Sharon and me, an undercurrent of feelings we didn't talk about. We sometimes met at the movies on Sunday afternoons. Her father would drop her off for the matinee with her friends. She would join me and we would sit next to the far wall so we would have only one neighbor even in a full house. We had done this a few times and we held hands during the whole show. At first our feelings made their way through our hands. Our palms would become sweaty and we would have to dry them off and then clasp again so our fingers were tightly wrapped around each other's. We graduated to kissing passionately. But there was nothing permanent about our relationship and we didn't let any emotional attachment ruin our studies or our friendship. I think we were in a stage of exploration, getting experience with the feelings stirred up during the teenage years. It might have been an intellectual affection for each other rather than the mindless hormonal passion that sometimes overtakes you. We would talk about books and the projects at school. Sharon was pretty but modest in her dress and she didn't believe in makeup claiming it was subjugation of women. Girls in our freshman class were already developing figures that merited fashionable clothes and makeup. But Sharon shielded herself from any peer pressure to follow that accelerated path to adulthood. She had seen me talk to other girls and I did sit with one or two of them in the theater during Sunday afternoons. She knew that I was not going to develop a stable relationship with her or anyone else.

The Plan—February 11, 1957

Today Mr. Wainwright called our first organizational meeting with the four of us and said that other teachers in the high school were not going to volunteer their time to mentor students for the ADNU contest. Many of them felt there was little time available and it would take too long to prepare any of the students in their classes for the contest. They also felt students were already booked solid with commitments in athletics, extracurricular activities like band, cheerleading or part-time work. Hence, the four of us were probably going to be the only applicants from Fernandez High School. He said that he had already lined up meetings for next week with the local ADNU Board of Directors and with the San Isidro Village Council. We would interview the respective members with two questions from each of us. These meetings would give us an opportunity to hear what the village elders thought about the "manifest destiny" theme and how the Valley and state related to it. The idea was that we could use the data from the interview as a starting point for our essay. We could do more research in the library to flesh out the points made during the interviews. We were to take the rest of this week to develop the questions we would ask. He asked us to show him drafts of the questions by Thursday so he could work with each of us to make them relevant, clear and succinct.

Sharon told me her questions would be on music and literary contributions by southwestern artists. I had thought about questions on land, politics, major historical events or the economy but I was going to think about this and maybe discuss the topics with others like Mr. McNair, the Latin teacher and Ms. Bell, my homeroom teacher who also taught Freshmen English. That night I wrote two questions on each of the four topics.

The Advice—February 12, 1957

I got a hallway pass from Mr. Wainwright and found Mr. McNair in the library. We found a corner where we could talk and I proceeded to brief him on Mr. Wainwright's plan for entering the ADNU contest. He nodded as I relayed the information but after a while a frown developed and he asked questions about the interviews with the ADNU and village council. I couldn't be very specific about the interview arrangements so I proceeded to show him my questions. He read them carefully and said:

"Do you know any of the board members of the ADNU?"

"No, I don't think so," I answered. "Why is that important?"

"I know three of them well and I have no use for them. They are a bunch of jingoistic fools who hide behind love of country to further their personal agendas. They see Communists behind every bush. And they are pretty quick in calling someone a "pinko." I think they enjoyed having the Rosenbergs fried. I would be very careful about the information you get from them. First thing, check their facts. They go around saying things that are at best, half true, if not out and out false. One or two of them may even be closet racists. They are smart enough not say anything overtly but I would be cautious in using any material they give you."

"Could you give me an example of a personal agenda?"

"Well, Mr. Douglas is a member who owns the gas station over in Mesa Blanca on Highway 84. He is also an investor in the advertising weekly—*The Mesa Shopper*. He has confided to people that he would like to take over the local newspaper, *The Valley News*. He says he would like to expose the political corruption in town and what he calls the "depravity" of the people in the Valley. He is a "hallelujah" Christian and says the Catholic Church has kept people believing in superstition. He rolled into town about five years ago with family money. He bought the gas station and put in an auto repair shop. He hired local workers and apparently got burned with thefts and employees not showing up for work every day. Most of workers he had trouble with were Hispanic and so he proceeded to think that all Hispanics were not fit to work for him. He has since hired only Anglo workers both at the gas station and at the newspaper that he co-owns with a fellow named Jack Morgan."

"But there are bad workers in town. That's nothing new."

"Yes, but most people do not declare a whole ethnic group off limits, especially since most come from a ranching and farming background and they may have needed time to show him what they could do. He is going to punish a big population segment for the wrongs done to him by a few bad eggs."

"What exactly were the wrongs done to him?"

"Several shiftless workers stole tools, expensive tools no less. He claims that workers had funerals to attend to and gave him short notices when they would be absent. The other thing we do not know for sure is how he treated these workers in the first place. He had no business experience as far as we could tell. So he may have ordered people around rudely."

"Is there no turning him around?"

"What I have heard is that he is set in his ways. Now he thinks that Hispanics in town aren't loyal to America. He thinks that they shouldn't speak Spanish, for example. He thinks it's un-American. What is dangerous is that he may use the newspaper, even though right now it is only an advertising rag, to promote his prejudiced views. It could get worse if he gets a hold of the *Valley News*."

"But we've had Anglophones living in the Valley for nearly a hundred years and they have intermarried with Hispanic and Pueblo Indian families."

"Yes, but with more population movement occurring in America today, like people moving to the west for retirement and health reasons, there is danger that these people will use latent prejudices to inflame the situation."

"But I have got to believe that this isn't the first time that an Anglo has had a problem with a Hispanic stealing from him. In a hundred years surely there have been incidents like this and things have been worked out. Over time is it not possible that he will see that Hispanics are no different in work ethic than any other ethnic group?"

"Well, in the past, unlike the colored people in the South, Hispanics have owned land for centuries and they were self-sufficient in either farming or ranching. I think they were able to withstand any temporary prejudice from an outsider. Further, again unlike the colored in the South, I think Hispanics dominated politics here in the northern part of the state so there was a counterbalancing force to any new group trying to impose its will on the native populations. But we are in a new age where land ownership and political power are no longer enough to avoid conflict. The colored people in the South are starting to band together. Look at what the Rosa Parks incident has started a little over a year ago. The Land Grant issues here in New Mexico may be enough to galvanize a similar movement."

"But I have never heard of physical conflict between Anglophones and Hispanics in the recent history of Northern New Mexico."

"And I do not think there will ever be physical conflict now or in the near future. At least not out in the open. The conflict I fear is silent and devious like preventing people getting jobs or advancing in their careers, getting loans, being trained in good jobs, discrimination in housing and so on. Since the economy is changing over from farming and ranching to business, finance, and knowledge oriented work like science, law and medicine, Hispanics are vulnerable because the new economy will require more and more education, something that has never been a priority for them."

"Who are the other members of the ADNU board?

"There is Wayne Whitehead, an ex-military guy who is still active in veteran affairs with the state. Another anti-pinko fool, he believes educators are all socialists if not Communists. Women don't belong in the workplace. He's originally from Oklahoma, married a Cherokee Indian lady who has since passed away. They never had any kids and he's taken her death very hard even though it happened about five years ago. He's a hard drinker and don't be surprised if he's a little tipsy at the meeting. He is in the all the parades that involve military figures and is an officer in the local veterans club. Basically a good soul but he waves the flag a little too much."

"Does he have trouble with Hispanics?"

"Not overtly. He's condescending to women and minority groups. But you can make the judgment for yourself when you meet him."

"But he married a Cherokee lady."

"That doesn't mean he thought of her as an equal. I met her once and she looked like she was the kind of woman who supports her husband no matter how he treats her. A lot of women still do that and I'm not sure that's going to continue. Today women are demanding rights. They're asking to be admitted into many more professions than the traditional ones like nursing and teaching. There's a women's liberation movement underway in America."

"Who else is on the board?"

"You'll probably notice a woman, Lucy Montauk, who's an outspoken member on the board and represents what I call the pilgrim crowd. She's totally against any equal rights vision for women. She still believes in the traditional role of women in marriage, the nurturing, stay-at-home Mom, charged with household chores. Homosexuals are depraved and anti-Christ. She's President of the Ladies of American Heritage Association or LAHA that meets in White Canyon, that development community just outside Los Alamos. They form a local, rabid contingent that hates Communists. She doesn't want Russian language taught at Los Alamos High School and carries on a campaign to fire the poor teacher. I understand LAHA members are all Anglophones with no Jews, Italians, Asians or colored allowed. Membership applicants are screened and have to be approved by their recruiting committee. Like the DAR they associate themselves with the Mayflower heritage or the royalty of Anglophone society. All other Anglophones are "white trash." They distance themselves from the Valley and rarely shop in San Isidro. They buy whatever they need in Santa Fe and Albuquerque."

"All right. I see that I have to be careful with my questions," I said. "You haven't given me your comments on my questions that I have drafted for them."

"Look, it doesn't matter what you ask them. They will give you their stock answer about how America is great and they don't understand why anyone should protest against the federal government."

"But I'm not protesting against America."

"In a sense, you are, simply because you're Hispanic. There have been protestations since 1848 when New Mexico representatives asked for recognition of their human and property rights just after the Guadalupe-Hidalgo treaty. Many of those representatives were Hispanic who wanted land grant ownership protected, full citizenship rights given to those who spoke only Spanish, guaranteed education for their children, and political representation at the federal level. They thought they could achieve that through statehood. Those land grant protests are still going on today even though statehood was finally granted in 1912 after sixty-four years of delay, mostly subsidized by unscrupulous carpetbaggers. Many in the state still believe this humiliation was deliberate. All other western states with fewer residents had already been admitted to the union. The New Mexico territory that included Arizona, also admitted finally in 1912, had been bypassed many times. Unlike any other state, New Mexico still recognizes the right to transact legal documents in Spanish. Land grant rights are still under dispute and federal officials look the other way when a Hispanic claims his or her citizenship rights have been violated. Part of the reason for the delay in statehood was the demand for the human and property rights by Hispanics."

"Mr. McNair, I have heard about these problems but there are two sides to any argument, isn't that true? I have pledged allegiance to Old Glory my whole school life, in fact, every single day when I was in grade school. I studied American History over and over again. I have heard the pilgrim story countless times as well as the history of the southwest since the Spanish settlement four hundred years ago. I have heard the good and bad—slavery of the colored people in the southern states, the virtual decimation if not elimination of Indian tribes in the Eastern and Midwestern parts of the American continent. There were Indians being killed for fun by white hunters, forced resettlement of whole Indian nations. The Spanish also did terrible things—stole food from the Pueblos, mistreated the southwestern Indian tribes, coerced the Christian religion on them, suppressed their love of nature and confiscated their land. I am not sure anybody's hands are clean in the settlement of this country of ours. I have been taught, perhaps indoctrinated, to love this country. I don't see the point of arguing over these points after nearly a hundred years since we've been under the American flag."

"I am glad you feel this way but please understand that other members of your ethnic group do not agree with you. It is likely they will continue to fight for what they believe has been taken away from them. Don't be surprised if the Hispanic community considers you someone that has abandoned them and its cause, that you have sold out and joined the enemy and, in a sense, forsaken them. You are the equivalent of an Uncle Tom for the colored people. Get a hold of George Sanchez' book *The Forgotten People* and see what he says about this issue. Listen, I have to go now to my next class. If you want to talk more about this, let me know and we can find the time. I want to encourage you to enter the contest. It will be a good experience for you. I think you are a good student, probably one of the best to come along in a long time. I see a great future for you."

I wasn't sure the conversation with Mr. McNair gave me any significant feedback on my questions. Instead, it had gone in several other directions and gotten a little personal. His insight into ASNU board and how they might view my essay was intimidating. I respected his judgment and intelligence and it was hard for me to dismiss much of what he had to say altogether. Maybe he shook me into a state of reality. The Valley was where I lived and this is the environment I had to contend with, like it or not.

I met with Ms. Bell in the afternoon just after my last class. She stayed after school and I joined her in the same classroom where I started every school day—homeroom. Miss Bell had been at the high school for a number of years and was close to retirement. She had been a staunch supporter of mine since I came to high school and she had been very helpful in improving my English pronunciation and writing.

I went over with her the same briefing on the contest that I did with Mr. McNair. She told me that she had been to ADNU activities like the speaker series they had once a month. At this event they invited a notable person in American politics or history to give a talk on a conservative topic like fiscal responsibility, states' rights or supporting a strong military defense. Although she had voted for Adlai Stevenson in both 1952 and 1956, she was not unhappy with the first Eisenhower term. She had lived through WWII and the Korean Conflict and she was grateful that Ike had not provoked or responded to any more war inducing political action. She said she didn't know the ADNU board very well and she had met with Lucy Montauk only once. The lady had tried to recruit her to the LAHA but after reading their constitution and bylaws, she had declined. Miss Bell said she considered herself too independent and belonging to such a conservative group would "cramp her style." I showed her my draft questions and she commented on each of them. She suggested changes in wording when I explained what I really wanted to know from the interviewees.

She knew no one on the village council but felt the members were provincial in their outlook, judging from their comments published in the Valley News, the local weekly tabloid. Miss Bell was encouraging with her remarks on my questions and was glad that I would write a serious essay and develop a speech that would be given at a public meeting. She would be sure to attend it and wished me luck in the contest.

Bearing the Cross—Wednesday, February 13, 1957

The next day, during a short hallway discussion while going from one class to another, I told Sharon about the discussion with Mr. McNair and she nodded while I reviewed many of his comments. At the end she said, "So? We've heard that stuff before. My skin color is a lot darker than yours and I see that kind of behavior from Anglophones a lot more than you do. You look European and white and I don't. I am also short whereas you are rather tall for a Hispanic, almost six feet tall. Your hair is a light brown, not black like mine. If you read enough, you learn that shortness and dark skin will earn you a lot of prejudice, no matter what country you live in. It's human nature, I suppose. I'm also a girl. Women have limited opportunities in this country. We're condemned to do only certain things with our lives, housework mostly. My mother reminds me of how impertinent I am with all my books and records. My intelligence can become a handicap or so she tells me."

"I thought I was the disadvantaged one, coming from the poor side of town, a welfare kid."

"Remember you're male. That makes up for a lot more than you think. Hey, you got a cross to bear? I got one too!" She turned and hurried to her next class.

The Preparation—Friday, February 15, 1957

After reviewing my questions overnight I decided to go with the economy oriented questions and turned them in to Mr. Wainwright on Thursday, the fourteenth. On Friday afternoon after school we met with him and he gave us back the questions with comments. He said that we had all chosen different topics and the draft questions were fairly good. Sharon had gone the artistic route, Marla had gone the agricultural road, Tom chose politics and governance and I went with the economic focus. Mr. Wainwright then gave us a rundown of the first meeting next week.

"Listen, we meet at 7PM at the Franklin Lodge near the high school on Tuesday evening, February 19. We'll meet with the board of the ADNU local chapter. Three of the five members have already confirmed that they'll be there. We are still waiting for confirmation from Mr. Cochran, Vice President from the Monte Chama County Bank and Dr. Blair, the San Isidro Hospital Administrator. I will introduce all of you, give the board members a brief review of what we expect from the interview and then turn it over to you one at a time. You can ask both questions at once, let the board members think a bit and ask for a volunteer to start responding to the questions. I am hoping that all of them will give you a response but you never know how the panel conversation will go. I will act as a moderator, making sure that we keep the responses to the point. I expect each of you to take notes on the responses you get. Ask for clarification if you wish. By no means should you contradict or argue with any member of the board. Keep to yourself any emotional response on your part to anything they say. Act cordial and respectful. Remember these people will be reviewing your submissions in March and they'll be among the people in the audience that'll judge your speech-making ability as well."

"Are they going to ask us questions?" Sharon inquired.

"Probably, but they'll be of a general nature, I'm sure."

"What are we really trying to get out of this meeting?" Tom had a quizzical look. "Is there a conflict of interest in even talking to the judges before the contest?"

"You ask a terrific question. No, there is no conflict. First, this is a private contest and there is no governmental agency involved where you have to be careful about disclosure. Second, you are not showing them your submission. Third, the entire board will be there or at least a board quorum so that they all receive the same information from you and hear the exchange with other board members. You are not trying to curry favor with any one board member. Finally, they can choose to give you whatever information they want about your questions, perhaps even nebulous information. What you are after is a sense for what they are seeking in a good submission. This is much like reading a teacher and trying to figure out what will be on the exam. All of you are good at that; at least you've proved that to me."

"What if we don't agree with what they say?" Marla spoke up after remaining silent up to this point. "Many of these people aren't even from the Valley. They're newcomers. What do they know about our history and culture?"

"Marla, this contest is about our country, not just about the Valley. These people will be judging your understanding of what the country stands for and how the Valley or our state fits into that bigger picture. In that sense, they have as much right as anyone else to judge your work. It could be argued that they can be more objective since they have been to other places in the country or are originally from other states."

"I think Marla is making a bigger point," I interjected. "There can be inherent prejudices in people especially if they come from regions in the country where bigotry is entrenched. Look at the officially sanctioned separate facilities for coloreds and whites in the southern states. Look at Texas where people of Mexican heritage are discriminated against in public establishments. The recent movie "Giant" had a few scenes depicting that awful prejudice. I understand Mr. Douglas on the board is from Oklahoma where a similar prejudice against Mexican-Americans exists."

I might have come off more strongly than I wanted to and it might have been because I was adding to what Marla had said. I defended Marla, many times needlessly, simply because I had known her since her seizure in church during San Pablo Day many years ago. She had been treated by my uncle, Don Filigonio, presumably for an evil spirit that had caused the seizure. She told me that she had never suffered one since that time in church.

Mr. Wainwright shook his head in disappointment. "I urge all of you to focus on America. This contest is an activity where we have to put our suspicions aside and work on finding areas of agreement. We want America to succeed. If we focus on differences and carry around these built-in suspicions, we will never reach our full potential as individuals or a country. We have to count on young people like you to rise above the errors of the past, the prejudices that have held us back. Over time I believe things will get better as we begin to see the potential of working together. I agree that coloreds and Mexicans are targets of bigoted individuals. I still believe that society as a whole will eventually win over those people who harbor these prejudices."

By this time we had become a little apprehensive about Mr. Wainwright's plan to interview ADNU board and maybe even about entering the contest at all. But we didn't argue with him possibly because we had respect for his judgment.

He had earned it with his fairness and consistency of behavior so we all nodded and left for home.

I had had a chance to look through the high school library to see if I could find anything concerning the economy of Northern New Mexico, my chosen topic for the ADNU contest. The only reference material we had were bound copies of *Time* and *Life* magazines and the index card system led me to general articles about the state but nothing about the economy. The local town library was even worse. They only carried this month's copies of national magazines such as the *Saturday Evening Post* and *Reader's Digest, Look* Magazine and *Time* and *Life* again.

The Research—Saturday, February 16, 1957

My mother and my sister took me on their weekly shopping trip to Santa Fe. While they went off on their own, I spent about two hours at the city's public library and found good reference material. There were state and county statistics about employment categories and tax revenues on different types of businesses in each county by monthly or yearly summaries. Other governmental bulletins led me to similar national figures. I wrote down figures that I could use for my essay. I was careful to note the sources of the material I planned to use.

The Outline—Monday, February 18, 1957

Today, during Mr. Wainwright's class, I worked on an outline for the essay. First, I would talk about the economic power that the United States had become in the one hundred and eighty years of its founding, acknowledging its natural resources of land, minerals and transportation infrastructure of rivers, lakes and deep-water ocean ports. Its temperate climate with an abundance of arable land and natural rainfall had allowed bountiful harvesting of grain, dairy products and livestock. Manufacturing had grown due to skilled immigrant labor from Europe and machinery that had been imported from more industrially advanced countries like Britain. Then I created a middle portion of the essay that would go into how New Mexico played a role in the economic development of the United States. As one of the forty eight states, it had been among the top ten producers of oil and gas, sheep and cattle, fertilizers such as potash and guano, lumber and rare minerals such as molybdenum and uranium. The last portion would become a future view of how the state would continue to contribute to America's greatness and economic well-being.

The Interview—Tuesday, February 19, 1957

After school I went home for a quick supper so I could get back to the high school grounds and wait for the others so we could join Mr. Wainwright in walking over to the Franklin Lodge. The building was rather large and had only side windows. The windows were so high and narrow that their design discouraged anyone from trying to break in that way. The front door, which was a double door to allow large furniture to go in and out, was made from thick metal. It also looked like it would be a formidable barrier to breaking in by kicking or ramming it with a log. The lock had a double welded shield on it so a crowbar couldn't be used to pry the doors open. There was no back door to the building but there was another heavy metal door on the side of the building that was exposed to the street. It was also made from heavy metal and had similar anti-burglary aspects to it. The building was a veritable fortress. It spoke loudly to non-Franklin members like me that I was not getting in unless I was invited.

The Franklins were known as a secretive group and their membership drew from the Protestant citizens in town. No Hispanic or Pueblo Indian had ever been a member of the secret society. Mr. Wainwright knocked on the door and we were led into a large room that formed the lobby of the building. There were double doors on either end of the lobby that led into what could have been an auditorium or additional rooms. A large table had been set up in the middle of the room with five comfortable chairs on one side. There was a smaller table placed perpendicular to the large table with folding chairs on both sides. The gentleman who let us in asked us to sit at the smaller table. He identified himself as Colonel Whitehead. He was a tall and heavy man with a ruddy complexion from the tiny capillaries on his cheeks that were virtually crimson in color. He wore a khaki shirt that looked U.S. Army issue, dark pants and thick soled black shoes, also possibly of military vintage. His eyes were puffy and he wore a folded military cap that covered a patch of his freckled, mostly bald head. His dirty blond hair on the sides of his head came out in wisps from underneath the cap that had pins and ribbons on it, ornaments and hardware that probably had military significance. Most noticeable about him was this high perspiration-soaked odor that emanated from him. His breath reeked of alcohol, possibly whiskey, that he was trying to mask with a cup of coffee that he held in his hand.

"Mr. Wainwright, I am glad that you've taken an interest in the contest," he said as he took the middle comfortable chair at the big table. "We've never had an entry from Fernandez High School and we've talked about how we could get students interested in the contest that's pro-American. We want to see more students interested in the Constitution and what it stands for. Personally I would like to see more students enlisting in the Armed Forces as well." He burped as he adjusted his chair and went on. "I think the contest gives them an awareness of America's strength that leads to patriotism and the need to protect the country from Communism. We'd all but given up on your school. We've had plenty of entries from St. Stephen's Academy over on the other side of the river and a couple of their students have made it to the district competition."

"Thank you, Colonel, it is a pleasure to meet you and we're here to talk a bit about the contest rules so that I can be a liaison for the ADNU contest at the school." Meanwhile three other gentlemen and a lady entered the room from the double doors behind us. While Mr. Wainwright was talking they took the other comfortable chairs. The Colonel took another sip from his coffee cup and looked to his colleagues.

"Well, it looks like we are all here and let me take time to introduce the other board members and then you can introduce your students." He proceeded to speak glowingly about each of the board members and the contributions they each had made to the Valley. He said that although ADNU was not affiliated with the Franklin Lodge of San Isidro, all the board members were members of the Franklin community so it was easy for them to use the facility for their board meetings. Each board member smiled as the Colonel addressed each of their backgrounds.

After he was introduced, Dr. Blair kept looking at the table top, apparently lost in thought. He was the youngest of the bunch, probably not a day over forty, but the bags under his blue eyes made him look tired and older. His hair was dark with modest sideburns. He had a casual suit on, light colored with a woolen thin tie that had no tie clip so both tails floated.

Mr. Douglas sat with his arms crossed, looking like he didn't want to be there. He looked impatient, glancing at his watch absentmindedly and his chin virtually touching his chest. He had worn a hat to the meeting and had taken it off. It now rested in front of him. It was black with a fancy hat band with silver buttons. His hair was plastered on the sides from wearing the hat. He had an intimidating look as he looked up from his downcast head position. His face sagged from wearing a perpetual frown. He had crossed his legs and they showed his brown cowboy boots with solid, elevated heels.

Mr. Cochran sat next to Mr. Douglas and looked very professional, wearing a dark blue suit with a silk tie. He had a pin on his suit's lapel, gold colored that matched his tie clip. His heavily waxed hair was graying and combed straight back. He wore wire-rimmed glasses that made his eyes look larger than normal. A large mole on his left temple looked out of place on an otherwise distinguished face.

Mrs. Montauk was an older woman, probably well into her sixties. She wore a beige business suit with a rose-colored blouse whose collar showed through her jacket. A string of pearls provided an accent to the blouse that had a ruffled neck collar. She had a gruesome turkey neck that the blouse ruffles tried to hide. Her mouth had a natural frowning expression, the kind you imagine in storybook witches. Her blue eyes looked piercing in a face that had heavy makeup with rouge cheeks and bluish upper eyelids. Her hair was done up into a bun that sat up on the back of her head. It had a beautiful tortoise shell comb stuck through it that had sparkly stones set on its edge. She had brought a pad and a pen for note taking.

Mr. Wainwright reviewed his background in teaching and interest in having students learn more about regional and national history. He believed the contest would be an excellent way for the students to do research in history and develop their writing and speaking skills. We were introduced as interviewers each with two specific questions for the board who would act as panelists and respond in any order to the prepared questions. The intent was to have the students learn from community leaders, like themselves, their views of America and how the state of New Mexico, and more specifically, the northern part of the state could contribute to national success. He asked for questions from the board and there were none.

"I am going to ask Sharon Archuleta to pose her two questions. Sharon, let's have you start."

However, Dr. Blair spoke up. "Wait a minute. I want to make sure that the students understand that whatever we say is not to be taken as something we want to see in the essay. We are expecting a creative essay that was entirely written by the student. I personally do not want to see anything I say quoted in the essay or even paraphrased."

Mr. Wainwright responded. "I believe the students understand that and we did discuss the very point you raise. The students will also interview the village council members and we will explain to them that the students are here only to get ideas for research that they will conduct on their own."

"Shall we move on?," the Colonel urged. Sharon stood up at the end of table and posed her first question.

"My interest is in the contributions that Northern New Mexico has made in the field of artistic works. For example, the Pueblo Indians have developed a highly sophisticated art in pottery design and natural firing. The Spanish settlers improvised and developed the art of *bultos* and *santos*. The chants of the Pueblo Indians are both mysterious and embedded with the love of nature. The descendants of the Spanish settlers developed folk songs that are still sung today in mountain villages. I want to know if you believe these contributions have been significant in elevating the cultural richness of America."

The board members looked puzzled and a couple of them looked at each other, unsmiling.

Finally, Mr. Douglas spoke. "I think your question is way off base, young lady. The contributions you speak of are of minor significance and really have become cultural artifacts, perhaps of interest to archeologists and anthropologists who study such things. The art that is significant in America hangs in the finest of museums like the works of Winslow Homer or in modern times, the great American Norman Rockwell."

Mrs. Montauk chimed in. "I agree with Mr. Cochran. I think the art you mention is amateurish and represents the doodling of primitive cultures similar to the carvings of aboriginal people in jungles or isolated villages. Mainstream America will never accept such primitive art as representative of its best creative works."

Then Mr. Cochran, the banker, spoke. "I am not sure I agree with my colleagues totally. Folk art is interesting and I have a couple of pieces myself. But I see the art you mention as having little commercial value. It just doesn't appeal to a lot of people. The artists you mention do come to the bank and ask for loans to start a business in marketing their works of art. None have any business experience nor can they tell me what kind of demand there is for this type of art. Selling this art on the side of the road or peddling it in the pueblo to tourists is a far cry from declaring it to be significant art in America."

The Colonel looked at Dr. Blair to see if he wanted to respond but the Doctor showed no sign of interest in responding. "If there are no more responses let's move on to your next question."

Sharon stood up again once she finished writing on her tablet. "My second question has to do with predicting the future in a sense. I would like each of you to give me your opinion as to what kind of artistic works in music, theater, the plastic arts, etc. should Northern New Mexicans be encouraged to practice their creativity on. Can any city, town or village in Northern New Mexico become an artistic center of any kind? If so, what is the artistic area? We know that Santa Fe and Taos have a few art galleries although not many; D. H. Lawrence attracted writers and artists during his time here about thirty years ago. Georgia O'Keefe, although developing her art in Abiquiu, is still here."

This time the Colonel took the floor. "Young lady, I do not think that you heard Mr. Douglas earlier about esoteric works of art. Now you bring up the distorted works of strange people who either passed through here or are still trying to make our beautiful region into a haven for perversion and maybe Communism. Many of these writers and artists have been trust fund babies or their beneficiaries who are infatuated with the terrain. They have cared little for improving the local economy and have acted condescendingly toward the Hispanic and Pueblo residents."

Mr. Wainwright tried to salvage the conversation. "Colonel, it is hard to describe Peter Hurd as a strange person. Born in Roswell and educated back east, he is a national figure in western art and he has spent a lot of time here in New Mexico."

"Who?" was the Colonel's response.

Mrs. Montauk broke in. "I have to admit that there are artists who favor painting great scenes here in New Mexico. Peter Hurd is certainly a notable figure. But it is hard to believe that Santa Fe or Taos could ever be an artistic center to compete with New York or San Francisco. I wouldn't bet on it. To answer your question more specifically, I think that New Mexicans should study the works of Norman Rockwell. He has captured the essence of American Life. He will be remembered as a great artist."

The Colonel broke the silence and said. "Let's move on to the next student."

Marla stood up and identified her topic. "I am studying agricultural history of New Mexico so my first question concerns the transition that seems to be occurring in America. In 1910 ninety percent of Americans lived in rural communities. In 1950, we were down to 40%. With the advent of powerful machinery, farms got a lot bigger and more productive to the point that small farms now find it difficult to compete against them. This has caused a massive rural to metro migration. Here in the Valley the arable land is along the river and it is difficult to create large farms. Farming has always been difficult here anyway due to the arid environment and the need for irrigation. My question is this. What can the farmers and ranchers do in the Valley to contribute to America's need for a domestic food supply that is safe and reliable?"

Mr. Cochran from the bank jumped in first. "What has happened is that the families that had owned land were well off when they were able to sell their crops. Now they cannot compete so they are now among the poorest families. Many of their children have had to leave the Valley for jobs in California where aircraft companies need thousands of workers. This means that the current generation of farmers will die off eventually without someone to take over the farm. I have had dozens of farmers in my bank trying to mortgage their land. I cannot grant loans because I think their land is almost worthless in today's economy. I foresee that the Valley farmers will be unable to grow crops beyond what they can use themselves. They cannot compete against the large farms of the Midwest and farms from overseas even with the inherent high transportation costs."

Mr. Douglas followed up. "I think farmers here are wasting their time trying to grow crops to sell. They haven't learned that we are in another age where land is not that important. These land grant claims we hear about are a ridiculous waste of time. Dwelling on this Hispano heritage that dates back to 1598 is silly. Who cares what happened back then? In my view, I think Mexico got the better part of the deal when the United States took over New Mexico. Mexico got $15 million in 1848 money for signing the Guadalupe-Hidalgo treaty." We all noticed that the board members started to fidget as Mr. Douglas continued. His face was now beet red.

"It doesn't matter what your heritage is, what matters now is what can *you* do to earn a living. How can you contribute to the economy and society. I think the poverty that has overtaken the farmers in the Valley has made them desperate and immoral, perhaps even vulnerable to Communism. Too many of the men have become alcoholics. I understand there is a growing marijuana and drug problem as well." He shifted his weight on the chair and leaned back a little.

His face was grimacing, his lips tight around his lips like a person in anger. But he continued.

"There are too many thefts in the Valley by people trying to survive. Moral structure has broken down. Maybe it wasn't ever there. The work ethic is awful. They haven't realized that they have got to get with modern society and find another occupation and work hard at it. People in other states have done so already. We're behind the times here."

Mrs. Montauk broke in as well. "My observation is that farm cooperatives may be the answer. It has worked with dairy farming in the Midwest and in New England. But in those regions there is a willingness to band together and establish a trust among the farmers. It is not a form of socialism which requires forced implementation by law. This cooperative is an entity based on voluntary trust. I just don't see that happening here. The culture in the Valley is one of *distrust*. Everyone for himself, family first and don't get in my way. The newspaper is filled with stories of petty bickering among families that has led to fistfights and killings. I just haven't seen a culture in the Valley that's amenable to cooperation among farmers and ranchers. I agree with Mr. Douglas. The farmers should look for other employment opportunities, maybe on a part-time basis and forget this la-di-da business with land grants."

Colonel Whitehead cleared his throat and started down another path in the conversation. "I think that the young from the farming families should try to enlist in the armed forces to fight the scourge of Communism. The Korean Conflict has taught us how pervasive Communism is and there is great need to contain it. We can only do it with our youngsters pitching in and fighting the evil that it promotes. There's a career there for the young folk and useful training that will help them get a job in office work or in a factory. I haven't seen a lot of enthusiasm for serving our country. We are not at war now but the Ruskies have just put up that Sputnik contraption in the sky and that may lead us to war with them. That's why Los Alamos has become so important to our national defense."

The Colonel saw that nobody seemed interested in continuing the responses to Marla's first question. "Now what's your next question?"

Marla stood up again after finishing her note taking.

"The Valley has a cuisine that is different from that found in Mexico and even in southern New Mexico. It has developed because of a merging of foods cultivated by the Pueblo Indians and those that the Spanish settlers brought into the region nearly four hundred years ago. My question is this. Can these dishes significantly contribute to the rich diversity of foods enjoyed by Americans?"

Mrs. Montauk quickly addressed the question. "I am convinced that these dishes will remain interesting for the Valley residents but irrelevant to the rest of the country. The dishes you speak of are similar to Mexican dishes found in Texas and California and they are enjoyed mostly by Mexican immigrants and the *bracero* gangs brought in to harvest crops in both those states. I just don't see Americans giving up the traditional dishes they enjoy—meat and potatoes, fried chicken, white bread and so on—in order to eat what I consider very spicy food, ground corn and beans."

Colonel Whitehead added his thoughts. "Myself, give me a steak and a beer with a baked potato on the side. That's real American food. There're places in Albuquerque offering very cheap fast food, ten cents for a burger. I think that's where the country's going, maybe with fries on the side. Coca Cola is now being served from a fountain more so than from bottles. I can see that people in this country will buy food that's provided conveniently. We are a nation on the go and we need a food service that's cheap, quick and delicious. Mexican food is seen as heavy and gas inducing, good for the poor folk mostly."

He saw that nobody was interested in pursuing the subject. "Can we move on to the next student?"

Tom stood up and brought his first question to the floor. "I am interested in the political process and governance of the state. My first question has to do with local politics and is this. Does the local political process reflect the governance beliefs of the U.S. Constitution?"

Mr. Douglas spoke first, despite the indication that the Colonel was ready to respond. "The local political process compared to the Constitution of the United States is like night and day. They are totally unrelated. The local political process is broken with no formal oversight of voter legitimacy, no verification of vote totals and what is worse, and no initiative to fix things. Frankly, I have given up voting in local elections because I think it is pointless. We have had county officers including the sheriff who have held offices like it was their birthright. I doubt they have read the Constitution. Further, I do not see any urgency on their part to meet the Russian threat. The Communists are testing Hydrogen bombs bigger than ours. They have every intention of destroying our country if we show any sign of weakness. I would like to see an awareness of the dangers of Communism in the political campaign. The candidates should tell us how they are going to contribute to our nation's safety from the Red Menace."

The Colonel added his indignation. "I agree with Mr. Douglas. There is political corruption that's rampant in our county of Contra Mesa. It's a shame that the citizens of the county are subjected to this outrageous form of government where our taxes pay for elected officials to hire their relatives who are incompetent so that very little government work gets done. It's a patronage system at its worst. Elections are rigged, votes are bought left and right. There is no respect for the law. I also agree that the officials should tell us what they are prepared to do to offset the Communist threat to our country."

Mrs. Montauk spoke next. "I believe that the local political process is not based on constitutional principles. It has deteriorated to the degree described by my colleagues and resembles the laughable democracy you see in corrupt countries all over Latin America. Personally, I think it is due to a lack of leadership among the Valley residents. Perhaps anyone with leadership potential leaves the county. Very few, if any, of the elected officials have a college education but what is deplorable is the absence of ethical behavior and moral rectitude. This has been going on for a long time. The tolerance for ineptitude is deeply entrenched and it may take several lifetimes to root it out. The lack of respect for ethics and the law will keep the Valley down. Poverty and drug use will become more entrenched and political corruption will continue unabated. I have not seen any improvement in the forty years I have lived in New Mexico. There is a lackadaisical attitude toward Communism as well. This is extremely dangerous. It is no accident that the Rosenbergs were able to get away for so long without being detected in New Mexico."

Mr. Cochran turned to Tom and asked the following question. "Son, why did you phrase the question in that manner? Were you already aware of the problems we have with local politics?"

Tom looked at Mr. Wainwright and then stood up to answer the question. "No sir, I did not phrase the question with any other motive except to hear what the board's view was on the local political process. I am aware of the nation's history of satire and ridicule heaped on elected officials everywhere. The board's comments are not unusual when taken in that context."

The Colonel regained control of the floor. He looked a little dazed and taken aback at the maturity of the response from Tom. "Let's move on to your next question."

Tom looked at the other students and detected muffled giggles. Mr. Wainwright was beaming, obviously proud of Tom's composure. "My second question has to do with how the rest of the country views New Mexico. The state is in its 45th year after joining the union. What advice would you give the state's leaders in making it a prominent contributor to America's greatness?"

Mr. Cochran approached the question using his business background. "It is important that Governor Simms take the initiative to exploit the tremendous mineral resources we have in the state. He should establish incentives for companies to come in and invest in mineral extraction and processing. It's time for the state to become more American. It's been wrapped up too long with this Spanish heritage thing. It's time to let it go."

He frowned when he said this and looked directly at Sharon, someone he obviously associated with the Valley's historical mania. He continued.

"The state needs investment from the outside. This will create jobs for us but the state can contribute significantly to the nation's industrial growth by being more business friendly and by becoming a prodigious supplier of copper, oil, gas, and uranium. Another business area that the state legislature can support is health care. We are already prominent in the treatment of tuberculosis and other pulmonary diseases. We have more sanatoriums than any other state, especially in treating tuberculosis. This is not rocket science. I mean, in what to do. But as you have heard before, there is a lack of leadership here, especially among the Hispanic community." Just then Sharon broke a pencil she was holding with both hands. There was a brief silence in the room.

Dr. Blair spoke up for the first time since his opening remarks. "We are blessed with the peacetime under President Eisenhower and I was happy with his recent announcement about the national highway system he plans to present to Congress for approval. The state is isolated from the rest of the country due to its arid countryside and great distances between cities. This national highway system will help integrate us into the American mainstream. US Highway 66 has brought a lot of tourism to the state and the national interstate system will enhance that industry. Arizona has sponsored legislation and public support for retirement communities. This kind of political support has been lacking in New Mexico for attracting older families who want a warmer clime in their senior years. Florida has done the same thing. The governor should take up the same cause in bringing retirees to our beautiful state. Health care facilities will be necessary for these older folks but we have a jump start with the many sanitariums that have already been built."

The Colonel had been fluttering his eyes, apparently a result of a drowsiness overtaking him. "Wayne! Wake up, we aren't done yet!" Mrs. Montauk exclaimed. The Colonel turned beet red in embarrassment. "Yeah, sure, any more comments for the young lad?"

"Well, I am not sure that the state is a land of big opportunity," drawled Mr. Douglas. "There is so much to overcome. We've got this heritage of farming and ranching that's dying out, so many lands tied up by Indian reservations, the federal government or by Hispanic land grant claims. We've got big water problems with Texas demanding so much of the Rio Grande and the Indians again being vested with permanent water rights they can't use. We've got an Indian population that chooses not to assimilate and dependent on federal aid and the majority of the state's population that is Hispanic, much of which clings to speaking Spanish, and whose members have been pretty slow in cultural assimilation as well. The mineral extraction and the tourism industries just don't pay the workers very much so there just isn't much to build on. Minerals? They die out eventually and you're left with a hole in the ground and no jobs. Health care and older folks? Again, it seems to me that those are service industries not different from what other southern states can offer. The state needs manufacturing with products that are sold to other states and internationally. The problem is we got no train tracks and no major highways to transport the goods. Air travel may be the way to go but air freight charges are pretty steep right now. The national laboratories in Albuquerque and Los Alamos are good to have but all the scientists are from somewhere else and the state only supplies the low level workers who don't earn much. Education in the Valley doesn't seem to be very important. It's true that the state doesn't give the Valley schools adequate funding but the Hispanic legislators don't seem to care. They appear to be more interested in themselves, relatives and friends. Absenteeism in schools is high and the dropout rate has been going through the roof."

He leaned forward and pounded his fist on the table as he said the following.

"And I cannot find workers who take the job seriously. That is not a function of education but of cultural morality. Integrity doesn't seem to be important. I can't rely on them to come to work regularly. They've got a sick relative or they have to go to a damn funeral. Worse, they seem to think I should be thankful that they work for me, not the other way around. Many don't even care about the quality of their work on the job. If there is a work ethic in the Valley, I haven't seen it."

Mrs. Montauk smiled broadly first and then took up the line of thought. "You gentlemen are really party poopers. The key to making our country great is people power, good hard-working folks who have high moral standards and who value the family life. I see a lot of broken homes in the Valley, women being abused, unwed teenage girls having too many babies, the male students dropping out of school. The fathers in families are able to do only menial work and are given to drinking their wages away. Women are then forced to work to support the men. This breaks up the family even more. I just don't see a strong family unit. It's a shame. Many immigrant groups have hit our American shores—Asians, Europeans, South Americans—and they have achieved success because they wanted to do a lot better than what they had left behind. Italians had many of the same problems that Hispanics have, marginalized because they spoke a different language, clung hard to Catholic teachings, family relationships and ethnic foods. They were stereotyped with crime, violence and wanton behavior. But they rallied to overcome the prejudice with a far reaching anti-defamation league, learned English and entered the professions—medical, legal, engineering—and became competent contributors. I just don't see the same ardor, the same passion, the willingness to do what it takes in this state, particularly in the Valley. There doesn't seem to be a high value placed on education, on training, on doing a great job, not just a good job, but coming to work committed and focused. The Valley has to get the lackadaisical attitude turned around. There is no entitlement, no easy path to success except through discipline and hard work. That's been the American way, starting with the Pilgrims and Jamestown, but all the immigrant groups have adopted it in order to be successful. I find people love working for the government here, a sad state of affairs. Back East, people are embarrassed to say that they work for the government. I would tell Governor Simms to get moving on motivating the state's residents on delivery of quality work. That will get investment here, not tax breaks."

The Colonel kept awake by tapping his fingers on the table while the others talked. Shaking his head as if to clear out the stupor caused by his earlier drinking bout, he declared, "Well if that's all for the young lad's questions, let's move on to the final student."

Mrs. Montauk interjected. "Listen, you all, it is way past eight o'clock and

I really have to go. I've got an appointment in Los Alamos at nine o'clock tonight with friends." She rose from the table, adjusted her skirt, picked up her purse from the floor and grabbed her notepad all in one continuous ballet-like motion. At the same time Dr. Blair and Mr. Douglas both quietly said something to the Colonel.

"Well, it looks like we have run out of time. Three members are asking to be excused so I am going to call this meeting adjourned. Mr. Wainwright, I hope that you have gotten the kind of information that you and the students were looking for."

He stood up and blessed us with a partly suppressed burp. All the board members were now walking over to Mr. Wainwright to shake his hand. Several of the board members gave us students words of encouragement for entering the contest. Dr. Blair was the only board member that greeted Sharon and me. The Colonel stayed with us and showed us out. We heard the front door slam shut as we walked away from the Franklin fortress. Sharon was quiet. She was obviously fuming and didn't want to talk to anybody.

I lived near the high school so I parted company with the rest of the group. The students were going to walk back to the high school to call their parents to have themselves picked up. Mr. Wainwright was going to make sure an office would be open for them to use the telephone.

The meeting had dejected me and I kept trying to understand what exactly had made me feel this way. Although the comments made by the board members tended to be on the pessimistic side, there had been observations that rang true to me. I was also disappointed that I didn't get to ask my questions but the board comments did cover a lot of ground including job creation, one of my topics. As I walked home, I saw that the Valley was a small part of the state and the state was a small part of a big nation. I was really dealing with how I was going to fit into this big complicated picture. It was scary all right and that was what bothered me.

A Post Mortem—Wednesday, February 20, 1957

Mr. Wainwright met with the four of us the next day. He asked for our opinions on the meeting with the ADNU Board. Sharon, probably the most outspoken of the four, said, "I'm out. I talked it over with my parents and I will not be entering the contest. The meeting convinced me that I have nothing

163

to learn from those people and I really don't want to give any of my time to a contest they oversee. I think their dismissal of the culture here in the Valley is shortsighted and borders on racism. They don't seem to understand what poverty does to people. Instead of trying to improve the Valley condition by creating jobs and making investments here, they blame the people who are struggling. They seem to think that the Hispanic culture is inherently corrupt and beyond hope. They forget that all countries have poverty and each country deals with it differently. People do not choose poverty, they are born into it and then struggle to escape. We can feel superior to them and virtually ignore them or we can work together to assist them in finding good jobs with counseling, training and ongoing support."

Mr. Wainwright answered her in a quiet voice. "I am disappointed that you have come to that conclusion. I don't want to seemingly defend all their remarks but I'm afraid that they represent a segment of the population in the Valley and the state that does not have a high regard for traditions that are foreign to them. I believe you did a credible job in presenting your case of celebrating cultural diversity in the country."

Marla joined in as well. "I don't think I am going to continue as well. I had not talked to Sharon but I thought that the responses they gave to my farming and cuisine questions were rude and prejudiced. They didn't just disrespect me but they sneered at long standing traditions here in the Valley developed because of the survival instincts of the early settlers and the Pueblo residents. The Valley behavior they denigrate is partly due to the harsh environment. I agree we are in a different age with advancing technology but behavior doesn't change at the same rate. It takes generations. I don't think they would appreciate my essay on the farming and cuisine topics. I'm glad that we had the meeting because I have saved myself a lot of work that would have gone for nothing. They don't have an open mind about my topics."

Tom spoke next. "They are an odd bunch but I think they are okay. I don't think I would be friends with them but I agree with Mr. Wainwright. We have to learn to deal with people like them. Frankly, I think they could have been a lot worse. I now see better where I have to go with my essay on politics. I started this thing and I am going to finish it. I will work with you, Mr. Wainwright."

"What about you, Ray? Are you still interested?" Mr. Wainwright looked at me as he asked the question. All the others waited for my response as well.

I had been leaning against the wall while they had talked and I straightened myself out and came closer to the group.

"Well, I certainly didn't agree with everything they said and I too was disappointed that they don't appreciate parts of our culture and they think lowly of our potential to adjust or even work together. But there were remarks, although seemingly offensive, that were hard to argue with." Sharon looked down at the floor and I could see she was ready to ignore the rest of what I would say. Marla sat with her arms crossed, unsmiling with twisted eyebrows. Whatever I said was not going to change her mind. It would be too much of an effort for her to deal with those people.

"I think there are going to be many more people like them that I am going to have to deal with in my life and the sooner I begin to do it, the better. There's too many of them who believe they can look at things objectively. Because of their experience, or perhaps their money, they hold influential positions. Although I'm not going to change their mind about a lot of things, there are enough things we can work on together where our joint efforts can make a difference. I owe it to myself to try to learn from them and understand why they think the way they do. It would be a tragedy for me to dismiss them altogether simply because they have different views than I do. They obviously don't like aspects of our Valley culture, maybe because they are unusual—like speaking Spanish, holding dear our family and religion, and preserving traditions that in their view really don't add to quality of life in America. As I am part of those traditions and continue to value them, I won't rub those things in their face. Nobody likes to be poked in the eye."

"Well, I don't like to be poked either! You are just turning yourself into a *Gringo*! Screw you." Sharon almost shouted as she picked up her books and left the room. Marla also sat up, put on her jacket, grabbed her books and followed Sharon without saying anything.

After looking at Tom and then me, Mr. Wainwright quizzed me. "I take it you are going to stick with it also?"

"Yes, but I am going to take a more abstract position in the essay. I am going to strip it of any reference to the Valley. I think I know what I have to do."

"Okay, okay, let's continue meeting twice a week until just before the deadline. I want to see a finished draft seven days before the submission date, an outline next week, and we will have daily rehearsals of the speech that last week.

I will have an audience at least once in the week before the submission date. I will use a stopwatch every time you rehearse. One last thing. The Village Council cancelled our meeting. Their next meeting is after our deadline so they won't be much help. But I encourage you to seek advice from others, friends, relatives, teachers. Good luck and I'll see you next week."

The Final Stretch—Week of February 25

We continued meeting with Mr. Wainwright according to his plan. Tom and I turned in our drafts and he gave us a few suggestions for improving them. I had joined the spring school play, a comedy called "Desperate Ambrose," and I was getting a lot of public speaking experience in English. I had the lead in the play and the part was demanding—lots of lines and lots of antics. Acting was relaxing for me and it gave me a chance to get away from the regular studies. We were all friends in the cast and got along well. There didn't appear to be any competition among the cast members and we were all having fun.

The time on my speech was averaging a little over ten minutes so I thought I was prepared for delivering it two weeks ahead of time in the case I became a local finalist in the contest. Tom and I met with Mr. Wainwright after all our practice sessions and he seemed to be pleased with our performances. After one session, Mr. Wainwright told me that he had closed his eyes to hear me more clearly and he said that he didn't hear any Spanish accent in my voice. Since the first grade I had tried hard to learn English and to pronounce the words like the Anglophone teachers. Early on I had noticed that Spanish-accented English was a tell-tale sign that Anglophones used to consider the speaker as handicapped in the English language. I had wanted to be considered an equal in the mastery of English. I was convinced that facility with the language was a requirement to getting a good job. That had become an embedded belief in my quest to improve my chances for a good job. My mother didn't make it any easier. We only spoke Spanish at home and it was discourteous to her to even use English words as substitutes for Spanish terms. So I practiced English pronunciation when I was alone, walking to school or going home, saying the difficult phrases over and over so I could hear the subtlety in the sounds.

Tom and I gave our submissions to Mr. Wainwright on Wednesday and he mailed them using school stationary.

The Finalists—Week of March 4

After a week of trying to get back into a more normal schedule, we heard from Mr. Wainwright that there had been twenty submissions to the local ADNU and there had been five finalists chosen. Two were from St. Stephens, the private school run by the Presbyterian Church across the river, and one was from Taos High School, and the other two were Tom and me. We were to deliver the speeches on Friday afternoon, March 8, at the St. Stephen's auditorium, one contestant at a time beginning at one o'clock with the speeches given every half hour, the last one starting at three o'clock. Tom had the one o'clock time and I had the slot following it at 1:30PM. The decision on the two winners that would advance to the District competition would be announced on Monday morning at 9AM. The contestants would not witness the speeches by the others. There would be seven judges, four of them from the local ADNU board and three from the Valley—the mayor of San Isidro, its chief of police and the minister of St. Benedict's, the Methodist church in the Valley.

Tom and I practiced our speeches for Mr. Wainwright one last time. Tom delivered an excellent talk on how the Constitution of New Mexico was modeled on the U.S. Constitution. He spoke of essential freedoms guaranteed by the original constitution and the bill of rights and how they were embodied in the founding document of the state. He used examples and spoke in a resonant tone, giving emphasis to passages with the rise and fall of his voice. He wore his suit and looked impressive. I didn't own a suit but my mother had bought me a sport jacket in the fall because I was starting to go to more formal events that required that I at least wear a tie. I had already worn it to a youth conference in Farmington associated with my work in the student council.

Showtime—Friday, March 8, 1957

On Friday we went with Mr. Wainwright to St. Stephens. The campus was old and was built to look like one of those private schools you read about in novels that are set in New England. Many of the original building were made of stone and were at least two stories high with steep pitched roofs made from copper that had a green patina. We walked into the lobby of the auditorium a few minutes before one o'clock. Mr. Wainwright asked us to wait in the lobby while he went and checked on the schedule. He quickly came back and said they were ready for Tom. I was to remain in the lobby until they were ready for me approximately a half hour later. There was a padded bench in front of a large bulletin board and I indicated that I would wait there.

While I waited I tried to relax and finally got up and walked around the lobby. My heart was pounding and I started feeling uncomfortable and alone. The loneliness grew because I was entering a new world. I thought about what Sharon said. I was becoming a Gringo, in her mind—a traitor of sorts. It didn't seem like I belonged here, among white, English-speaking people. They didn't look like me. They hadn't seen the things I had seen; they hadn't spoken the words I had said, especially in Spanish. It felt like it was impossible to succeed. I could see why so many had failed to be accepted and why so many didn't even try.

I thought of what Don Filigonio had said a long time ago about learning from the Anglo. Learning English was the first priority. Without it, it was impossible to learn the American culture that was "the law of the land." The first years of my life spent in the Pueblo of San Pablo had set me off on a course that would keep me in the old ways. It was possible to survive if I continued on that path. But there had always been something inside of me that wanted more than what my mother or my ancestors had achieved. They had endured hardships and had worked hard. I was willing to be just as strong and work just as hard but I wanted more as a reward. I needed room to grow, to see what I could do. What I saw in front of me was not enough. There was a chance of failure. I had handicaps. My wings could melt, like Icarus in my Latin class. If this was offensive to the Valley culture, so be it. It was a gamble I was willing to take and I was willing to be stubborn about it.

And I *was* obstinate as my mother pointed out. I refused to accept my station, whatever was expected of me in the Valley. She left me to learn on my own, to fail by myself and then I would accept what I was meant to be. She was surprised every time I came home with a small victory. She would never celebrate it with me, probably for fear that it may encourage me and I would then fail later, when it would be more debilitating. She had not known anyone to be successful in what I was trying to do. She didn't interfere and that's all I needed. That was enough indirect support.

I had told my mother the night before that I was in this contest and I was going to give a speech. She looked at me blankly. She wanted to empathize and she hugged me. I knew she didn't understand what the fuss was about.

She knew that finishing high school was important even though she had only finished second grade when her father pulled her out to help with the farm. She was home schooled by her older brothers and sisters who had advanced a little further than second grade. She could read fairly well in Spanish and could write at maybe the sixth grade level. Her English was poor, both in oral and written form. She was practically illiterate in that language. She couldn't follow normal conversations in English, even if the words were simple. The vocabulary knowledge was missing.

I walked around the lobby thinking that I should play the scene out. Sure, I could lose the contest but I had done one more thing toward being competitive. I would do my best and not make it easy for people to reject me. I would learn English, develop a stronger vocabulary, and achieve a mastery of language that rivaled the level of native speakers. I would write with polished grammar, complex sentence structure and with creative flair. I must not give up. In speaking, I had to practice my pronunciation until it became natural and my Spanish intonation did not creep in.

Mr. Wainwright and Tom came out about twenty minutes later after they had gone into the auditorium. Tom's face was flushed but he was smiling and seemed relieved. Mr. Wainwright grabbed him by the shoulders and told him he had done very well. He was proud of him. I too shook his hand and put my arm around him in congratulations. Mr. Wainwright turned to me and asked me if I was ready. By that time my head was spinning and I was feeling ill but I said "sure." He patted Tom one more time and led me into the auditorium.

We walked up to the front of the auditorium. I had never been there and it seemed that I was about to play an "away" game—a strange court, someone else's ball, someone else' rules. No practice, no warm-up, no settling down. The microphone had been placed in front of the stage at the orchestra level. There were about twenty people in the audience. The seven judges were seated in the first two rows several seats apart from each other. They each had clipboards in their hands and were apparently still writing notes about Tom's performance. I was greeted by Mrs. Montauk, the member of the ADNU board I had met at the Franklin Lodge. She was wearing her hair up like before but she had a tortoise shell comb on the bun this time. Her suit was a dark green with a full beige blouse whose frilly top partially covered her awful neck. Her single strand necklace had a large carved ivory pendant. Her face reflected a no-nonsense attitude. I tried to smile at her but she wasn't looking directly at me. She asked me to stand in front of the microphone. I recognized Colonel Whitehead and Dr. Blair from the ADNU board and I nodded when our eyes met. My heart was still pounding and my throat had become dry. I tried hard to relax by thinking about the pleasant times I had in my youth—going to the river, eating apples at harvest time, the good times with Tito at the Pueblo. I felt my face becoming hot and wondered whether I was going to faint. I heard Mrs. Montauk announce my name—Reyes Córdova—to the judges and the other people in the audience. She pointed to Mr. Wainwright and said something about Fernandez High School. Finally, she addressed me and said that she was going to take her seat and start a large clock that was in front of her. If my speech went past 12 minutes she would raise her hand and ask me to stop. She asked me if I understood the instructions and I nodded. She then said, "You may begin."

I had given my speech so many times that the words flew out of my mouth. I remember thinking that I was going too fast so I paced myself and started to get into a smooth delivery, perhaps a little too casual but keeping my voice at a stage loudness. I remember using my hands and arms to make the points that were critical in the speech about job creation and entrepreneurship. I saw that Mr. Wainwright was smiling and trying to communicate signs of encouragement. I was three quarters though the speech and I saw that eight minutes had passed. The last part of the speech had to do with the economic success of America in the twentieth century due to the many skills that were brought together in steel making, the auto industry and electric appliances that were now second to none in the world. Suddenly, my mind went blank. I looked at the floor, trying to remember a key word that would lead me into the last part of the speech. But the harder I tried to remember, the worse I felt and nothing came out. After what I thought was an interminable lapse of time, I repeated the last spoken thought in different words and the rest of the speech came to me. I finished self-confidently but I knew that I had committed a fatal error in speech making.

Mrs. Montauk came up, half smiling, and shook my hand thanking me for the presentation and handed me over to Mr. Wainwright who had a pained expression on his face. He put his arm around me and led me out of the auditorium. He tried to give me comfort by telling me that the substance of the talk was outstanding. "You slipped up a little in your delivery but you came back! I am still proud of you. Both of you were outstanding!"

He went back into the auditorium, presumably to say goodbye, and on our way out we met the St. Stephen's students who were going to follow us in the schedule. By now I was calm but still dejected. I told Tom that I froze up for a minute and it looked bad for the school. I told him that I didn't know what happened. I knew the speech cold. Mr. Wainwright was listening and he tried again to put the mishap in perspective. "Hey, you were a finalist in the contest. You had a well thought out speech. It happens to the best of us, even professionals. Take it in stride. You will have plenty of other opportunities to show your stuff. You and Tom will go far. I know it!"

On Monday we learned that Tom was going to join a St. Stephen's student in representing the Valley in the district competition. Tom did well there too and he went on to the state level and took third place. The important thing was that Fernandez High School had made it to the big time. I nursed my wounds and eventually got over it. I have never had a speech lapse since. Mr. Wainwright would be proud of me.

14
Miquo
Summer 1957

What are you guys doing? Come on;
let's see what's happening in the world.
                                    —*Miquo*

"**W**e need a car," Fidel declared. "We've got to see what's going on in the rest of the town."

"We're fourteen and we can't drive for another couple of years," I said.

"My brother drives but he won't take us anywhere. Anyhow, my father won't lend him the car anyway," Fidel said with a sigh.

The time had come when Fidel realized we were at the no-drive zone of life, those three or four years of life between the time when you weren't interested in going anywhere that's farther than an hour's walk away and the time you are eligible to drive a car, legally of course. It is a time when we know we are tethered to our home and there is an inexplicable yearning to do something interesting far, far away. It was time to expand our horizons—meeting new people, hearing new conversations, coping with new challenges. We had to look at the world from a new perspective. Curiosity was the main driver but our boundless energy and naiveté were irrepressible catalysts.

Neither of us owned a bicycle or had access to one. They weren't very useful anyway because so many of roads in town were unpaved and the sandy soil made for difficult pedaling. The other problem bicyclists faced in town were the seeds of a pervasive weed—*tribulus terrestris*– the goatheads. The weed, whose leaves were claimed to enhance testosterone levels in men, hugged the ground and grew in all directions, bearing seeds whose spiky spears could easily puncture a bicycle tire.

Often when we talked about why we wanted to go somewhere, we couldn't pinpoint exactly what we would do when we got there. We really didn't have anyone to visit. We had no errand to run and no business to be anywhere else. Yet there was something out there that beckoned us although we couldn't describe it and we couldn't tell where it was.

It was also a time when the fear sets in that we're no longer kids but we're not adults either. We didn't qualify for anything significant—vote, go into the service, get married, and most importantly—drive a car. The hormones had arrived, of course, with us growing hair where it wasn't there before, muscles beginning to show, our sweat becoming sour, our voices changing in pitch and girls becoming much more interesting but still untouchable. These changes led to confusion about who we were, who we would become and where we would go. Without a father and with a mother who dropped out after second grade, the uncertainty was probably greater for me.

I thought it was survival that I should have as the goal. In translation, it was a question of simply earning enough money to support my mother and me. One of my half-brothers had gone to California after high school and landed a job in an aircraft company. The other had gone into the U.S. Army and gotten married. My sister, the eldest, still worked in Los Alamos as a maid and basically lived there, visiting us occasionally on weekends. There weren't a lot of jobs in the Valley and those in the national laboratory nearby required a college education or were of a menial nature—janitor, clerk, construction, etc. My mother had no real expectations of me since she didn't really understand the new world that was no longer based on farming or ranching. All she knew was that a job was important and she encouraged me to find part-time jobs not only in the summer but during the school year as well. Her view was that our finances could only get better; at least that's what she hoped. In a sense, that gave me free rein to head in whatever direction I wanted for a career and go as far as I wanted. Of course, the disadvantage was that there was nobody to help me, provide moral support or better yet, mentorship.

I looked at the adults around me and wondered when I would be transformed into one of them. The few who stayed in the Valley were able to find a position in a local service company or worked for the government. Although the talk was that the government jobs were boring, the wages were reasonable, the position was stable, and there was a good pension at the end. I had doubts about my fitting well in that kind of position. My problem was that I was unwilling to settle unless I had to, a situation I feared could happen very soon. Fidel didn't express it that way but it was the same thing.

And then there were my clothes, another symbol of growing up. My mother had complained that my clothes seemed a little small although they weren't as worn as those she had recently thrown away. She had stopped buying my clothes and now wanted me to tag along and choose colors in addition to trying them on. We couldn't afford more than a couple of changes for me so the fit was critical, at least from her point of view. I wore the basic blue jeans; Levi's mostly, except that I would rip off the leather label that showed the sizes. I was embarrassed to have a size 28 waist. My shirts were made from a sturdy cotton blend, the kind that wears forever and requires minimal ironing. They weren't exactly stylish but my mother washed them often enough so that they looked more or less presentable. She said that having clean clothes, even if they were simple, gave me a look of being honest, a trait she felt would get me ahead, maybe even a job. She said I had to have pride in my appearance. If I didn't believe in myself, how could I expect others to believe in me?

My shoes had a persistent coat of fine, whitish grit acquired by the endless walking I did across the pale, dusty earth of the Valley. There were few sidewalks, even in town. If you walked for almost any length of time in the Valley, you risked getting a film on your shoes, not the sandy kind but the powdery stuff that crawls into the nooks and crannies of the shoe's upper contours. People carried a kerchief around to wipe off the inevitable blanched patina as they entered a house or a business. Business owners would sweep the dust off the sidewalk in front of their establishment. Others would use a water spray to wash it off. But the infernal dust was everywhere because of the swirling storms we would have during the seasonal changes of the spring and fall. In the hollow between the heel and sole of my shoes I usually had a hardened cake of clay that would come off only with the use of a dull knife. It didn't rain much in the Valley but during the late summer we would have rainstorms that turned the dust into a paste that would harden when it dried and then once ground up by our footsteps, would become dust again.

The summer rains could be torrential which created a flooding problem because there was little groundcover to absorb the water that fast. Water would accumulate on the surface and flow into the *arroyos*, or natural gulches that would empty into the river basin. Where the terrain was hilly, the rushing water accelerated erosion and would bring down silt down to a natural drainage area. After such a summer rainstorm, a pond would form in front of our house since the highway, fifty yards from our house, had been built up and acted as a dam.

The street to the side of the house was also built up so the water had nowhere else to go. The bottom of the pond had many layers of silt so it became impermeable to water. The pond would take weeks to dry out. The area would then show cracks where the silt and clay contracted. Of course, a day after the rainstorm we would be greeted with cries of the tadpoles that eventually matured into little frogs. It was such a loud chorus that you could hear it for miles. The town never provided any drainage for the pond until many years later when a storm sewer system was installed.

Fidel and I grew up together. Fidel and I were the same age but they kept him back in first grade due to his poor progress in reading. The difference in grades didn't affect our friendship. We would wrestle, swim in the river, play football and baseball, but mostly we would play basketball the year round. In winter, we would use the bouncing ball itself to harden the wet clay court we used for playing in the 50 degree weather. We seemed to be exercising all the time in our fight against the onset of boredom, stretching our adolescent muscles in fear of body atrophy that would leave us smallish and weak. Fidel was a little taller due to his long neck. He couldn't jump any higher than me and he wasn't any faster but he did have that small height advantage.

There was less than a month left in the summer vacation and we would be off to school again all too soon. Fidel and I were sitting on the library steps near town hall after several hours of playing basketball on a warm Wednesday afternoon. We were waiting for the library to open at two o'clock. It was relatively small with only a few shelves of old books and it was staffed by volunteers and was open only for three hours during the summer. It was a small miracle for a town our size to even have a library at all. It was one of the few places in town that had an evaporative cooler and it was great to go there and feel the soothing air. Fidel and I would read newspapers and magazines for a half hour or so, dwelling longer on the pages with girls in swimsuits.

Suddenly, a vintage white Cadillac four door sedan pulled up in front of us and its passenger side window rolled down. The car was the classic 1949 model with the small tail light fins, the triangular vent windows, single curved windshield, a V8 engine and a body more compact than the monstrous one that had just come out. It was seven years old but in very good shape.

"Hey guys! How about going for a ride around town?" It was Joseph Ortiz, younger son of Harold Ortiz who owned the furniture store in town. His nickname was "Miquo," and he was one of those boys who attended private school out of town and didn't much associate with the likes of us. So I was surprised that he had stopped. I was apprehensive.

Families with means did not send their children to public schools in town. Most of those families sent the girls to Loretto Academy and the boys to St. Michael's. Both were located in Santa Fe and there were vans that would transport the students every day. But Miquo didn't go to St. Michael's. He went to a school in St. Louis, Missouri that was private and Catholic.

Miquo was a little older, possibly sixteen since he now had a driver's license.

Fidel jumped up from the steps before I could even fully understand what Miquo said.

"Yeah, that's great!" I heard Fidel say as I slowly came back to life.

"Where are you going?" Fidel added as he jumped into the front seat. They waited for me to get in the back seat. I was still stunned from the sudden ride offer. I didn't know whether we were doing the right thing getting into the nice car.

"Just around town," Miquo said as he pulled away and turned onto the main street of town.

"Dad let me have the old car and I just got off work so I thought I'd go for a cruise," he explained. "What are you guys doing? Come on; let's see what's happening in the world."

"Well, we were just saying that we needed a car and you showed up. Maybe you were listening," Fidel laughed as he turned up the radio in the car that had an Elvis tune playing.

"*Oh let me be, …*"

"*Let me be youurrr teddy bear…*"

Miquo told us he had been working at his dad's store all summer, the eight to two o'clock shift with no break. He was snacking on a sandwich for lunch as he was driving. As summer was drawing to a close, he knew he would be leaving soon for the boarding school in St. Louis. He hated the school and wished that he went to school in town. But his older brother and sister had both gone to the boarding school and they thought the world of it. His parents thought the school had better teachers than the public school in town.

Miquo had heavy lidded eyes, freckles, thin light brown hair and wore wire rimmed glasses and a white shirt with a tie. His pants were gabardine, well pressed and pleated and his shoes were shiny, black wingtips. He was clean shaven with hair neatly combed and he looked like a young adult.

Although many of their customers spoke only Spanish, the Ortiz family preferred to transact business in English, resorting to Spanish only if absolutely necessary. Fidel and I had not been in their home. It was a large house at the top of the ridge where the San Isidro church was located.

Miquo had always been very friendly the few times we had met up with him. His family didn't go to the Catholic Church in town and we rarely saw him around town. We liked him because he didn't seem to have a snooty attitude towards people from our side of town.

"Let's take a ride through the Valley and see what's happening. You guys go to school here and probably know what everybody's doing but I don't," Miquo said as he turned to Fidel and then to me.

"Actually, Ray and I have lost contact with a lot of our friends in the summer because we don't have a car. A few of their families have telephones but neither Ray nor I have one at home," Fidel explained.

We drove several of the Valley roads that lead to the farming villages that embrace the feeder streams of the Rio del Norte. As we whizzed by the villages and their fruit orchards I could see that we were still a few weeks away from harvesting apples and peaches. I hoped silently that a farmer would hire me to help him pick the fruit. It was hard work but I loved being in the trees, on a tripod ladder, reaching for the full bodied fruit firmly in my hand that I would pick and store in my apron bag. During the harvest season, the early autumn air was clean-smelling, the sky would be an azure blue, a hue not found at lower elevations. The sun would warm us during the early morning hours when we would start. We would shed our light jackets around eleven o'clock as the sun neared its zenith and we would work in our tee shirts during the afternoon until dusk. A light lunch of a sandwich and a soft drink would keep us going, snacking on an apple or a peach until supper. The work of a few days of picking fruit would provide me with money beyond the meager amount I earned while working as a counter clerk at the theater. We had not had a spring freeze this year so the fruit crop was bountiful and there would be plenty of work to go around.

The fresh air coming in the rear window had the scent of the alfalfa and corn fields that we passed. There was more moisture in the air of the farming villages than that in the town proper. I leaned back in the soft rear seat and closed my eyes to enjoy the ride even more while Fidel chatted with Miquo in the front seat. I wondered if I would be able to own a car like this, ever, even a used one. I had never been in a Cadillac before. My relatives all had Chevrolets and Fords, most of them pickups. We drove around for about an hour and Joseph dropped us off again at the library. Fidel and I thanked him for the ride and let him know that we were available anytime he needed company.

"He's got everything," Fidel said. "Boy, a nice car, nice clothes, spending money. Wow! I could use some of that."

"He's a nice guy to give us a ride. He didn't have to do that." I said. I brought us back down to earth with a reminder that we were not in his class of people. I didn't even own a pair of gabardine pants with pleats.

"Yeah, yeah, I know." Fidel said. "We have to keep looking for a way to get out. I mean get out and look around. I'm tired of the same old thing."

I knew that Fidel was talking about getting a ride but his complaint went further than that. What was the long term plan for me? Could I ever earn enough money to buy a car of my own? Where was I going to work to earn that kind of money? I had trudged all over town at the beginning of summer and all I could find was part-time work at the theater. I managed the candy counter and popcorn machine. I had to wear my Sunday clothes in order to work there. But it felt good to just have any job. I didn't earn much but it taught me a responsibility for handling money and making correct change. Could I do better when I graduated from high school?

I should have expected that we wouldn't see Miquo again that summer although we kept an eye out for his white Cadillac and getting another ride with him. Occasionally we hung around the library a little longer. When we were near his father's store we would look in the window to see if Miquo was working, hoping that he was about to complete his shift. We didn't see him again the rest of the summer.

Fidel and I continued our routine of grinding out the remaining days of summer by playing ball, walking around town and doing small projects for his parents like painting and cleaning out the garage. We complained about not having access to a car and no one cared. We yearned to go away and visit places and found no one to drive us there. I did get to go to the Santa Fe Fiesta during the Labor Day weekend with my mother but I met up with none of my friends. Fidel' parents didn't go to the Fiesta. I would walk around the plaza by myself, around and around, looking for someone from the Valley. There was a food stand that sold great steamed *tamales*. I would buy one and peel the corn husk and eat it like a candy bar, slowly, a small morsel at a time to make it last. I could walk around for almost an hour all the while consuming a single *tamale*. Occasionally I would get a lean one, with very little pork; just a hint of red chili in its inner core but the corn meal was firm and starchy. I probably didn't look cool eating one but I didn't care.

After Labor Day we went back to school and hooked up with friends from Valley villages and met new teachers in the high school. I did get a job picking apples for a farmer during the weekends in October. I made a little money that fall and I saved most of it for use as pocket money the rest of the school year. Fidel and I got busy with the activities of the new school year and soon we were into winter and chilly weather so we saw less of each other.

It was during the Christmas vacation that we heard the news from friends about Miquo. The weekly town newspaper had played the story down and the item was buried with others that were barely newsworthy. All the item reported was that a young man was found dead in his bedroom apparently the result of an accidental rifle wound. There was no identification of the young man or where the accident occurred.

However, information from the police investigation and the coroner's office did leak into town. That is how our friends had heard about it and there was verification that it was Miquo who was found dead. His body had been taken away to an out of town mortuary and cremated. There was no wake or funeral held in town.

We heard that Miquo, apparently despondent, did take a rifle from his father's firearm collection and shot himself. The blast sent a bullet through his mouth and skull. Blood spray and brain splatter were found on the wall of his room. The family gave no explanation nor described the circumstances that led to the tragic death.

Fidel and I talked about the suicide when we saw each other again during the holiday season. We were so far from the world that Miquo lived in that we couldn't understand the conditions that would lead to his decision to end it all. On the surface it didn't make sense, perhaps suicide never does. Miquo had so many things I didn't have, at least that I thought important. He had a father, a comfortable home, nice clothes, spending money and access to a car. All these things I had thought would give him a chance for worldly success.

Miquo had not known any of our friends so the incident didn't cause the same shock in them that Fidel and I felt on hearing of Miquo's fate. That summer ride in his car had given us a connection with him, shallow but firm, the kind that only youth can deliver. It made his death more personal to us even though it was alien in a way since we were still struggling to understand our place in the world during those odd years. We were more afraid of the life that lay ahead of us than the death that only happens when you have a rare accident. There was talk about nuclear war with Russia. Was there even a future for us? Sometimes it looked so bleak. Maybe Miquo, to a degree and for different reasons, was also afraid more of life than death. Fidel and I never spoke about Miquo again but I knew that the memory of the summer car ride would stay with us for a long time.

15

Miss Jane Bell
September 20, 1957

First, you have to help yourself before
you can help the Valley.

—*Miss Bell*

"Mind your pace!," Miss Bell said, as I tried to keep the pot steady so the hot water wouldn't spill and drench me. "I should have worn other shoes. These twist in the street gravel and hurt my ankle," she complained. "I can't see as well with these street lamps so far apart."

Miss Bell and I were walking back from her apartment to the high school athletic field where we were selling hot dogs and apples at a football game. Miss Bell was our class sponsor and she was generous enough to help us raise money for our class. I wasn't sure what the money was going to be used for but I had volunteered to work the concession stand at football games. The stand had a low pitched roof and had open windows on three sides. It had no heat and only had a single power outlet and the hot plate that was available to us didn't get hot enough to boil water, at least not hot enough to cook the hot dogs. So she was kind enough to let us cook the dogs at her apartment and then transport them back to the concession stand. This was not sustainable, I thought, but so many other things at Fernandez High School were like that.

She was a stout woman who had been at the high school for about ten years, originally from Kansas. She taught English and was my homeroom teacher as well. Our school superintendent had a policy of hiring English teachers who spoke the language natively. Many of them were young and came with energy, wanting to make a difference in teaching. The newspapers described the new trend of educated women venturing out into unusual places, part of a flexing of intellectual muscles that women ached to do. It was said that women wanted challenging jobs. Teaching school in rural New Mexico was seen as out of the ordinary certainly.

Northern New Mexico was indeed a different place with its multi-cultural history. *Life* magazine had done an article on the region, calling it one of the last frontiers of the American West. The recruited teachers stayed a year or two and then went elsewhere, possibly to get married and be where their husbands worked. None married young men in the Valley, at least that I knew about. Of course, we didn't have many college educated men living in the Valley. Most of them who left for college rarely came back. The young women who came to teach were smart and patient. They knew about the challenges in teaching bilingual students. We would show up in first grade not knowing much English, often absolutely none, like me. At that time we had no kindergarten and no other form of transition from an all-Spanish speaking culture to the modern English of America, our new home, a little over a hundred years after the Guadalupe-Hidalgo Treaty. We would soak up the English as fast as we could, often knowing just enough to get to the next grade. Some of my friends stayed behind in first grade if the total immersion technique didn't work as well on them.

There were no books at home, not even a Bible, and education was not a priority. Many of the students lived on farmland tracts with no electricity or phone. Fortunately, the Superintendent had the foresight to know that the next generation was not going to live on the farm or ranch. They had to get a job, probably in the city like Albuquerque or on the west coast, and for that the pupil needed to know good English. He also believed that we could mask our Spanish accent better by learning English from teachers who came from outside the state.

Miss Bell didn't quite fit the model of the young Midwestern teacher-recruit since she was now well into her sixties. The story was that she had come to the Valley after catching the wave of the women's liberation movement late in her teaching career. No one knew the motivation for her migrating westward into the high desert country, pretty far from her native Kansas. But she seemed to be happy being here. Maybe she came looking for the magic of Cíbola also. People in town figured she would retire soon and every fall they were surprised when she would appear in the fall to start school again. I was amazed that, despite her age, she could manage to keep us in line both in and out of the classroom.

She had shown us pictures of her summer vacation taken in Venice last year, a trip she had planned for many years. She told us she enjoyed the trip immensely and encouraged us all to plan trips abroad for both our education and pleasure. She had a picture taken of her on a gondola on the Grand Canal. It was clear the trip had been the culmination of a plan. She had learned some

Italian the year before so as to make sense of signs in Venice and get along with phrases she could master.

"You have to plan if you want to accomplish what you dream about," she would say to the English class. "The plan reveals all the obstacles you may encounter in achieving your goal. The plan should list what you have or plan to have in resources for overcoming the obstacles. If you can control gratification, you can accumulate the resources to accomplish whatever goal you set for yourself. The first three steps to success is plan, plan and plan."

She wore glasses and was always professionally dressed with her hair neatly done. Most of the girls in the high school believed she wore a wig because they couldn't believe she could tame her hair that well day after day. Her wrinkled face had a tense look but she smiled often so it wasn't as intimidating. Her eyes were a deep blue and perhaps her best facial feature. Age had been unkind to her, the neck now droopy and deeply lined and layered, her heavy upper arms flabby. She would lean over my desk with her hands spread on the desktop. I could see the large veins bulging on her hands, pulsing as they turned bluer the more she leaned. Her skin on her lower and upper arms was already like crepe paper, still very white despite being out in the sun when she walked to and from school.

I had been in her apartment several times as part of my concession stand duties and it was always at night. It was a one room studio, a kitchenette to one side with a window facing south so I imagined that she saw a lot of late morning sun when she sat at a table there. Her bed was on the other side of the room set against the wall that separated the bathroom from the rest of the apartment. The bed was a three quarter bed which appeared strange to me since a full sized bed could easily fit there. There were two pictures on the wall—one was a landscape with a pond and trees surrounding it, certainly not a scene from our area but maybe something that reminded her of Kansas, the other was of a young girl, seated and pensive with dark hair that was shoulder length. I wondered why she would have a picture of a young girl. The rest of the apartment was plain, even stark. The kitchen area had an old brightly colored dinette set with vinyl covered chairs with padded seats, the refrigerator dated with the upright pull handle, all popular in the early fifties. I imagined a quart of milk, some butter, slices of ham and pieces of fruit behind its door. It was enough for nourishment, thought, rest and getting by.

The apartment was a place for contemplation or redemption. What was her past like? What were the hardened memories that haunted her? There was plenty of time to relive the joy or pain in the place where there was no other amusement. In solitude there is no shelter from a nightmare. I saw some books on a nightstand. Did their stories remind her of past desires forming then a prelude to nightly dreams? Was there a death punctuating them, creating a breathless night? How was her life to end? Were there friends or relatives? She never spoke of them to me or other students that I knew.

She did not own a car which explained why she wanted to live near campus. I used to see her riding in other people's cars, frequently with fellow teachers on their way to a concert in Santa Fe or to do some shopping. The weekends must have been long with no one to breakfast with, telling stories of family and friends between the slices of toast and jam. Was there coffee to brighten the weekend morning and enliven nerves to plan the coming week?

She would occasionally share a joke with us. I always thought a person had to be upbeat and basically a happy person in order to live alone. Her life, consisting of teaching English at a struggling high school, living in a studio apartment sparsely furnished, with no obvious friends just seemed stoic to me. Her humor betrayed an inner peace that I hoped I could have someday.

She was a teacher who believed in a long term plan—one that required research of what's possible, determining realistic goals and timelines, and putting in place a strategy for execution. She could separate wants from needs and parse away the frivolous and vain of the former. I had known stingy people in my family but, unlike Miss Bell, they did not seem to have a goal for the resources they were piling up.

"I saw your mother the other day," breaking the silence as we walked. "She was walking home in work pants and a jacket,"

"She has a plastering job in the south side of town. She's been working there for the past couple of weeks," I responded.

"You've got to do well in your studies so that you don't have to do that kind of work. I've told you that since you were a freshman. How are you doing in your classes?"

"I'm okay. Latin is my hardest subject but you know Mr. McNair is hard on everybody."

"Just tell yourself you can make it. Education can get you a better job."

"There aren't too many openings here except the national laboratory with their menial jobs for us. Most of my relatives that work at the lab are janitors, drivers, and construction workers—that kind of thing."

She stopped and looked at me while she put her hand on my shoulder.

"How bad do you want to live a life better than your relatives, than your mother?" she raised her voice with eyes that asked the question again.

"I am not sure I can break away. There are so many things that get in the way. I've got to support my mother. I'm the baby of the family. My sister can help but I don't know for how long."

The pot I was holding seemed to be getting heavier. I turned and started walking again.

"Listen, don't walk away. You have to focus on your goal of doing something better, of not accepting what the Valley will do to you if you choose the easy way. You have the talent to do something different. You have to trust yourself, invest the time and energy. You understand that, don't you?"

I didn't want to encourage her in the lecture with me while I was a captive audience carrying the pot with hot water. So I tried another subject.

"I feel I need to work and save money for a car," I said.

"A car! What do you need a car for? Don't you see that wish is what locks you up! I see so many young people borrowing money to buy a car, needing more money to fix it, pay for the gas and then being stuck sometimes for years in paying it off. And what you do get in the end? The need to buy another one! Ask yourself—what is this car going to do for getting me a better job? Is it an investment or an expense?"

I saw I wasn't getting anywhere with her. It was always that way. She identified the factors that propagated life here in the Valley. She continued on a subject that often caused me to walk away from my mother and Miss Bell.

"What about Sharon? She asked as she finally started walking back to the game.

"We're friends," I said. "She likes books and we trade them."

"Well, it's important that you keep it at the friendship level. It's too early to get serious. You have to finish college before girls can become important. It is a big step in your life, getting involved with a girl. It takes you in a different direction of responsibility. It's expensive. Do sex and it owns you. From that moment on and there's no turning back. You have to choose. What's more important? And it goes back to how badly you want to break away from here."

"This is my home, Miss Bell. I can't say I *want* to break away. My relatives would be mad if I ever said that."

I saw that this was a perfect opportunity for her to tell me what was on her mind. What she saw in me convinced her that I had the potential to do something different. My arms were getting tired from carrying the pot. I couldn't walk too fast because that would make the water come through the edges of the lid. So she continued.

"I don't say this to everybody. But I say it to you because you can understand what I am saying. You understand the big picture about the Valley. What I mean is this. You don't have to repeat what's been going on for generations, the endless cycle. I don't know how far you can go. It really is up to you. The education I talk about may not be obvious to you. It is *the* answer, trust me. But you have to put the car and the girls aside for a while. I know the culture here tells you the opposite. A girl came to me last week and said she was pregnant and had to leave school. Her mother was very happy because she was going to be a grandmother. I was heartbroken because that girl will probably not finish high school. She will be a single parent, most likely handicapped with few skills to get a job. This was no accident and it's a shame," she sighed. "This happens generation after generation. It's a curse where there is poverty and education is undervalued."

"You have said this before, Miss Bell. But we do need money. Welfare assistance stops when I reach eighteen. It's only thirty dollars a month but that sum is important right now and my mother is counting on me to replace it when it stops."

"I don't want to encourage you to fight with your mother. You have to find a way to reason with her that you are worth investing in, that you have the potential to earn a lot more but you need to continue your education. You have to believe in that first. You can't convince her if you don't believe it yourself. We can only tell you so many times. We can support you in this goal while you are in school but then you have to take over. It's hard, I know. There is a greater burden on your shoulders when you are so young. But I have seen you grow while I've known you. You can do it. There will be obstacles because of your ethnicity and you come from a poor family. Others would give up hope. You don't give up easily. I have seen you perform when others were afraid to take it on."

She slowed her walk and complained about her shoes again. This gave her an opportunity to pause in her speech that I had heard before, fragments here and there but this was the first opportunity for her to put it altogether. The pot in my hands had given her my undivided attention.

"I should wear lower heeled shoes," she said as I continued my quickened pace with the pot held steady.

"The gravel on the road really makes it hard to walk with these shoes."

She continued talking about shoes and the inevitable dust that gets into all the crevices that shoes have nowadays. I wasn't sure I could contribute so she continued her monologue and I focused on carrying the pot.

"Don't let the lab lure you with an immediate job with promises to help you with your education. They are a long way from accepting people from the Valley as scientists or engineers. You'd probably end up as a staff person with a boring job. You have more potential than that. You have no chance there. There won't be a laboratory director there from the Valley for a hundred years, if ever. You're a townie, a local and there's an inherent prejudice there. It happens all over the country. They're no different. It's not a racist attitude, necessarily. It can be, though. It's just that you're different from them. You have a culture, a religion, a language that's different. You have to go and start a career where people do not care who your father is, what your last name is. You have to go where the real question is: 'What can you do and how well can you do it?' It may have to be the east coast where there are hundreds of ethnicities, thousands of surnames and where a meritocracy is more likely to be found because it becomes hard to be prejudiced against so many groups. Back east you can still find discrimination but it's a lot better than it was before. Now there'll be competition, sometimes world class competition. But you can compete. I don't know where you will end up. It's up to you. But you can go as far as you want to as long as you educate yourself and work hard. I know you can do it."

"I can see that getting a better job can help my mother but how does it help the Valley?"

"First, you have to help yourself before you can help the Valley. Forget the Valley for a while. It's existed long before you came along and it will get along and it probably will not prosper without more people like you. But we have to start somewhere. You can be one person to do it. The Valley has too many problems for one person to handle. And it's going to take a long time to make it better. If you try, it will pull you down and you become indistinguishable from the rest. Valley residents have not found a way to help each other. It will break you and everyone else that you get to work with you. If you are successful after being away for a spell and you have seen how things can work better, you could decide to come back and join others in leading change, real change that can make a difference. But even with the experience you will have gained, energy and passion that you can put in, and maybe financial resources, it will still take a couple of generations before we can see the difference."

It was a fair distance we walked from her apartment to the football field. And I really had not expected the heavy discussion we were having. It was something that I was going to think about whether I wanted to or not.

I always thought of her as a strong person, possibly because of her serious nature and consistent attitude. She was not particularly motherly, at least not the nurturing sort, condescending and expecting us to fail. I had seen some teachers fall into the educational trap of blaming the lack of learning on the student, especially one that came from an underprivileged home. Of course, the majority of us in the public school fell into that category and we had a dual language handicap as well. I never detected any prejudice of that sort in Miss Bell.

She had taken an interest in my schoolwork from the time I met her when I entered high school. She had seen the scores on my eighth grade achievement exams at that time and sought me out and told me that she expected a lot from my time in high school. After her long monologue, she said less as we approached the football field.

"Despite these shoes, this walking is good exercise for me and I know I need it," she said.

"I can smell the autumn in the *bosque*. Winter is not too far away and I have got to get my winter clothing and air it out."

"There must be twenty dogs in the pot and I know we can sell them. We should make twenty dollars for the night." I said.

I had held the pot very level and I had not gotten any of the greasy water on me. We were nearing the concession stand and we could hear the cheers from the crowd more clearly now.

"Yes, we must have sold forty already," she said as she caught up with me and entered the stand together.

I put the pot on the hot plate. The other students had been waiting for the new pot and I saw them quickly sell at least five dogs to patrons who had been waiting for them. Another three or so came over as soon as they saw that a new batch had arrived.

"Look, I am going to sit in the stands awhile and see the rest of the game. If you need me, you know where I am. We can go cook some more at my home if necessary. We can talk some more during school if you want."

And she left. I watched her walk away while she put on a light jacket.

She had developed a slight limp, possibly from the gravel her shoes had trouble navigating. She may have twisted an ankle, I thought. It was just her nature to not tell me.

The light jacket reminded me of the slight chill in the air. I couldn't get her image out of my mind. She had supported me through my freshmen year. It was obvious that some teachers wanted to find students that showed potential and could prove to be good learners of their respective subjects. She taught English so she sought students with good verbal skills. I would find her often in her assigned classroom, alone, staring through the window due east at the *bosque* and the mountain range that stayed snowcapped through most of the year. There was a mystery in her past and there was no clue as to its nature.

"Have you read Maugham?" she asked me one day after homeroom. "Here is a copy of *Of Human Bondage* and you can keep it after you're finished with it. But I want you to come back and tell me what you think of it."

I read the book, a few pages every night and after a couple of months I had finished it. I couldn't connect the story with Miss Bell or why she had asked me to read that particular book. I did sit down with her and gave her my review of the book. She looked at me as I talked about the Phillip story line, the setting and Maugham's prose style. She was looking for something in my face or my voice. Maybe the book was supposed to transform me, recognize a part of life that I was ready for. I had turned fifteen but I felt the same, still trying to figure out where I was and why things were happening to me. It was puzzling and didn't know what to make of it. I didn't know where to go for help in sorting things out. She may have recognized in me that I did want to get out. I didn't want to go through the life in the Valley my mother had. I was tired of being poor.

I had come to believe what she had always advocated, namely, the key was to master English as best I could. I had signed up for the fall play to improve my elocution and there was a speech contest I had planned to enter in the spring. My Latin class had already strengthened my vocabulary and I was determined to read a classic novel every week. At home I was still speaking our Valley Spanish and with many of my friends that language was still the default tongue. I had to figure out how to manage enough time to accomplish my goal. Maybe this was where Miss Bell's planning skills could help me. I would talk to her about next week when I would also ask her about her limp and get her started on New York again.

16
Califa and Green Apricots
June 5, 1958

And I don't want to be a janitor my
whole life.

—*Abrán*

Abrán was my first cousin, third son of my mother's older sister, Maria Elena. He was born in June and I was born in December of the same year—1942. When my mother visited her sister which was often in the summer and the fall, the time for harvesting corn, chili and apples, Abrán and I would get together and catch up on the latest games, comics and books. He lived in the farming village of Nambroca, one of the early settlements of the Spanish colonists, near San Gabriel established in 1598 on the western banks of the Rio del Norte.

Abrán's mother had inherited land in the village from our grandfather. Abrán's father had built a house on the land near the county highway but the family also owned a farming strip about 100 feet wide that extended all the way to the Chama River near its confluence with the Rio del Norte, the strip encompassing an area of ten acres. His father had given up trying to make a living out of the farm and had taken a custodial job at the national laboratory just like a lot of farmers and ranchers in the Valley. His father was vocal in saying it was a boring and demeaning job but it gave the family a steady income. This attitude might have been a factor in his heavy drinking, especially on weekends. There had been fights with the older boys and they had left home and joined the army when they were old enough. One of them, Ernesto, now lived in California or "Califa" as the Valley residents called it. Abrán was the only boy left and he had two younger sisters.

"I am going to Califa," he said when I saw him a couple of days after his birthday.

"You're barely sixteen. What are you going to do there?

"I'm going to live with Ernest. He's got a job in Burbank, fixing cars and he says he can get me part-time work in a car wash."

"Will you finish high school over there? You have two more years to go."

"I hope not. I look old enough to be eighteen. They probably don't care."

"But it is harder to finish once you drop out. Sooner or later, somebody's going to want to see the high school diploma."

"I'm not learning much in school. Besides, *no tengo interés. [I'm not interested.]*

"What does your father say about this?"

"He doesn't care. He would have one less mouth to feed. He's already giving me a hard time about getting a job during the summer."

"Did you try?"

"Damn right I tried. I went to every store from the Pueblo all the way to San Isidro. I even tried a couple of places in Santa Fe although I don't know how I would have gotten there every day. Maybe I could have lived with one of our relatives there. There's nothing out there for me. The store owners hire their relatives. Even in the village offices, the relatives come first."

"What about waiting a couple of more years and getting your diploma then trying to get something at the national laboratory? Your father can help you get a position there."

"He hates his job. And I don't want to be a janitor my whole life. You've got to have a college degree to get anything better besides construction, a watchman or a janitor. There's no college for me. I don't have the grades or the money. That's why California's the place."

He got up and walked away from me. We had been facing the sun, leaning on my mother's car. After a few steps, he turned and said, "Let's go get green apricots down near the *acequia*."

I hurried to join him.

You had to have a strong stomach to eat green apricots. A few wouldn't hurt you but I had seen friends of mine throw them up violently when they over-ate. We had become addicted to the fruit of the Valley and we ate green peaches, green apples and green pears long before they showed any signs of ripening. Apricots were the first fruit to mature so we went after them in June when they started showing up in the Valley trees. In Nambroca the apricot trees grew wild. People didn't cultivate them because there really wasn't a local market for them. The fruit was rather small and the markets would rather get the fruit from California, much larger and better looking but tasteless. The apricot trees had blossomed in May and now little apricots were starting to appear. They wouldn't ripen until July but there were so many apricots, it was wise to take a few off so the rest would grow to a reasonable size. Even the ripe apricots from Nambroca were a little tart and had big stones so there was little meat. However, the ladies of the Valley made great apricot jam out of them. By partly cooking the crushed and deboned fruit the Pueblo Indian ladies made *empanadas* or turnovers along with those made from boiled sweetened prunes.

Abrán continued explaining why he intended to move to southern California. He said that many other young people from the Valley had not found work in San Isidro or in Santa Fe and had chosen to join a family member who had gone to the Los Angeles area and found a job in the rapidly expanding metro area. The prodigal sons and daughters would come back and visit the old folks for a few days. They would speak well of their new lives with good jobs, great weather and the exciting city life. They talked of palm trees, ocean beaches, a big zoo and the many new stores. No wonder other young people like Abrán would decide to take their chances there too. But there were a few who did come back, dejected, with plenty of stories to tell of being stuck in a menial job with overbearing supervisors. Going to California was not the solution for everyone but there were many more success stories than failures. I always wondered whether it was work ethic that explained the gap between success and failure. Abrán never showed an exemplary work ethic when we harvested crops, made chili *ristras*, washed cars, fed the animals or even in weeding the garden. He was severely underweight, had a thin, almost emaciated face and tired easily. My aunt was not the disciplinarian that her sister, my mother, was with me. I always thought Abrán's family had more income than my mother and me. I mean a lot more income. My frustration was with the poor living conditions that my mother and I endured. I understood that it came from the lack of steady work. Although our welfare check helped a bit, it did not approach the comfort that a regular paycheck provided.

"What about staying here and working on the farm? A bunch of farmers are forming a cooperative so they can sell to the stores in San Isidro and Santa Fe," I said.

Abrán turned to me with dejected eyes and cleared his throat like he wanted to get something big off his chest. "The time of farming in the Valley is past. It is very hard work to try to do everything yourself. When our grandfather farmed, there were lots of kids to help out. Your mother still talks about being held back from going to school. She only finished second grade because her parents thought she was old enough to work on the farm. It was a time when it was okay to be barely literate. Superstition was acceptable. You sang to make yourself happy because the work was so hard. You felt good because you owned land and you were the captain of your soul. The work you put in was for your family. The reward was that you had a home and the family ate well." Abram was starting to make me feel like there was no solution for the young people like me. He continued in a barely audible voice.

"My father feels bad that he doesn't farm much anymore. The land fills up with weeds and we plow only to keep the weeds down. The land looks tired. It's been worked hard for nearly four hundred years. It needs to be fertilized or at least lay fallow for a while. The same crops—corn, chili, and squash—have been farmed for years and years. My father tried apple trees but they require trimming, mulch and most importantly—spraying. Otherwise, the apples are distorted, wormy and small. Nobody will buy them. My father even tried cattle but we didn't own enough land for pasture or alfalfa and the few it could sustain didn't make it worthwhile. He's frustrated and mad at the change that's happening. That's why he drinks. He married my mother and was happy because they were getting land, farming land with access to an *acequia*. They thought they had it made because that's the way people prospered here in the past. People with land were rich. Look at the difference with your mother. She inherited no land and then married a man who had no land and who eventually became a sheepherder. Then she separated from him. She chose a life of poverty. Maybe she didn't know how bad it was going to be."

"How do you know it's going to work out in Califa?"

"I don't know. My brother will open a door. I'll take that job and I'll keep looking for a better one. At least I won't have to stare at this depressing place. I look at my father and I see myself twenty years later. My mother can't help. She has never worked anywhere else. She took care of us, stayed home, and was the loyal housewife. I don't think my father's going to last long with his heavy drinking so my mother will probably end up living the rest of her days with one of my sisters. I have got to figure out where the best place for me is. Maybe Califa, maybe not. But I know I can't stay here."

I wanted to try out what I thought was a strategy that would work. I really wasn't trying to argue with him. I knew he had made up his mind.

"You know that I believe education is the answer. My teachers tell me that.

What I read in newspapers and magazines all say that. I have to go to college." I surprised myself that I used the same words my teachers had said to me. I guess I wanted to believe in something that, inevitably, would also take me out of the Valley.

"Well, it may be the answer for you. You believe in that and you have the brains for it. But we are not all the same. Education can help to the degree that we have the talent for it. You have done well in school and you have the intelligence. But I don't have that talent or interest even though we have the same grandfather."

"Education can mean training like fixing airplanes, working in a factory or on a complicated machine," I explained. It was clear I wasn't making any sense to my cousin.

"There's nothing like that here in the Valley. Even Albuquerque doesn't have any factories of any size. There is no manufacturing in the state. There is mining going on. Copper near Silver City, potash down south, uranium near Grants but it's a dead end job. The mines peter out and you haven't developed any skill you can use somewhere else. Ray, the handwriting's on the wall. We have been a bunch of small farmers and ranchers for centuries. We speak Spanish and we're getting better in English. We learn carpentry in high school, home economics for the girls. What kind of training is that? Where are we going to get a job with that kind of training? We have an FFA club at the school. Maybe the club gives us a little self-respect to call ourselves future farmers but small farms can't make it anymore, not here anyway. You can't raise a family with the size farm we have. Farming may become a hobby that families may want to pursue for pleasure but not for making a living."

We had reached the large apricot tree and there was an abundance of green apricots on it. Both Abrán and I were tall enough to reach quite a few by simply standing on our toes. We grabbed a few of them and stuffed our pockets with the fuzzy fruit. They were the size of a walnut or smaller. Their centers had not formed into a hard bone so you could pop one in your mouth and work away the crunchy meat without hitting something hard and without worrying about choking on the bone. We sat down on the bridge over the *acequia* while we snacked on the green apricots. We had done this for years, being friends as well as close relatives, enjoying the fruit of the Valley, growing up together, sharing secrets and figuring out the world.

The tan hued water from the Chama River was running in the irrigation ditch. The color indicated that it was carrying the silt from the San Juan Mountains and the upper range of the Jemez peaks. There were good minerals in that silt, my mother used to say. Weeds and alfalfa clippings would drift by, like souls trying to ride the waves of life. This conversation was a lot more serious than usual.

"I've thought of joining the army if Califa doesn't work out, Abrán continued. My brothers did all right in the service. I will be eighteen in another couple of years and they'll take me. I'm a little low in weight but I can bulk up when I hit the west coast. If I'm lucky I could get training in the service that could get me a job when I get out."

I decided to change the subject. "You were going out with Erlinda. What does she say about all of this?"

"That was a mistake. I should not have gotten involved with her. Even though she's nothing great to look at, I got all excited with her. Before I would catch the late bus from school I would walk her home. She and her mother live near the theater in San Isidro, you know."

"What do you mean, you got excited with her?"

"We were kissing and stuff in the theater on Sunday afternoons like a lot of kids. But I started going for more and soon I was feeling her breasts and then I got under her skirt and finger-fucked her. I got turned on and I couldn't stop."

"She let you do that in the theater?"

"You cross that bridge and it is hard to turn around and go back to kissing. One Sunday afternoon we showed up at the theater but we left just as the movie was starting. We went to her house. She said that her mother was going to be gone for the afternoon. We were there for almost two hours and we did it three times. We went back to the theater, paid to get in again and left when the matinee was over."

"Cheez. You could have gotten her into trouble," I said with unmasked envy. Frankly, I was also shocked with his courage to take such risks. He and I had never talked about sex except maybe superficially. He had given me a pornographic comic book once, the miniature kind that you can stuff in your pocket and hide from prying adult eyes. It didn't last too long with me. My mother found it and destroyed it without bothering to tell me.

"We got that out of our system and we didn't do it again. In fact, we have not gone to the movies together since then."

"Did she say something to you after you guys did it?

"Well, we stayed away from each other for a while. She told me she had missed her period and I went into a panic. That day I threw up when I got home and my mother asked me what the problem was. I told her I had eaten something bad at school."

"Wait a minute. I thought girls threw up when they got pregnant, not boys." I felt a little uneasy myself. I had eaten too many of the green apricots because my pockets were empty and my mouth was very sour. Abrán's story could have been my story. I felt I was looking in the mirror. This could have happened to me. I took a deep breath of the clean moist air coming off the nearby orchards, meadows and vegetable gardens. I was sorry I said that after I realized it was uncomfortable for Abrán to talk about what happened with Erlinda.

"Very funny. My stomach was tied up in knots for a couple of weeks. I didn't know what to do. She came back and said that her period had just been late and wasn't pregnant. The sex must have upset her rhythm."

"So it's over with Erlinda?"

"We avoid each other in school. I feel revulsion for her. It's stupid."

"You liked her, didn't you? I mean you kissed her at the movies. She liked you back. I don't understand the revulsion."

"It's crazy. I don't know why I feel this way. Yes, I liked her a lot. There are people that you just like, you know. There is compatibility. It happens when you meet them. It could be a boy or a girl. The opposite can happen too. You just can't stand someone. It's a kind of magnetism or energy. It attracts or repels. With Erlinda, I felt good being with her. We talked about teachers, books and songs we both liked. Then the kissing started that led to the sex. It was like the attraction collapsed. It got ruined and now it's gone. There's nothing there. I can't explain it. Maybe it was all kid stuff, nothing serious. "

"She was the first one for you? And you for her? The whole thing sounds pretty serious to me."

"I guess we both didn't take it seriously enough. She was exploring just like I was. Maybe I was the first one to really like her. We didn't stop to think, I guess."

"I remember her mother was very thin and had a goiter. They had come to town from Rio Blanco, the village near Medanales. They were on welfare and her mother had a number of gentlemen callers, including one of my married uncles. One time I spotted him with her. They were parked in his car in front of her house one evening."

"Yes, her mother had it removed and she looks better, maybe gained weight. They are both still on welfare. She was nice to me. She trusted me with her daughter."

"Did Erlinda tell her mother or anyone else, you think?"

"It doesn't matter and I don't care. I can always deny it. Anyway, she doesn't mean anything to me. Like I said, the whole thing was both of us experimenting. We played with fire and we're lucky that nothing happened."

"Well how was it, the sex I mean?"

"I probably came too fast the first time when she got me so hot by sucking my cock. She was kind of tense when I went into her. I was able to come again a couple more times but it wasn't any more enjoyable. Maybe we were afraid her mother would find us."

"Why do you avoid her now? Can't you just be friends?"

"Like I said before, once you cross the bridge, it's a different relationship. To me it's ownership. She will own you. Or maybe I own her. Maybe it's a bad habit that keeps you going back to it, again and again, like a drug. I think girls know that it's a hook. Life changes with sex, even if you don't have a kid. It changes everything."

"Are you going to California to get away from her?"

"I hope not. Like I said, she and I aren't especially interested in getting together again."

"That's a shame. It looks like it was serious for a while."

"But I do look at girls a little differently now. The pure sex thing is over for me. I want to have a friend that's part of me and I'm part of her. Maybe I've learned something. It can't be just the sexual attraction. That can obscure the real reason to care for someone. I don't know what the reason should be but it isn't just sex."

We both got up from the bridge and starting walking back to his house. It was getting close to lunchtime and our mothers would be expecting us soon. But I didn't know whether I could eat anything after having so many green apricots. Every time I felt queasy I took a deep breath as if that commanded my stomach to settle down. I tried to focus on what Abrán was saying and I wanted to be the friend that he needed now.

It was a clear, sunny day and there was a slight breeze, quietly bringing the fragrant scent from flowering trees, the grasses in the river meadows and the mint that grows along the *acequia*. As we walked, more silently now, Abrán's confession made me realize that the kind of visit I had made in the past to

Nambroca was over. This may be the last one, not because Abrán was leaving but because we were now living in a different world, one that we had to think about and not just enjoy. It was a time of decision, of figuring out what was right, when to act, what to say, and to think about others. There was something inside of us that had matured. It pushed us toward passion, despair and hope at the same time. It made us feel things more deeply, veering us this way or that, without a frame of reference. It was a time of transition where we couldn't look at what had happened in the past and steer our lives by it. We were in uncharted waters with little room for error. We were doomed to fail if we did nothing. Parents were no help because the world had changed, changed a lot. They would tell us that there were truths that never change and they apply no matter when we live, a hundred years ago or now. But the way we earn a living does change and every generation has to adjust. The change is big as Abrán's father found out. And Abrán has to learn new things too if he is going to survive.

We walked by the little chapel that was built near the *acequia*. The cemetery behind it was filled with our ancestors' gravestones reminding us of *their* lives, in times when working the land was the only option to live, marry and raise a family. We were passing markers of several generations that had lived that way. My mother showed me a family tree with her ancestors who lived on these farmlands since 1764. Church records before that date had burned in a fire but she was confident that during the second Spanish resettlement of 1692, Nambroca welcomed back its descendants of its first settlers of the sixteenth century. I had always been in awe of their resolute belief that they could make a living here despite the harsh climate—dry, frigid winters, scorching summers, windstorms in spring and fall. Rainfall was scarce and the keeping of sheep and cattle was hard work with little natural feed and so many predators like mountain wolves to deal with. Indian raids by Commanches were brutal on the Pueblo Indians as well as on the European newcomers until the mid-nineteenth century when the U.S. Army slaughtered most of them. Our ancestors must have been from a tough breed. Theirs was a time of sweat that comes from being in the sun, nurturing the meager crops, irrigating the soul with the love of a spouse, the children hugging your leg, the church calming your fears because the next day will be the same as the last one. The mountains and river do not change and you sense that time is like a drumbeat that keeps life simple and in rhythm.

Post Script

Abrán did leave for Califa and things didn't work out well. He didn't last long at a car wash; then he became a night watchman at a factory, then finally working as dishwasher at a fancy restaurant. After two years, soon after reaching the age of eighteen, he enlisted in the service. He was assigned to Fort Ord and did his training there. I lost track of him after I left the Valley to go to college. In December of 1960 I heard that Abrán had been assigned to an Okinawa base and while there he had been in an accident. He and another soldier were wounded when they triggered a land mine left over from the Japanese occupation of the island. They had been on a military exercise in a wooded area. He came back to the Valley a disabled veteran and never married. He still lives in Nambroca.

17
Death in Cibola
Summer 1958

You can see how she died. Murder/
suicides get me sick. There's been too
many for me already.
                        —*Officer Mondragon*

Chris and I would play cards or checkers in the garage where they parked the ambulance and the fancy hearse used during funerals. It was a huge space with enormously high ceilings. It was cold in the winter because it wasn't heated and during the summer it became uncomfortably warm and stuffy. But it was great during the fall and spring for simply practicing our basketball dribble or sitting down at a table and playing a board game. From the garage you could go into a couple of sleeping rooms used by the men who worked the night shift. A bathroom was next door and the door into the embalming room was further down the corridor leading to the garage exit.

Chris was home from the military high school that summer and I had just finished the sophomore year at Fernandez High School. We had gone to junior high school together but had gone on to different high schools and so the summer was the time when we could spend time together and review the stuff we did during other nine months.

Chris took me into the embalming room one day. Windowless, it was dark and cave-like even with the indirect light from the garage shining through the door as he opened it. We stepped inside and Chris flipped the light switch. An array of fluorescent bulbs lit up the room with dazzling light and a buzzing sound. Once my eyes adjusted to the glare, I saw how the room was filled with cabinets and drawers attached to white-colored walls. The cabinets had glass doors and you could see tools and bottles and small boxes stored in them. Prominently placed in the middle of the room, three human-length tables were set on pedestals. Each table had a smooth one inch lip encircling its top with a drain located at one end that emptied into a sink on the far wall. The middle table, tilted slightly with the lower end toward the sink, had a sheet over what appeared to be a human form. The others were empty and level. Each sink had a tall looped faucet and several flexible hoses.

I followed Chris over to the occupied table. He stood over it on one side and I was opposite him looking down on the shielded human form. I had attended many funerals by that time so I had been up close to dead people, mostly distant relatives, elderly and little known to me. The departed one was always dressed in formal garb, the face ashen except for the obvious makeup used around the cheeks and to hide any discolored areas on the skull.

I gasped as Chris lifted the sheet covering the body. He lifted it high so that I could see the torso all the way to the lower abdomen and thighs. I could remember only once or twice when I had felt that breathless sensation, that of an unexpected discovery, chilling your brain, your eyes pulsing to take in the meaning of what you are looking at. The shock was total, the world becoming a different place, sending doubts as to whether I was really there, standing and dizzy as I gazed at the nakedness of death. There was an antiseptic smell mingled with an unmistakable fleshy odor that you find inside a meat store. The body was colorless, the rough stitches still showing across the entire torso where the Y-shaped autopsy cuts had been made. The stitches squeezed the pinkish skin edges on the long incisions. Her breasts seemed deflated, a shadow of what they might have been in her youth, small hairs now surrounding her widely round and darkened nipples. Her pelvic area also seemed empty, the hip bones jutted out, the belly life drained and pallid like a waxen image. The public hair was a light brown like her washed out hair that she had worn short. It was still curly although matted and unsightly. Her neck was pale and unbecoming yet her face bore a serene look, her lips symmetric and full, complementing a pristine nose, pleasant eyes and forehead despite age lines weathered in years ago from the elements of life.

I felt sick and my legs were weakening. But I was ashamed to show any signs of faintness to Chris. I took a deep breath silently. The sight was made more frightening because of its stark presence. It made me feel that I was looking into the future, an empty darkness. The cold, slightly tilted porcelain table she lay on put a dread into me that I would be there someday, drained of blood, violated and pumped full of fluid to preserve my body for a few more days. I tried regaining a bit of composure.

"What happened to her?" I managed to blurt out. My heart was still beating fast from the shock I had just experienced. Chris was still looking at the stitch lines.

"No one knows. She was found dead in a local hotel room so the sheriff ordered an autopsy. I see that it was an extensive one. We don't see these very often."

Chris was nonchalant about the scene. I was sure he had seen many naked corpses but I wondered how he could become so dispassionate about seeing them like this. The starkness of the scene had disrupted not only my senses but basic functions like breathing, speaking and staying on my feet.

The woman was probably around forty, tall and a bit thin. She didn't look Hispanic, her features unlike those of Native Americans also. The Valley had attracted a goodly share of Anglo residents, many of them spilling over from Santa Fe where rents were higher. We were twenty four miles away from that city down a two lane highway and a good thirty five minutes by car observing the speed limits. "Was she a tourist or a visitor?" I asked, swallowing hard to hide my inner turmoil.

The embalming room was refrigerated but it wasn't the cold air that gave me goose bumps on my arms and legs. Death had been a part of life that had not scared me up to this point, perhaps because I had lost no one close. Looking at the naked corpse brought it closer to me. I knew that I would remember this scene forever. It was strange that the remains of a person I had never known would do this to me.

"She could be. Let me look at her file."

Chris finally put the sheet back over the body but I could still see the silhouette of death it represented. I was still trembling but not visibly. Chris walked over to the cabinet area and looked through the contents of a clipboard.

"Her address is in Illinois so she might have been passing through, a tourist perhaps. The autopsy samples will probably tell us what happened to her. She didn't have any marks on her body so they probably have ruled out foul play."

Chris said this so authoritatively that I had not realized until now that he had learned a lot about the mortuary stuff by just hanging around the garage. His oldest brother was the chief mortician.

I wondered what had brought her here to San Isidro. Had she heard of Cíbola and wanted to see what our Valley was really like? Her life may have ended prematurely before she could take it in. Or maybe she knew she was dying and wanted to end it here. It was a mystery.

It took me time that summer to get over the vividness of the scene in the mortuary. I thought about death more often and wondered how I would die. It was no longer an abstract concept for me but an ultimate state that I would reach and that I imagined being grotesquely still, cold and empty when I got there. I would be motionless on the porcelain table. I could not hide and I would be there for anyone to see. I could not cry or laugh or feel pain or joy. Death was the opposite of motion and freedom.

I still went to see Chris often at the garage and we did things together like go to movies and take in a party or two. One night I decided to stay over at Chris' house because we had gotten home late from a double feature at the drive-in movie. My mother was out of town and she knew I might stay over. His parents had a big house because they had had so many children and many of them were gone now except for Chris who was the youngest. It was almost one o'clock in the morning and we were having a late night snack in the kitchen. His parents had gone to bed already when the phone rang. It was Albert who was on ambulance duty. Chris answered the phone. All I could hear was Chris saying "Yes" and then another "Yes," moments later.

"Let's go," he said. "They need us at the garage; there's been a shooting."

What happened after that is still blurry, even today. I remember riding in the ambulance, the siren blaring, going for miles and stopping at a junction on the way to Chimayó, a village about ten miles from town. Albert left the ambulance on the side of the road behind a state police car with flashing lights. Albert and Chris took the stretcher; I took a small bag that contained plastic wrappings and harnesses and we headed toward the house that was all lit up. A small dog barked at us as we approached the house, not very loud, a token bark performed out of habit. He came up to us, unsure whether we were friend or foe. I petted him and got a friendly wag of his long tail. He had a quizzical look on his face.

There was a classic 1952 Chevrolet coupe in the driveway, presumably the homeowner's. It was a two-toned low-rider with the car's front end slightly lower than the rear, equipped with fender skirts and whitewall tires on chromed wheels with spinners and it had a rounded hood on the windshield. It was obvious that a lot of investment had gone into restoring the car as well as turning it into a possible prizewinner at a car show.

A police officer was standing in the doorway, talking to a man who later identified himself as a neighbor. Both the officer and the neighbor were smoking cigarettes, the small plumes of smoke twisting as they rose up into a violet sky. The officer had a name tag on his shirt—Sgt. P. Mondragon.

"It's too late," Officer Mondragon said to Albert as he blew cigarette smoke to his side while lifting his head slightly. He threw the butt on the ground and smashed it with his ankle-high boot. "Gunshot to the head and it looks like murder/suicide. The coroner's on his way." The officer continued talking to the neighbor and occasionally took some notes.

Albert, Chris and I had to wait for the coroner before we could touch the body. So we placed the stretcher down near the house entrance and stood around listening to the conversation between the officer and the neighbor. The dog came over and sat down and was just as attentive. He apparently belonged to the owners of the house. As I looked at him, he tilted his head sideways and whimpered in a way asking 'What's the matter?'

"Yes, I did hear two quick gunshots and then another one later," repeated the neighbor. "The second volley was louder and a single shot. It came several minutes later after the first two quick ones. The later gunshot really got my attention and I came over and knocked on the door. The lights were on and the door was unlocked so I came in and discovered the body."

"When was the last time you saw either one of them?," the officer asked.

"I hadn't seen either of them for a couple of days, you know. He had been discharged from work over at the national lab for drinking. I guess that happened about a week ago. I remember they had a terrible fight that night. I could hear them all the way down the highway to my house. She had left the house and was yelling from the road. I couldn't make out what they were saying but it was clear she was mad, really mad about something."

"Was it because he had lost his job?" "Well, she didn't have a regular job, just took in sewing and ironing for ladies in town. So I imagine they weren't going to have a lot to live on. She was such a nice young lady, Concha, the daughter of Jose Lucero from Chimayó. They had been married about two years, no kids yet. Maybe that's good."

"When did he start drinking?"

"Eliseo picked it up as a teenager. He was a good athlete, playing ball for the Crusaders in Santa Cruz. After the games were over, he'd go partying too much. My son, Moises, played on the same team. After high school he took an internship at the national lab and we thought he would quit his drinking. It was a good job in the security section with lots of promotion potential. He and Concha bought this house from her uncle. But he acted like things weren't going the right way." The neighbor threw his cigarette butt on the ground and stomped on it once with his right foot.

"Besides last week's fight, did you hear about any other serious arguments?"

"Well, there was a rumor that he was flirting with an old flame of his and Concha had heard about it. I'm sure there were words exchanged over that issue. It could have set him off to drinking heavily again. She had talked about getting a job and helping out with the household expenses. But he was a proud man and wouldn't hear of it. She was unhappy with his attitude. He was a macho type, you know."

By that time the coroner had arrived. The dog had disappeared.

"Hello, hello. Officer Mondragon, *que tal*?" [How goes it?] the Coroner said.

"*Orale, orale [Hey, hey.].* We got another bad scene here, a double, kinda messy."

The Coroner was introduced to the neighbor after greeting Albert.

"Let's go see what we have here, Albert. Why do these things happen so late at night?" the Coroner said.

Albert followed him and led Chris and me into the kitchen and then the large room where the body was. The officer had stayed outside with the neighbor. The dog tried to come in the door but the officer shooed him back.

It was a gentleman, probably in his thirties, lying in the space between a small coffee table and the couch, his arms entwined with a hunting rifle. His jaw rested on his chest and there was blood on his shirt from the wound on the side of the neck. The jolt from the shot must have made him fall from the couch where he had been sitting. A pool of blood on the floor had formed from a head wound at the back of his skull. His eyes were still open with a vacant look. He had black straight hair, most of it combed straight back but the jolt had loosened strands that now covered his forehead. His face was thin and tanned, like he had been out in the sun working in the fields. He had a thin moustache but was otherwise clean shaven. You couldn't tell how tall he was because of his folded position. He wore a dress shirt, long sleeved and neatly pressed. His pants were pleated, khaki colored and his shoes were wing tips, oxford-colored and very shiny.

"*Que triste*, Albert. Such a young man too. Let me take photos first before we touch him." The coroner examined the scene, taking pictures and carefully going over the body. He shook his head and mumbled under his breath. He wrote notes and looked around the longish room that served as both a dining area and a more formal living room. It was modestly furnished mostly with store bought furniture of a boxy modern style, the walls a neutral beige color with a couple of pictures of pleasant landscape scenes in the dining area.

The coroner stopped to look at the picture of the Last Supper hung over the couch. It was too large for the area and it had a nice carved wooden frame with a glass surface. He shook his head again.

"I am looking for any evidence of a struggle. Do you see any, Albert?"

Albert started looking around the room. There was a table and four chairs at one end of the room that served as a dining area. Atop a buffet cabinet were portraits, probably of family or friends. There was a round carpet, shag style, underneath the table area. Toward the other end of the long room were the couch (where the body was found), an easy chair and a straight chair forming a u-shape around a coffee table with a glass top. The TV set was on the opposite wall in front of the sitting area. It was not an expensive set. It had a twenty one inch screen, a portable model perched on top of a nicely finished wooden table, the kind carved in a woodworking class..

"No, I don't see anything out of place. He might have straightened things out before he killed himself. That's seems unlikely, though," said Albert.

There was a thick Mexican blanket underneath the coffee table, couch and easy chair. A few pale crocheted pieces made the furniture look a little more homey. There were windows at either end of the room with thick, three quarter length curtains that were used for both privacy and heat insulation. The coroner looked through the window and examined the sill to see if the lock had been unlatched.

The coroner and Albert went into the kitchen and talked to the Officer Mondragon at length about the call to the Sheriff's department and the sequence of events leading up to this point. The coroner questioned the neighbor about the times of the shots and when he placed the phone call to the police. He sat down at the kitchen table, shoving aside a napkin holder and a tall salt and pepper shaker set. He wrote more notes. The coroner looked around the kitchen, opened the cupboard and the refrigerator, opened the back door and then closed it. He said something to the police officer that I didn't quite hear. They conferred in subdued voices and at the end nodded in agreement. Finally, the coroner turned to Albert, Chris and me.

"Yes, you can take him away. It's okay. It is pretty obvious. But you have to come back for the wife. I will take a look at her now in the dark," he said. "It may be getting light when you come back and we can all get a better look." Just then the dog gave a mournful, sustained yelp like someone had stepped on his tail. He had been outside the door. Through the officer's legs he had seen the stretcher as we entered the kitchen. The dog backed away from the door, still uttering a high pitched howl, like a coyote.

Albert had prepared a plastic sheet on the stretcher by that time and we moved the body onto the stretcher and carried it out to the ambulance. Half the sheet was underneath the body and the other folded half was used to cover it. The gentleman was about six feet tall, an above average height for the Valley but his weight couldn't have been more than one hundred and sixty pounds. Albert had guessed the height and weight and written them down on a form that the coroner signed. On the way we passed the dog, now whimpering as if licking his wounds. He was sitting down on his hind legs, his front legs straight and anchored with his paws. He watched as we took out his master and then followed us to the road where he stopped. After loading the body into the ambulance and closing the back gate, Chris got in and sat next to Albert. I got the window seat and as we drove off, the dog was still watching us.

Chris and I were silent as we rode back to the mortuary to deliver the first victim of the tragedy. It took us over an hour to get there, unload the body, help Albert undress the gentleman, and inventory the items in his clothing. Although it was nearly dawn and we hadn't slept, Chris and I were wide awake and assisted Albert where we could.

By the time we got back to the murder/suicide scene it was getting light but sunrise had not occurred. I looked around but the dog was nowhere to be found. The police car was still there with flashing lights and the scene had attracted several curious neighbors. The coroner was gone but the policeman led us to where the dead woman was.

She was 200 yards or so due west, across the highway, in a sandy field filled with river brush, willowy reeds and cottonwood trees. The Santa Cruz River that ran parallel to the highway at that point was only 100 feet away from her body. "She ran when she saw he had a gun and was going to use it," Officer Mondragon explained. "She took off into these bushes at the edge of the *bosque* but he caught up with her. He shot her twice in the back. The coroner said one shot caught her lung and she collapsed. You can see how she died. Murder/suicides get me sick. There's been too many for me already."

Although the site had reeds and undergrowth, the brush was not thick enough to shield her from the pursuer. He had enough of a view that he had time to aim and shoot the fleeing human target who was desperately trying to get traction on the sandy soil.

"We have to turn her around away from the bushes first. Then we can see if she'll straighten out without getting too much sand on her," Albert instructed. As Chris and I positioned ourselves as Albert instructed, we heard rustling in the nearby cottonwoods. A large bird, white breasted with a beautiful black set of feathers, had spread its wings and then settled on an outstretched branch, perched at an angle where he could oversee our activities. We gently turned the body and slid her carefully away from the bushes.

She was wearing a long, pleated skirt and a festive embroidered blouse and leather sandals with heel straps. Chris and I took her from her crouched position and slid her limp body onto the stretcher. She must have knelt after being hit the first time, and then slumped forward with the second fatal shot, trying to breaking her fall. Her elbows had held her up for a while and then the top of her head hit the sandy soil. Her eyes were partially closed and blood had oozed out of her mouth. Her brown hair was drawn back, tied with a multi-colored kerchief. Her tresses touched her shoulders and covered the collar of her blouse. We were able to get her atop the plastic sheet, face up.

As I tried to catch my own breath after taking in the grisly scene, the sun finally peeking over the San Felipe Mountains, I saw ants on her face crawling up into her eyes and nostrils. Albert saw the insects and removed them using a brush from the bag we had brought with us. "Goddam ants," he said. The bird emitted this screechy sound as he said it.

The ants on the face were simply another indignity, another vulnerability of death. They attacked a sacred place, the eyes we use to understand the world. Her once pretty face, now pale and bearing an eerie stare, showed the scars of tension and pain.

After we folded the rest of the sheet over her, the three of us picked her up and placed her on the stretcher. "Okay, I get one end and the two of you get the other end. I lead with my back to the stretcher," ordered Albert. We trekked through the sand and reeds and made our way to the ambulance. The bird fluttered his wings and made weird muffled sounds from his elevated perch where rays from the dawning sun made him almost invisible.

As we walked I wondered what uncontrollable rage drove the husband to threaten and then chase down the woman that shared his bed. The youth was gone; the dreams of happiness, comfort and fulfillment slipped away in a moment of anger. I tried to understand what I had seen, take in the horror and tragedy, the reality of dying young in a place where life is hard but certainly far from hopeless. After sliding the stretcher into the ambulance and securing it, we closed the rear door. I turned around and saw onlookers near the house. The officer had cordoned off the scene near the river so no one had gone there. The bird had disappeared.

Albert had walked back to the house and said something to the officer. I looked for the dog. Like the bird, he was gone too, maybe starting a search for another home, sadly accepting the fates of those who used to feed him. Chris and I hadn't talked to each other during the whole evening and early morning. I broke the silence.

"What do you think made him do it?" I said. As I spoke I thought of the lady I had seen earlier in the embalming room and of Miquo, my neighbor who had killed himself a couple years ago, and the eerie similarity to my father's death as told by my mother. I had gone to the newspaper archives in Santa Fe to read about the incident. It had happened in April when he was 26 years old and I was born eight months later. Chris continued looking straight ahead as we waited for Albert to come back.

"No one will ever know," Chris said, without turning his head toward me. I knew when he didn't want to talk. But my head was throbbing for lack of sleep, filled with crazy images of death that scared me. I remembered what I had read in the newspapers.

My father owned a tavern and after closing up one night he went to visit his estranged wife. There had been an argument and she had fled the house. Picking up a rifle, he followed and caught up with her as she tried to hide among the *Chamisa* bushes. After killing her, he went back to the house and shot himself in the head. No one seemed to know what the argument may have been about.

This couple, just like my father and his wife, paid the penalty for despair so intense it robbed them of reason. It came in the night like a sleuth, waiting to pounce on their souls in one unguarded moment. Could those seeds for rage be in each of us? Would I repeat my father's actions? I covered my face with my hands and rubbed my eyes, trying to stay the swirling images in my brain.

Albert came back and started the ambulance but didn't turn the siren on. "Nice looking couple," he said as we got on the highway. "They went crazy last night. With the autopsy we'll see if he was drunk when he did it. You're not yourself when you're boozed up." Chris and I didn't respond.

Maybe Albert was right. Alcohol can cause turmoil in the human spirit that leads one to commit unspeakable acts. The turmoil gathers strength from itself like a tornado. The lives become entangled in a struggle whose only resolution is death for both. We rode back to the mortuary in silence again, this time in the bright early morning light.

18
Science in Montana
June 1959

President Eisenhower thinks we need
more scientists and engineers to catch
up with the Russians.

—*Reyes*

We had lunch in Worland, Wyoming and had gotten back on the train. The cafeteria at the train station had served us a Salisbury steak with mashed potatoes and green beans, the typical special plate that you got at any F.W. Woolworth counter. It seemed to be the current faddish meal of America, our way of massifying the menu for everybody. I had a Coke with it so it wasn't so bad. You always got a slice of white bread with the dish or one of those brown-topped rolls that can be split three ways. The bread came with a single pat of butter on a piece of wax paper. I didn't have much of a breakfast in Casper where we had stopped for half an hour around seven in the morning. I was still groggy after trying to get some sleep on the overnight ride from Denver that I boarded around ten o'clock the previous evening. There had been a five hour layover at the Denver terminal after arriving from Lamy, the station closest to Santa Fe. Most of the time in Denver I spent on a bench after making sure my suitcase had been transferred over to the Billings train luggage rack. I was surprised at the number of people still walking around in the station late in the evening. But I did manage to get a bench to myself so I could get a nap in before train boarding was announced. I went to sleep soon after we left the station and woke up an hour before we stopped in Casper. The Burlington line had no dining car, at least not on the Denver-Billings route, so the train waited for us to finish our hot lunch in Worland and then resumed the journey.

The car had few passengers. There was the lady with a toddler that slept a lot when not sucking on the bottle. She kept busy changing its diaper, keeping it occupied, feeding it and holding it while it slept. She smiled and appeared to be happy taking care of the baby. In the back of the car was a gentleman who had a pile of books, magazines and papers spread out over the seat next to him. He wore reading glasses and seemed content to be left alone to his extensive reading material. An elderly gentleman sat across the aisle from me and had been asleep, like me, for most of the morning. He had taken his lunch by himself in a corner of the cafeteria and had eaten very little of it. He appeared to be pensive most of the time and had greeted me when I got back on the train.

We heard a couple of train whistles after which we felt the sudden jerk when the train started rolling again. The train car was old and spartan, with wooden seats, its windows with a yellowish tinge like you see when you don't brush your teeth. The aisle was topped with a glued on rubber runner that spanned the entire length of the car. The pull cord on either side of the car drooped between its eyehooks and had darkened from the pulls it had sustained in its lifetime. The doors that isolated the car interior from the connecting passageway between train cars were banged up with some smears from rubber soles or heels that had been used to kick it open or slam it shut.

"Where you going, young feller?," the elderly gentleman said as he leaned over to make sure I could hear over the din of the rolling car.

"Billings first, then Bozeman," I answered.

"Well, that's mighty interesting. I'm headed for Helena, yessir. Are you visiting in Bozeman?"

"No, not really. I'm going to a science camp at the college there for high school students."

"Is that so? What kind of camp?"

"The program is supposed to convince us to go into science when we go to college next year. The government is sponsoring these programs because of Sputnik."

"You mean that ball the Russians put up in the sky? Everybody's now afraid that we're going to get bombed from outer space? Those Communists are dangerous."

"President Eisenhower thinks we need more scientists and engineers to catch up with the Russians." I had heard a scientist from Los Alamos say that during a visit to our high school.

"Well, I'll be damned. We're spending all this money for getting you and other kids interested in science?"

"That's about it."

"What are they paying you?"

"They're not exactly paying us. They're paying for my trip there and back and my expenses at the college for a month."

"What are you going to get out of it?"

"Well, there's about seventy five of us from several western states and I would say that most of us simply want to be better prepared for college."

"You're Mexican, aren't you? I hadn't heard of Mexican kids going to college."

"Well, I am from New Mexico of Hispanic heritage. I'm not from Mexico although the state was part of Mexico for about twenty two years until the American forces took it over in 1846. That part of the country was settled by Spain in the sixteenth century, mostly land north of Santa Fe."

"I don't know too much of the history of that part of our country. Mexico and Spain are the same to me. What's the big difference? All I know is that most of the folks there are called Mexicans. I never went to college, no sir. I didn't need it to work on the Union Pacific Railway Company for thirty five years. I retired about three years ago."

I saw that he was like a lot of older folks. He could hear but he had lost his ability to listen, especially to young people. I went along with his train of thought. "There aren't too many jobs in the railroad business now that President Eisenhower put in those interstate highways. A lot of stuff is moving by big trucks."

"You're a pretty smart kid for being a Mexican. You don't look like a Mexican. They're mostly darker than you, shorter too.

I had learned not to respond to comments of that nature. There was no winning comeback. I tried to act unaffected even though it stung every time I encountered it.

"But you're right about the trains being cut back. That's one of the reasons I retired. They didn't need me no more. Sad, though, we did a lot of good things with the trains. Connected America in many ways. People aren't riding trains anymore either. Airports being built everywhere. Still expensive to fly though but prices may come down in time."

"Where are you going, sir?"

"I'm retired, lost my wife last year and I'm trying to get on with my life. My kids are all grown and gone so I'm off to see the sights. This time it's the "Gates of the Mountains" up near Helena. We live in a great country, son. I don't reckon I'll see it all but I'll see what I can."

The gentleman told me his name was Jack Wilcox and his doctors had told him he had a bad heart and to take it easy. He figured he had traveled 100,000 miles already on the trains during retirement. Because of his old job he had a lifetime pass to ride on any passenger train for half price so he aimed to take advantage of it while he could. He had visited most of the western states already with Montana and Idaho still to go. We talked a little about all the sites he had visited and enjoyed. By the end of the summer he figured he would go home to Pueblo, Colorado and do volunteer work in a hospital or library and probably worry about the Russians. He slid back to his seat and took a nap.

I looked out the window at the vast prairie and off in the distance, the Rockies. As we turned a little more westward we got to see the Tetons with their snow-capped peaks. I eventually dozed off also and awoke hours later when the train slowed down and stopped for track changes as we approached Billings. We arrived at the train station close to six o'clock. I was going to try to catch a bus to Bozeman that left at seven. I said goodbye to Mr. Wilcox and wished him luck on his sight-seeing trip. I pulled my bag off the arrivals cart and hurried off to the bus station which was located only a few blocks away. I bought my ticket and checked my bag and went in to the snack bar and ordered a hot dog and a Coke. It was Sunday night and there were a lot of travelers getting on or off both the *Trailways* and *Greyhound* buses. The station also served as a terminal for a regional bus service—Great Falls Bus Company—whose line would take me to Bozeman. Although we boarded the bus on time we were delayed another ten minutes while another connection arrived and the passengers boarded. It was dark inside the bus and very few people had turned on their reading lamps. I sat a couple of rows behind the driver so I could be sure to hear when we got to Bozeman.

After retrieving my bag from the bus at the Bozeman station, a gentleman came over and asked if I was with the science conference. He turned out to be Dr. Larsen who was the Director of the Science Camp. We went inside the bus station and joined two other students who had arrived from North Dakota for the camp. We exchanged greetings and got to know each other's names and followed Dr. Larsen to a van that would take us to the college. One student was Mark Cornwall from Grand Forks and the other was Monica Johansen from Minot. Mark was a bit taller than me, around six feet or six one, dark hair, horn-rimmed glasses and he wore a plaid woolen jacket. Monica had light brown hair, drawn straight back with no bangs and tied in a short pony tail. She had brown eyes and wore glasses with clear plastic frames. She had a sensuous mouth and a comely figure. As we looked at each other, I felt a mutual attraction but we both kept our composure.

Mark sat in the rear-most seat of the van while Monica and I took the middle bench seat. There was a hint of a girlish scent—mild perfume or lotion—from Monica that felt good as we took off. Dr. Larsen talked about the plans for our first day at the camp—a general orientation session for everyone, introduction of all the counselors and an explanation of the calendar events for the next 28 days. The three of us were so tired of traveling all day that we said very little as we drove to the campus. We dropped off Monica at the girls' dorm. Dr. Larsen checked us into the boys' dorm located on the opposite side of a quadrangle. Mark and I were assigned to the same dorm room that had a single bed on either side of the room with small desks adjacent to the beds. Near the door, again on either side of the room were a closet and a small bureau with four drawers. When you opened the closet door, you found a mirror mounted on the rear side of the door. We quickly made our beds and were sound asleep in minutes. I hadn't even had a conversation with Monica yet but she appeared in a dream.

We had our general assembly meeting at 9AM the next day after breakfast in the campus cafeteria. The college was a small land grant institution and the third largest school in Montana in enrollment after University of Montana and Montana State University. It was known as a teaching college with a strong science and technology curriculum. Dr. Larsen had received a large grant from the National Science Foundation for holding the science camp for high schoolers who would be seniors the following school year. The mission of the camp was to recruit students into technology fields in college and to improve their science and math skills. The camp would have lectures in the principal science areas of biology, chemistry, physics, geology, earth science and computers in addition to math and English composition. The approach would be hands on with lots of labs and workshops. There would be field trips taken to complement lessons in various fields as well as to visit natural attractions around the Bozeman area. The only free time or non-scheduled time we would have to ourselves would be all day Sunday and several evenings after 7PM. There were seventy five of us and we were divided into three cohorts—Red, Blue and Green—of twenty five students each. The three cohorts would alternate classes, field trips, and other activities but we would come together for campus meals and a general assembly meeting once a week at 9AM on Mondays.

Most of the students were from northern western states—Washington, Idaho, Montana, and the Dakotas. Only a handful came from the other western states. I was one of two students from New Mexico and most significantly, I was the only Hispanic student out of the seventy five. But there were many other ethnicities represented, especially the Scandinavian ones. I learned Monica had a Swedish last name.

What I really appreciated from the group of students was that there was no sign of prejudice. We accepted each other as equals, regardless of skin shade, facial features, stature, name, speech dialect or accent. Having grown up in Northern New Mexico, it had become second nature to me that I was judged by my name or appearance before I could interact with anyone. It was strange to be accepted here as an equal by so many different people.

The talks with Miss Bell had encouraged me to look for such a situation. "Realize your potential," she would say. The camp would give me a chance at bat. Maybe I would strike out but at least I'd get to the plate. Mr. Wilcox on the train had reminded me of the stereotype that plagues someone with a distinct ethnicity, religion or language. I needed to be where I could show what I could do without seeming to be an overachiever. I didn't want to be the first one to break an ethnic barrier, a Jackie Robinson. Maybe I believed this because I knew I wasn't a superstar, as he had been. He had to be much better than his white peers in order to be accepted. I didn't want to carry a massive racial weight on my back. I felt I had too many handicaps already—welfare kid, illegitimate and fatherless, Hispanic, English as second language, marginal schooling. Thinking about handicaps was so self-defeating. It was easy to just give up and accept the general stereotype and work as a janitor like so many of my relatives, the fear that my cousin Abrán had. I wanted a well-paying job, a nice home and reliable car. I wanted to marry my equal in intelligence and temperament. I couldn't do any of this in the Valley back home. I didn't want to try. Failure was almost inevitable if I stayed. I saw it in my relatives and a few had had more going for them than I did.

I found the Bozeman area greener than the San Isidro countryside although both areas had scenic mountain ranges with snow-capped peaks in the early summer. The town was set at about the same altitude and the sky was just as blue. The air was clear and smelled crisp with a hint of pine scent that might have come down from the mountain forests. Although I was a thousand miles away from home, I felt great after a good night's sleep and I looked forward to the summer camp.

Mark and I were not in the same cohort which we thought was an advantage because we could compare notes on at least two different cohorts. He was a pretty good basketball player and he also played chess so we got along pretty well. During our camp days we spent time comparing life in Grand Forks with that in San Isidro. He read D. H. Lawrence a lot and he knew the author had lived in Taos for a little while. He was reading Lady Chatterley's Lover in the early weeks at Bozeman. I was still working on Hemingway's "The Sun Also Rises" during the little free time we had at the college. He said he wasn't into girls much but that he had gone to the junior prom with a neighbor of his that he had known his whole life. His father, who was an accountant, and her father worked in the same firm so the families knew each other pretty well. He had been in the JV basketball team like me. Next year he really wanted to focus on studies so he could go to an eastern school like Williams, Amherst or Colgate and major in chemistry. I told him that my mother and I were on public welfare and I would have to be pretty lucky to get a full scholarship somewhere, especially coming from a rural school. If nothing came along maybe I could enroll at a local college in Santa Fe or Albuquerque on a part-time basis.

Every night, as we lay in bed trying to sleep, Mark and I would recount the day's activities and describe to each other what we had learned, the characteristics of every teacher we had, the type of quiz or exam they gave, and the antics of some of our fellow students. Among the students was the quiet, withdrawn type, socially underdeveloped, afraid to look you in the eye, wouldn't hang around with others and generally wanted to be left alone. The other extreme was the loquacious type, talking a mile a minute, always drawing attention to himself/ herself, hanging around with the teachers, usually being a nuisance to the other students. We both agreed that there were a few really bright students who would be successful and that we were somewhere in middle. We would always have to work hard to try to keep up but we were committed to make something of ourselves despite our handicaps and external barriers we faced. Talking to Mark helped me understand how far I had to go. The different classes and teachers helped assess my skills and extent of the holes in my education. Comparing what I could do with what other students could do was enlightening. But it was all brought together by talking to Mark at night. We didn't bullshit each other, maybe because it didn't matter. We probably wouldn't see each other again after the camp. Being in Montana was like being on an examination table and a bunch of doctors poking at me to see if I was good for something.

Mark saw that I was drawn to Monica and I had to admit that I was happy that she was in my cohort. We took classes together but we didn't sit next to each other. Occasionally we would have lunch or dinner together and we enjoyed each other's company. I admitted that on the first field trip to Virginia City I sat next to her on the bus and in the night-time darkness of the return trip I had kissed her. But during the entire camp it didn't go beyond a close friendship. We went to the movies once and we spent quite a bit of time on a secluded park bench on the campus simply talking and enjoying an occasional kiss. I liked her a lot and she appeared to be happy with me although we would be together for only a month. Once the camp was over, the separation would be more than just distance. There were other barriers. But we both loved learning new things. She had had a better education. She'd taken calculus already and was enrolled in advanced classes in biology and chemistry for the senior year. She had not been in any plays but she played the piano and sang fairly well. She entertained me one Sunday afternoon with her talent, after which we had a passionate kissing interlude.

The college had a small computer lab and every student was asked to write a short FORTRAN program, debug it and have it run successfully on an IBM 650 mainframe. It had a state-of-the-art rotating magnetic drum memory with 2000 words and it used magnetic tape for archival memory. We learned to punch the deck of cards with the computer instructions, compile the program and fix any card and associated program instruction errors. It could take days to get the program to run correctly. The simple exercise taught us the importance of precision and patience in working with machines that have no conscience or sympathy.

We were subject to the instructional talent of the college faculty. While many faculty members were organized and well-rehearsed in their delivery of the material, none of which was simple and easy to learn, there were some members that should never have been let into the classroom. One poor fellow, amply degreed and obviously very intelligent, tried to teach us geology and actually went on field trips with us to the eastern slopes of the Sawtooth Mountains. He was unable to finish a thought without saying "Ahh." It was distracting and some irreverent boys in the camp would each tabulate and then compare the number of "Ahhs" in a lecture. But the general consensus from the attendees was that it was a good camp and it conditioned all of us for college level classes that would soon be coming our way in a little over a year.

We had a party the last day of camp. We had made friends with a few members of our cohort and we exchanged addresses so that we could write to each other. Most of us knew that it would be unlikely that we would write more than once or twice. Mark and I had been honest with each other from the very beginning and we wished each other well. The next morning I saw him go off with Monica and a few others to catch the Greyhound bus to Billings. It was much harder to say goodbye to Monica. We had talked for more than two hours the last night we were together. Despite our efforts to not get so involved, it was tearful for both of us. We kissed passionately and started some heavy petting until we realized what we were doing. We stopped and continued talking, standing only a few feet apart. We knew it was over and we wanted it to end well so we could begin anew when we got home. There was no point to pine away a thousand miles apart with other differences that would stand in the way. The next morning our eyes met only briefly and we both smiled. Her scent had become so much a part of me that anything close to it still evokes a faint memory of her.

I took the train from Helena through Salt Lake City on my way home. Then I boarded the Union Pacific to go to Denver and called up a cousin of mine and stayed there overnight. I had written my mother earlier of my change in plans so she could meet me in Lamy a day later. I remember arriving amidst a dust storm. I saw my mother standing near her car waving at me. I waved back and hurried to get my suitcase from the porter who retrieved it from the baggage car. My mother hugged me for a long time, the dust spray enveloping us. She had been crying. It was unnecessary to say anything. It was as if she knew that I had grown older, much older than the actual time I had spent learning science in Montana.

19
The Dam Kids
April 20, 1959

*Is it not time to forget the past and get
on with the present.*

—*Ron Stallman*

They came when the Abiquiu Dam budget was approved by the state and the U.S. Corps of Engineers, all nineteen of them enrolling in the high school, five as freshmen, six as sophomores and eight as juniors joining me in my class. There were no seniors, presumably because those stayed at the last town to finish school. They were the children of the heavy construction workers who had been hired to build the third dam on the Chama River, this one providing hydroelectric power to the northern part of Contra Mesa County in New Mexico. Their fathers were the heavy machine operators, the surveyors, surveyor crewmen and engineering technicians and whose employment with the general contractor depended on relocating to where the latest contract award was. The local newspaper said that it was a $50 million dollar project with a completion date of June 30, 1961.

The eight students in my class of 140 had assimilated well, joining clubs, making friends with lifelong Valley students, trying out for sports and plays, and volunteering for community activities. Their parents were from all over the country—Illinois, Pennsylvania, Georgia, Louisiana, Montana, Washington and California. Their arrival provided a shock to the class, the new students accustomed to coming into a new school system and fitting in, not being shy about making their presence known and working fervently on acceptance by administration, faculty and students alike. Although gregarious, not all were honor students nor were they particularly good at sports, but they were welcomed and soon were treated as regular students. Nevertheless they were a disruption to the status quo, bringing new attitudes about music, movies, books and recreational activities. Strangely, none were troublemakers, nor did they bring a penchant for alcohol parties, marijuana smoke-ins, or promiscuity. Looking back, I guessed that their parents had done a good job in reining in bad habits that could cause a job loss through a bad image in the community for the general contractor.

The students had lived in several states in cities, suburbs and in rural areas, been educated in private and public schools, and generally were a lot more cosmopolitan than the average student at Fernandez High whose lineage in the Valley spanned several generations. They were Americans as we were trying to be, ever since August 18, 1846, the date of General Kearny's march into Santa Fe. Their invasion presented an opportunity for us to see how different we were, how far we were from America, maybe even question as to whether we were going to make it. They represented itinerant America, going to where the jobs were, taking skills and experience with them, spreading the tastes and trends from other places, colonizing the frontiers with the homogeneity and uniformity of the country. They were friendly enough, perhaps too friendly, leading us to question their sincerity, like being on a first date. Being President of the Junior Class, I got to know all eight of them (junior class) through Student Council, the Drama Club and sports but I became especially friendly with only three of them—Ron, Debra and Winston.

Ron Stallman was a tall, lanky guy who had taken Intermediate Latin at a Catholic high school and had decided to join our Advanced Latin class with Mr. McNair. I saw him at church with his father who was a civil engineer and one of the managers of the Abiquiu Dam Project. They had rented a house on the west side of town, near my neighborhood and close to the downtown area. His mother lived in Pennsylvania and had divorced his father many years ago. I saw him often in the morning when we would meet on the way to school. We became fast friends after he confessed that he had been trying to learn Spanish and he wanted to practice it with me. He had met Marla Garcia and had started spending a lot of time with her at school, sitting with her at football games, that sort of thing. He knew that I had gone to school with her for several years and that she considered me a friend. He was smart, making the honor roll the first semester, and had become a candidate for the National Honor Society. One day we were walking home from school and he asked about the junior play that was having tryouts the following Monday.

"I want to be in the play but I've never acted before," said Ron.

"Well, even if you don't get a speaking role, there are a lot of openings in the stage crew. They help with the props, building scenery, getting the stage set up for each scene and just being useful to the stage manager and the director. They have just as much fun as the actors and they learn about putting on a play."

"The play is *The Mousetrap* by Agatha Christie. I've read it and would like to try out for a speaking part, maybe a minor one."

"You probably won't have any trouble getting one. Mr. Calvin, our Drama Club Advisor, is fair in assigning the roles. The problem we normally have is that some students who try out for parts have such a heavy Spanish accent that they are a poor fit for any speaking role. You don't have that problem."

"You mean because I'm an Anglo?"

"Well, yes. Does the term bother you?"

"Not really. But I noticed that there is sensitivity about labels. People from the Valley don't like to be called Mexicans, for example."

"That's true. Calling them that is an insult on several levels and it appears to be confusing to the typical American visitor to the area. First, Valley people do not associate themselves with Mexico, they never have. The colony here was established long before there was a country called Mexico, more than two hundred years before, as a matter of fact. Second, when Mexico did declare independence in 1821, that country's administration had a lot of trouble stabilizing itself that it virtually ignored its northern lands. Spain had tried re-taking over Mexico until 1836 when it conceded defeat. That enabled Texas to declare its independence in 1836, even laying claim to the eastern part of our state, and opened the way for President Polk to aggressively pursue the "Manifest Destiny" policy and occupy and annex not only Texas but all the lands west including California. Mexico's government was still not stable enough to defend those territories and eventually conceded the lands for modest compensation with the Guadalupe-Hidalgo Treaty. Third, families in this area never really supported Mexico's independence and never received any assistance from Mexico's fledging government in fighting the warlike Indians or defending ourselves against American or Texas invaders. During the tenuous claim on New Mexico by Mexico all but one governor of New Mexico was native born. Mexico sent an army officer named Perez in 1837 to become Governor. Native New Mexicans revolted and beheaded him and re-installed Manuel Armijo who governed for the next nine years until he heard Kearny was on his way in 1846 and he skipped town. Basically, we were too small and 1600 miles away for Mexico City to bother with us. We revolted against American occupation as well and in January 1847, insurrectionists in Taos tortured and scalped Charles Bent, the first American-appointed Governor, in front of his family. He tried to escape with Kit Carson, the long-time American sympathizer, but Bent was eventually murdered. Today, we live with monuments to Carson and Bent; the names of the protestors are long forgotten.

"So you associate yourselves with Spain more than Mexico?"

"Not really. I suppose there are pretentious people out there who can trace their roots back to Spain claiming our dialect here is closer to Spain's language rather than the Mexican version. I'd say we are more like a lost tribe, nominally cut off from Spain in 1821 and from the short connection with Mexico in 1846. The society here intermarried freely with Pueblo Indian and American families over the years. I would say that very few Valley people have any allegiance to Spain and much less to Mexico, especially after the stupid Perez incident. You won't see any September 16 celebrations here. You can understand why calling us 'Mexicans' is an insult."

"So how do the Valley people distinguish themselves from others who are Hispanic in heritage?" I could see that the conversation could go on forever. Ron appeared to be really interested in the Valley's history and I didn't really want to appear defensive. People were going to call us whatever they wanted, regardless of what the truth was.

"Well, Ron, that is a complicated question. People with an inclusive agenda want to call everyone "Latino" and we probably respond to that, although it is alien and nondescript. Self-deprecating Hispanics call themselves "Chicano" which is really a combination of "chico" or small and "Mexicano" or Mexican. This generally is seen as a derogatory term, much like "nigger" to a Negro. It may be okay to use it among themselves but it is inflammatory when used by others due to its reference to stature and being from Mexico, neither of which really applies to people from Northern New Mexico. Maybe it works in Texas and California but not here."

"So is there any term that is acceptable to the Valley people?"

"Hispanic refers to the lineage that we were, and to a large degree still are, namely Spanish speaking. It says nothing about ethnicity because there has been a mixing, whether forced or not, with the Indian tribes of the area and later intermarriages with American traders and settlers. Until 1846, the European settlers, not just the Spanish, were subject to Indian hostilities, caused by the imposition of the Christian faith, theft of crops, subjugation of native people, rape of women or invasion of arable land. There was reprisal by natives in the form of rebellion and slaughter of missionaries and families of settlers. The Pueblo Rebellion of 1680 is notable because most settlers went to El Paso for twelve years until the Re-conquest of 1692 when Santa Fe was re-taken.

"Is it not time to forget the past and get on with the present?"

"If you read the history of Europe, Africa or Asia, you find this sort of battle going on for hundreds if not thousands of years. Look at the extermination of Jews in Germany just a few years ago. Every time you have ethnic, religious, language, or skin-color differences you will probably have conflict of one form or another. History confirms that over and over. In Northern New Mexico we are blessed (or cursed) to have several of those factors at work and doing damage and preventing harmony. There are people who look at the landscape and see a blend of three cultures; these are tourists mostly or naïve residents who have not probed beyond the surface of everyday transactions.

We have Spanish land claims that have gone on for over a hundred years. We have resentment from Indian tribes of what Coronado, an early Spanish Conquistador did back in 1540. We have resentment from the American invasion in 1846 and the subsequent land grab by greedy speculators and carpetbaggers, mostly from neighboring Texas. We have protests against big employers, like Los Alamos National Laboratory, who have allegedly not hired people from Northern New Mexico on an equitable basis." By this time I saw Ron was ready to call it quits. This was way too much information about being an Anglo and wanting to be in the next play.

"Where did you learn this stuff? asked Ron.

"We have been taught New Mexico history in several grades before high school. Of course, current events are covered in the newspapers, like the ongoing land grant claims and the protests against worker discrimination at Los Alamos."

"Will there ever be harmony in San Felipe?

"Not in our lifetime. Assimilation takes many generations and there's got to be a force or crisis to make it happen. There are natural barriers to assimilation like the Indian reservations, like land ownership for Hispanics, the slow progress of the political process, the pervasive poverty that has set in with the decline of small farms and ranches." I said this as I was trying to be positive and not leave Ron with a hopeless attitude.

"I guess in Pennsylvania we have the Amish who have set up self-imposed barriers to assimilation," said Ron. "They don't use electricity and stick to farming." The Jews in Philadelphia and other eastern cities have protested discrimination as have the Italians. They both have anti-defamation organizations. The Irish in New York and Boston were discriminated against in the 1800s. The recent Negro movement in the South has highlighted the terrible prejudice against people descended from former slaves."

"Look Ron, I don't want to give you the wrong impression about the Valley and its people. I invite you to talk to Pueblo Indian students, other Hispanics, Anglos, long-term residents and short term ones and certainly read about the history yourself. This is a sensitive subject and you deserve to hear other points of view."

"Okay Ray. Let me ask you a question so I can calibrate what you've told me a little better. "Why is it that in many parts of America, actually where I have lived, probably now about 12 different states, there is harmony among the people? They have different surnames and appear to get along with each other. My question is: why is there harmony there and not here?"

"You know the answer. You said so yourself. Were there Negros in the area? Were there ethnic groups banding together, forming ghettos? Probably not. You were living in areas where assimilation into a general American culture had established itself so that ethnicity and other divisive factors were almost non-existent."

"Yeah, the key is assimilation, getting to an American culture, whatever that means," said Ron.

"Listen, I gotta get home now. Remember what I said—talk to others," as I left him and started to run the rest of the way.

The conversation with Ron was heavier than I wanted it to be, especially since a lot of the topics could unduly emphasize differences in our backgrounds. I enjoyed his company and wanted to learn from him. He personified the America I wanted to get to know, especially from a young person. He had learned to survive, going to different schools, making friends quickly, learning about the new community and having an open mind. He didn't seem to have a bone to pick, fear to pester him, or something to prove. There was a definite interest in education, something instilled in his psyche by his parents perhaps.

On Monday night Ron joined me in trying out for the Junior Play. He read for Mr. Calvin along with the other students hoping to land a part. I had already been cast as the Inspector and the next day we learned that Ron was going to be Mr. Paravicini, a not insignificant part. Marla was a member of the stage crew so it worked out great for Ron. I didn't see much of either of them except when Ron was on stage. I had heard that Marla had fallen for Ron real hard, telling some of her friends that she "loved" him. I was apprehensive at hearing that bit of gossip but I didn't say anything to Marla.

Another student I got to know well the first year of the Dam Kids was Debra Corbin. Originally from Ohio, she had attended a school in Louisiana during her sophomore year and was hoping to graduate at Fernandez High. Her father operated a bulldozer and her mother had gotten a job as a cashier at a grocery store. Debra had a younger sister who was into gymnastics in junior high school. Debra was at the awkward age with a body that was still stretching, freckles slowly disappearing, untamable hair and feet so large that shoes looked like boats. She was in my math class, Trigonometry, with Mrs. Barber. Debra was ready for Calculus but Fernandez High didn't teach it. The best the high school could offer her was Trig so Mrs. Barber would often pull Debra and me aside and give us more advanced homework, special quizzes and exams. Debra was shy at first with me and then opened up after a few homework problems that we worked on together. She told me about the problems she had had at other schools where she had to take certain subjects like American History several times. She had lived all over the Midwest—Missouri, Iowa, Michigan, and Illinois—and then spent two years in Louisiana. She had lived in a trailer park most of her life, her family finally buying a fifty footer with two bedrooms several years ago that they hauled from project to project. They had stationed it in a trailer park at the edge of town along with other white families who worked entry level jobs at Los Alamos.

"Listen Ray, I can't work on trig homework today. I'm meeting my mother after school. She wants me to look at a sweater she found for me at a downtown store. I'm sorry. I do appreciate the time we spend on the homework," she said.

"I do too. Hey, no problem. I can hang out at the snack shop with friends before I head for home."

"I've got an idea. Why don't you join me? My mother's been asking to meet you."

"Go shopping? I'm not sure I could help you."

"No, silly. Just walk with me to the store where my mother works and meet her. You can be on your way in a few minutes." There was an extra dose of pleading in her eyes and there was no reason for turning her down. I didn't read any romantic overtures in her invitation either. I wasn't looking for any but I was still trying to understand the subtleties of American behavior, especially from one of the Dam Kids.

"Okay, okay. I'll meet you at the gym entrance right after the last period."

After school we walked to the grocery store together and we talked about our class fundraising activities for the month. She had volunteered to sell "sloppy joe" sandwiches at noon with Mrs. Munroe, one of class sponsors. The high school had no cafeteria and most students either had to walk home for lunch or use the gymnasium to eat any lunch they had brought on the bus. A hot sandwich was appealing to those who were tired of brown bag meals. She slowed her pace and turned to me in a more serious tone.

"Compared to other places where I've lived, I notice that the families in the Valley are really down on their luck," Debra said. "I say this after noticing that the students who buy our sandwiches don't seem to have a lot of money. Some students have confided that they are on public welfare or their parents are on unemployment insurance. I guess the Pueblo families get a stipend from the federal government?"

"There really aren't many big employers here in the Valley except for the state government and the laboratory in Los Alamos," I answered. "This has been a farming and ranching community and you know that those occupations really can't support a family. The farms in the Midwest are getting larger and larger and the ranches in Texas and Florida grow most of the livestock nowadays. "Bigness is the trend for business, no pun intended." It had become clear that Ron and Debra as newcomers had already noticed the major symptoms of the Valley—slow societal assimilation and economic constriction that comes during a time of transition—agricultural to non-agricultural.

I was introduced to her mother, a thin, sallow-faced woman in a plain print dress, her hair done in short braids, making her look younger but odd. She took a short break from her job and walked outside the store with us, lighting up a cigarette from a pack she carried in her store apron.

"Debra tells me you're pretty good in math," she said.

"Your daughter isn't bad herself," I answered.

"I'm glad she was able to meet you. It's hard for us traveling around, having Debra and her sister make new friends. We like it here in San Felipe and we hope that Debra can finish her schooling next year." She put her right foot slightly forward and her left hand under the right arm pointing straight up, her wrist flexed so the cigarette ash wouldn't fall on her. Her eyes narrowed, a smile showing wrinkles around her mouth; she blew smoke to her right side away from me, awaiting my response. But I had none. Finally, Debra spoke.

"Ray is going to be in the Junior Class Play, Mother. I think we ought to go. It starts in a couple of weeks. Maybe Linda and Dad would join us."

"I don't know, honey; your Dad gets home so tired. All he wants is to take a bath and then have a beer. But we can ask. Is it on during the weekend?"

"Yes, we have a Saturday night performance and a Sunday matinee," I answered.

"Good, that increases our chances on going. I better go back to finish up and punch the time clock." She stamped out her stub with her foot, looking down as she continued. "Listen, Ray, I'm glad that you're in the same class with Debra. I know it's helped her in school." She extended her hand to shake mine, pulling me toward her, so she could kiss me on my left cheek, whispering "thank you."

Debra and I didn't relate beyond a warm friendship. She didn't seem interested and I was not attracted to her. I was attracted to quite a few girls but there was no magic with Debra. We had "sock hops" in the gymnasium once a month, playing hit tunes on the PA system. I saw Debra there once and I did dance with her a couple of times. I remember her arm was stiff when I tried to turn her during the swing steps. She obviously hadn't danced very much.

My friend Manuel took her to the Junior Prom and I saw that they were having a good time. He bragged about kissing her at the drive-in theater but she didn't let him go any further than that. Debra seemed happy and well-adjusted during the rest of the year. I didn't see her much during the following summer and her mother had taken another job in Riverside, across the river.

Debra and her family had achieved a modest version of the American dream, ensconced in a mobile home, probably living from check to check, but the parents had jobs and pride in what they could control.

Winston Donahue was the athletic member of the three, six feet tall, weighing two and quarter, with a red-headed crew cut and a neck thick from lifting weights. He became the starting fullback on the football team, earning more yardages on the ground than all other ball carriers combined. The rest of the team wasn't very big so the football season had its usual so-so season. Winston had an outdoor voice so one of the teachers asked him to have his hearing checked. He didn't change his volume so I imagined that his hearing was found to be normal. I sat next to him in my American History class. An average student, he did his homework and did volunteer to answer questions in class but they were unimaginative and succinct. We played basketball after school with friends of mine. His eye was a little off so he wasn't a shooter but he held his ground on rebounds, blocking others with his strong body and using his height well. Normally good natured, he reacted badly when pushed or treated unfairly. He was intimidating when angry. He shouted his outrage first, and got even later, when the sport allowed contact that led to retribution. I remember restraining him once during a rough basketball outing with a hot headed friend of mine.

"I don't know what his problem is," he said as I put myself between him and my friend.

"Why don't we call it a day? Huh? It's getting a little dark anyway," I said, hoping to calm things down.

"Yeah, yeah. Let's go, Ray."

We found our schoolbooks and started walking toward downtown. His breathing wasn't as hard but I could see he was still upset.

"I see there's an anti-Anglo attitude with some of your friends," he said. "What is their goddam problem?"

"Well, it really isn't you that they have a problem with. It's their home life, mainly. That was Mario who was guarding you. His father's a drunk who beats up his mother all the time. He's picked on Mario a couple of times. There's little money at home, just his father's pension from being a disabled veteran. The family owns a small farm that had great apple trees on it. But it was too much work to water them, spray them and there's not much of a market for apples around here. People got used to getting them from the store. They look great, being from the west coast, but they're tasteless. He resents you because your dad has a job, a steady one. He thinks that you have an unfair advantage, having a dad that works, you speak good English and you'll probably get a good job when you graduate. That's the image of an Anglo, in his eyes and, for that matter, by many other students who come from a farming or ranching family"

"Well, why don't they do something about it? Look for another job?"

"You're right. Initiative could be the answer. But there aren't too many unskilled or low-skilled jobs in the Valley. Knowing good English is essential for a good paying job. It's been difficult for a lot of people here."

"What about you? You don't even have a father and your mother's on welfare. Why don't you have a problem with me?"

"I guess I've come to realize that you are not the enemy. It's really up to me to make it happen. Getting a job, I mean. I don't have connections, certainly no family money. You may have an advantage but only I can make myself competitive."

"I'm going to call my mother from the store up ahead. She'll come and get me." I could see that he was still upset; his ears were still flaming red from the skirmish with Mario.

"Sure. We'll see you tomorrow in History class, I said.

There are times when one gets the
impression she thinks the class is a joke.
—*Reyes*

Dennis C de Vaca had died in an auto accident on his way to Santa Fe near the turnoff to La Mesilla. The state police had found no evidence of alcohol and no other car had been involved. They assumed that Dennis had lost control of his car. He was the only son of Corina C de Vaca who had employed my mother for several years. She had been generous in paying my mother to clean the house and do occasional ironing. About a month after the accident, she told my mother that she had ordered an expensive suit for Dennis from an Albuquerque tailor a week before he died and she had now received word that it was ready for pickup. She had explained to the tailor the sad circumstances concerning her son so the tailor had agreed to make alterations—free of charge—to the suit so it could fit another young man. Her idea was that I should be the beneficiary of the tailor's kind offer. My mother thought it was a blessing because she knew we couldn't afford to buy a suit for my high school graduation.

When told of the gift, I was apprehensive that everything would work out the way Mrs. C de Vaca and my mother planned. Dennis was six years older than me, was two inches taller and weighed 50 pounds more than I did. At five feet ten inches carrying 135 pounds I only sported a 28 inch waist during my senior year. I still remember the kidding I received from the summer science camp I had attended in Montana the year before. A girl I had befriended, Monica Johansen, was able to encircle my upper arm with her forefinger and thumb. She thought I was too skinny. After coming home from camp I bought a cheap weight lifting set and had tried to bulk up over the course of the high school senior year. I did gain about ten pounds and my neck went from 12 inches to 13 and one half in girth. Still, I was not sure I was ready for clothes befitting an adult male. My sizes were still found in the "Boys" department of the dry goods stores. Mrs. C de Vaca had offered a pair of new shoes as well and my mother brought them home—a beautiful pair of black Florsheim wing-tips that were size ten, a size and a half too big for me. My mother was able to sell them to a relative for ten dollars to buy me something more appropriate.

We made the trip to Albuquerque about a month before the graduation date to see the tailor. He appeared puzzled when he saw me. Although he didn't say anything negative, I think he wondered how he was going to alter the suit for me. He took my measurements, first for the pants and then moved on to my shoulders, chest and sleeve length. I was asked to try the jacket on. It was at least a couple of sizes too big for me. After marking the jacket with chalk lines he wrote notes on a pad. He put the suit away and then came over to talk to us. We had already told him that our plans were to have me wear the suit for graduation day.

"Well, it's going to entail a lot more work than I thought," he said. "But we will see what we can do. It's not going to be a perfect fit, especially with the jacket. The difference in shoulders is just too big. The pants will be okay but the jacket will be a little broad on the shoulders. I can have the suit ready in two weeks."

My mother had rehearsed me on what I was supposed to say.

"We appreciate you taking the time to alter the suit for me. Dennis was a good friend of our family."

"*Dank you, very mucht, dank you*" my mother said in her heavily accented English with a slight laugh, bowing her head as she spoke.

We did go back two weeks later and the suit was indeed ready. It was a beautiful dark blue suit with a satiny lining in the jacket. The pants were also lined down to the mid-thigh with the same material. The pants had a flat front with no pleats and also had the inside two buttons for preventing the fly area from doubling up or sagging. The single breasted jacket had the right sleeve length and the chest closure was not bad. But the shoulder breadth made me look like a footballer. The tailor kept closing the jacket a little more in the collar but my lack of shoulder lift let the jacket droop so the shoulders went out too much. Although not the greatest fit, my mother declared the suit acceptable, probably because it was "free." We thanked the tailor again and he shook my hand and wished me well on my graduation. On our way home to San Isidro I convinced myself the graduation gown would hide most of the suit so the shoulder problem would not be a big deal. I remembered to send a thank you letter to Mrs. C de Vaca.

Mr. McNair, acting as our guidance counselor, called me into his office the same week that we had picked up the suit. I remember he had a frown when I walked in and I thought that I had done something wrong. He had been a supporter of my schoolwork and had found school money to send me to student council conferences in other cities. He had nominated me for representing the school at Boys State, a week-long camp in Roswell that reviewed governance principles and the political process in the state.

"Ray, I wanted to talk to you about the designation of valedictorian for the Class of 1960. You remember that we talked about it after the end of the seventh semester in January? I had told you that you were clearly the designee because you had the highest grade point average in your class."

"Sure, I remember that meeting. I learned that the seventh semester was normally the time when the valedictorian is named."

"Yes, I've been here fourteen years and I don't remember waiting any longer than the seventh semester to inform the public who will be the valedictorian. The traditional thinking was that we really do not have enough time to re-calculate the GPA for your class the last week of the semester. In fact, graduation is the day after the semester officially ends. Further, students have unusual schedules during the eighth semester like special projects and can be absent during the semester interviewing at colleges they hope to enter."

"I understand all that. I believe we discussed that during our meeting in January."

"Yes, we did. But Principal Granger and his administrative staff had decided to deviate from the norm. It turns out that your grade in Senior English will likely be a "B" this semester. Miss Johnson has informed the administration that Charlene Mansfield will get an "A" and you will get a "B." Principal Granger is reconsidering the normal procedure in naming the valedictorian."

"What does this mean? Am I going to be valedictorian or not?"

"Well, the discussion has gone on for a considerable amout of time and the decision has been made. Technically, even with a "B" in senior English, your GPA is still a bit higher than Charlene's but the difference is so small that there is fairness issue that has been brought up. The thought is that the GPA for each of you is nominally the same. For that reason, the decision is that you and Charlene will be co-valedictorians."

"Does this have something to do with anything else? I have had my differences of opinion with the Principal on how he handles Student Council matters. And with Miss Johnson, it's no secret that I've been unhappy with her unorthodox exams and unprofessional treatment of fellow students. She called Frankie Garcia, a very good student, 'the smiling ghost' simply because he doesn't participate in class discussions."

"Well, it's true that Mr. Granger has been disappointed with your attitude towards him. He doesn't trust you. He wouldn't sign a letter of recommendation for your college application to Purdue University. He believes you deliberately went out of your way to criticize him on his views of the Student Council resolutions you sponsored. But I cannot tell that this action is any kind of reprisal. He knows that you are a very good student and that many teachers have praised your work for its creativity and high quality. I am sure you were honest in handling the conflict with him."

"Well, despite his reluctance to sign the letter, I did get into the engineering school at Purdue and they offered me a scholarship but the amount wouldn't have supported my living expenses. I had several long talks with the Principal—one on one—and there is a disagreement between us on how he approaches student rights, school discipline and confidence. We are young adults that deserve a little more respect than he gives us. I have no basis for believing he is ethnically biased. I know a lot of people think he is a racist but I haven't witnessed any justification of that view. And I think our discussions were not personal in nature. I often got the feeling that I presented a threat to him."

"You bring up Miss Johnson and whether she has a problem with you. What I know is that she thinks you are a gifted student but you lack a sense of humor. You take things too seriously. She is new here. This is her first year in teaching. We hired her just out of college and she doesn't know the Valley. She comes from Seneca, a little town next to the Oklahoma border. They probably don't have a lot of Spanish speaking students up there. Several students in her class have already complained about her alleged insensitivity to the Valley culture. Knowing her, I'm sure she meant no harm in the jokes she tells in class to try to get people to relax and have fun in class. There may have been jokes that had an ethnic side to them. Students have already told us exactly what she said. You never complained about her but she could tell that you were upset with her comments. Apparently you rejected any attempt on her part to have a friendlier attitude in class. She thinks that students are too sensitive about their ethnicity. She says she's trying to lighten things up."

"I don't believe I've ever complained formally about any teacher at the high school. And I've suffered through plenty of first-timers who were obviously uncomfortable with the students for one reason or another. In her case, I could see that the Hispanic students felt she had a blatant, special interest in the Anglophone students, both in class and out of class. It was obvious she had a kinship with them. There was one exam she gave, which I thought was unfair, that had a key to the foolish answers that the Anglophone students quickly discerned while the Hispanic students took the questions seriously. Of course, the questions were nonsensical and the students who didn't get the key were lost and got a bad grade. I would not have protested if she had thrown the grades away but she decided to count them as real, including mine which was not that great."

"But her decision to give you a "B" is not based on one exam, is it?"

"I don't know her grading system. We've had very few exams and we have had composition exercises, book reviews, etc. She gave me an A for my research paper on "Unitarianism" which meant she recognized good work, even from me. It is hard to tell with first timers. The student is the guinea pig in a sense. There are first timers, whether Anglo or Hispanic, who really go out of their way to understand the problems that students have in learning the material. She comes up short when compared to them. There are times when one gets the impression she thinks the class is a joke."

"Are you bitter about having her as a teacher?"

"No, I don't think so. I believe every student in school will tell you that he or she has had a number of very good teachers and only a few that were really bad news. What seems to make the difference is the feeling, sometimes only an illusion that the teacher is really interested in having you learn, that they're speaking to you individually. It's like having a switch turned on. You do more for that teacher because you're engaged. Someone cares that you learn, not just your parents."

"Well, what drives you to do well, regardless of who the teacher is?"

"You probably know the answer to that question before you even asked it. I've known you for the four years I've been here. You know where I come from, the bad side of town, a single mother on welfare, living in a house with minimal plumbing, wood-fired heat, etc., etc. Frankly, I am committed to have a better life than any of my relatives. I don't know how I'm going to do it but there's no stopping me. Sitting back is not an option."

"You've told me that several times. People claim you wear it like a badge. It's often taken the wrong way, like having a chip on your shoulder. You should be careful how you express your ambition. It's good to have that goal. I've probably had something to do with encouraging you to have it. You've chosen the field of engineering for your career. Is that an Eisenhower thing?"

"Well, you remember I went to the Montana science camp last summer. Last year, a scientist came down from Los Alamos and told us that President Eisenhower had encouraged NASA to hire more scientists and engineers as a result of Sputnik. He doesn't want America to be left behind, especially by the Communists. The scientist told us that there would be a lot of scholarship money for those of us who would choose science or engineering as a field of college study. He didn't explain what engineers do but I got a better idea of that kind of work at the Montana science camp."

"Did you also learn that engineering is probably the toughest field of study in college? You have to learn advanced math, physics, chemistry and the property of materials. The dropout rate is extremely high." Mr. McNair sat back and looked concerned. For a moment, it looked like I was losing his support.

"Yes, I did. It scared me at first when I saw that other high school students at the Montana camp already had taken calculus, knew how to program IBM mainframes, and had done nifty plasma projects. Although I was far behind on all of those things, I could keep up with the best of them on subjects that were new to all of us. I convinced myself I could catch up over time."

"Ray, I'm glad you have confidence in yourself. That is a strength you need in education. Listen, I've got to write notes on this meeting and submit them to administration. Do you have a problem with the valedictorian decision?"

"No, I am not going to protest, if that's what you mean. This isn't the first time that I've faced a questionable decision and probably won't be the last. I suppose if I had parents with connections, it could be a different matter. It's not worth it to me. I have confidence in myself. I know what I've accomplished by myself. Many teachers have been great for my learning. But there's nobody behind me, ready to defend me. I am sure this won't be the last time I raise an eyebrow and wonder why this is happening. My only recourse is the quality of my work in pursuit of a goal I take on. If people choose to dismiss it or consider other factors over which I have no control, then I have to go elsewhere. My only chance is seek an environment where reward is based on merit, not on who your father is."

"So you think you are getting shafted?"

"I didn't say that. I don't have all the facts in front of me and I don't think that will matter. I've got bigger fish to fry than to pout about being a co-valedictorian rather than valedictorian."

"You know, I've noticed that you have been more serious since the student council election last September. Do you feel a difference this year from last year when you seemed to be on top of the world—President of Junior Class, Yearbook Editor, Boys State, Drama Award Winner?"

"You hit a sore point with me. I had a great year last year and I expected to have another one this year. Many teachers went out of their way to acknowledge my accomplishments last year and I thought I had the student body behind me. Perhaps I wanted to be recognized by my fellow students, especially those from the Hispanic community, that we could achieve whatever we wanted by simply focusing on a goal and working smart and with plenty of effort. I had been elected overwhelmingly as Junior Class President."

"Well, what happened at that Student Council meeting? Miss Harding told me about it with few details. She just shook her head when I asked."

"In my mind, an important part of my world collapsed. There were about thirty student representatives in that room. We were to choose the President of the Student Council who represents the entire student body. He or she is the first student consulted on any high school matter—curricular, governance, scheduling, counseling, student handbook, in session activities and extra-curricular activities. I thought I could bring change to the level of student involvement. I felt I had credibility with many of the teachers. At that point I had not had any serious problems with the administration. I thought I had mentored a lot of the lower classmen and their leaders during my junior year."

"Were you nominated?"

"Yes, I was the first to be nominated by one of my supporters. The cheerleaders came in a little late, just as nominations were being accepted. Miss Harding re-started the meeting and said that one nomination had been made for President, namely me. Surprisingly, one of the cheerleaders nominated Charlene Mansfield. What was amazing, looking back now, was the change in atmosphere of the meeting when the cheerleaders came in the room. They were wearing their uniforms, bright colored, effusing school spirit, positive and bigger than life, however shallow that may have been. There were no more nominations so Miss Harding asked to take a piece of paper and vote for either candidate. I was so sure that I would win on the first ballot, I didn't even vote. The shock came when Miss Harding counted the ballots and then counted them again. She said that the vote total for each candidate was too close and we should vote again."

"Didn't she give you a chance to appeal to the representatives? Did Charlene talk? Was there any campaigning?"

"No, I don't think anyone really considered it necessary, including Miss Harding. We all knew each other. Many of those students had been in the Student Council last year."

"What happened in the second ballot?"

"That was my epiphany. I voted for Charlene the second time around. I conceded defeat in a sense. If the overwhelming majority of these students were not voting for me, then I really should not be President. They were the most active students, many of them always on the honor roll. I do not know whether my vote made any difference. I never asked Miss Harding. She counted the ballots and announced that Charlene would be the President of the Student Council. The students clapped. We went on to nominate and elect people for the other offices. My name was again nominated for VP and I was elected by acclamation. After setting the next meeting date, Miss Harding adjourned the meeting. As the students shuffled out of the classroom, Miss Harding went over and congratulated Charlene and then asked to see me in her office."

"Did she give you details on the balloting?"

"No, and I really wasn't interested. She said it was a shock to her that the students did not vote for me. She went on to recount a lot of my scholastic and service accomplishments. It was obvious she had been looking forward to working with me. The last thing she said was 'I don't know what happened in there.'"

"I listened to her and it was comforting to hear her words. But I was beginning to understand the dynamics of the meeting. I had lost an important connection to my peers and their confidence in me. The students represent the larger community, not just of students but of the Valley. The local newspaper had been full of stories about me during the last school year. All that notoriety had created a separation that I had not been aware of, at least not to the degree that showed itself at that meeting. There was a cultural tie that I had lost and I didn't know it. I was no longer part of my native community. I had ascended, or descended, whichever way people might look at it, into a different realm. I was being pushed out from the Valley culture. It was a release from Cíbola, the land of the ancients. I had embraced too many things that are alien to my community. I was no longer a representative for them. We use the word '*faceta*' to denote a haughty attitude. The word implies that the ostracized person thinks he or she is no longer a member of the group and perhaps even considers himself or herself 'better' or 'different' from the group."

"Have you been able to verify your suspicion this year?"

"We don't like to come out and say it. The answer is that there will never be a definitive yes or no. These things happen anonymously, probably for fear of reprisal. I certainly would not do that to anyone. We have enough challenges already. But it may explain a phenomenon that is attributed to our culture in the Valley. Namely, the belief is that when someone tries to climb out of the proverbial snake pit, we collectively drag him or her down again. We don't tend to help each other out. The only exception is being a relative but even that is not universal. There are other ethnicities and cultural groups who do go out of their way to further each other in whatever way makes sense. That is considered rare in the Valley."

"That's very interesting. Have you been able to accomplish your goals this year despite this setback?"

"Coming from my background, I've learned to accept setbacks and simply apply my efforts to something else that would advance the cause I told you about studying engineering, getting a good job and having a better life. I know that the students were not interested in what I could do for them. So I redirected my efforts during the senior year."

"On the valedictory change, are you going to want to talk to Principal Granger or Miss Johnson?"

"No. I really do not see any point to it. If they are doing this deliberately, they are revealing a petty side to their personality. If they are doing this out of fairness, where were they when other incidents happened in the past to cause a change in the eighth semester? They have to live with this on their conscience, not me."

I saw that the conversation was at its end so I thanked Mr. McNair for the information and we shook hands. He saw me to the door and I walked down the empty hallway to my locker. I could hear the school band rehearsing in the gym. The sound was faint but it was clearly the graduation march. There was only a little over a week to go. We would have finals next week and then it would be over.

At graduation I would be delivering a co-valedictory speech, not a valedictory one. I hadn't even started writing one but there was time.

That night after supper I explained to my mother the change in the designation of valedictorian. Although she had rarely taken an interest in any of my academic achievements she took it badly. She asked me why I hadn't protested. I went through my reasoning and she dismissed it before I had even finished. She said I had become timid of late. I had been more aggressive in the past. Something had caused me to take things in stride instead of fighting back. I told her that I fight when there is a good chance of winning. I pick my fights more carefully now, especially those that matter. What was important was what I had learned in school. Grades are supposed to be an indication of that. If Charlene had learned as much as I had, so be it. I have to respect that. But my suspicions were that we weren't even close in that department. But there was a scoreboard and I was told that the score was tied. What matters now is the score not how well you played. The real game had just begun. I knew college would be a lot harder. The summer in Montana had shown me that. You were on your own. Nobody would be there to support you, encourage you and help you with the homework. On that basis I was far ahead. My mother had no concept of what I was trying to do. She was not an impediment either. She took care of me— washed clothes, fed me, never demanded that I put household chores ahead of school. I couldn't complain. She told me that she had my suit pressed and she had bought me a new tie for graduation. She wanted me to try out two white shirts that she had gotten from her clients. She suspected that they may not fit my new neck size due to the weightlifting regimen I had been following.

I thought I could put the valedictorian thing behind me and simply concentrate on the finals for the other courses besides Senior English. I already knew what my grade was going to be no matter how I did on the final. I studied every night, giving up going to movies or even watching television.

During the final week of school I also worked on my co-valedictory speech. We were going to be limited to five minutes due to the crowded program. They gave the commencement speaker 30 minutes. She was a local woman who became the first female County Clerk for Santa Fe County. Again, we would be subjected to the thought that working for the government was a great achievement. My speech would start out on acknowledging the great achievement that graduation represents. For many of us, we would be the first in the family to graduate from high school. Few parents had gone that far. There would be 125 of us, the largest graduating class of Fernandez High School. In fact we would be the largest class of any village or town north of Santa Fe except for Farmington, the gas and coal mining town near the Colorado border. The second point was that this point in time was the beginning of something new—college, military service, a job, marriage or something that is or will be our contribution to society. The third point would be the most poignant and that is the acknowledgement that we couldn't have done it without our parents, guardians, mentors and teachers. Every one of us could remember someone who was special to us, who kept us going. The more I thought about the three points, the more they seemed the standard framework for a valedictory speech. What I really worked on was making it specific to us, San Isidro and the Valley, the culture we have and what we need to do to have it prosper in these times of change and uncertainty.

On Friday morning, the last day of class, Mr. McNair sent for me. I was in the gym looking over the podium and arrangements for the graduation exercises that would be held tomorrow, Saturday at 9AM. The graduation committee, consisting of the senior class advisors and school counselors, had walked us through the program and showed us where to sit and the sequence for entering and exiting the exercises.

I went into his office and it looked like he had the same frown he wore the last time we met. He greeted me and asked me to sit down.

"I know this is kind of late to meet on this matter but Principal Granger asked me to speak with you."

"Really? What about? I mean we're one day away from graduating. He won't have to see me again."

"Look, Ray. That attitude is what he is concerned about."

"What does he have to worry about? He holds all the high cards. What could I do to him?"

"Well, I tried to reason with him but he's adamant. He wants to see your valedictory speech."

Instinctively I wanted to laugh but out of respect for Mr. McNair, I held back. I leaned forward in the chair and held my midsection with both hands and arms. I was fumbling for words that would not sound impertinent. I think Mr. McNair had prepared me for the ridiculous request with his short preface regarding my attitude. I looked at him and didn't say anything for a minute or so. Again, I wanted to choose my words carefully. I certainly didn't want to lose my cool, not at this late date.

"Okay, I understand. What would he be looking for?"

"I am going to say something I may regret. It could cost me my job if you repeat it. I have never entrusted a student with this kind of privileged information but I think you know me well enough that this thing will not get settled unless I talk to you in a straight manner."

"I understand. What is this about? Is he still stewing over the student council resolutions?"

"Well, he's become convinced that you may try to embarrass him with your speech. He wants to make sure you're not planning to say something that he would have to explain to the superintendent and the school board."

"I didn't know I had that much power."

"The way I see it, you have two things that could hurt him and the school. You are the co-valedictorian and that represents a high honor and with your background, it is a superlative achievement. Many teachers have come to admire your hard work, service, creativity despite the handicaps you've had. That, the scholastic honor I mean, gives you a lot of credibility. You may not appreciate it now, especially with the last minute change in designation. Second, you represent a large and important part of the community. I know you think that it's abandoned you. But to the rest of us, you are still a visible member, not only in name that goes back centuries, but that you're bilingual, and you look like you belong here. Everyone is aware that the Valley is a poor region; its per capita income is lower than the rest of the state. *Life* Magazine declared Northern New Mexico a "frontier" or "third world" in America. The administration and the faculty all believe we are here for people that you represent. You understand that if you say we are not doing our job, it looks bad."

"Why does he think that I'd do that? Doesn't he understand that I wouldn't do something to hurt the school? I mean, he really underestimates me in my resolve to better myself. I tried to help others in the school and they didn't want my help. That's fine. I'll continue on my own, relying only on people who do want to help me. And I am grateful to you, Mr. Wainwright and Miss Bell and many others who have done much more for me than I could have ever expected. But he has gone the other way. He attributes malice to me."

"Look, we could debate why he is the way he is. I am not in a position to judge him because I don't sit in his chair. He's in charge of things I know nothing about. He's our representative to the Superintendent and the School Board. I don't know the relationships there. All I know is that we've come to this. I need to see your speech."

"Is it just you or is he supposed to review it as well? You initially said that he wanted to see it."

"I will argue that I have seen it and reviewed it. He will trust my judgment. But it's true that he did request to see it himself."

"And are you supposed to impose censorship if you find something distasteful? How does he know that I won't change it between now and when it actually gets delivered?

"Ray, I am trying to be reasonable here. I'm not going to change your speech if it's unnecessary. I am asking you to trust me on this matter."

"How long are you going to take to review it and do you need a copy?"

"It can't be that long since we only gave you five minutes. I can review it in front of you and no, I don't need a copy."

"Okay, okay. I happen to have a marked up version in my locker and I will go get it now. Can you wait a couple of minutes?"

"Sure."

I left the office in a surprisingly calm manner. As I walked to my locker, I started shaking my head in disbelief, half of me wanted to start laughing at the ridiculous request and the other half was becoming increasingly furious. Principal Granger had the audacity to ask to see my speech. Should I revel in the fearful power that request represented? Or should I be incensed that I couldn't be trusted to deliver a lousy co-valedictory speech? I wasn't sure it was worth being bothered about. I looked through my notebook and found the two page speech. I had cleaned out my locker the day before and had left behind only one book and my notebook so it didn't take me long. I was back in the office in a jiffy. I sat down and was prepared to hand him the speech. "I want to ask you one question before I hand this over."

"Sure, what is it?"

"Are you requesting to see Charlene's speech as well?"

"No. Principal Granger is not particularly worried about her."

"This is between you and me now. Isn't that a clear case of discrimination? To be asking me for my speech and not hers? How would that look to an independent observer? To the school board, for example? Am I such a subversive individual that I'm the only one to worry about?"

"If we were in a perfect world, I guess that would be the right protocol.

But we are here, in this resource limited environment, trying to reason with an unreasonable person, running out of time, and trying not to upset too many people. I have already indicated to you that I am uncomfortable having to talk to you, requesting to see the speech and then convincing him that he's got nothing to worry about."

I handed him the speech and watched him read it. I felt sorry for Mr. McNair. I didn't think I'd made it easy for him. Perhaps my mother's "timid" speech had taken an effect on me. I'd given in but I wondered what would've happened if I hadn't. Would they have prevented me from giving the speech? I felt I'd done the right thing. I trusted Mr. McNair. He hadn't given me reason not to.

"Very nice. You wrote a good speech. I like the things you say about the Valley, preserving the heritage but contributing to its development in the modern world. I know what I can say to Principal Granger. Thanks, and you can go. Good luck tomorrow."

He handed the speech back to me and we shook hands again. I walked out of the office, cleaned out my locker for good and left the building. Walking home I wondered if this was going to be the end of it. I would see Principal Granger tomorrow and I had to decide how I would respond to anything he said to me.

I revisited the speech again that night and made minor changes, adding a little melodramatic phrasing, and figuring out where I could pause for effect and where to raise my voice. Being in all the plays at school had taught me that timing was everything if you wanted to make an impact on the audience. Of course, the gymnasium was not exactly a theater for drama, the acoustics being as bad as they were.

For commencement I wore Dennis C de Vaca's suit that had been altered for me. It still made my shoulders look bigger than they really were. My mother had broken down and bought a new shirt for me. She had measured my neck. She claimed that I was now a size 14 and my sleeve length had reached 32 inches. She asked me if I was going to continue lifting weights. She didn't want to buy more shirts at that size if I was going to grow a thicker neck.

The bleachers were filled with parents, relatives and friends. This was a big event for San Isidro. The *Valley News*, the local newspaper, had good pre-event coverage, publishing quotes from Charlene and me. Mr. Granger and I shook hands but we didn't exchange any words beyond the "congratulations" and "thank you." It was a more emotional and tearful meeting with my teachers who had done a lot for me. I thanked them profusely. I don't know whether they had heard about the panic from the administration about my speech. They didn't let on and I didn't bring it up. As far as I was concerned the panic never happened.

Glossary of Spanish Terms in Northern New Mexico

Acequia—Irrigation ditch. The main ditch that branches off the river is called the "acequia madre" or mother ditch.

Adiós—Farewell, literally translated "to God."

Anglo or Anglophone—Refers to an English speaking person either male or female. It is not used in a derogatory tone.

Atole—A blue corn meal cooked in hot water to form a mush eaten for breakfast with milk and sweetened with honey or sugar.

Barbacoa—Meat cooked for many hours in a barbeque pit, commonly mutton, pork, venison or beef. The drippings are collected in a pan and consumed as a broth.

Boracho—a drunken person.

Bosque—River forest usually consisting of stands of cottonwoods and Russian Olive trees. The forest can be as wide as a mile when the river bank is flat and sandy and only a few feet above the water line.

Bulto—A carved image of a saint. Spanish settlers and their descendants carved the images in a crude but artistic way due to a lack of tools and artistic materials.

Cabrón—A male goat. Curse word used to humiliate a cuckolded man.

Canale—Roof spout usually made from wood or galvanized metal.

Capilla—a small chapel found in a village without a full time priest.

Carne seca—Literally "dried meat." The phrase refers to jerky (or pemmican made from mutton, venison, buffalo or beef. Before drying in the open air, the jerky is marinated in brine or brine with red chili flakes or powder.

Chamisa—A sage-like shrub, otherwise known as "rabbit brush."

Chico—A sage-like brush, prickly that matures to a man's height.

Chicos—Dried sweet corn. Pueblo Indians commonly pulled up the leaves wrappings, bound them and dried the entire husk in the sun.

Chimajá—Wild parsley used by New Mexicans as a medicinal herb.

Chingada—Curse word, more common in Mexico, whose root is *Chingar* or to "screw" or "fuck."

Chongo—A hair braid worn by Pueblo Indian men sometimes interwoven with a colored sash.

Cuidado—Carefulness so that "con cuidado" translates "be careful."

Curandera—Woman knowledgeable in curative herbs and potions. Male version is "curandero."

Diós –God. "Diós te bendiga means "God be with you.

Ejido—Common lands royally established for the use of a settlement. Such ownership was never recognized after the invasion by United States armed forces.

Empanada—A turnover, usually of fruit, commonly apple, apricot, cherry, prune or mincemeat.

Estufa—A stove, usually wood or coal burning with a griddle on top for cooking.

Frijoles—A bean dish made with pinto kidney beans grown in southern Colorado, notably the San Luis Valley. Anasazi beans or the common kidney beans can substitute for the pinto variety.

Gringo—A derogatory term for a non-Hispanic man, "gringa" for a female. Its use became so common that the derogatory nature became less pronounced.

Güerito—Dimuniative version of Güero, referring to a person with blond or light brown hair. A female with white skin is referred to as "blanca."

Horno—an earthen oven used for baking bread and pastries. The oven is about five feet in diameter and five feet high with a hearth that is about a foot above the ground and is built with adobes and plastered with clay. It is totally enclosed except for a small opening in the front where the bread loaves or pastries can be inserted and extracted with three foot long paddles. The oven has a four inch hole at the top that acts as a chimney for the fire that was started inside in order to warm the oven floor and walls. The entrance hole is covered with a wooden plank until the fire goes out whereupon the ashes are removed and the unbaked loaves and/or pastries are placed on the oven floor. The wooden plank is again used to prevent heat from escaping.

Jodido—Done in or "fucked" in the English vernacular.

Llano—A plain or flattened expanse of land.

Madrina—godmother. Baptism ties families together. The father and the godfather refer to each other as "compadre" while the female analogy is "comadre."

Manzana—Apple. Various varieties are grown in Northern New Mexico the most common is Delicious. Others include Jonathans and Winesaps. The apple tree is the "manzano."

Masa—Dough made from bleached or unbleached wheat flour. Dough made from corn meal is called "masa harina."

Necio—Silly or stupid.

Oro—Gold. The Spanish exploration of the sixteenth century of the southwestern section of North America was in part due to the search for gold (oro) and silver (plata).

Pachuco—An outrageous dress style by a Hispanic male in the early 1940s and again in the early 1950s distinguished by baggy pants, moustache and a long key chain.

Partera—midwife.

Pelamela—Literally, "peel me it." A curse word from a man to another man asking him to peel the first man's foreskin back, an insulting sexual allusion.

Penitente—Literally, penitent. The term usually refers to the unsanctioned Lenten rites in which men subject themselves to the torture endured by Christ before crucifixion, notably whippings and the carrying of a large cross. This tradition has been carried on in isolated villages in Northern New Mexico.

Piñon—A shrub-like pine tree that bears small pine nuts. It is native to New Mexico, now recognized as the state tree.

Posole—A hominy-like dish made from a large kerneled white corn sometimes referred to as "Indian corn." Lime is used to remove the thin film on the kernel. After washing the lime off, the kernels are cooked until they pop and chicken or pork broth is then added.

Santo—A painted image or icon of a saint done in a crude manner associated with the early Spanish settlers of New Mexico.

Tetone—the nodule that grows in a cluster of the cottonwood tree. When ripened, it erupts into a cotton ball that floats away in the air.

Tewa—One of several dialects of the Pueblo Indian tribes.

Tortilla—A flattened piece of dough that is toasted on both sides on a hot griddle. It is used as an alternative to bread at a meal. It is commonly used as a wrap for seasoned meat, minced vegetables like onion, garlic, beans and green chili.

Trapo—Dish towel.

Viga—Roof beam usually made out of a pine tree trunk that has been debarked.

www.ingramcontent.com/pod-product-compliance
Lightning Source LLC
Chambersburg PA
CBHW031058020726
47495CB00007B/1936